Ethan

"A sweetly redemptive story… Well written and thoroughly enjoyable. I loved, loved, loved it!"

—*Eyes.2C Reviews*

"A tender romance novel of learning to trust. Fans of Grace Burrowes's *The Soldier* (book two in the Windham series) will absolutely adore *Ethan*."

—*The Royal Reviews*

"Lovely, gentle book about the healing power of love… The sexual and emotional intimacies are brilliantly interwoven."

—*The Book Vixen*

"Imaginative, eloquently written, meaty, and just plain fabulous!"

—*Ck2's Kwips and Kritiques*

"Characters whose chemistry was electrifying…a plot that resonates long after the covers are closed… wrapped in profound imagery that is only enhanced by the sensational witty dialogue."

—*Romantic Crush Junkies EZine*

"An emotional plot that tugged at my heartstrings, putting tears in my eyes at times… I couldn't put it down."

—*Night Owl Reviews* Reviewer Top Pick

D0355697

Praise for *New York Times* bestseller Grace Burrowes's rule-breaking, unforgettable Regency romance

Darius

"Delightfully different… Burrowes brings to life a deeply moving romance that's sure to be remembered and treasured."

—*RT Book Reviews* Top Pick, 4.5 Stars

"This rising author handles powerful romance and complicated family life with skill in romances with great appeal."

—*Booklist*

"Page-turning, breathtaking reading… Once I started reading this tale of redemption, I didn't want to put it down… Grace Burrowes enchants."

—*Long and Short Reviews*

"Steamy…very compelling…a scorching tale of seduction and intrigue."

—*Night Owl Reviews* Reviewer Top Pick, 4.5 Stars

"Brilliant… The plot was unlike any romance novel that I have previously read and yet the romance arc was both realistic and believable."

—*The Royal Reviews*

"[Burrowes's] writing is sublime and even more importantly, so is her characterization."

—*All About Roman*

Nicholas

"Exquisite…breathtaking and heartwarming."
—*Long and Short Reviews*

"Infused with secrets, humor, betrayal, tender romance, sexual tension, and love, this story will have readers eagerly turning the pages amid tears and laughter."
—*Romance Junkies*

"Red-hot chemistry that's sexy as heck, yet sweetly romantic."
—*Drey's Library*

"Grace Burrowes creates characters that are emotionally damaged but still manage to be the most forgiving and caring and courageous individuals you could possibly imagine… I always find myself wanting to step into the pages of the book, so I can simply hug the dickens out of these characters, and I'm betting you will, too."
—*Novels Alive*

"Another beautifully written story. The characters are wonderful, and the story definitely holds your interest…"
—*Romantic Historical Lovers*

"Ms. Burrowes continually presses the bar and goes above and beyond the normal to give her readers phenomenal love stories that keep us manic for more."
—*Romantic Crush Junkies EZine*

the
CAPTIVE

GRACE
BURROWES

sourcebooks
casablanca

Copyright © 2014 by Grace Burrowes
Cover and internal design © 2014 by Sourcebooks, Inc.
Cover illustration by Jon Paul

Sourcebooks and the colophon are registered trademarks of Sourcebooks, Inc.

All rights reserved. No part of this book may be reproduced in any form or by any electronic or mechanical means including information storage and retrieval systems—except in the case of brief quotations embodied in critical articles or reviews—without permission in writing from its publisher, Sourcebooks, Inc.

The characters and events portrayed in this book are fictitious or are used fictitiously. Any similarity to real persons, living or dead, is purely coincidental and not intended by the author.

Published by Sourcebooks Casablanca, an imprint of Sourcebooks, Inc.
P.O. Box 4410, Naperville, Illinois 60567-4410
(630) 961-3900
Fax: (630) 961-2168
www.sourcebooks.com

Printed and bound in Canada.
MBP 10 9 8 7 6 5 4 3 2 1

D0361083

*To those at war, especially the wars
nobody sees, may you find peace*

One

IN HIS PERSONAL HELL, CHRISTIAN DONATUS SEVERN, eighth Duke of Mercia, considered the pedagogic days the worst of a horrific lot—also the most precious. The days when his captors used his suffering to teach the arcane art of interrogation might cost him his sanity, even his honor, but they also ensured he would some day, some night, some eternity if necessary, have that sweetest of satisfactions—*revenge*.

"You see before you the mortal form of a once great and powerful man, Corporal," Girard said, pacing slowly between the table his prisoner had been lashed to and the damp stone wall where the corporal stood at attention.

Girard was a stranger to hurry, a necessary trait in a torturer. A big, dark, lean acolyte of the Corsican, Girard lived in Christian's awareness the way consumption dwelled in the minds of those it afflicted.

"Our duke is still great, to my mind," Girard went on, "because His Grace has not, as the English say, broken."

Girard blathered on in his subtly accented French, and despite willing it to the contrary, Christian

translated easily. As Girard's ironic praise and patri-
otic devotion blended in a curiously mesmerizing
patter, Girard's superior, Henri Anduvoir—the actual
intended student—lurked off in the shadows.

Bad luck in a man's superiors was not the exclusive
province of Wellington's army. Girard made a science
of extracting truth from those reluctant to part with it,
and pain was only one tool at his disposal.

Anduvoir, a simpler and in some ways more-evil
soul, was plainly addicted to hurting others for his
own entertainment.

Christian filled his mind with the lovely truth that
someday Anduvoir, too, would be made to suffer, and
suffer, and suffer.

"*Yet*. Our duke has not broken yet," Girard went
on. "I challenge you, Corporal, to devise the torment
or the prize that will break him, but be mindful that our
challenge grows the longer His Grace is silent. When
the good God above put Mercia into our hands all those
months ago, we sought to know through which pass
Wellington would move his troops. We know now, so
what, I ask you, is the point of the exercise? Why not
simply toss this living carcass to the wolves?"

Yes, please God, why not?

And then another thought intruded on Christian's
efforts to distance himself from the goings-on in that
cell: Was Girard letting slip that Wellington had, in
fact, moved troops into France itself? Girard played a
diabolical game of cat and mouse, hope and despair,
in a role that blended tormenter and protector with a
subtlety a better-fed man might find fascinating.

"We yet enjoy His Grace's charming company

because the duke serves another purpose," Girard prosed on. "He did not break, so we must conclude he is sent here to teach us the breaking of a strong man. One might say, an inhumanly strong man. Now…"

The scent of rich Turkish tobacco wafted to Christian's nose, cutting through the fragrance of lavender Girard favored and the perpetual damp of the Château's lower reaches. Christian's meager breakfast threatened a reappearance, a helpful development in truth. He focused not on Girard's lilting, philosophical French, but on holding the nausea at bay, for he had reason to know a man could choke on his own vomit.

A boot scraped, and by senses other than sight, Christian divined that Anduvoir had come out of his shadows, a reptile in search of his favorite variety of heat.

"Enough lecturing, Colonel Girard. Your pet has not told us of troop movements. In fact, the man no longer talks at all, do you, *mon duc*?" Anduvoir sucked a slow drag of his cigar, then gently placed the moist end of it against Christian's lips. "I long for the sound of even one hearty English scream. Long for it desperately."

Christian turned his head away in a response Girard, who was by no means a stupid man, would have predicted. Anduvoir was an infrequent visitor, though, and like any attentive host—or prudent subordinate— Girard trotted out the best entertainments for his guest.

Anduvoir moved into Christian's line of sight, which, given the careful lack of expression on Girard's face, was bad news all around. Anduvoir was short, dark, coarse featured, and behind his Gallic posturing, suffused with the glee of a bully whose victim could not elude torment.

"A quiet man, our duke." Anduvoir expelled smoke through his nose. "Or perhaps, not so quiet."

He laid the burning tip of the cigar against the soft skin inside Christian's elbow with the same care he'd put it to his prisoner's mouth, letting a small silence mark the moment when the scent of scorched flesh rose.

The blinding, searing pain howled from Christian's arm to his mind, where it joined the memory of a thousand similar pains and coalesced into one roaring chant:

Revenge!

৵৹

"Lord Greendale was a man of great influence," Dr. Martin said, clearing his throat in a manner Gilly was coming to loathe, the way she'd loathed the sight of Greendale lighting one of his foul cheroots in her private parlor.

"His lordship enjoyed very great influence," Gilly concurred, eyes down, as befit a woman facing the widowed state.

The bad news came exactly as expected: "You should prepare for an inquest, my lady."

"An inquest?" Gilly gestured for her guest to take a seat, eight years of marriage to Greendale having taught her to produce an appearance of calm at will. "Theophilus, the man of great influence was universally disliked, approaching his threescore and ten, and the victim of an apoplexy in the midst of a formal dinner for twenty-eight of his most trusted toadies. What will an inquest serve?"

Since Greendale's apoplexy, Gilly had dared to order that the fires in her parlor be kept burning through the day, and yet, the physician's words chilled her more effectively than if a window had banged open.

"Lady Greendale…" Martin shifted a black satchel from right hand to left, making the contents rattle softly. Gilly was convinced the only items of interest in that bag were a selection of pocket flasks.

"Countess, you must not speak so freely, even to me. I will certainly be put under oath and questioned at length. I cannot imagine what the wrong words in the hands of the lawyers will do to your reputation."

His wrong words, over which he'd have no control, of course. A just God would afflict such a physician with a slow, painful death.

"Reputation matters little if one is to swing for murder."

"It won't come to that," Martin said, but he remained poised by the door, bag in hand, as if lingering in Gilly's presence might taint him not with her guilt—for she was innocent of wrongdoing toward her late spouse—but with her vulnerability to accusations. "I had Harrison consult on the case, and he confirmed my diagnosis by letter not two days after the apoplexy."

Dr. Theophilus Martin had observed this precaution not because he was intent on safeguarding Greendale's young widow, but because his late, unlamented lordship had created an air of mistrust thick enough to pollute every corner of the house.

"What am I to be charged with?" Stupidity, certainly, for having married Greendale, but Gilly's family had been adamant—"You'll be a countess!"—and she'd been so young…

Dr. Martin smoothed a soft hand over snow-white hair. "You are not accused of anything."

His lengthy, silent examination of the framed verses of Psalm 23 hanging over the sideboard confirmed that Gilly would, indeed, face suspicion. Her life had become a series of accusations grounded in nothing more than an old man's febrile imagination, and he'd made those accusations where any servant might have overheard them.

"They will say I put a pillow over his face, won't they?"

"They can't. You had a nurse in the room at all times, didn't you? Lovely stitch work, my lady."

Gilly had been accompanied by two nurses, as often as possible, and the stitch work would go to the poorhouse as soon as the inquest was over.

"If I was with his lordship, a nurse was always present—or you, yourself. Will the nurses be suspect?"

She did not ask if Martin would come under suspicion, because quite honestly, she was too afraid to care. He'd been summoned to Greendale Hall on many occasions, and had socialized with Lord Greendale as often as he'd treated him. His solicitude of Gilly now likely had to do with seeing his substantial bill paid.

"I hired the nurses based on my personal experience of them, so no, I shouldn't think they'll come under suspicion," Martin said.

Because the physician was eyeing the door, Gilly fired off the most important question, and to Hades with dignity.

"Who's behind this, Theophilus? My husband is not yet put in the ground, and already you're telling me of an inquest."

Though thank a merciful Deity, Martin's torpid humanitarian instincts had resulted in this warning, at least. Another smoothing of his leonine mane followed, while the fingers of his left hand tightened on the black leather handle tellingly.

"I thought it the better part of kindness not to burden you with this news prematurely, but Lord Greendale himself apparently told his heir to see to the formalities."

And to think Gilly had prayed for her husband's recovery. "Easterbrook ordered this? He's still in France or Spain or somewhere serving the Crown."

"As heir to Lord Greendale's title and fortune, Marcus Easterbrook would have left instructions with his solicitors, and they would in turn have been in communication with King's Counsel and the local magistrate."

Men. Always so organized when bent on aggravation and aspersion. "Greendale was the magistrate. To whom does that dubious honor fall now?"

"Likely to Squire Gordon."

Gordon was a hounds-and-horses fellow, and he'd never toadied to Greendale. A fraction of Gilly's panic eased.

"Shall you have some tea, Theophilus? It's good and hot." Also strong for a change, Gilly's second act of independence from the infernal economies Greendale had imposed on her.

"Thank you, my lady, but no." Martin turned toward the door, then hesitated, hand on the latch.

"You needn't tarry, Theophilus. You've served the family loyally, and that has been far from easy." He'd served the family discreetly, too. Very discreetly. "I suppose I'll see you at the inquest."

He nodded once and slipped away, confirming that he would not call in even a professional capacity before the legalities were resolved, not if he wanted to maintain the appearance of impartiality. Not if he wanted to keep the Crown's men from turning their sights on him as well.

Gilly added coal to the fire—rest in peace, Lord Greendale—and stared into the flames for long moments, weighing her very few options as best one could weigh options when in a flat, terrified panic.

As her strong, hot tea grew tepid in the pot, she sat down with pen and ink, and begged an interview with Gervaise Stoneleigh, the coldest, most astute, most *expensive* barrister ever to turn down Greendale's coin.

And that decision very likely saved her life.

❦

"Girard gave me final orders concerning you."

Christian turned his head slowly. He was still recovering from the last teaching day, a sorry effort on the corporal's part, consisting of familiar tortures enthusiastically applied the better to impress Anduvoir, while Girard had stood bristling with silent censure.

Girard did not approve of brute maneuvers that produced no results, and one had to respect Girard's sense of efficiency.

"You don't care that Girard might have given me orders to kill you, do you?"

The jailer sounded Irish, or on rare occasions when nobody else was about, Scottish, and Christian admitted—in the endless privacy of his thoughts—to being grateful to hear English in any accent other than French.

And typical of Girard's cunning, the jailer was also a frequent source of small kindnesses intended to torment the prisoner with that most cruel weapon: hope.

"Girard said I'm not to allow you to suffer, on account of what's gone before. Said you'd earned your battle honors, so to speak, though it would be a mercy to allow you to join your duchess and your son. He said you're a man who can trust no one, and the life that awaits you won't be worth living for long, assuming your enemies don't ambush you from the hedges of Surrey."

Ah. The old lie, for Christian had no enemies in Surrey, and his wife and son yet thrived at home in England. Severn was a veritable fortress, staffed by retainers whose loyalty went back generations. Girard was simply a petty evil allowed to flourish in the bowels of the Grand Armée's outpost on the slopes of the Pyrenees, and this claim that Helene and Evan were dead was merely a blunt weapon in Girard's arsenal.

Which Girard would pay for using.

Christian focused on ignoring the man speaking to him, a big blond fellow with watchful green eyes and a wary devotion to Girard. Girard referred to him as "*Michel*"; the other guards quietly referred to him in less affectionate terms.

The jailer held a gleaming, bone-handled knife,

its presence a matter of complete indifference to Christian—almost. The knife had become something of a friend to Christian—for a time—until Anduvoir had found a use for it no man could contemplate sanely.

"Orthez fell in February," the jailer said, still lingering near the open door of the cell—a taunt, that, leaving the cell door unlatched when Christian was powerless to escape. "That was weeks ago, not that you'd know, poor sod. Bordeaux was last month. Toulouse has been taken, and we've heard rumors Napoleon has abdicated. Girard's gone."

None of it was true. These fairy tales were a variation on the stories the jailer told from time to time in an effort to raise hopes. Christian knew better: hopes that refused to rise couldn't be dashed.

The jailer came no closer.

"I've seen what went on here, and I'm sorry for it," he said, sounding Scottish indeed, and damnably sincere. "Girard is sorry for it, too. This was war, true enough, but when Anduvoir came around…"

But nothing. Christian was tied to the cot, a periodic nuisance he'd long since become inured to. Girard's greatest cruelty had been to show his prisoner only enough care to ensure Christian wouldn't die. The mattress was thin but clean, and Christian probably had more blankets than the infantry quartered elsewhere in the old château.

He was fed.

If he refused to eat, he was fed by force. If he refused to bathe, he was bathed by force as well. If he refused his occasional sortie into the château's courtyard, where fresh air and sunshine assaulted his senses every bit as brutally as the guards assaulted his body, he was escorted there by force.

Eventually, the force had been unnecessary, for a man strong enough to escape was a man who preserved the hope of revenge, and Christian wanted to remain that strong. He endured the fresh air and sunlight, he ate the food given him by his captors, nourishing not himself, but his dreams of revenge.

Girard had understood that too, and had understood how to manipulate even that last, best hope.

Christian was required to heal between sessions with Girard or the various corporals, and he was given medical care when the corporals—or more often Anduvoir—got out of hand. Now he'd earned a simple, relatively painless death.

He tried to muster gratitude, fear, relief, something. *Anything* besides a towering regret that revenge would be denied him.

"I'm sorry," the jailer said again. "I'm so bloody sorry."

Girard had said the same things, always softly, always *sincerely*, as he'd lowered Christian carefully to the cot where the mandatory healing would commence.

Christian felt the knife slicing at the bindings around his wrists and ankles, felt the agony of blood surging into his hands, then his feet.

"I'm sorry," the jailer said again.

And then Christian felt…nothing.

Two

"Orders fly in all directions once the guns go silent."

Devlin St. Just—Colonel St. Just, thank you very much—was complaining about peace, one of the career soldier's dubious privileges. "During wartime, the paperwork was limited to one side of a line," he went on. "Now we're galloping the length and breadth of Europe because pigeons simply won't do."

"If you brought Baldy orders, they must be important," Marcus Easterbrook observed—though he was finally *Lord Greendale* now. He would not bruit the title about until he'd received word of the final outcome of the inquest, bad form being an offense among Wellington's officers tantamount to treason.

Easterbrook took a nip of brandy, then passed his fellow officer the bottle, because a victorious army was supposed to be a gracious, cheerful institution—also because, like many who rode dispatch, St. Just had the ears of the generals. Brandy, alas, constituted the sum total of the amenities available in Easterbrook's tent, unless one counted the occasional camp whore.

Colonel St. Just was built like a dragoon, big, muscular, and capable of wielding rifle or sword with deadly intent. Easterbrook did not envy the larger man his dispatch rides, though. For the sake of the horse, the rider traveled light, and for the sake of the orders, he traveled hard, taking routes more direct than prudent.

"One shouldn't swill decent brandy, Easterbrook." St. Just tipped a finger's worth into his glass. "Bad form."

St. Just had been born on the wrong side of the blanket, but it had been a *ducal* blanket. Easterbrook poured himself three fingers into a chipped glass and moderated his reply accordingly.

"One develops a certain tolerance for lapses of form during war."

"Does one bloody ever." St. Just swirled his drink, held it under his not-exactly-delicate nose, then set it on the table untouched. "Tell me about this lost duke. He's the talk of the entire camp, though we hadn't heard of him up in Paris."

A small mercy, that.

"The lost duke is a legend here in the South and around the passes," Easterbrook said, wondering why, of all vices, St. Just had to be willing to gossip. "The eighth Duke of Mercia was attached to Wellington's Peninsular Army, serving mostly on His Grace's staff. He'd produced his heir and bought a commission in the family tradition."

"One baby does not a ducal succession ensure."

No, it did not, alas for the poor duke, though if memory served, St. Just had a proper litter of legitimate siblings.

"You'd have to have known Mercia," Easterbrook said. "Had all the brass in the world. As arrogant as only a duke born and bred can be, and as his cousin, I can assure you, the succession was not in jeopardy. My father was younger brother to the ducal heir, though Papa took the surname of his bride as a condition of the marriage settlements. I am every inch a Severn."

"You know His Grace?"

As if a duke would not associate with a mere cousin?

"He was my only living adult relation on my father's side, his father having been my eldest uncle. In any case, Mercia bought his colors and served honorably, but simply disappeared one morning last summer. We found his uniform, shaving kit, and his horse near a stream running north of the camp, and concluded he'd drowned while bathing."

Though as a boy, Christian had swum like an otter. Easterbrook had even said as much to the investigating officers, who'd viewed it as possible evidence of desertion.

Desertion, by a peer and an officer. The board of inquiry hadn't been very fond of their ducal comrade. Pity, that.

St. Just was apparently not impressed with the brandy, for he ran his finger around the top of the glass rather than consume his portion. "A grown man drowned in a stream?"

"You served in Spain?"

"For years, clear back to Portugal," St. Just said, that finger pausing in its circumnavigation of the rim. "Yes, I know: sudden floods, tinkers, locals sympathetic to

the French, French deserters… His Grace would have
been well blessed to die by drowning."

"He might agree with you, were he still alive.
Smoke?" Easterbrook certainly agreed with him.

"I don't indulge." He didn't indulge, he rode like
the wind, and he'd paused a moment, eyes closed,
before consuming his midday peasant fare of black
bread, butter, boiled potatoes, and beef cooked to
mush. After the belching, farting company in the officers' mess, such a paragon should have been a refresh-
ing change, and yet, Easterbrook was not enjoying St.
Just's company.

Easterbrook clipped off the end of a cheroot,
because he *did* indulge.

"A few weeks after Mercia disappeared, we heard
rumors the French had captured a high-ranking
English officer out of uniform."

St. Just shifted his stool a foot closer to the tent flaps
tied back to catch the prevailing breeze. "Poor sod."

"I know men who wouldn't bathe, lest they lose
the protection afforded them by their officer's uniform." For the French considered any English officer
captured out of uniform a spy, and indulged their
interrogatory whims on such unfortunates without
limit or mercy.

"I certainly kept my colors handy," St. Just mused.

Easterbrook passed the cut end of the cheroot under
his nose and took a whiff of privilege and pleasure,
however minor.

"I was seldom out of uniform myself. When the
rumors died down, a letter was carried from parts
unknown to one of Wellington's aides, unsigned,

but purporting to be from a French doctor. Said a titled English officer was being held under torture and should be quietly ransomed."

St. Just paused, his glass halfway to his lips. "That's unusual."

Ransom was unusual and officially unavailable, both sides having decided to hold prisoners for the duration of the hostilities. At last count, some Englishmen had enjoyed the dubious hospitality of Verdun for more than ten years.

"Suspiciously unusual," Easterbrook allowed, though Christian had been lucky from the cradle, and protocol regarding prisoners was often honored in the breach. "Word of the letter disappeared into diplomatic channels, but spies were sent out who apparently reported to Wellington that they found nothing, heard nothing, saw nothing."

Thank God.

"And yet, you began to hope?"

"Hope for what? By that time it had been months. Mercia was raised with every privilege and wasn't shy about indulging himself. Even in the officers' internment up in Verdun, he would have fared badly. How would a man like that cope with torture? How would any man? And after that much time, one had to wonder if Mercia would even want rescuing."

St. Just studied his drink, when most officers would have long since tossed it back and helped themselves to a refill.

"His Grace had a wife and son. Why wouldn't he want rescuing?"

"Cleaning up after Soult, we've freed some prisoners of war, and they did not fare well in the hands of the French."

"The French themselves did not fare well," St. Just countered, peering at the label on the brandy bottle as if actually reading what was written there—in French, of course. "One doesn't expect prisoners to enjoy full rations, regardless of whose care they're in."

"The deprivation is only part of it." Easterbrook used the oil lantern on the table to light his cheroot, then poured himself more brandy and cast around for a change of topic. "Is there any pleasure more gratifying than decent libation, a lusty whore, and a good smoke?"

"A lasting and fair peace," St. Just said, his gaze off to the northwest, in the direction of Merry Olde England, no less. "But you were telling me about your cousin."

The colonel would rather discuss a missing duke than naughty women. War did strange things to some men.

"The lost duke, whom I believe to be with his Maker as we speak. When Toulouse fell a few weeks ago, some half-soused Paddy of questionable loyalties let slip that a titled English officer had been held in some crumbling château in the foothills of the mountains. Seems the place was built on the site of a medieval castle, complete with dungeons. He said the prisoner was freed when the castle was abandoned by the gallant French."

"They're the defeated French now."

"So they are." Easterbrook lifted his glass in salute and took a drag of pungent tobacco.

And made another effort to change the damned topic. "You shipping out for Canada with everybody else?"

"I have family obligations, though I doubt I'll sell out. You've concluded this Irishman was lying?"

This was the same tenacity that ensured orders entrusted to St. Just reached their destination, no matter what. Easterbrook was beginning to hate his guest nearly as much as he respected him.

"The Irishman was…" Easterbrook paused as the acrid smoke curled toward the tent's ceiling. What to say? To crave a wealthy dukedom wasn't a sin, was it? "The Irishman was none too sober, and his motives were questionable. What was he doing inside that château, hmm? And where is this lost duke now, when every soul knows the Emperor has abdicated."

St. Just twitched the tent flap, as if to let in a bit more light, though Easterbrook took small satisfaction from the smoke bothering his guest.

"If Mercia was tortured at length, his mental faculties might not be at their sharpest," St. Just said. "And what would he gain by marching even this far north, as opposed to making his way directly home from the coast?"

"How could he afford passage home? How could a man subjected to deprivation and torture for that long travel any distance on foot? Assuming he's alive— which I have not for months—he's a bloody hero. As for those impersonating Mercia and claiming to be the lost duke, we give them a hot meal and nominal courtesy, until I can assure the generals we've another charlatan on our hands. Then the mountebank is run off to make shift with some other scheme."

And still the damned man merely sat back, folded his arms over a broad chest, and watched the smoke curling upward.

"For a French physician to put something in writing like that… He'd have been shot as a traitor to the *Republique* if the letter had fallen into the wrong hands."

Tobacco was said to calm the nerves. Easterbrook inhaled deeply, until the tip of his cheroot flared bright red, then let the smoke ease out through his nose.

"Mercia might have been taken prisoner, but what are the chances the French would capture a man naked from his bath, deny him the chance to get into uniform, realize he's a bloody duke, and continue to hold him for interrogation against all policy to the contrary? That would exceed *bad form* considerably."

"Besides," Easterbrook rose as he went on, because it was time to run his guest off, "we suffered no lapses of intelligence that suggest this prisoner might have been Mercia. Mercia was in on all the meetings, consulted on strategy, had even scouted some of the passes. He's a canny devil—*was* a canny devil, for all his arrogance—and the French would have been well served if they'd laid their hands on him."

"If he broke."

Easterbrook tipped the bottle to his lips, because it would somehow be empty when he returned to his tent, victory and graciousness notwithstanding.

"I'd break," Easterbrook said quietly. Perhaps he'd had too much brandy, or perhaps he'd spent too much time in the company of Colonel Paragon St. Just. "I'd try to hold out, but one hears stories, and I'm sorry, St. Just, one officer to another, I'd break."

"You don't know that." St. Just rose too easily for a man who'd ridden the distance from Paris. "My thanks for the hospitality, for the meal, the drink, and your company. I'm off to check on my horse."

Bless the beast. "Your horse?"

"I ride my own mounts. I'm safer that way, and as much ground as we've covered the past few days, I need to take him out and stretch his legs, keep him from stiffening up. You're welcome to join me."

"Excuse me, Colonel Easterbrook, Colonel St. Just?" A subaltern who might soon be of an age to shave came puffing to a stop right outside the tent, then saluted with the exaggerated enthusiasm of the young and never injured.

"Anders." Easterbrook took one last drag on his smoke, tossed the stub to the ground, and rubbed it out with the toe of his boot. "Are you on an errand for Baldy?"

"General Baldridge has another lost duke for you, sir. We put him in the officers' mess."

"Famous." Easterbrook chugged the dregs from the brandy bottle and tossed it aside. "Does this one at least speak English?"

"He doesn't say much at all, sir, though his eyes are a frightful blue."

"Well, the poor devil got that much right. Fetch my horse, Anders. St. Just and I will hack out when we've dispensed with His Latest Grace. Come along, St. Just. Lost dukes only show up once a week or so in these parts. They're our entertainment, now that the Frogs no longer oblige."

❧

Christian stood outside the tent, the spring breeze nigh making his sore teeth chatter—though it hadn't obscured a word of the exchange that had taken place inside.

"He's another lost duke." The subaltern had kept his tone expressionless as he passed along the message to some general. "Third one this month, but we've sent for Colonel Easterbrook, sir."

"Poor Easterbrook." The senior officer blew out a gusty breath, and Christian heard what sounded like a pen being tossed onto a table, then a chair creak. "I suppose this one has a tale as well?"

"Not that I've heard, sir. He looks... Well..."

"Permission to speak freely, Blevins."

"If I were claiming to have wandered the heights for months, living on nothing, perhaps crazed from a blow to the head or captured by Frogs, it would help if I looked like him, sir."

"Elaborate."

"He's skinny as a wraith, and his eyes look like he had a front-row seat in hell. He isn't babbling and carrying on like the last two did."

"The last four, you mean. I suppose Easterbrook will be forced to denounce this one too, but a bit of Christian charity won't go amiss. Take the man to the mess tent, observe the proprieties, and get him a decent meal. One never knows, and it doesn't do to offend a duke, particularly not a mad one."

Interesting point, suggesting this commanding officer had a grasp of strategy.

"Aye, sir."

Blevins stepped out of the tent, conscientiously

retying the flap, though it continued to luff noisily in the breeze.

Sounds were something Christian was getting used to again. Sounds other than iron bars clanging open and shut, rats scurrying, Girard's philosophizing, his jailer's doleful brogue-and-burr mutterings...

"You're to be fed while we await further orders," the blond, ruddy-faced Blevins said. From the crisp look of his uniform, Blevins either came from means, was particularly vain of his appearance—thinning hair could do that to a young fellow—or he'd only recently bought his colors.

Christian mustered two words. "Your Grace."

"Beg pardon?" English manners had Blevins bending nearer, for the fifth lost duke spoke only quietly.

When he spoke at all.

"You're to be fed, *Your Grace*," Christian said slowly, each word the product of a mental gymnastic, like tossing separate pebbles into the exact center of a quiet pond.

"Oh, right you are, sir, er, Your Grace." The man's ears turned red and he marched smartly away, only to have to slow his step when Christian didn't quicken his own. Blevins's embarrassment was not the product of a lapse in manners, but rather, pity for one who had parted from both his reason and his shaving kit some time ago.

"Afraid the fare is humble, Your, er, Grace. Well-cooked beef, boiled potatoes with salt and butter, the inevitable coarse bread, but it sustains us. Things are better since old Wellie put Soult in his place. The locals are happy to feed us, you see, because we pay them for their bread, unlike their own army."

The words, English words, flowed past Christian's awareness like so much birdsong at the beginning of a summer day. Easterbrook was coming, and Easterbrook could see Christian to England, back to the arms of his devoted if not quite loving duchess, and their children. Evan would be walking and talking by now, losing his baby curls, perhaps even ready to be taken up before his papa for a quiet hack.

Christian had enjoyed many discussions with his infant son while enduring Girard's hospitality. He'd chosen the boy's first pony—a fat, shaggy piebald—read him his favorite bedtime stories, and picked out a puppy or two.

In his mind, he'd gently explained to the child that papa had a few Frenchmen to kill, but would be home soon thereafter.

The scent of roasted beef interrupted Christian's musings like a physical slap. He categorized his perceptions to keep his mind from overflowing with sensory noise. Scents were English, or rural, or French. Cooked beef was definitely English. The pervasive mud smelled merely rural. The damned orange cat with the matted fur stropping itself against Christian's boots was French.

He bent carefully and tossed the cat—he did *not* pitch it hard, as he wished to, or wring its neck—several feet away. Cats were definitely French.

"Shall I fetch you some tea, Your Grace?" Blevins's adoption of proper address had become enthusiastic, if not quite ironic. "The wives are good about keeping us supplied with tea even when the quartermasters can't."

"Hot water will suffice. My thanks." For even the thought of tea sent Christian's digestion into a panic.

This time, Blevins succeeded in keeping a straight face to go with his, "Very good, Your Grace."

Did dukes no longer thank their servants? Blevins's expression cleared, and he hustled away. Perhaps the man thought Christian would finally be shaving.

Soon enough, Easterbrook would come, and then on to England, where Christian could begin to plot a just fate for Anduvoir and Girard, and all would at last be well again.

❧

"Not hoping must be hard," St. Just said as he and Easterbrook made their way toward the officers' mess. The tent lay on high ground, and gave off the same beguiling, smoky aroma as every mess St. Just had had the pleasure of approaching from downwind. "Mercia is your cousin, after all."

He kept his observation casual, because something about Easterbrook's reaction was off. If any of St. Just's family had turned up missing, and then been reported found, he'd be dancing on the nearest fountain and bellowing the good news to the hills.

While Easterbrook's mannerisms suggested dread.

"Mercia is a young man," Easterbrook replied. "If it is him, and he still has his reason, and his health is not entirely broken, he could get back to his life, or a semblance of it."

Anybody held by the French for months would have reserves of resilience St. Just could only envy, though the creature they found in the mess tent was pitiful indeed.

He sat alone at the end of one table, taking small bites of boiled potato, setting his fork down, chewing carefully, then taking another bite. His beef was untouched, his appearance unkempt, his bearded features sharp, like a saint newly returned from a spate of praying and wrestling demons in the wilderness.

"A real duke has pretty manners," Easterbrook said, approaching the table, "but he'd be tearing into that beef if he'd been kept away from a good steak for months. I'm Easterbrook."

He sat across from the skinny, quiet fellow with the brilliant blue eyes, and crossed his arms over his chest.

"My teeth are loose, Colonel," the man said. "I cannot manage the beef, because the French became too parsimonious to feed me the occasional orange. Or perhaps they ran out of oranges themselves."

"Ah, but of course—shame upon those niggardly French." Easterbrook shot a long-suffering glance toward the several officers malingering two tables over. "Perhaps we should take this discussion outside."

St. Just would have preferred to shoo their audience away, because the cool mountain air would cut right through the wraith at the table.

"We should take the discussion outside, Your Grace, Marcus," said the wraith—softly. *Ducally*, in St. Just's informed opinion.

"My apologies," Easterbrook replied, "Your Grace, indeed." His tone was so punctiliously civil as to be mocking.

The man rose slowly—perhaps he could not abide leaving his potatoes unconsumed—and nobody moved to help him. St. Just discarded the notion given the determination in those blue eyes.

"Look here," Easterbrook said when they'd drawn a few steps away from the mess tent. "If you were Christian Severn, Duke of Mercia, you'd bloody well not be sporting that beard. You look like you haven't shaved in weeks, your hands are dirty, and without putting too fine a point on it, I wouldn't want to stand downwind of you on a hot day."

None of which, in St. Just's opinion, had any bearing on the present situation.

"My hands shake too badly to wield a razor, Cousin, though less so now." His Grace—why the hell not refer to him as such?—held out a right hand that did, indeed, suffer a minute tremor. "The French would not shave me, because I might succeed in slicing open my throat against the razor, regardless of the barber's skill. They clipped my beard occasionally instead."

This was more logic, but Easterbrook waved an impatient—and also slightly unsteady—hand.

"The Duke of Mercia was a man in his prime, for God's sake. You're skin and bones and you have no uniform, no signet ring."

Which, of course, the French would have taken possession of immediately upon capturing the fellow. Inside the mess tent, shuffling and murmuring suggested the audience had shifted close enough to hear the exchange.

"I was fed enough to keep me alive, not enough to keep me strong. You insult your cousin, Easterbrook." The man spoke softly, as if he refused to entertain a lot of bored officers who at midday were not yet drunk.

"Half the camp knows I was cousin to Mercia," Easterbrook spat as Anders led his horse up. "Having me identify the imposters has become a standing joke. My cousin was left-handed, you ate with only your right hand. Explain that."

The explanation had St. Just itching to hop back in the saddle and ride anywhere—Paris, Moscow, Rome—provided it was far, far away. His Grace held up his left arm, on the end of which was an appendage bearing five fingers; the last two of them bore old scars and curious angles at the joints.

"As a gift to the commanding officer, the guards decided in his absence that I was to write out a confession to present their superior upon his return from Toulouse. My captors neglected to realize I was left-handed." The lost duke spoke slowly, each word chosen to convey the most information with the fewest syllables.

"The guards limited their attentions to the hand they thought I could not write with," he went on. "I did not write out the confession in any case. When Colonel Girard was done having his guards beaten for their cheek, he was effusively apologetic." That last phrase was flourished with subtle irony and such a perfect enunciation of the final consonants, that St. Just paced off a few feet, the better to curse quietly.

"Anybody who reads *The Times* would know the story of the lost duke," Easterbrook said, a bit desperately, to St. Just's ears. "My cousin was a robust man, handsome, fastidious, vain about his person. His family connections would be listed in *Debrett's*, and known to anybody who moved in good Society. You're skinny, dirty, disgracefully turned out…"

He ranted on, for he was ranting, his voice rising, likely for the benefit of the officers inside the tent, but St. Just had heard enough.

"Easterbrook, mind your horse."

Anders held the reins of a grand chestnut beast, solid, but with a hint of Iberian grace and refinement. The horse was pawing and curling its upper lip while craning its neck forward.

Toward the lost duke.

"Aragon?" Easterbrook was apparently not that canny a fellow. Beside Aragon, St. Just's mount was standing perfectly calm.

"Not Aragon," the lost duke said, walking toward the horse. "Chesterton. You took my horse, Cousin, and changed his name. I suppose I am to thank you for looking after him when God knows what might have befallen him had he remained in French hands."

The beast pawed repeatedly, and wuffled, a low, whickering sound of greeting.

And the love of a mute beast was, to St. Just, better evidence than any interrogation would ever yield.

"You've found your duke," St. Just said. "Either the horse has read *Debrett's* and colluded with an imposter, or that's his master, plain as day." A half-dozen officers had shuffled out of the mess tent, their uniforms declaring them cavalry, and not a one argued with St. Just's conclusion.

Easterbrook scowled as the horse nuzzled at the lost duke's pockets, each in turn. The duke scratched at the animal's shoulder. Had the bloody horse been able to, it would have purred and hugged its owner.

"By God…" Easterbrook took a step toward a man

whose death would have been convenient, if tragic. But the duke held up a hand—his good hand.

"Do not, I pray you, embarrass us both with an excessive display of sentiment comparable to that of this lowly beast. If you would show your welcome, fetch writing utensils that I might communicate with my duchess posthaste. A change of clothes would be appreciated as well, as would a bucket, cloth, and soap."

The horse gave up nuzzling empty pockets, but was either too well-bred or too canny to nudge more strongly at a master who would likely topple at such attention.

For the first time, Easterbrook's expression conveyed consternation and...shock. "You don't know, then. God help you, nobody told you about Helene."

Three

"YOUR GRACE, YOU HAVE A CALLER."

Christian had been at his London town house for three days and nights, and still his entire household, from butler to boot boy, seemed helpless not to beam at him.

He'd been *tortured*, repeatedly, for months, and they were grinning like dolts. To see them happy, to feel the weight of the entire household smiling at him around every turn made him furious, and that—his unabating, irrational reaction—made him anxious.

Even Carlton House had sent an invitation, for God's sake, and Christian's court attire would hang on him like some ridiculous shroud.

The butler cleared his throat.

Right. A caller. "This late?"

"She says her business is urgent."

By the standards of London in springtime, nine in the evening was one of the more pleasant hours, but by no means did one receive calls at such an hour.

"Who is she?"

Meems crossed the study, a silver tray in his hand bearing a single note of cream vellum.

"I do not recall a Lady Greendale." Though a Greendale estate lay several hours ride from Severn. Lord Greendale was a pompous old curmudgeon forever going on in the Lords about proper respect and decent society. An embossed black band crossed one corner of the card, indicating the woman was a widow, perhaps still in mourning.

"I'm seeing no callers, Meems. You know that."

"Yes, quite, Your Grace, as you're recovering. Quite. She says she's family." Behind the smile Meems barely contained lurked a worse offense yet: hope. The old fellow *hoped* His Grace might admit somebody past the threshold of Mercia House besides a man of business or running footman.

Christian ran his fingertip over the crisp edge of the card. Gillian, Countess of Greendale, begged the favor of a call. Some elderly cousin of his departed parents, perhaps. His memory was not to be relied upon in any case.

Duty came in strange doses. Like the need to sign dozens of papers simply so the coin earned by the duchy could be used to pay the expenses incurred by the duchy. Learning to sign his name with his right hand had been a frustrating exercise in duty. Christian had limited himself to balling up papers and tossing them into the grate rather than pitching the ink pot.

"Show her into the family parlor."

"There will be no need for that." A small blond woman brushed past Meems and marched up to Christian's desk. "Good evening, Your Grace. Gillian, Lady Greendale."

She bobbed a miniscule curtsy suggesting a miniscule

grasp of the deference due his rank, much less of Meems's responsibility for announcing guests. "We have family business to discuss."

No, Christian silently amended, she had *no* grasp whatsoever, and based on her widow's weeds, no husband to correct the lack.

And yet, this lady was in mourning, and around her mouth were brackets of fatigue. She was not in any sense smiling, and looked as if she might have forgotten how.

A welcome divergence from the servants' expressions.

"Meems, a tray, and please close the door as you leave."

Christian rose from his desk, intent on shifting to stand near the fire, but the lady twitched a jacket from her shoulders and handed it to him. Her garment was a gorgeous black silk business, embroidered with aubergine thread along its hems. The feel of the material was sumptuous in Christian's hands, soft, sleek, luxurious, and warm from her body heat. He wanted to hold it—simply to hold it—and to bring it to his nose, for it bore the soft floral scent of not a woman, but a *lady*.

The reminders he suffered of his recent deprivations increased rather than decreased with time.

"Now, then," she said, sweeping the room with her gaze.

He was curious enough at her presumption that he folded her jacket, draped it over a chair, and let a silence build for several slow ticks of the mantel clock.

"Now, then," he said, more quietly than she, "if you'd care to have a seat, Lady Greendale?"

She had to be a May-December confection gobbled

up in Lord Greendale's dotage. The woman wasn't thirty years old, and she had a curvy little figure that caught a man's eye. Or it would catch a man's eye, had he not been more preoccupied with how he'd deal with tea-tray inanities when he couldn't stomach tea.

She took a seat on the sofa facing the fire, which was fortunate, because it allowed Christian his desired proximity to the heat. He propped an elbow on the mantel and wished, once again, that he'd tarried at Severn.

"My lady, you have me at a loss. You claim a family connection, and yet memory doesn't reveal it to me."

"That's certainly to the point." By the firelight, her hair looked like antique gold, not merely blond. Her tidy bun held coppery highlights, and her eyebrows looked even more reddish. Still, her appearance did not tickle a memory, and he preferred willowy blonds in any case.

Had preferred them.

"I thought we'd chitchat until the help is done eavesdropping, perhaps exchange condolences. You have mine, by the way. Very sincerely."

Her piquant features softened with her words, her sympathy clear in her blue eyes, though it took Christian a moment to puzzle out for what.

Ah. The loss of his wife and son. That.

She pattered on, like shallow water rippling over smooth stones, sparing him the need to make any reply. Christian eventually figured out that this torrent of speech was a sign of nerves.

Had Girard blathered like this, philosophizing, sermonizing, and threatening as a function of nerves?

Christian rejected the very notion rather than attribute to Girard even a single human quality.

"Helene was my cousin," the lady said, recapturing Christian's attention, because nobody had referred to the late duchess by name in his presence. "The family was planning to offer you me, but then Greendale started sniffing around me, and Helene was by far the prettier, so she went for a duchess while I am merely a countess. Shouldn't the tea be here by now?"

Now he did remember, the way the first few lines of a poem will reveal the entire stanza. He'd met this Lady Greendale. She had a prosaic, solidly English name he could not recall—perhaps she'd just told him what it was, perhaps he'd seen it somewhere— but she'd been an attendant at his wedding, his and Helene's. Greendale's gaze had followed his young wife with a kind of porcine possessiveness, and the wife had scurried about like a whipped dog.

Christian had pitied her at the time. He didn't pity her now.

But then, he didn't feel much of anything when his day was going well.

"Here's the thing..." She was mercifully interrupted by the arrival of the tea tray. Except it wasn't simply a tray, as Christian had ordered. The trolley bore a silver tea service, a plate of cakes, a plate of finger sandwiches, and a bowl of oranges, because his smiling, hopeful, attentive staff was determined to put flesh on him.

His digestion was determined to make it a slow process.

"Shall I pour?" She had her gloves off and was

rearranging the tray before Christian could respond. "One wonders what ladies do in countries not obsessed with their tea. Do they make such a ritual out of coffee? And you take yours plain, I believe. Helene told me that."

What odd conversations women must have, comparing how their husbands took tea. "I no longer drink tea. I drink…nursery tea."

A man whose every bodily function had been observed for months should not be embarrassed to admit such a thing, and Christian wasn't. He was, rather, humiliated and enraged out of all proportion to the moment.

"Hence the hot water," she said, peering at the silver pot that held same. "Do you intend to loom over me up there, or will you come down here beside me for some tea?"

He did not want to move a single inch.

She chattered, and her hands fluttered over the tea service like mating songbirds, making visual noise to go with her blathering. She cut up his peace, such as it was, and he already knew she would put demands on him he didn't care to meet.

And yet, she hadn't smiled, hadn't pretended grown dukes drank nursery tea every night. Whatever else was true about the lady, she had an honesty about her Christian approved of.

He sat on the sofa, several feet away from her.

She made no remark on his choice of seat.

"I suppose you've heard about that dreadful business involving Greendale. Had Mr. Stoneleigh not thought to produce the bottle of belladonna drops for the magistrate—the full, unopened bottle, still in its seal—you might have been spared my presence permanently. I can't help but think old Greendale did it apurpose, gave me the drops just to put poison in my hands. Easterbrook probably sent them from the Continent all unsuspecting. Greendale wanted me buried with him, like some old pharaoh's wife. Your tea."

She'd made him a cup of hot water, sugar, and cream—nursery tea, served to small children to spare them tea's stimulant effects.

"I'll fix you a plate too, shall I?" A sandwich, then two, as well as two cakes were piled onto a plate by her busy, noisy hands.

"An orange will do."

She looked at the full plate as if surprised to find all that food there, shrugged, and set it aside. "I'll peel it for you, then. A lady has fingernails suited for the purpose."

She set about stripping the peel from the hapless orange as effectively as she was stripping Christian's nerves, though in truth, she wasn't gawking, she wasn't simpering, she wasn't smiling. The lady had business to transact, and she'd dispatch it as efficiently as she dispatched the peel from the orange.

And those busy hands were graceful. Christian wanted to watch them work, wanted to watch them be feminine, competent, and pretty, because this too—the simple pleasure of a lady's hands—had been long denied him.

He took a sip of his nursery tea, finding it hot, sweet, soothing, and somehow unsatisfying. "Perhaps you'd be good enough to state the reason for your call, Lady Greendale?"

"We're not to chat over tea, even? One forgets you've spent the last few years among soldiers, Your Grace, but then the officers on leave are usually such gallant fellows." She focused on the orange, which was half-naked on the plate in her lap. "This is just perfectly ripe, and the scent is divine."

The scent was good. Not a scent with any negative associations, not overpowering, not French.

"You are welcome to share it with me," he said, sipping his little-boy tea and envying her the speed with which she'd denuded the orange of its peel.

Peeling an orange was a two-handed undertaking, something he'd had occasion to recall in the past three days. This constant bumping up against his limitations wearied him as Girard's philosophizing never had. Yes, he was free from Girard's torture, but everywhere, he was greeted with loss, duress, and decisions.

"Your orange?" She held out three quarters of a peeled orange to him, no smile, no faintly bemused expression to suggest he'd been woolgathering—again.

"You know, it really wasn't very well done of you, Your Grace." She popped a section of orange into her mouth and chewed busily before going on. "When one has been traveling, one ought to go home first, don't you think? But you came straight up to Town, and your staff at Severn was concerned for you."

Concerned for him. Of what use had this concern been when Girard's thugs were mutilating his hand? Though to be fair, Girard had been outraged to find his pet prisoner disfigured, and ah, what a pleasure to see Girard dealing with insubordination.

Though indignation and outrage were also human traits, and thus should have been beyond Girard's ken.

"You're not eating your orange, Your Grace. It's very good." She held up a section in her hand, her busy, graceful little lady's hand. He leaned forward and nipped the orange section from her fingers with his teeth.

She sat back, for once quiet. She was attractive when she was quiet, her features classic, though her nose missed perfection by a shade of boldness, and her eyebrows were a touch on the dramatic side. A man would notice this woman before he'd notice a merely pretty woman, and—absent torture by the French—he would recall her when the pretty ones had slipped from his memory.

"Now then, madam. We've eaten, we've sipped our tea. The weather is delightful. What is your business?"

"It isn't my business, really," she said, regarding not him, not the food, but the fire kept burning in the grate at all hours. "It's your business, if you can call it business."

Something about the way she clasped her hands together in her lap gave her away. She was no more comfortable calling as darkness fell than he was receiving her. She'd barely tasted her orange, and all of her blather had been nerves.

Lady Greendale was afraid of him.

Perhaps she'd heard the rumors about the lost duke's madness; perhaps she hadn't recalled he'd be a good foot taller than she; perhaps she hadn't expected the staff to leave them so very much alone.

In any case, he didn't like it. Next to hope, fear was the tormentor's most effective weapon.

"Lady Greendale, plain speech would be appreciated." He spoke not only quietly, but gently, the way he might speak to a child or the elderly. "I'm sure you'd rather be home at such an hour, and I would not detain you unnecessarily."

Unfortunate word choice. An English civilian caught in France when war broke out was a *détenu*.

"You should have gone home to Severn first, Your Grace, and then it would not fall to me to remind you of your duty, but here we are."

She was stalling rather than scolding, suggesting the lady was quite unnerved. He waited her out. He was a master at waiting, and at silence. Girard's ill-treatment had bequeathed a legacy of patience, in addition to scars.

And she apparently had some passing familiarity with silence as well. All her fluttering and shifting about ceased. A few beats of quiet went by, and Christian abruptly missed her blathering.

"It's your daughter." She turned limpid blue eyes on him, a world of worry shining out of them, but the worry, for once, wasn't for him, and that was a curious relief. "I am very concerned about your daughter."

❧

Gilly had gathered up the last of her courage to get her to this elegant, toasty London parlor, for what she recalled most clearly about Mercia was that he was tall. Her husband had been tall.

Tall men had self-possession and reach. Neither was a good thing.

Thin as he was, Mercia looked even taller now than he had when he'd danced with Gilly upon the occasion of his wedding to Helene. His eyes, the famous Severn blue eyes, were sunken, and his blond hair was pulled back into a loose, old-fashioned queue. Helene had been uncomfortable with what she called her husband's cool intensity. She'd said he was too serious by half, and much taken with himself.

Coming from Helene, who'd been taken with herself indeed, the comment had lodged in Gilly's memory. Greendale had been nothing, if not taken with himself.

"Tell me about my daughter."

His tone was encouraging, and he'd asked the right question—or given the right command—but Gilly had the sense he couldn't recall the name of his only surviving child. Or maybe he could, and saying that name pained him too much.

"Lucille will be eight this summer," Gilly said. "She's very bright, she reads well, shows some talent at the piano, and is much loved by her governess and nursery maid."

Also by her mother's cousin, or Gilly would not be bearding this gaunt, quiet lion in his den.

Though how many lions drank nursery tea and folded a lady's wrap as if it held precious memories?

"And yet," His Grace said quietly, "the girl suffers some problem, else you wouldn't be calling upon me at such an unusual hour."

He made a simple deduction, rather than delivered

a scold, so Gilly gave him an honest answer. "I was told you sleep during the day, Your Grace, and you're refusing all callers."

Which admission would alert the duke to the fact that his staff was more concerned about him than about discretion. Gilly felt a spike of protectiveness toward her host, in part because everybody needed privacy, and in part because he was so quiet. He spoke quietly, his movements were quiet, and his eyes were the most quiet of all.

Greendale had seldom been silent for long, and all his tirades had had the same focus.

"And now," His Grace said, putting down his empty teacup, "you will have the more daring among my peers calling upon me at night."

Was he making a jest? "Not if you come down to Severn with me."

And again, silence fell between them, filled only with the soft roar of the fire. The lack of conversation should have unnerved Gilly, but the quiet moments allowed her to truly study him.

The Times had heralded Mercia's return with front-page articles, but all they'd really said was he'd been held by the French and denied the privileges of an officer. That was likely male code for something more dire than a scrabbling, parole liberty in the town of the *Republique's* choosing, but Gilly was without men to translate for her.

Thank God.

"I intend to remove to Severn," he said, "but not until the bankers see that I live, have possession of the relevant faculties, and have returned my duchy to good financial health."

They'd likely said that to his face, too, the rotters, and held his own money clutched away from him as they said it.

"Bother the duchy's financial health. You are clearly competent to administer your own affairs." Gilly reined in her temper by fixing him another cup of his nursery tea. She would not have minded a cup herself, insomnia being a widow's frequent burden. "Your daughter's health is precarious, and that should take precedence over all."

"If she is ill, I will certainly retain physicians to examine her."

"I already have." She passed him his tea and then had nothing to do with her hands.

"Perhaps you'd peel me another orange?"

Excellent notion. He'd eaten his already, steadily ingested one section after another, and yet, his hands weren't sticky.

Taking a small plate, Gilly peeled the fruit and tore it into sections, wiped her fingers using the finger bowl and a serviette, then passed him his orange. The whole process took several minutes, which allowed Gilly to organize her thoughts.

"You are capable of silence," he said, taking the plate of orange sections. "I had wondered." He might have been mocking her, in that soft, musing voice. Or he might have been trying to communicate something else entirely.

"One doesn't usually make a call to sit without speaking like a pair of Quakers at meeting."

He saluted with his teacup. "You were telling me about my daughter."

"Lucille, yes. She grew quite withdrawn when her brother died, and we feared she might fall ill as he did."

"He was ill, then?" A quiet question, the inflection coming across as almost…French?

"He was colicky, then started running a fever. Not typhoid or lung fever, that we could tell. Influenza, most likely."

He rose and went to the window, keeping his back to her, which struck Gilly as rude, until it occurred to her nobody would have discussed his son's death with him, and Helene's letters had—if she'd written any, if he'd received any—been no doubt worse than useless.

Gilly was in the presence not only of a duke—a tall, quiet duke, with silent eyes and clothing that fit him far too loosely—but also a grieving father and husband. She nearly envied him that grief, which suggested her grasp of reason had become tenuous.

"Evan did not linger, Your Grace. He was ill seven days and nights."

"You were with him?"

Still the duke kept his back to her, and his voice was the same. Soft, aristocratic, no emotion whatsoever, as if somebody gravely ill slept elsewhere in the house.

"I stayed for the duration, and for a few days afterward. Even Greendale understood my place was with my cousin at such a time."

"And this was hard on the sister?"

The sister? Lucille, his daughter, but Evan's sister.

"Very. Helene did not cope well. Greendale would not let me linger at Severn indefinitely."

"Coping was not Helene's greatest strength."

Diplomatically put, but what did the man find so fascinating beyond the darkened window?

"With her mother's passing, Lucy became even more withdrawn. Losing her mother and brother was difficult, and she hasn't known what to make of your situation."

No small child could have made sense of a father imprisoned, far away, and unlikely to return.

"I was hard put to make sense of my situation myself." This observation bore the quality of an admission, not a joke. By no means a joke.

Gilly let the silence stretch, not knowing what to say. She studied the lines of his evening attire that hung on him like so much damp, oversized laundry. Perhaps his situation still made no sense to him?

"What are Lucy's symptoms?"

"She speaks very little, and she does not leave the schoolroom unless forced to do so by me or her nurse. Her appetite is poor."

He turned, his expression for the first time yielding to an emotion—consternation. "She has gone into a decline. I did not know children could."

Gilly's opinion exactly, but the doctors had scoffed. "She has lost weight. She no longer plays, but rather, dresses and undresses her dolls by the hour, sits and stares, or draws."

"What do the physicians say?"

"That she is being stubborn and willful and attempting to dictate to the adults around her." Stubborn and willful were apparently the most frequent complaints men made against females of any age, and yet, where would Gilly have been without a full complement of stubbornness to see her through her marriage?

"What do *you* say, Lady Greendale?"

Gilly was so used to keeping her opinions to herself, every one of her opinions, regardless of the topic, that His Grace's question caught her off guard.

His expression suggested he truly wanted her view of the matter. Mercia was tall, and he was male, but if his question was any indication, his resemblance to Greendale ended there.

"Lucy has lost her family, Your Grace. She needs family, and until recently, I could not oblige." And Greendale had enjoyed ensuring it was so.

Mercia ran his hand over her jacket, which he'd folded across the back of a chair. "Your bereavement is recent?"

Whatever else Mercia was doing, he wasn't catching up on gossip. "More than a month past. Lord Greendale succumbed to an apoplexy, according to the official inquest."

He twisted the gold signet ring about the middle finger of his right hand, an unusual location for such a piece. "My condolences. Perhaps you'd like more tea?"

His Grace had not yet addressed the problem Gilly had brought to him, and the hour grew later. "Bother the tea."

He was not offended by her lapse in manners. Maybe after wintering with the French, little offended him, and yet, Gillian was a guest in his home, at a peculiar hour, and clearly, His Grace was not faring well.

She extended an olive branch, for the child's sake. "We're family, Your Grace. You are welcome to call me Gillian. To Lucy, I am Cousin Gilly."

More consternation shone in his remarkable blue eyes, as if to whom and when familiarities might be granted had been misplaced on some French mountainside, along with the roles of husband and father.

And the ability to appreciate a strong cup of tea.

And the ability to sleep through the night.

His Grace resumed a place beside Gilly on the sofa, settling carefully, like an old fellow who had not enough padding on his bones to tolerate even a short tenure on a hard chair.

Or perhaps the duke was too exhausted to stand for more than a few minutes?

"I am inclined to take your suggestion that I remove to Severn sooner rather than later. The curious and inconsiderate have been leaving their cards by the dozen, and I am summoned to Carlton House several days hence for a private audience with the Regent. My health is not much better than precarious, and I am loath to subject myself to the remaining weeks of the Season. At your prompting, I will repair to Severn at week's end."

"Thank you." She nearly told him he should observe mourning for Helene—Evan had been too young—because mourning kept the curious and the inconsiderate away for a few months.

"I have a condition."

With men, every concession came at a price, and yet, Gilly did not anticipate an onerous request from the weary, soft-spoken duke. "Name it."

"You will accompany me, and until I go, you will act as the lady of this house. You will deal with the invitations, you will deal with the squabbling, smiling housemaids. You will see to the closing up of the household, and you will assert your presence during daylight hours so I needn't bother with housewifery all throughout my nights. If you are disinclined to meet this request, I will take that much longer to make the journey south."

Again, he'd surprised Gilly.

His condition called to the long-denied part of her that delighted in the role of caretaker, a part of her that had shrunk to a husk under Greendale's criticisms, that had wished even if Greendale were the father, Gilly might have had children to raise and love.

And yet, what came out of her fool mouth? "What of a chaperone, Your Grace?"

He did not smile. Gilly's sense of his amusement was unsupported by anything save the way he turned that signet ring, played with it almost, the band loose around his finger.

"First, my lady, we are family, as you've noted yourself. You are Helene's cousin, and widowed. If your own family could not provide for you, I would naturally expect you to apply to me in their stead. Second, you have apparently been a frequent visitor at Severn in my absence. As a kinswoman, you would be the logical choice for my hostess, were I to entertain. In any case, you are beyond chaperones now, are you not? Third, you are the logical choice of female to take a continuing interest in Lucy's development, because you are the only one who might sponsor her come out ten years hence."

Quite a speech from him. Gilly sorted through his words and concluded he was offering her a home at

Severn, however temporarily. Absenting herself from
Greendale represented the closest thing Gilly had to a
goal, besides seeing to Lucy's welfare.

Mercia had some ulterior motive, of that Gilly
was certain, but no matter. She'd been dealing with
men and their motives for years, and Lucy had no
other champion.

Gilly rose, which meant the duke had to come
to his feet as well, and gracious, he was tall. "I'll
collect my things and remove here in the morning,
Your Grace."

Some flicker of emotion in the vicinity of his thin
mouth suggested he was pleased, or possibly relieved,
but apparently he'd left the ability to smile on that
French mountainside, too.

"Send for your things. I'm sure a guest room is kept
in readiness, and the hour grows late."

⁓

Gillian, Lady Greendale, was fretful, busy, and only
distant family, but if she kept mostly to daylight hours,
cajoled the child out of her megrims, and spared
Christian mountains of painstaking social correspondence, then he'd consider the bargain well met.

That she could peel oranges and didn't regard him
as a freak because he eschewed tea was to her credit
as well.

Lady Greendale regarded him, her head cocked at
an angle like a biddy hen sizing up the new egg girl.
"You want me to stay here tonight?"

He did, and not because a craving for more oranges
might beset him. "Shall you sit?"

She went back to the sofa, resuming her place before the tea trays.

"You're sure you wouldn't like some sustenance?" he asked. Except for a few bites of orange, her ladyship hadn't eaten a thing, and offering food was as close to charming as he could be.

"Am I delaying your dinner, Your Grace?"

"You are not." He wasn't capable of eating a dinner. She'd find that out soon enough if she joined his household.

"Well, then yes, I could do with a sandwich. Will you join me?"

"No, thank you."

Her spine stiffened.

"Well, perhaps…" He surveyed the offerings, and knew he ought to be hungry. More to the point, the lady would take it amiss if he didn't eat. "A buttered scone."

She beamed at him with every bit as much guileless goodwill as his staff showed, and Christian had to look away. He resumed his slouch against the mantel, where the fire's warmth could work its magic on the permanent ache he'd absorbed from the cold, damp stones of the Château's lower reaches.

"You mentioned an inquest, my lady." He'd already forgotten her name again, though it would come to him when he was trying to recall where he'd put his pocket watch.

She dabbed butter on his scone and considered the effect, much the way some women held their embroidery up, the better to admire it, then added a bit more butter.

"I was told an inquest was a formality, Lord Greendale being a peer. Nonetheless, it was unpleasant in the extreme, Your Grace, and were it not for the assistance of my barrister, I shudder to consider the consequences. Jam?"

He'd missed most of what she said, because his attention was fixed on the fourth finger of her left hand, which sported a slightly odd bend to the second joint.

"You're not wearing a ring." Perhaps her rings no longer fit. His certainly didn't.

"I'm no longer married."

Neither was he. The thought still caught him by surprise and unsettled him, which would have pleased Helene. "I gather your union wasn't happy?"

"No, it was not, hence the unpleasantness at the inquest. Your scone." She brought him the plate with its pastry, the closest she'd come to him, close enough for two things to register in his awareness.

She was physically small. He'd gathered that in some casual way when she'd stormed his desk and swept past Meems, who boasted a certain dignified height. *How* small she was surprised him.

She seemed larger when she was in motion, her hands moving, her voice crisp and demanding. Maybe that was part of what kept her twitching about, making noise—the need to cast a larger shadow than the Creator had given her.

The second fact to register as she held up his scone to him was that it took resolve on her part even to approach him. Her hands were steady, and her eyes held no particular emotion, none at all.

How often had Christian labored to the limit of his soul for a taste of indifference?

And yet, Lady Greendale carried a wonderfully feminine scent, the sort of scent that would get her noticed in close quarters rather than ignored. Her fragrance was sweet and floral, though neither cloying nor faint, but also held a hint of the exotic, if not the daring.

No one and nothing had smelled good at the Château, excepting possibly, in the opinion of the cats, Girard's damned lavender.

Christian took the scone from her. "My thanks."

"You weren't always so ducal," she said, stepping back.

"Ducal, am I?" He was exhausted and unable to sleep; he no longer registered things like hunger or thirst, and he could barely write his own name legibly. Pity the peerage if those attributes were now ducal.

"All the silences, the hauteur, the brooding glances. You do them very convincingly. I hope you don't plan to approach your daughter like this."

She was casting that big shadow again, instructing him from the superior height of her familiarity with a child Christian did not know as well as he should. "I will deal with Lucy as I see fit, and so will you."

He half sought an argument with his small invader, but she merely resumed her seat on the sofa and tore off a bit of orange peel.

Then munched on it—on the orange *peel*—as casually as if she were a prisoner bent on avoiding scurvy.

"You call your daughter Lucy. Her mother wouldn't allow nicknames. She was Lady Lucille to all and sundry, even me."

"She liked to be called Lucy when she was younger." He had no idea from whence that assurance came, but he trusted it. The girl was his firstborn, after all. For the early years of Lucy's life her parents had had no heir to distract them from their only baby.

"Then I shall call her Lucy too." She smiled at him, not the fatuous, beaming-idiot smile he saw so often, but something softer and more personal, more inward.

A door slammed down the hall, and Christian nearly dropped his damned scone right on the carpet and vaulted behind the sofa.

"Oh, do come sit." She rose, took him by his left wrist, and tugged him to the sofa, releasing his hand as quickly as she'd seized it. The riot of reactions that caused had him setting his plate down with an audible racket.

God in heaven, what had he got himself into?

Four

GILLY DECLINED MERCIA'S OFFER OF IMMEDIATE HOSPI-
tality, took her leave on a silent prayer she'd done the
right thing for her young cousin, and repaired to the
Greendale town house.

Her London residence—her former London
residence—was a comfortable, even opulent town
house, but every room reeked of old Greendale's
cigars, and his effects were everywhere. Humidors,
bootjacks, snuffboxes, and riding crops littered the
premises like so much scent from a prowling tomcat.

She would miss none of it, and neither did she
make any effort to organize or pack away Greendale's
personal property. Let Marcus deal with the lot, and
may he have the joy of it.

Gilly departed from the town house the next morning, trying to dredge up some pang of loss at leaving
one of her marital homes, the staff, anyone…in the
end, she stooped to pet a black-and-white house cat,
but the beast tried to bite her as she scratched its chin.

She wanted to swat the wretched feline into next
week—Greendale would have kicked it into the

street—but she patted its coarse head and climbed into her coach.

When she arrived at Mercia's town house—mansion, more like—she was surprised to find him at breakfast in his library.

"Your Grace hasn't slept." Not that Gilly had slept much, either.

"A tea tray, Lady Greendale?" He gave the butler a pointed look before his arctic gaze settled back on Gilly.

"No, thank you, Your Grace." The butler hovered, despite Gilly's demurrer, which would not do. "It's Meems, isn't it? Perhaps you'd be good enough to attend me in the family parlor in twenty minutes or so, Meems? And I'll need to speak with His Grace's housekeeper as well."

The butler bowed, his face expressionless, and withdrew while Gilly appropriated a chair across from the duke's enormous desk.

"One should begin as one intends to go on." She offered Mercia a smile, and got exactly nothing in return. His expression suggested English was no longer his first language, and he had to mentally translate all communication—words, gestures, everything—into some system known only to him.

He would not appreciate displays of compassion—Gilly never had herself—so she made none, though at his wedding, he'd been a much sunnier gentleman; also likely a much healthier gentleman.

"One should, indeed, begin as one intends to go on." His plate held half a buttered scone, nothing more, though the library was redolent with the scents of ham and bacon.

"You truly do stay up all night, don't you?"

"I do not sleep much at any hour. Today, when I might have napped the morning through, I must away to the tailors, lest my court attire embarrass those who behold me in it."

His own embarrassment was apparently of no moment.

"You dread this outing." And that was puzzling, because lazing about the tailor's was supposed to be as much gentlemanly fun as hanging about at Tatt's or Jackson's.

"I most assuredly do not look forward to being poked and turned and handled like so much puppetry. Here." He pushed a daunting stack of papers across his desk at her. "You will politely decline these invitations. Pressing matters require my presence at the ducal seat, et cetera."

"You have no secretary?"

"He had the great good fortune to marry well in my absence. Were I not serving King and Country, I would no doubt have prevented such insubordination."

Was he *joking*? Complaining? As he tore off a small bite of scone, Gilly had no way to tell.

"You'll hire another, though?"

He chewed his bite of scone while Gilly waited for an answer and wished she hadn't been so hasty in declining a reprise of breakfast. The bacon smelled divine, and that scone looked as light as summer clouds.

"Hiring an amanuensis, my lady, would involve running an advertisement, or notifying the agencies, wouldn't it? And that would require lingering here in Town, and *that* would require accepting at a minimum

the invitations extended by the other ducal house-
holds, and *that* I am unwilling to do."

His voice, always pitched softly, dropped even
more as his scold continued.

He was not her husband, to scold her for no reason.
This fact somehow got tangled up with Gilly's longing
for the bacon she'd declined, with the lingering smart
to her finger from the cat's bad behavior, and with
years of sleepless nights.

"Your mood leaves something to be desired, Your
Grace." And in lieu of bacon, Gilly would not mind
being served an apology for that state of affairs.

He paused with another small bite of scone halfway to his mouth. Greendale would have been on
his third scone by now, crumbs everywhere, butter
streaking his chins, and that realization only made
Gilly more irritable.

"I beg my lady's pardon."

"Don't do that with me." Gilly got to her feet, and
braced her hands on the desk, as if she might appropriate some of the furniture's bulk and weight. "I spent
eight years married to a man who thought his every
flatulence and eructation should be greeted with awe,
when in truth he was a cretinous excuse for a human.
I understand that you're tired and cranky, but so am
I. If you beg my pardon, you do it sincerely, not with
exquisite condescension that implies I have the wits of
a small child."

Mercia's chewing slowed, then came to a halt.

Oh, *feathers*. This had happened twice already since
Greendale's death. Twice before, some furious creature with no sense had taken control of Gilly's mouth

and flown into a rage over nothing. The first time had been with Mr. Stoneleigh after the inquest; the second time had been when the vicar had come round after the funeral, apple cordial on his breath, inquiring after Gilly's spirits.

Mercia had committed no such blunder, and yet, Gilly wished Meems would return with the damned tray.

"I'm sorry," she said, straightening. "I don't sleep well, and the cat ripped my glove, and I wanted bacon—" He'd think her daft, and not be far wrong.

Mercia patted his lips with his serviette and rose, bracing himself on his hands as Gilly had. He leaned close enough that Gilly could smell sandalwood over the ambient scent of breakfast.

"Can you ply a needle?"

"Of course." Hadn't he heard her outburst? She'd used the word *flatulence*, for pity's sake, and Mercia was a *duke*.

He leaned farther over the desk, only inches between his nose and hers. "Can you sew with sufficient skill to spare me a trip to the tailor's?"

Where was Meems? Where were her wits? "If you want me to alter an existing set of clothes, I can do that, provided I have some time."

He stayed right where he was, allowing Gilly to note that His Grace had a white scar across one earlobe.

"I am due at Carlton House the day after tomorrow for a private audience at two of the clock."

The day after tomorrow was…soon. "Well, then, yes. You put on what you intend to wear, inside out, and I can take in the seams."

And the whole time they'd had this exchange, his

expression had been as unreadable as a sphinx's. And yet, Mercia was more concerned about dodging this outing to the tailor's than he was about Gilly's rudeness.

"I'm more than competent with a needle, Your Grace." She'd had to be, as few clothes as Greendale had permitted her.

"I'll meet you in my sitting room in an hour. The maids will help you get settled."

He left her just like that. A slight bow, and he was gone, the remains of his scone forgotten on the desk. Gilly shifted around to his side of the desk, sat in his chair, and started to pour herself a cup of tea, only to find the pot was filled with hot water, not tea.

An unpeeled orange sat near a plate of crispy bacon and an artful pile of translucent slices of ham.

No eggs, no toast, no kippers.

Eccentric, then. Lucy's poor papa had become eccentric.

Gilly ate the orange and half the bacon, which was every bit as good as bacon could be, and spent twenty minutes each with the housekeeper and the butler explaining that His Grace would be removing to the country early for the summer. Next she organized the invitations by date and collected the household sewing kit.

When Gilly knocked on the door to the ducal sitting room, she heard nothing granting her permission to enter, so she pushed the door open a few inches.

"Your Grace?"

"I said come in."

"I didn't hear you. You might consider speaking above a whisper, you know. My goodness, you have dropped some weight."

"In the neighborhood of four stone."

He stood near his dressing-room door, barefoot in white satin knee breeches and a white linen shirt, both of which were turned inside out. The shirt was cut to billow gracefully about his arms and looked merely very loose, but the breeches were in danger of falling off his person.

What had those dratted French done to him?

"Whatever you do, please do not allow your pins to pierce my flesh." He spoke with an odd, measured cadence, as if the same words, spoken by a lesser man, might have escaped through a clenched jaw.

Did tailors have so little understanding of their thimbles?

"I will not stick you," she said, unwilling to bait him when he was so obviously dreading the exercise. "We'll start with your breeches, because they're the more complicated."

He paced off to the window, his shirt billowing, one hand on the waistband of his breeches. "Now? Don't you want to measure something, or consult your pattern cards first?"

"Now," she said, slipping a pincushion onto her wrist. "All you need do is stand still." She dropped to her knees and patted the rug before her, as if she were coaxing a puppy out from under the sofa. Even though it was early summer, he had a fire in his hearth, and Gilly was grateful for the warmth.

He crossed the room and fisted and flexed both hands, like a pianist preparing for an opening cadenza, or a prizefighter about to step into the ring and put up his fives. Gilly slipped two fingers under the hem of the right leg of his breeches, her knuckles sliding along the skin of his bony male knee.

His Grace inhaled as if she'd jabbed him with a pin.

"What do you recall of Lucy?" she asked, because conversation was all she could offer him by way of distraction.

"Very little. She seemed a bright child, but Helene was not well pleased to have produced a girl, at first. I rather liked my daughter. She was a baby, nothing more, but she was my baby."

Had Helene ever called the child "my daughter" or "my baby"? The girl, Lady Lucille, her ladyship, our firstborn—Helene had used any of those—but not "my daughter." And Gilly was certain Helene had never admitted to liking the child.

Though Gilly liked the girl—had liked her ferociously at first sight and still did.

"Who chose her name?" Gilly pinched up the outside seam of the breeches, appalled at how much extra material there was. Did charging around after French infantry cause a man to drop nigh sixty pounds?

"I chose her name, for Lucifer, bringer of light. Her mother hated it." His Grace reported a dispatch from the marital past rather than a regret or a boast.

"But Helene doted on the girl." Rather than turn him, which would require touching the duke or ordering him about, Gilly scooted around him on the floor.

"That came later, and I am convinced Helene's attention to Lucy was mostly because Helene was jealous of the baby."

"Jealous of her own child?" Gilly rose on her knees to gather the seam over his bony hip. At his sides, his hands flexed again.

"I took to stopping by the nursery at odd times during the day. Lucy was a jolly child, and I enjoyed her company. Helene got wind of—*what* are you doing?"

"Taking in the waistband, lest your breeches come down when you bow before your sovereign." She slipped her finger inside his waistband and gathered a substantial tuck of fabric.

"I appreciate that my clothing should fit, but must you—?"

"Done," she said, withdrawing her hand. "We'll do the other side now. Helene objected to the attention you showed your daughter?" And what topic should she throw at him next, because an abundance of fabric needed to be taken in.

"Not objected, exactly. But she informed me my interest in the child was unseemly. A daughter's upbringing was her mother's province, and I was not to make a nuisance of myself. By that time Helene was carrying again, and I humored her."

"Most of us humored Helene," Gilly said around a half-dozen pins, though she'd loved her cousin, even if Gilly had been thrust at Lord Greendale while Helene had become a duchess.

"Will this take much longer?"

"Not if you hold still. I told Meems you'd be removing to Severn. He said he hasn't heard from the house steward there for several months. Mrs. Magnus suspects foul play."

She started up the second outside seam, pondering Helene's version of Lucy's upbringing. Helene had claimed Mercia had lost interest in Lucy, not that he'd been shooed from the nursery. Somehow, Gilly could not see anyone, not even Helene, shooing this man anywhere.

But then, she couldn't see him in a nursery either, much less dandling a baby on his bony knees.

To take in the second side of his waistband, she rose and gathered the material as she had the first side, her fingers inside the waistband, next to his shirt.

Up close, he was still solid, for all the weight he'd lost. He stood motionless, not even breathing, and she soon had his breeches done, sporting pins all along his outside seams.

"Now you change breeches," she said, stepping back. "You remove these carefully so as not to disturb the pins. We cut the seams open, sew them up as they've been pinned, and they'll fit more closely. Leave your shirttails out all around when you come back."

He stalked off to his dressing room—where was his valet, and why couldn't that worthy tend to this little exercise in sartorial expedience?

The shirt was more complicated, because taking it in required Gilly to stand directly next to His Grace as she pinned and tucked. She positioned him with his side to the hearth, his hand extended so his fingers rested on the mantel.

Across his shoulders, the garment fit well enough. On the side where Gilly worked, the duke obligingly kept his hand outstretched. On the other side, he was back to opening and closing his fist in a slow, unhappy rhythm.

"Other side," Gilly said, feeling a pressing need to conclude their business. She might have done so without incident, except she'd left the wrist cuffs for last.

"Shall we sit?" she suggested when he was sporting pins up both side and arm seams. "We're almost done."

"You're faster than the tailors."

"I'm not as exact, and I have no need to impress you with the care I take," she said, finding a seat on the sofa. "Give me your hand." He sat and offered the right one first. She put his knuckles against her thigh and gathered the fabric around his wrist. "One doesn't want to have to move the openings for the sleeve buttons…" She took a pin from her cushion and marked how much to take in. "Other one."

He hesitated, then extended his left hand. She took that one too, put it in her lap, then drew in a breath.

This single, prosaic appendage was some sort of key to the rest of the man. The palm was broad, the nails clean and blunt. As male hands went, this one should have been elegant, and the first three fingers were. The fourth finger was scarred, however, as if burned, the nail quite short. The smallest finger was missing the very tip. Not enough was gone to disfigure the nail, but enough to suggest a painful mishap. The joints of the last two fingers weren't quite right either, as if they belonged on the hand of an arthritic coachman.

Gilly tugged at the fabric, intent on completing her task. She'd come across her share of disfigurements, as the lady of any manor might. Stableboys' toes got mashed, scullery maids suffered the occasional burn, smallpox survivors abounded, and children with less than perfect features were born to the tenants.

But Mercia wasn't a stableboy, scullery maid, or yeoman's eleventh child. On him, such an injury was blasphemous. Gilly hadn't wept since long before her husband's death, and the ache in her throat and pressure behind her eyes took a moment to decipher.

"It isn't pretty," the duke said. "I should have warned you."

"You're probably lucky to still have these fingers," she replied, but inside, inside she was collapsing with outrage on his behalf. He wouldn't want pity though, no fawning, no tears.

Certainly, no tears. Tears were never a good idea. Gilly's husband had wasted no time instructing her on the matter of useless tears.

"I can no longer write comfortably with it," he said, as if his hand were a quill pen in want of attention from a good, sharp knife. "With a glove on, it suffices for appearances' sake."

"It pains you, then?" Of course it hurt. Any visible scar hurt, if for no other reason than it reminded one of how the scar arose, and memories could be more painful than simple bodily aches.

"I rarely feel much with it, though I can predict approaching storms. Are you quite through?"

"Almost." She put in one last, completely unnecessary pin, and let him withdraw his hand before she could weep over it.

She didn't even know Mercia and might not like him if she did know him, but to have endured such suffering made her hurt for him. Men did stupid things without limit—duels, wagers, horse races, dares, bets—and war had to be the stupidest.

"My thanks." He stood as soon as she sat back, no doubt glad to be done with the whole business.

"Can you get the shirt off without stabbing yourself?

It wants caution. Here." She didn't wait for his invitation, but started lifting the hem. She was presuming, but she'd been married for years and years, and his valet was not on hand—if he had a valet—and the shirt was full of pins…

"Really, Lady Greendale, you needn't." He reached out as if he would still her hands, but stopped short of touching her. "I can manage, if you'd simply…"

"Close your eyes." She wasn't tall enough to lift the shirt over his head unless he bent forward, which he did, allowing her to extricate him from his voluminous, pinned up, inside-out shirt. She stepped back, glad to have the maneuver safely concluded, and carefully folded up the shirt. "There. All done."

He turned toward his dressing room, and Gilly couldn't help the sound that came from her. She moaned, an involuntary expression of dread and horror and even grief. He turned to face her, shirtless, and his eyes were colder than ever.

"You insisted, my lady."

That he'd taken his back from her view helped not at all, for his chest was every bit as disfigured as his back.

❧

Over Meems's sniffy, tenacious protest, Gilly had insisted Mercia be allowed to rest right through dinner the previous night. Meems was in the same excellent rebellious form the next morning, and perhaps of the opinion that a mere interfering countess needed to learn her place in the household.

For Meems was male and must inflict his opinions on all in his ambit.

"His Grace hasn't stirred, your ladyship, not that we can hear."

"Not that you can hear?"

"He sleeps with his doors locked, milady."

Meems's grave deference notwithstanding, he was happily anticipating how Gilly would see His Grace awakened through a pair of locked doors.

"You've tried calling out?"

"If the sitting room door is closed, that would do little good, milady."

"Then I'll wake him myself." She set her teapot down as quietly as she could, when she wanted to bash the thing over the old man's head. "You're heating His Grace's hot water, are you not?"

"But of course." He had the temerity to fall in step nearly on the heels of her slippers, until Gilly turned and glared at him at the foot of the stairs.

"Surely you'll see personally to the duke's breakfast tray, Meems?"

He indulged in a peevish sniff, then took himself back to the kitchen stairs without a word. Meems was piqued because he wanted to show his duke off before Polite Society for what remained of the Season, but Mercia was not an exhibit in a public circus.

Gilly tapped on the door to the sitting room and heard nothing in response. "Your Grace?" She leaned her ear against the door, and still…nothing.

And yes, the door was locked.

She extricated a hairpin from her bun and went to work. The lock was well oiled—give Meems credit—and Gilly was skilled, and soon the mechanism gave with a satisfying click. The bedroom door was even easier, and there he was, the eighth Duke of Mercia, facedown in his great four-poster monstrosity.

Gilly closed the door behind her, mindful of His Grace's privacy, and approached the bed.

If she hadn't known better, she might have thought the duke dead. He was that pale, as if he'd wandered beyond even the reach of the sun. In his utter immobility, he looked exhausted, like he'd been on forced march for weeks. A castaway quality to how he sprawled among his crisp, white sheets and blue satin pillows suggested he was resting deeply.

"Your Grace?"

His hand—the right hand, the perfect one—slid under his pillow, and his cheek twitched.

"Mercia? Your Grace?"

She was on the verge of reaching out to shake his shoulder, when he rolled onto his back. Gilly took a blinking moment to comprehend he held a wicked-looking knife in his hand. The blade gleamed in the morning light, brighter than any tea service, bright as jewels.

"Good morning, Your Grace."

"What the bloody *hell* are you doing here?" Not his near-whispered drawing-room voice, but the rasp of a savage, one who'd use that lethal knife on any and all comers.

He'd snarled a question at her.

"I'm leaving, of course, in a moment. Your tray is on its way, though, and when you've broken your fast, I'll await you in the library."

❧

Though she'd seen many of his scars—by no means all—the countess hadn't left Christian's household, and this pleased him more than it should. Of course, she might depart still, probably would, in fact, but she hadn't run off, a silly note in her wake referencing pressing business or whatever polite fiction women resorted to when terrified out of their wits.

By a scarred, emaciated duke wielding a knife, may God have mercy upon him.

Christian dressed in waistcoat and shirtsleeves—hang the bloody cravat—and stepped into a worn pair of Hessians that had once been nearly painted onto him but fit him loosely now. As he brushed his hair back into its queue—barbering required proximity to scissors too—a footman appeared with a breakfast tray.

The scent of bacon in close quarters, of any cooked meat, nearly drove Christian to retching. "You will please take that down to the library."

"Of course, Your Grace."

He didn't recognize the man, didn't recognize half his staff, and it had been only two years since his last leave had sent him pelting through London on a lightning spree of self-indulgence.

Helene had disdained to come up to Town for more than a week of it, and he'd applauded her stubbornness, if anybody had cared to ask. What an idiot he'd been, and what a silly twit he'd married.

And yet, he'd give anything to be that idiot again, and for the silly twit to be at his side now, sniffing and judging and trying to tell him what to do.

He paused outside the library and rolled his shoulders as if he were loosening up for a cavalry charge.

The countess, being widowed, no doubt had a dower house, but she'd struck him as a woman who'd rather be around family than moldering away on her late husband's estate.

He opened the door, rehearsed contrition at the ready.

"I do apologize for intruding on your slumber, Your Grace." The countess was in good looks this morning, dressed in a black gown that showed her figure to great advantage. Three years ago, he would have stolen a kiss to her cheek.

Idiot did not begin to cover the matter.

"You need not apologize in the slightest, my lady, nor do I sense that you are genuinely sorry." His breakfast tray waited on the low table before the countess, so he took a place more or less beside her. "Your intent was to rouse me, else you would not have gone through two locked doors to achieve that end."

"Your orange?" She handed him a plate of fruit, the orange peeled and divided into sections for him. "I've told the kitchen they'd best be seeing to the preparation of the foods you enjoy regularly. They're happy to do it, you know, even to peeling your oranges. I did this one myself. Tea?"

"Without the tea."

Cautiously, he took a bite of orange. The scent of it was appealing, particularly when blended with the countess's soap-and-flowers fragrance.

"I've basted up your clothes from yesterday's fitting. If you can spare the time, we'd best see how they do. Scone?"

"Please."

"Meems is moping," she went on. "He wants you

to sport about Town for a bit so the household might have bragging rights on the lost duke."

"Lady Greendale—"

She wrinkled her nose, as if a foul scent had wafted in through the open window, which was silly when the window looked out on the gardens where honeysuckle bloomed in riot. "You can't blame them, really, but I told Meems you were needed at Severn, which you are. Butter?"

"Countess."

She wound down, as he'd hoped she would, and sat with the scone on the plate in her lap, the butter knife balanced beside it.

"I apologize for what you saw yesterday."

Before he'd fallen asleep eighteen hours earlier— and before he'd nearly held the lady at knifepoint— he'd come at the problem a dozen different ways in his head. To apologize or express regrets? To apologize deeply, profoundly, sincerely? To be heartily sorry, most sorry, most heartily sorry... Endless words, and none of them sounded quite the note he wanted.

He was not sorry to be alive—only living men could achieve revenge—but he was sorry his misadventures had visited themselves on her in even a minor, indirect, visual way.

"I was married for some years, Your Grace, and to a man who thought a wife's first responsibility was to valet her husband on all but formal occasions. I would not have taken your shirt from you had I not been prepared to see you *en déshabille*. Any apologies are due you from me, and you have them."

He considered forcing the point, but she was

passing him his scone, the butter having been liberally applied.

"Might I have a bite of your orange?" She didn't
meet his eyes, and Christian had the sense her question
was some kind of test.

Women were the subject of many a campfire
discussion among Wellington's soldiers, and a point
of rare agreement among men who drank, fought,
swived, and killed daily: there was no understanding
women. Not their minds, not their moods, not their
passions or lack thereof. Christian was confident the
French soldiers, the Dutch, the Russians, the Hessians,
they all had the same discussions, and all came to the
same conclusion. .

"I am happy to share." He held up a section, and
she leaned over and took it between her teeth, as he
had previously.

And she chewed tidily, sparing him a small, smug
smile.

She was staying. That's what her little demonstration was about. She wasn't running off because of an
awkward moment, wasn't succumbing to matronly
vapors, wasn't flinching at the sound of distant cannon.

He offered her another section.

Five

THE LAST NIGHT BEFORE CHRISTIAN AND DEVLIN ST. Just had arrived in Paris, they'd camped beside yet another farm pond, and St. Just had bluntly asked Christian when he planned to bathe properly.

"My scent offends you?"

"You're as tidy as a man can be when he bathes regularly in a bucket," St. Just said. "But you face the generals tomorrow, and you'll want to look your best for them."

A great deal went unsaid around Devlin St. Just: *you'll want to look your sanest for them*, for example.

"I was accosted at my bath," Christian said, unrolling his blankets. "One moment I was in that frigid, clean water, scrubbing away, thinking dirt was the worst part of soldiering, the next I was surrounded by grinning Frenchmen, a half-dozen rifles aimed at my naked backside."

St. Just rummaged in his saddlebags. "And that was the start of it. Thereafter you were probably denied the opportunity to be clean, or it was forced upon you. Shall I throw you into yonder pond?"

The offer was as sincere as it was insightful. St. Just was an inch or two taller than Christian's six feet and two inches; he was as fit as the devil and damned quick.

"That won't be necessary."

"Fine, then." St. Just pitched a bar of hard-milled French soap at Christian's chest, but Christian's right hand wasn't up to the challenge of catching it. The soap smelled of roses and mint. "In you go. I'll just clean my weapons here while you scrub up."

St. Just offered one of his rare, charming smiles, this one with a bit of devilment in it. And then he extracted a knife case from the same saddlebag and opened it to reveal six gleaming throwing knifes. A brace of elegant pistols that looked to be Manton's work followed, a short sword, and of course, his cavalry saber as well.

"Point taken."

Christian would be well and thoroughly guarded while he bathed, and still, he dreaded the necessity to strip down before another human being.

"I can't guard you if I don't watch what you're about," St. Just said, unsheathing his saber. "Else I'd politely turn my back."

"You aren't guarding me. The only threats I see are a lot of bleating sheep and two brindle heifers. You're playing with your toys."

"Right. You could also wait until dark, but then the sea monsters might come out and gobble you up."

"Fuck you, St. Just."

"So many wish they could." He heaved a theatrical sigh and went about polishing his sword as if Christian weren't kneeling on his blankets, feeling like a complete buffoon. The legacy of his tenure among the French would accrue usurious interest—if he allowed it to. Christian pulled his shirt over his head, shucked out of his breeches, and took his damned bath.

And to be clean again, really truly clean, had been worth the humiliation.

Except St. Just hadn't said a thing about the scars, the eccentricity of a titled officer being afraid to bathe, or the need for a grown man to be reassured of his own safety in the bucolic surrounds of the French countryside.

Christian's heart had still been thundering against his ribs when he emerged from the pond and toweled off.

"Shall I trim your beard?"

"Are you trying to provoke me?"

"I'm trying to tidy you up. You look like a wild man from darkest Africa in your off moments."

Of which there was an abundance. "Perhaps I always looked like something escaped from the jungles."

"Not you." St. Just tucked his pistols away, and Christian was sorry to lose sight of them. "I was two years ahead of you at university. You were as vain as a peacock ten years ago."

"We all were."

"We were boys; it was our turn to be vain."

Except Christian abruptly recalled St. Just as a much-younger man, a duke's by-blow who was cursed with a stutter. He hadn't been vain in the least, and when the situation had called for it, he'd let his fists do the talking.

"So you either give me permission to trim you up

now," St. Just said, "or I'll have a go at you while you sleep."

"You wouldn't dare."

"Nighty-night then." He ran his thumb across the blade of yet another knife—this one likely resided in the man's boot—and his teeth gleamed in the fading light. "Or we could go best out of three falls." He tucked the knife away. "I'm a decent wrestler, growing up with four brothers. For a while I had a slight advantage, being the oldest, but they'd come at me in twos and threes."

"Get out your kit, then, and shut up."

"Wise choice. You wouldn't want my death or dismemberment on your conscience."

He pulled a shaving kit from his saddlebag—Aladdin's cave of wonders for the traveling cavalryman—and produced a pair of grooming scissors.

"Don't think," he said. "Just sit there and hate me for doing this, hmm?"

"What hatreds keep you going?" Christian asked the question mostly to keep St. Just talking.

"I am haunted by the abuse I see of good animals," St. Just said. "They never asked to go to war. They never asked to attempt a goddamned winter march on Moscow. They never asked for the artillery barrages to frighten them out of their feeble little horsey wits. Hold the hell still."

For all his irascibility, St. Just's hand was steady and deft. Snip, snip, snip, while Christian wondered if he'd ever allow another to shave him again. To be assigned a valet when he'd come down from university had been a comfortable and pleasant rite of maturation, to start each day with the cheerful, careful ministrations of a man dedicated to the proper care and grooming of the young duke.

"Your cousin took good care of your horse while you were unable to," St. Just said. "You're done, and I expect a solid recommendation from you as a barber when I muster out."

Christian rubbed his hand along his jaw, finding the beard much closer to his skin, much tidier.

"My thanks." Because by insisting on this concession to proper turnout, St. Just had scrubbed away another layer of captivity.

"You'll set all the ladies' hearts to fluttering." St. Just tossed him a towel, using, of course, too much force.

And Christian couldn't catch it, not with either hand. "As if I give a hearty goddamn for the ladies' opinions."

"You will," St. Just said, getting comfortable on his blankets. "God willing, we all will again, someday soon."

Christian wanted to argue with St. Just, wanted to ask what that last comment meant, wanted an excuse to keep the man awake, really, because bathing and letting his beard be trimmed had left Christian's nerves shorn too. These mundane aspects of hygiene were accomplishments for him, reasons to be a little less worried for his sanity.

But something in the exchange with St. Just had tickled Christian's jumble of memories, something in the comments about horses. The words rankled, as so many things rankled, and still, Christian could not put a finger on why. Something to do with Chessie, with finding the horse whole and in good weight, even after months of campaigning against the French.

Christian eventually fell asleep, feeling bodily clean for the first time in more than a year, though feeling clean was by no means the same as feeling safe.

❧

Christian found Lady Greendale in the family parlor, sitting at the escritoire by the window.

"The clothing fits," she said, rising as she surveyed him. "A bit loosely, but well enough."

"And my thanks for your efforts." She looked so…composed, sitting in the sunlight, the invitations scattered about on the desk. She wasn't a beautiful woman, but she had a domestic quality that went well with the tidy parlor and morning sunlight. "I must impose on you a bit further, though."

"Of course." She tossed her pen aside and came toward him, then circled around behind him. "You'll want this tied back."

"My hair?"

"You're going to Court, Your Grace. Some still powder their hair for such occasions. Hold still."

She withdrew a pocket comb and gently started tidying up his hair. He'd done the best he could with his own brush and comb, unwilling to ask anybody's assistance.

He hadn't thought to ask hers, though she was a widow and a relation, and a woman who, for all her chatter, possessed prodigious common sense. She'd comprehended he needed his oranges peeled, and he hadn't had to ask.

Nobody should have to look on the evidence of his captivity—he didn't want to see it himself—and yet, Christian was gratified that when she did look, Lady Greendale calmly accepted what was before her eyes.

So he suffered her to arrange his hair, tying it back with a simple black ribbon. Her diminutive stature helped him endure her attentions, but so did her tendency to chatter.

His *irritation* at her tendency to chatter, rather.

"You do not appear to be looking forward to this great honor, Your Grace. The day is pleasant, fortunately. Perhaps Prinny will be kept overlong at his tennis matches, and then you'll be spared the royal interview. Where are your gloves?"

He passed them to her, which merited him a frown.

"These are not riding gloves, sir."

His dignity suffered more than a pinch, but common sense did not make the woman prescient.

"I can't easily manage the change of gloves myself—I must use my teeth—and I don't want to risk…"

She didn't make him finish. "Dress gloves then. I daresay you've a pair or two. You were smart not to tart yourself up with too much gold, lest Prinny get ideas. You won't glower at the poor Regent like that, though, will you?"

She tugged the glove onto his right hand, and he submitted to her assistance as if he were a boy still in dresses.

"What do you mean, giving Prinny ideas?" He knew the man, had been introduced on a handful of occasions as the scion of any noble house might be in early manhood. The Regent was genial when it suited him, shrewd, and not as spoiled as the press wanted to paint him.

"He solicits donations for his causes, the parks, that pavilion by the sea. Some think it scandalous, while we've been waging war over half the globe for his papa's entire reign. Others consider him a visionary, but everybody knows to keep their coin out of his sight. Where are your sleeve buttons, that I might do up your cuffs?"

"Here." He extracted them from his pocket, and dropped them into her outstretched hand. He hadn't figured out quite how he was to don them—a footman usually assisted—and Lady Greendale was still blathering away.

"These are lovely." She slipped one through his cuff, then brought his hand close to her nose to examine his jewelry. "Are those sapphires?"

By virtue of her having appropriated his hand, his palm was near enough to her cheek he could have stroked her face with his fingers. Had he taken this liberty and dared a small touch of her soft, fragrant person, she would not have rebuked him, but she might have pitied him, and that would have stolen all his pleasure from the moment.

"Those are star sapphires," Christian said when she let his hand go. "On my personal signet ring, the lion's eye in the family crest is the same stone."

"What do you mean your personal signet ring?" She gathered up the right cuff, and slipped the fastener through, then patted his knuckles as if he'd been a good lad, not holding up the coach before the family departed for Sunday services.

"My father was sufficiently practical he kept various versions of the Severn signet ring at our principle houses. He said a groom shouldn't have to ride halfway across England because His Grace forgot a piece of jewelry and had a letter to seal. I liked the idea of one ring, though, *the* Severn ducal ring, so I had one made on my eighteenth birthday. Papa no doubt rolled his celestial eyes at my vanity. The sleeve buttons and cravat pin were made to go with that ring."

"And let me guess, the French took your ring from you?" She seized his left hand and attacked the cuff, his disfigurement of no apparent moment to her.

"My ring was the only thing I was wearing when I was captured."

Her hands momentarily paused, holding his. Her grip around his fingers was warm, firm, and lovely. Sensation in his left hand had become dodgy, but he felt her hold on him and made no move to withdraw.

"Then why did they torture you? Your ring gave away your identity."

Why, indeed. Christian had been weeks in Girard's dungeon before that question had occurred to him, emerging into his awareness in the middle of a dream about Chessie being led away by the grinning, laughing French.

"What ring, my lady? The ring disappeared, just as they claimed not to have seen my uniform drying in plain sight over the bushes. I was out of uniform, and therefore due none of the courtesies afforded an officer in captivity."

"A nation of lawyers, the French…" She retied his cravat and repositioned the pin, the whole effect more

fluffy and elegant than what Christian had managed.
Had she patted his left knuckles too? Christian was too
preoccupied with her casual use of the word torture.
Even in his mind, he shied away from the blunt term.

Misadventure, ordeal, difficulties, captivity…not
torture.

"You'll start a fashion with this beard." She brushed
her fingers over his cheek, a passing caress startling in
its familiarity. Mothers and sisters might touch their
menfolk thus, and wives certainly did, though duchesses did not.

Had not.

Her touch sparked none of the bristling and roiling in
his gut he might have expected, particularly when she'd
been making free with his person for some minutes.

"I'll soon be late," he countered. "My thanks for
your assistance."

"You'll be all right?" She went quiet, didn't follow
the question up with more of her patter or fussing.

He would never be all right, had stopped even
wishing for it, for then his Christian duty to forgive
his enemies might gain a toehold in his conscience. "I
beg your pardon?"

"Today, putting up with the nonsense of it all.
George means well, you know. I think he's really
quite a lonely man."

George…the Regent, the sovereign, the de facto
King. And the countess thought the man lonely.

And was very likely right. "I will manage."

"Yes, you shall." She linked her arm through his,
another casual touch that ought to have startled, but
didn't…quite. "If you find yourself in difficulties,

wanting to smash something, say, or scream profanities and take up arms, you put in your mind a picture of what you can look forward to, and you add details to it, one by one, until the picture is very accurate and the urge to do something untoward has passed."

He liked that she'd walk arm in arm with him, liked that she'd lecture him about how to endure… *torture*. "You do this when the morning calls become too boring?"

She looked down, as if puzzling something out.

"When I am vexed beyond all tolerance, but can do nothing to aid myself, when I want to descend to the primitive level of those who lash out in violence at blameless victims, then I do this in my mind. I think of Lucille, or my mother's flower gardens, or a nice rich, hot cup of chocolate on a cold and blustery morning when we might see the first snowflakes of the season."

St. Just had told him to endure by concentrating on his hatreds, but such guidance hadn't been particularly useful when the length of the list alone left a man helpless and overwhelmed.

Lady Greendale told him to endure by focusing on something he looked forward to.

Whatever that might be.

She walked him right out through the back gardens, to the mews, to the very mounting block where Chessie stood, one hip cocked, swishing a luxurious russet tail at nothing in particular.

"Safe journey, Mercia, and of course, my regards to dear George." Lady Greendale went all the way up on her toes and kissed not his cheek—his cheeks being covered with neatly trimmed beard—but his unsuspecting mouth. Perhaps because he'd had no warning, he felt that kiss. Felt the soft brush of her mouth against lips no longer chapped, the weight of her balancing against his chest, the momentary press of her breast against his arm.

She lingered near for a moment, long enough to whisper, "Courage, Your Grace."

Then she stepped back so he could mount his steed and tilt at the day's windmill.

He rode the distance to Carlton House by sticking mainly to the quiet paths through the parks, and when he arrived, he'd found one thing, and one thing only, to look forward to—another kiss from the countess, soft, sweet, freely given, and wholly unexpected.

❧

Mercia's eyes had been a trifle wild as the groom had tightened Chessie's girth, and Gilly had wanted to tell His Grace to stay home. This call on the Regent was a courtesy extended by the Crown toward a loyal—also wealthy and impressively titled—soldier. The soldier should have been free to decline the honor.

But men did not operate according to the principles of any logic Gilly could fathom, and so she did as women had long done—she waited. She finished the last of the polite replies to invitations, she consulted with Mrs. Magnus on which staff to send down to Severn and which to leave in Town, she embroidered the hem of one of her black handkerchiefs, using a pearly gray thread she liked for the way it caught more light than any true gray ought.

She started embroidering a cream silk handkerchief

with the Severn crest done in royal blue, and still the
duke didn't come home.

When it came time for late tea, and the afternoon
had passed into early evening, Gilly rounded up the
two largest footmen the household boasted and prepared to make a charge on Carlton House.

She conjured up any number of explanations.
Mercia had run into old chums from the army; he'd
been invited to join the Regent for tea; his horse had
turned up lame... But what if he'd taken a misstep,
perhaps pulled a knife on a footman, lost his patience
with the Regent himself, or lost his way? What if
he'd flown into a rage because he couldn't manage his
gloves or a cat had nipped at his finger?

Losing one's way was easy enough to do.

❧

When Christian had gone for a soldier, the cavalry
had been the natural choice because he'd long had
an appreciation for the horse. He'd been riding since
before he could walk, if being taken up before his papa
counted, and so he'd hidden in the Carlton House
mews after enduring a half hour of George's good
wishes and shrewd regard.

Prinny had prosed on about his uniform from the
10th Hussars, an outfit he'd designed himself, and
Christian hadn't known whether to laugh or weep at
the notion of military dress reduced to a flight of fashion.

When that interminable half hour had passed, the
grooms had let Christian sit on a tack trunk and pass
an hour in idleness, watching the comings and goings
common to a busy stable. One hour became two,

then afternoon became evening, and one old groom remarked to another that a man shouldn't be made to wait so long for his ladybird, no matter how pretty her ankles.

Time to leave then.

Christian signaled he was ready for his horse, and walked out into the soft light of a summer evening.

Without warning, his heart pounded, his ears roared, and the periphery of his vision dimmed. A sense of dread congealed in his chest, making him want to both collapse and run.

"You a'right, guv?"

"He's a bloody dook, that one. The missin' dook. Yer Grace?"

"He ain't missin' if he's standin' right cheer. Maybe missin' his buttons."

This exchange, quintessentially British in its accents and intonation, and in its cheek, helped Christian push the darkness back.

"Gentlemen, I can hear your every word."

"You looked a mite queerish, Yer Grace. Your 'orse is ready."

The groom held up Chessie's reins, as if the *queer-ish dook* might have forgotten he even had a horse. Christian reached up with his left hand out of habit, then had to switch hands to take his horse.

This enraged him, that a particular angle of sunlight should plummet him back to the day he was captured, that he was not able to use the hand God Himself had intended him to use, that his heart was ready to fight to the death when no enemy was about.

The elderly stable lad stood there, looking concerned

but also uneasy, and Christian wanted to wallop the little fellow into next week.

With his left fucking hand.

"My thanks."

The groom sidled away, sending one last leery look over his shoulder as Christian led the horse to the mounting block. He tarried, checking the girth, the length of the stirrups, each buckle and fitting on the bridle, because the sense of dread had not receded.

London was prone to riots, and Christian was out of uniform. This summer, everybody was in love with the soldiers in uniform. Hungry men or widows unable to feed their children might bear ill will toward a duke, but not toward a decorated cavalry veteran.

He should have worn a uniform. Again, he should have…

Some part of him watched as his mind prepared to launch into a flight borne of irrational fear and rootless anxiety, even as his horse stood patiently at the mounting block. Christian inhabited two simultaneous realities: the pleasant early evening in the stables, and the inchoate, amorphous disasters gathering in his mind.

Put in your mind a picture of what you can look forward to, and…add details to it, one by one, until the picture is very accurate and the urge to do something untoward has passed.

A snippet of the countess's chatter, and yet it had lodged in his mind like a burr. The western facade of Severn popped into his head, with its long, curving drive that ran past the smaller lake. This time of year, the rose gardens around the central fountain would be in bloom, and the groundsmen would scythe the park lawns twice weekly. The air would be fragrant with the ripening hay fields and the cropped grass, while the fountain made a soft, splashing undercurrent, different from rain but equally clear and soothing.

An occasional lamb would bleat for its mama…

His heart slowed. Chessie stomped a back hoof, and Christian swung up as he let his mind add detail after detail.

The sound of carriage wheels tooling over the crushed white shells of the driveway.

Light bouncing off the windows on the third floor at the end of the day.

The scent of the lake when the breeze shifted, how the surface rippled with the wind. The ducks rioting and taking wing en masse for no apparent reason.

By the time he found his own mews, Christian was breathing normally and looking forward to seeing the ducal seat.

And to his next sighting of the small, fierce countess who gave surprisingly good advice.

❧

"His Grace is riding up the alley, milady."

"Well, thank God for that." Gilly lifted her bonnet off and passed it to the footman, whose relief had been evident in his tone. The duke was a grown man, a peer of the realm, a decorated officer, and still, she'd fretted over him as if he were a child gone missing at the market.

"If you would tell Cook we'll take a cold collation out on the back terrace, I'd appreciate it. Lemonade, plenty of sugar, no tea. And tell her to make it pretty."

"Very good, milady."

When he'd left, Gilly checked her appearance in the mirror above the sideboard, hoping her own relief was not as obvious as the footman's had been. A hairpin had caught in her bonnet's black netting, which caused a thick blond curl to list down around her shoulder. She hastily tucked it up, fetched her embroidery hoop, and managed to be sitting on the terrace, stitching, when His Grace came trooping through the gate from the mews.

"You're back." She rose, planting a smile on her face despite the inanity of her words. "How was your visit?"

"These are ruined." He pulled off his dress gloves with his teeth, and passed them to her. "His Highness sends you his condolences. Have we anything to eat?"

"He didn't feed you?"

"He didn't…he…I forget." Mercia ran a hand through blond hair coming loose from its queue. Gilly did not offer to tidy him up lest he use his teeth on her.

"I've ordered a cold tray."

He muttered something as he wandered to the bed of daisies pushing up along the back wall.

"I beg your pardon?" Gilly raised her voice to carry over the clopping hooves in the alley beyond the wall.

"I said, you need not join me, Countess. I can take the tray inside."

Despite his snappishness, the duke should not be alone. "I want to hear of your call upon the Regent."

He wandered a few more steps, plucked a daisy, and began pulling off its petals, one by one. "You do not want to hear about my call on the Regent, which was perfectly prosaic, boring, in fact."

"Was it boring for four or five hours?"

"I beg your pardon?" He lifted his gaze from the half-dismembered daisy, and Gilly saw the depths of an arctic winter.

"You were gone for nearly seven hours, Mercia. Prinny observes the courtesies, but by bestowing a few words here, a few minutes there. You missed tea."

"I missed tea?" Those blond eyebrows rose, and Gilly steeled herself for a blistering set down. "So I did. Perhaps that's why I'll have something to eat now."

He hadn't said he was hungry, putting Gilly in mind of all the times she'd been too upset to eat. She was saved from concocting some reply when the footman arrived bearing a large tray.

"I'll set it out," Gilly said, offering the footman a smile. "My thanks."

He bowed, shot a puzzled look at the duke, and withdrew. Mercia's household endured a great deal of puzzlement of late.

"Come sit, Your Grace, unless you'd like to perambulate while you dine?"

He tossed away the denuded daisy and stomped over to the table.

"Strawberry?" Gilly held up a large red berry, wanting to stuff it in his unsmiling mouth. She'd worried about him, and here he was, no explanation, no apologies—nothing.

Mercia took the strawberry from her fingers with his teeth, and the air between them grew less tense.

"Please do sit, Mercia. If you loom over me, you'll spoil my digestion."

"Heaven forfend." He took a seat, despite his sarcastic tone.

"You are a duke," Gilly said, putting a half-dozen fat strawberries on a plate. "This petulance does not become you, despite what you may have heard about the privileges of rank. Shall I make you a sandwich?"

He eyed the strawberries. "Some buttered bread and cheese."

Gilly met his glacial gaze, and folded her arms across her chest. "You forgot to say please. You are being perverse, perhaps because your afternoon left you in the mood to brawl with somebody. If you must indulge a violent urge like a territorial beast of the jungle, take yourself off to Jackson's boxing salon, then. I am a lady. I do not brawl."

Though God knew, the very thought of plowing her fist into Greendale's soft belly had provided her a great deal of satisfaction. Restraining the urge had provided more satisfaction yet.

She passed the duke a roll, sliced in half and liberally buttered, a thick piece of cheddar tucked between the halves. She wanted to stuff it down his throat.

Also to cry, though she'd given that up years ago.

To think she'd worried over this…this…

"My thanks." He took the roll from her, and they ate in uncomfortable silence for some while. Gilly had to slow her own meal to allow for her companion's deliberate pace. His Grace was incapable of bolting his grain, even after a long, hungry afternoon with the Regent.

"You're coming undone." He made that observation in the same tone of voice as he might have asked for the salt.

"I am slightly perturbed with you, because you have been inconsiderate. I am not undone. I am trying to make allowances."

The light in his eyes changed, warmed a little. "No, your hair is coming down. Here." He brushed a hand over her shoulder, where the errant curl was once again free of its pins and bouncing at liberty behind her ear.

"*Feathers.*" To touch one's hair while eating was unladylike in the extreme, but there would be nothing for it.

"Hold still." He rose and removed a pin from her coronet, caught up the rebellious curl, and fastened it securely back in place. "Why are you trying to make allowances?"

"Because we hardly know each other," Gilly said. "You are not used to answering to a household, and I am not used to the least thing about you. You could not know I would…expect you back for tea."

He took the last bite of his cheese sandwich and dusted his hands, stopping to peer at his left hand.

"What?" The question left Gilly's lips unbidden.

"I ate with my left hand."

"You hold the reins with it."

"A single rein. I can't ride in a double bridle. I don't trust it for that."

"I've never understood why a horse must be made to suffer two bits at once," Gilly said. "As sensitive as the mouth is, one ought to suffice. You won't tell me about your afternoon, will you?"

"It was unremarkable. If you'll excuse me?"

And just like that, he was on his feet. No explanation for his delay, no apology for keeping the household guessing, no effort at making conversation.

"I was *worried* about you. I'll be ready to leave for Severn at first light," Gilly said, though she was having doubts about the wisdom of that plan.

"As will I." He went back to the bed of daisies and chose another victim. This one he held in his right hand, tapping against the knuckles of his left as the evening shadows gathered around him. "Prinny thanked me."

Gilly bit into one of the strawberries His Grace had disdained to eat. "He ought to thank you. You served long and well."

"He said…" Mercia tapped the daisy against his own nose. "He said the way I'd been treated was useful for shaming the French into concessions at the negotiating table. Useful."

"You were treated disgracefully. Shall you mutilate that flower too?" Gilly didn't want him to. Yes, the daisies were profuse, and only daisies, but she didn't want him to indulge in pointless destruction.

He looked down, his expression unreadable in the gloom. Then he strolled over to the table and tucked the flower behind Gilly's ear. His fingers grazed her jaw, probably unintentionally, but it was a sweet touch. Gentle and soothing, unlike His Grace's mood.

"My thanks for the food. I'm sorry you were worried. I'll try not to give you cause for it again. You'll excuse me if I don't join you for dinner."

He sauntered back out the gate, into the darkening

alley, off on God knew what ducal errand, while Gilly ate the last of his strawberries and wondered if anything she'd endured in her marriage to Greendale could be considered *useful*.

Six

GILLY HAD GROWN TOO USED TO THE QUIET OF THE countryside, and her attempts to sleep in Mercia's town house were fruitless. The streets grew quieter after dark, true, but the remaining sounds compelled the attention for being more isolated.

Then too, she was anxious. Anxious on Lucille's behalf, hoping the duke's reunification with his daughter lifted the child's spirits, and hoping the child might lift the duke's spirits.

Gilly tossed back the bedclothes and found her black silk wrapper. Was there any consolation to the new widow greater than black silk? She gathered her shawl around her shoulders and made her way to the library, intent on selecting a book for the next day's journey. She could read in coaches, in short doses anyway.

Except even in this small task, His Grace had to frustrate her.

She rapped softly on the open library door—startling a man who cuddled up with knives was not well advised.

"Come." He uttered the word without looking up from his desk.

"Good evening, Your Grace."

He set his pen down with the long-suffering air of a composer interrupted by the charwoman. "I thought you were a footman coming to trim wicks and build up the fire."

"Sorry to disappoint. What are you working on?"

"A report."

"I couldn't sleep."

"Obviously."

His foul humor was so palpable Gilly wanted to stomp from the room. No wonder Helene had despaired of the man, despite his former good looks.

"I came to find a book, something soothing to quiet my mind, something to take with me on the journey to Severn." She crossed to the bookshelves, which held more volumes than she could count in a month. "Shouldn't you be in bed if we're to be awake at first light?"

"Sleep eludes me as well." He was up, prowling around, then poking at the fire.

"When Greendale died, the physician left me with enough sleeping draughts to put down a small herd of horses. I tried not to be offended."

"He didn't mean for you to use them all at once." Now he tidied up his desk, capping the inkwell, opening and closing drawers.

"I've never been certain. Have you read all these books?"

"The ones in Latin, English, or French, probably. My Greek is rusty."

"Then you might show a hint of good manners—nothing binding or impressive—and help me select a book I can take to bed with me and read in the coach tomorrow."

"Poetry," he said, banging a drawer loudly. He came over to stand beside her, which meant they were in some proximity, the rows of shelves positioned to accommodate one person browsing, not two. "Here."

He took down a volume of Blake. "Bucolic, but with occasional nods toward the profound."

"Read me a few lines."

His scent came to her, rosemary and sandalwood, fresh, a little piney, male, and clean—even at this hour.

Had he eaten anything since he'd disappeared into the mews in the last of the day's light?

"'Like a fiend in a cloud, with howling woe,'" he quoted, "'After night I do crowd, And with night will go.' From the *Poetical Sketches*."

"Not very soothing. Try something else, and this time read it, please, do not draw upon the gloomy reaches of your memory." She leaned back against the bookshelf, crossed her arms, and closed her eyes, the better to hear the beauty of the poetry and ignore the grouch reading it.

"'He loves to sit and hear me sing, Then, laughing, sports and plays with me; Then stretches out my golden wing, and mocks my loss of liberty...' I cannot read this."

He held out the book, and Gilly would have bet her favorite silk shawl he'd never opened it. He'd been quoting all the while. The bleakness in his eyes was unnerving.

"Today? When I did not come home?" he said, staring at the little book. "I was waiting."

He was a foot taller than Gilly, battle hardened, and capable of meanness. He'd killed for King and Country, and endured all manner of privations in captivity, but at that moment, he was...uncertain.

"What were you waiting for?"

"The park...it wasn't safe."

She took the poetry from his grasp. "Explain this to me, Your Grace. I do not take your meaning."

"I rode to Carlton House through the parks, to avoid the streets, the shops, the people...at midday, nobody's in the park."

"And later in the day, everybody who is anybody is in the park." She took his arm and steered him back toward the fire, which was roaring merrily, thanks to his attentions. "You did not want to deal with the awkward questions and the well-meant stupidity."

He frowned down at her. "I have underestimated you."

"Most do. I prefer it that way."

"As a widow, you're subjected to awkward questions too, aren't you?"

Gilly wanted to see his eyes, because she sensed his inquiry had hidden, gnarled roots, so she took a seat on the sofa and patted the place beside her.

Had Helene intended that her husband be left with awkward questions? Had she grown weary of the awkward questions related to his captivity? Was that why she'd made the choices she had?

"One isn't supposed to be a happy widow," Gilly said, certain in her bones Mercia would not judge her for the admission. "One might be merry, after several years' bereavement, or peaceful, or content, but not happy. Perhaps you'll consider me unnatural and limit my influence on Lucille, but I am a happy widow."

He settled beside her, gingerly, as if the sofa were too hot to sit upon, and Gilly heard the poem again in her head: *"He stretches out my golden wing, and mocks my loss of liberty."* "What was your report about, Your Grace?"

"Nothing of any import, old army business."

"Then you won't mind if I sit here and read for a bit while you work on it?"

His expression shifted, as if he were frowning because he was thinking too hard, not because she'd displeased him.

"I'll be as quiet as a mouse," she said, opening the book to a random page. "I can keep quiet, you know, when I choose to."

"I've written enough for now."

"Then find your own book," she said, leafing through hers. "Find an old friend, and renew your acquaintance."

He wandered off while Gilly chose a nice long poem about flowers and skies and lambs. She would not have remarked his return, except this time, he sat down like he didn't expect the sofa to collapse under his weight. He sat close enough that the fold of his dressing gown casually draped over the hem of Gilly's shawl.

He held another small volume, but stared into the fire, the book unopened in his hands. When Gilly yawned a half hour later and looked up again, he hadn't moved in the entire time she'd been reading.

"I'm off to seek my bed. You should do likewise, Your Grace. Morning will be here before we're ready for it."

"I don't advise rousing me from my slumbers," he said, eyeing his book. "I take exception to violations of my privacy."

"I do apologize, and it won't happen again. Next time, you'll wedge a chair under the door in addition to locking it, won't you?" She rose and put her book on his desk.

He got to his feet as well and laid his unread book beside her Blake. "If there were a next time, which there won't be, I'd wedge a chair under the door and push a wardrobe behind the chair."

"I understand."

And if she meant anything she'd ever said to him, she meant those two words.

He must have sensed this, because he studied her for some moments. Perhaps because she'd been married to Greendale, perhaps because she was tired and the day had been fraught, Gilly did not divine the duke's intent until the very last instant.

He framed her jaw with one large, callused palm and held his hand to her skin long enough for the heat of him to seep into her.

"When I rode home today, what I put in my mind that I looked forward to," he said softly, "what saw me past the riots and mayhem and enemy patrols in my mind, was this." He turned his head at an angle, pressed his lips to hers, and drew back half an inch. "You brought me home today, my lady. For that you have my thanks."

He kissed her again, on the mouth, then in the center of her forehead, the slow, deliberate *reverence* of his gestures as stunning as it was surprising.

For one bewildered moment, Gilly held his face against her hand, then left him standing alone in the shadowed library. Before she was halfway up the stairs, she was crying for no reason she could discern.

❧

"I did not keep you alive for years on that godforsaken rock pile, despite the English battering at our door, Anduvoir wreaking his intrigues, the garrison whores in constant uproar, bad rations, disease, and cold, for you to throw it all away by taking ship for England."

Michael Brodie was the son of a wealthy Scot, though he'd found it prudent to tend toward his mother's Irish side of the family when in France. Robert Girard, as he chose to be called, suspected dear Michael had some bulldog ancestry in his lineage too—the affectionate variety of course.

"Michel, I have a desire to see once again the land of my father's people. You needn't accompany me."

Michael's green eyes lit with a zeal that boded ill for French colonels lacking an instinct for self-preservation.

"This has to do with that damned duke, doesn't it?"

"No, it does not." Girard waved the serving girl away, meaning no insult to the yeasty, frothy, tepid *weissbier* favored at the rathskeller. "My decision to travel has to do with being weary to my soul, and England being some place where the government will not seek to kill me, not officially. Proper fellows that they are, they have sent me letters to this effect."

In fact, the War Office had extended informal clemency to him, in order that France might offer the same courtesy to others whom the cessation of hostilities had left in delicate straits.

Michael waved the girl over, and because he was a good-looking devil who never bothered the ladies, over she came. That they spoke English also didn't hurt, the English being the most solvent among the nationalities thronging Vienna of late.

"*Drei biere, bitte.*"

"Michael, are you attempting to inebriate yourself with beer?" For it would take more time than Girard had to see that accomplished, and more than three beers.

"Two of them are to dump over your fool head. You will die a painful, bloody death in England. The English gentlemen are great ones for blowing each other's brains out or sticking one another in the lung or the gut on the so-called field of honor. The higher their title, the more likely they are to lack sense."

"I have had enough of violence, thank you sincerely." And to be honest, the welfare of a certain duke did also trouble him. Mercia had stayed alive for one reason—to kill his captors—and a man with such an agenda bore careful watching.

Revenge could keep a man alive against all odds, but it took a heavy toll on a fellow's common sense.

And thus Girard did, indeed, still worry about his favorite English duke.

The beers were delivered by the smiling, handsome

little brunette lady who looked about sixteen years old. They all looked about sixteen years old anymore.

Michael tipped generously, assuring both good service and privacy, and watched the serving maid as she scurried across the room in answer to a bellowed summons.

"You have a sister about her age, don't you, Michel?"

Michael left off watching the girl and took the kind of prissy sip of his ale that suggested the foaming head of the drink was a damned nuisance. "If you're going to England, I'm bloody well going with you."

He ignored the question thoroughly, revealing that the sister—sisters, in fact, there being more than one—were a sensitive topic.

"The English government will not officially try to kill me," Girard mused, "but that leaves a good dozen Englishmen who will take offense at my continued existence, your damned duke among them."

"He's home now, Mercia is," Michael said, hunching over his beer stein. With his blond hair and size, he fit in easily among the locals, but his conscience meant he was not at all compatible with the prevailing sense of opportunism and self-interest loose in an otherwise lovely city.

"You should go home too, my dear, though I will allow you to join me as far as England. I get good service when I drag you about with me."

"Are you going to England to kill him?"

"I told you, I have had enough of violence, and I am not given to dissembling," Girard said, shoving to his feet and leaving Michael with his three beers. He tossed some coins on the table and draped his greatcoat over his shoulders, because even in summer, Viennese evenings could be chilly, and weapons could benefit from concealment.

"You don't need violence to kill a man," Michael said, sitting back, one big hand wrapped around his drink. "As far as the English are concerned, Robert Girard doesn't even need a reason. He kills and torments for pleasure."

"None of them died, Michel. You alone can vouch for the fact that none of them died at my hands, though now," Girard said, settling his hat on his head, "it appears I continue living, without a reason to justify that either."

He took his leave, lest Michael's capacity for impromptu sermonizing overtake him, though the fellow had a point: Mercia's situation required resolution, and to see to that, somebody would have to die. On his good days, Girard rather preferred it not be him, and on his bad days…

On his bad days, he could think of no place he'd rather die than merry olde England.

❧

"Come." Lady Greendale took Christian by his ungloved left hand and pulled him toward Severn's main staircase. "You'll hide in the library, or with your stewards or your correspondence, and that child has waited weeks and weeks to see her long-lost papa. She needs to see you're alive with her own eyes."

"I beg your pardon." Christian planted his feet, stopping her forward progress—barely. The countess was surprisingly strong for her size, and apparently suffering no ill effects from having endured his kisses the previous night. "I would prefer not to be dragged up to the nursery like some errant scholar come downstairs to peek at Mama in her evening finery."

She smiled at him, appearing perfectly charmed by his mulishness.

"I'll bet you did exactly that, and your papa pretended not to see you until your mama bid you come give her a kiss. You were likely adorable, too. How we do change."

He had been adorable. His mama had told him so. With some effort and no little consternation Christian identified the temptation to...smile.

"Perhaps we might compromise?" He winged his left arm at her, his momentary good humor fading. This confrontation with the child really would be better put off to when he wasn't sporting the dust of the road, bone-weary from hours in the saddle, and completely without a plan as to how the reunion should be handled.

But thank God, the countess was filling her sails.

"...She writes to me regularly, and I to her, as I have a paucity of cousins worth the trouble, much less with legible penmanship. Hers is exquisite, though, even for a child."

"As mine is...was."

"Really? Well, we know she didn't get her penmanship from Helene. Why you never hired the woman an amanuensis is beyond me, Mercia. In any case, Lucy is very much looking forward to seeing her papa, and worried she won't recognize you. You must be sure not to look so forbidding to her. You can be the duke later, when her beaus and swains come calling. For now, enjoy being the papa."

She marched up the steps, a ship's captain determined to dock her vessel safely at the pier of her choosing.

"Excuse me, Countess, but refresh my memory: How many children have you had the pleasure of raising?" Perhaps if he scrapped with her a bit she'd be less nervous, and then *he* might be less nervous too.

She paused at the second landing, forcing him to do likewise.

"Low shot, Your Grace. Unsporting of you, though I raised my younger brothers because my mama was in a perpetual decline, which ought to be impossible. I will forgive you though, because you are anxious. A papa doesn't rise from the dead every day."

She'd taunted, dragged, and talked him to the nursery door.

"Hello, Nanny, Harris." Her ladyship nodded to the nurse and the governess. "Nothing would do but His Grace must come directly to the nursery to see Lady Lucy. His Grace has reminded me her ladyship prefers to be called Lucy. She's in the schoolroom?"

"At her letters," Harris said, bobbing a deep curtsy. "Your Grace."

He nodded in response, not recalling this Harris person in the least. Nanny was another matter, though, for she'd been Helene's nanny too.

"Nanny, I hope we find you well?"

"Better now, Your Grace. Better now that my lamb's papa is with us again."

"Where I much prefer to be," he said, wanting to run howling for the stables.

"Well, let's get on with it," the countess said, taking his hand again.

Since when had grown women been permitted to take the bare hands of grown men, so that said fellow—a duke, no less—might be hauled about like a load of garden produce? He counted himself fortunate Lady Greendale did not grasp him by the ear.

She guided him to the schoolroom, which enjoyed westerly windows that let in a good deal of afternoon sunlight. A child sat at an ornate little desk, carefully dipping her pen in the inkwell. Her tongue peeked out the side of her mouth, her lips were pursed in concentration, and her feet were wrapped around the legs of her chair. Her pinafore was spotless and nearly free of wrinkles.

She did not move, except for the hand guiding the pen, and she was so focused on her work, she didn't look up. She had the look of a Severn, blond hair, a lithe elegance to her little frame, dramatic eyebrows...

While Christian stared at his only living child, the countess silently melted back into the sitting room. Now, now when he needed chatter and brisk efficiency more than ever, the woman deserted her post.

Nothing for it but to charge ahead.

"Lucy."

She looked up, staring straight ahead at first, as if she weren't sure from whence her name had been spoken. She set her pen down and turned her head.

"Lucy, it's Papa."

She scrambled up from the desk and started across the room, her gaze riveted on him. He went down on

one knee and held up his arms, and she broke into a
trot, then came pelting at him full tilt.

"I'm home," he said, taking in the little-girl shape
and sheer reality of her. "Papa's home."

She held on to him tightly, arms around his neck
like she'd never let go.

"You're glad to see me, hmm?" He kept his arms
around her too. They were alone after all, and he
hadn't seen her for three damned years.

She nodded vigorously, nearly striking him a blow
on the chin with her crown.

"I'm glad to see you too, Lucy Severn, very glad.
What were you working on?"

She wiggled away, though letting her go was an
effort, and pulled him over to the desk—another
determined little female towing him about.

"'Welcome home, Papa. Love, Lucy,'" he read. "Your
hand is lovely, Lucy. What else have you written?"

She showed him, opening sketchbooks, copybooks,
and pointing out books she'd either read or was reading. He did as his father had done, exclaiming here,
praising there, asking a question occasionally.

But only occasionally, and all his questions were
answerable with a nod or a shake of the head.

Lucy led him into the sitting room, her expression radiant.

"Look who you've found, Lucy," Lady Greendale
said, rising from the settee. "He isn't lost anymore, our
duke, you've found him. Will you take him to see the
kittens in the stables now?"

"Really, kittens are perhaps more in line with a countess's responsibilities than a duke's, don't you think?"

Christian speared the lady with a look, but his daughter swung his hand and peered up at him with big blue eyes.

Severn eyes, but prettier for Helene's contribution to their setting.

"You come home from war only once," Lady Greendale said. "Why don't we all pay a visit to the kittens?"

She reached for Lucy's free hand, but the child drew back. At first Christian felt an unbecoming spurt of pleasure that Lucy wanted to hold only her papa's hand, not her cousin's, but as he led the child toward the door, she dropped his hand too, and shook her head.

"She doesn't want to go out," Lady Greendale said. "Nurse warned me it was getting worse."

"It's a lovely day," Christian said with a breeziness he'd likely never feel again. "I want to spend time with my daughter, and what's more, Chessie will want to see how much she's grown while he was off campaigning on the Peninsula. You recall Chesterton, don't you, Lucy?"

She nodded, her gaze going from one adult to the other.

"Well, come along then." Christian scooped the girl up bodily and settled her on his back. "We've a stable to visit."

The countess started in with her chatter, which was a relief, for the child continued to say nothing.

"Chesterton is quite the largest horse I've seen under saddle, but he seems a steady fellow, and very handsome. I would guess that did your papa take you up on such a horse, Lucy, you might be able to see clear to France."

Because he carried her on his back, Christian felt his daughter chortling—silently.

And by the time they'd inspected the entire stable, he was glad for the countess's patter, glad for her ability to comment on everything, from the knees on the new foals to the whiskers on the kittens.

For it became obvious Lucy had inherited her father's propensity for keeping silent, and she intended to remain that way for reasons known only to her.

Seven

CHRISTIAN APPROACHED THE NURSERY SUITE, LUCY still clinging like a monkey to his back. He set her down when they reached the sitting room, and she scampered off to the schoolroom, leaving Christian to wonder if his daughter's manners had lapsed along with her words.

"She's not normally given to rudeness of any kind," the countess said, looking worried.

Before Christian could frame a reply—what did he know of his own child, after all?—Lucy was back, her copybook and pencil in her hand. She held the book up to her father.

"Will I come tomorrow? Yes, if you wish it, and we'll visit Chessie again, or the kittens." He passed the book back to her.

Why wouldn't she speak, for God's sake? That she'd withhold her voice from her own father made him feel *punished*.

The child waved her book under his nose.

"Cousin must come too?" Excellent notion, given the awkwardness of one-sided conversations. "Countess?"

"Of course, I will be happy to come," she said, smoothing a hand over the child's golden hair. "Maybe you will have written a poem about clouds and lambs and kittens when we come back, or maybe about a great chestnut charger who can see to France."

This provoked a smile from the child.

"Until tomorrow, then." Christian turned to leave this maudlin little gathering only to find a pair of small, skinny arms lashed around his waist. The child's embrace held desperation, and ferocious if silent determination.

"I forgot," he said, lifting her up to his hip. "You will come down to see us after tea, won't you?"

Lucy shook her head, pointed at her father, and drew her finger to her own chest.

"I'm to come to you? No, I think not. I came this time. You must come next time, but it will be only two floors down. If you don't come, I'll realize you were too fatigued, and content myself with Cousin Gillian's company."

He set her down, not too hastily, and turned on his heel to go, then stopped. "Countess, may I offer my escort?"

She looked torn, but made no objection. "Thank you, Your Grace."

The door was safely closed behind them before he spoke.

"I suppose you think I bungled that, but making a great fuss over what might be nothing more than a child's stubbornness could be ill-advised. Of course, I'm assuming the child *will not* talk, though it might be more accurate to say she *cannot*."

Silence met this observation, unnerving coming

from the countess—Cousin Gillian—and how odd that silence—Christian's last, best, most trustworthy friend—was in some wise no longer welcome in his life.

৵৶

Over a substantial tray served on the terrace, Gilly admitted that the distinction between unwillingness to speak and inability to speak *mattered*. His Grace was brusque, troubled, and sometimes difficult, but he was neither stupid nor free of paternal impulses.

And for that reason, Gilly confessed a transgression to him.

"I saw you greet her, Your Grace. I apologize for peeking, but I didn't want you to start interrogating her when she's been so anxious about seeing you."

He sat back, a shaft of sunlight falling across his face. The sunshine was of the benevolent, early summer variety, but it illuminated both his fatigue and the white scar on his earlobe.

"And now you disclose your spying?"

He seemed amused, but Gilly did not trust her ability to read this man. She'd had no warning at all that he was about to kiss her, and she still had no idea why he'd done so or what she felt about his presumption.

"I wanted you to know what I'd done, and to express my apologies. I should have allowed you both privacy."

He'd been exactly right with the child, perfect in fact. So kind and understanding Gilly had wanted to weep with relief—and he'd been affectionate. Little girls needed affection, particularly from their papas.

"My privacy has suffered far worse violations, my lady. You should have given us a moment, true, but you're protective of the child, and one can't castigate you for that, under the circumstances. You aren't eating much. Does the company put your digestion off?"

Was he teasing her? She sat up straighter. "The company is agreeable."

He held up a section of orange, and rather than take it from his hand, Gilly took it with her teeth, a shockingly informal way to go on. Nonetheless, he'd started it, and something about the daring of such behavior—she might one day abuse his trust and bite him—appealed to her.

"The company," he mused, "is *agreeable*. Such profuse emotion, Countess. I assure you the sentiment is mutual." He took a sprig of lavender from his lemonade glass and pitched the garnish with particular force into a bed of daisies. "I will review the physicians' correspondence, we will have an outing with Lucy tomorrow, and I will consider where we go from here."

Mercia twitched his fingers together—the lavender had been wet with lemonade—and Gilly wondered what exactly had been done to his hand.

To the rest of his body, to his mind. His privacy, his heart, his soul.

None of her business, as she was none of his.

"We have other business to conduct, Countess. More orange?"

"No, thank you," she said, feeling off balance at his word choice—business, as in finances and ledgers. That sort of business. He'd eaten all but two orange sections, and put one on her plate.

"What are your long-term plans, my lady? I ask both as Lucy's papa and as the husband of your late cousin."

"My plans?"

Her bread and butter turned to sawdust in her mouth when she saw the considering light in his eyes. He'd ambushed her, the wretch, out here in the sunshine and beauty of a perfect summer's day. Greendale had been a master at the ambush.

Next Mercia would explain, politely, that he needed privacy with his daughter, and an extraneous cousin-in-law on the premises must needs be a temporary imposition.

Well, damn him. Damn him and his elegant, scarred hands and his beautiful, soft voice and his lovely eyes and his kindness toward the child. Damn him for all of it.

And especially for kissing her. Those gentle, nearly chaste kisses had been so…so… Gilly had lost sleep trying to find words for Mercia's kisses. One word kept careening into her awareness, no matter how stoutly she batted it away. Mercia's kisses had been *cherishing*, as if Gilly were the reason he lived, the reason he'd bested demons and nightmares to return to her side.

Which was balderdash. He'd meandered home from Carlton House through the park, and she was pathetic to make so much of a small late-night lapse between two tired adults.

He regarded her now with an expression so far from cherishing that Gilly's food sat uneasily in her belly.

"We've only just arrived at Severn, Your Grace. Must we discuss plans and arrangements now?"

"We must." He picked up one of the sections of orange and held it out to her. "Please."

Please eat, or please reveal her hopes and fears, as manifest in the next year's residential particulars? His blue eyes held an odd light, and Gilly abruptly wished she had the protection of her black silk shawl, for all the afternoon was pleasant. She used her fingers to take the orange from him and popped it into her mouth.

"The army enjoys a surfeit of discipline and structure, as if to counteract all the chaos and upheaval of its daily existence," Mercia said. "I have not had a settled life, a life to my liking, for more than three years. I impose on your good nature that we might coordinate plans, my lady."

She chewed her orange, trying not to blame him for wanting his household to himself.

"I have no set plans for the near term." Marcus had sent her a note of condolence upon Greendale's passing, and that note had not included assurances that she'd be welcome in the dower house. Maybe he'd assumed assurances hadn't been needed—she could occupy the dower house as a matter of right—but the Greendale dower house was little more than a ruin.

Across from her, the duke screwed up his thin-lipped, elegant mouth in a grimace of impatience.

"For the near term, you will stay here, my lady. We are agreed on that for the child's sake. I'd like you to consider making your home with us permanently, though. You are in mourning, and I certainly intend to live quietly. You know this household, and I have no hostess, no lady to see to the maids and the housekeeper."

He had no one to see to *him*, as far as Gilly could tell, which apparently mattered to him not at all.

"You would take me on as a charitable relation?" Her question held caution and surprise, for his invitation was as tempting as it was unexpected.

He pushed back from the table and shot her an annoyed look.

"I am the relation deserving of charity, Lady Greendale. I will be up to my ears in estate matters, for Easterbrook made it clear the stewards and tenants were as reluctant as the bankers to do anything on his say-so as my successor. I have no time for the household matters, no time for the child, no time for the social nonsense that ought to go along with my title. I quite honestly need your help, and I am asking you to give it on a more or less permanent basis."

For him that was a protracted and reassuringly loud speech. The part of Gilly that had wanted only to be useful rejoiced to hear it, but some other part of her—that had been briefly cherished in a shadowed library—was disquieted.

"You'll remarry," she said, drawing on that sense of disquiet. He should remarry, and not because he needed an heir. He needed somebody to sit with him in the library when he could not sleep, needed somebody to see that he ate regularly. Needed somebody to find him the perfect valet.

Needed, and deserved, somebody to cherish *him*.

"I might remarry eventually, particularly if Easterbrook doesn't sell out. I don't look forward to the prospect though, and intend to observe some mourning of my own. I learned of Helene's passing only when I met up with Easterbrook outside Toulouse."

This was news. "And Evan?"

"At the same time."

He was so matter-of-fact...so heartbreakingly matter-of-fact. Gilly was especially glad she'd seen him on his knees, hugging Lucy to him so tightly.

"I will think on this, Your Grace. You are generous, and as a place to bide during first mourning, Severn has a great deal of appeal." A place to be needed and busy, a place to heal from eight years of being Greendale's countess.

"First mourning is only six months for some, your ladyship." He held out the last orange section to her. "Give me a year. Give me and Lucy your full year of mourning."

In that year, would he give her more kisses? She took the orange and set it on her plate.

"I will think on this," she said again. "We will see what transpires with Lucy. You might well decide to send her to a convent, where her silence will be viewed as a spiritual achievement."

"No, I will not." He appropriated the orange section from her plate and munched it into oblivion. "I am disinclined to send her away for any reason. You have a scar, Countess."

What on earth?

He took her hand in his and rubbed his thumb over the back of her knuckles. For all his hand had been mistreated, his grip was firm. Also warm. Perhaps even cherishing.

"A burn, I think," he said, studying her hand. "A nasty burn, but old. Well healed."

His touch was a delicate, sweet caress to Gilly's nerves, like the summer breeze and the dappled sun. "Spilled tea. It happens."

He patted her knuckles and let her have her hand back.

"We do heal, hmm?" He did not smile, but Gilly had the sense they'd shared something, a wink, a joke, a secret, about scars and the stories they concealed.

Not a harmless secret, for some.

"You should tell Lucy you will never send her away. Harris no doubt threatens with every imaginable dire fate to try to inspire the girl to speak. I forbade the use of violence in your schoolroom, though."

Her presumptuousness caught His Grace's curiosity. "An occasional birching befalls most English school-children, and usually to good effect."

"According to whom? The tutors who've beaten the children to silence? The pious hypocrites who misquote Proverbs?"

She should not have broached this topic, not with him, not when he had so recently noted the scar on her hand. An outburst threatened, worse than any of her previous lapses.

"A stubborn child who is never disciplined cannot learn to govern himself," Mercia said, as if reciting some platitude he'd heard before his own backside had been caned.

"Helene was stubborn. Did you take a switch to her in hopes of eradicating the failing in your duchess?"

They were arguing. The last thing Gilly wanted was to annoy His Grace, and yet on this topic, she could barely be rational.

"I would never raise my hand to a woman."

"But you would raise that same hand to a small child, and expect brute force to teach her self-possession and restraint. I can assure you, resorting to violence for the betterment of those helpless to defend themselves is anything but an example of restraint."

She stared at the empty plate, her hands fisted in her lap lest she hurl the hapless porcelain against the nearest hard surface.

His Grace's handsome head, for example.

"No birchings for my daughter, then, and no more threats, either. Not from anybody." When Gilly dared a glance at him, his Grace's expression suggested talk of Gilly's eventual departure qualified as a threat. "I commend the lemon cakes to your excellent care, Countess."

He rose, bowed over her hand, then departed, his back militarily straight.

Leaving Gilly to wonder if His Grace's hospitality was a great and subtle kindness, or if—the notion chilled—he'd threatened her with a gilded cage.

Another gilded cage.

❧

Christian wasn't precisely glad to be alive. Surviving torture turned a man into a ghost toting a bag of memories that could not be shared, and inhabiting a body no longer reliable or easily maintained. That body, after torture, did not sleep well, did not exert itself unproblematically, did not ingest food easily, and certainly could not be relied upon to deal with amatory pastimes—not that Christian would be indulging in any of those.

Not soon. Not immediately.

But the hour he'd spent with his daughter made it plain the child, at least, was delighted her papa had survived, and this changed the complexion of Christian's existence.

For himself, he could be content to languish in bitterness, to wake up each day after a bad night's sleep—the countess would not permit a continued reversal of circadian routines—aching in body and soul, dreams of revenge his constant companion.

For his child, he would have to manage something… more, until Girard could be found and exterminated.

Lucy wanted her papa to take her up on Chessie, an exercise requiring the ability to guide the horse with his seat and one hand while he steadied the child with the other.

She wanted to hold her papa's hand—either one would do—and to ride about on his back.

She expected his appearance in the nursery on some predictable schedule.

If anything had assisted Christian to remain upright and breathing, despite Girard's mischief, it was the physical fitness of a seasoned cavalry officer determined to lead his men well. That part of military life—the physical challenge of it—Christian had foolishly thrived on.

The time had come to foolishly thrive again, insofar as a tired and tormented body would allow it.

So Christian began his first full day at Severn as his father and grandfather often had, by riding out. He started with the grounds of Severn itself, the bridle paths and park, keeping mostly to the walk. Yesterday's ride down from Town had tired both him and the horse, and the purpose of the morning ride was twofold.

He wanted to regain condition, or see if it was possible to regain condition, and he wanted to see his land. The countess had been right to bring him home, for southern England was beautiful in summer.

And her ladyship apparently intended to enjoy it to the fullest, for Christian spotted her walking among his mother's treasured gardens. For the first time, Lady Greendale wasn't in black—he delighted in knowing even her night robes were black—and she was out-of-doors without a bonnet.

He was inclined to leave her to her wanderings, except she looked so…pretty. She wore a high-waisted walking dress in lavender, her blond hair burnished gold in the morning sun, and she was humming as she occasionally bent down to sniff a flower.

"I know I've been caught," she said, kneeling to take in the scent of a red rose and getting a damp patch on one knee for her efforts. "You should not lurk in the trees, Mercia. Come into the sun, and greet the day with me."

She ran her nose over the flower's outer petals and gave him a soft, private smile that put him in mind of Italian Renaissance maidens who knew delightful, naughty secrets.

"Good morning, Countess. You're up early."

"As are you, as is the sun. And your dear friend, Mr. Chesterton."

"My lazy friend. We were useless above a sedate trot, weren't we, Chessie?"

The horse looked about, pricking his ears at the sound of his name. Christian swung down, gave the animal a pat on the neck, and fell in step beside the countess, leading his gelding by the reins.

"Did you sleep well?" she asked. "My mama said it's a polite inquiry, but the question strikes me as personal."

"I rarely sleep well," he said, simply for the pleasure of thwarting her small talk.

"Neither do I." Her smile became sad, and he wondered why they hadn't met up in the library again the previous evening, where something more interesting than sleep might have befallen them. "Restless nights are the price of adulthood, perhaps." She slipped her hand through his arm, uninvited, as if she would... comfort him?

He stepped aside, untangling their arms, and lifted his hand to his lips to fashion a piercing whistle.

Except the fingers of his left hand no longer accommodated their boyhood competence. What came out was an odd huff that would in no wise get the attention of the stableboys. His right hand did no better, and he wanted to kick something—Anduvoir's privy parts would do for a start. He took no consolation from the stray thought that Girard alone might understand why.

"We need a groom?" her ladyship guessed. "I'll try."

She put her fingers to her lips and got off a stout, shrill peal, which had the stable lads looking up from across the sprawling back garden and Chessie standing quite tall in his gear. A groom scampered over, swung up on Chessie, and took the horse off toward the stables.

The sight of the groom trotting Chessie away to the stables tickled recollections Christian couldn't quite retrieve, though the moment of déjà vu passed as quickly as it had arisen.

"What a good soul," the countess said as Chessie

obligingly decamped in the direction of his oats. "With a good memory too."

"Very good," Christian replied. "If Chessie hadn't recognized me, I'm not sure I could have survived more stumbling about the French countryside, trying to prove my patrimony to the authorities."

For some starving French farm wife would doubtless have killed the bearded scarecrow who'd forgotten how to talk.

"I'm glad Chesterton's memory did not fail him." Her ladyship slipped her arm through Christian's again, then slid her hand down to encircle his left wrist. "What exactly befell your hand?"

War. Pain. Evil in the form of drunken corporals who likely could not have understood his English if he *had* broken his silence. "The French."

They strolled along without further words, the lovely summer morning making the memory of the torture obscene, but less real too. Without him willing it, Christian's mouth formed more sounds.

"The guards sought to wring a confession of treason from me, so even if I did escape, my own people would put me to death. The idea was not to cause physical pain for its own sake—though a certain variety of soldier enjoys torturing prisoners for that reason—but to destroy my sanity. A dream of escape often sustains a prisoner, and Girard wanted me to have that dream, probably to torment me as much as comfort me. Girard was livid when he realized what the guards had done with his pet duke."

"The torture was merely a means to an end?" She spoke the word so casually, and her fingers laced through his.

Gently, but unapologetically. The way Girard had handled him after Anduvoir had departed to terrorize the camp whores.

"The goal of my captors was to rob me of my reason, to reduce a proud little dukeling to a puling, begging cipher. Breaking me became a game for them, and to some extent for me, too."

As best he could figure. Why else would Girard have alternated inhuman treatment whenever Anduvoir came around with punctilious care and feeding?

"A game, like a duel to the death."

"My death, or the death of my reason."

She brought his hand up, holding the back of it against the extraordinary softness of her cheek. Until he'd taken liberties with her in the library, he'd forgotten how wonderfully, startlingly soft a woman's cheek could be. As soft as sunshine and summer rain, as soft as the quiet of the English countryside.

"Shall we sit?" he asked, though she'd likely release his hand if they sat. He was a widower, though, and she ought not to begrudge him simple human contact when he'd been so recently bereaved.

She let him lead her to a shaded bench near the roses, the morning air faintly redolent of their perfume. When Christian seated her, the countess kept his damaged hand in hers.

"I was not allowed to garden at Greendale," she said, fingers drifting over his knuckles. "The estate had gardens, because his lordship would not be seen to neglect his acres, but I was forbidden to walk them, or to dig about in the good English soil, or to consult with the gardeners regarding the designs and plantings."

Based on the studied casualness of her tone, this prohibition had been irksome.

"You are free to garden here all you like. I ask only that you not disturb my mother's roses."

"They are lovely."

"She was lovely."

Another silence, while Christian became aware of his surroundings beyond the small hand holding his. The roses were in their early summer glory, and why Polite Society insisted on staying in Town through most of June was incomprehensible, when the alternative was the English countryside. The sunshine was a perfectly weighted beneficence on his cheek, the scent of the gardens heavenly, and the entire morning aurally gilded with the fluting chorus of songbirds.

He wanted to kiss the lady beside him again, not in thanks, not as a good-night benediction, but for the sheer pleasure of the undertaking.

"You were right about Severn," Christian said. "I rode a few of the home-farm fields, and those are in good repair, but the bordering tenant farms are not as spruce."

"You'll soon put matters to rights." She patted his hand, didn't squeeze it. "My goal this morning was to inspect the family plot and the chapel grounds."

"You wanted to tend the graves?" He didn't like this idea, instinctively loathed it.

"I doubt Nanny or Harris have thought to bring Lucy to see them. When Lucy visits, all should be pretty and soothing."

What about when *he* visited? Though Helene had apparently taken her own life, and no amount of flowers would pretty that up.

"You would bring Lucy to see the graves?"

"I'll tend the graves first," she said, her chin coming up. "Lucy's father ought to take her to visit them."

He disentangled their hands, which required an odd little struggle. The countess didn't seem to understand what he was about until he shook his fingers free.

"I am of no mind to linger about graves, my lady, not now." Not ever. Children succumbed to flu, so Christian could not directly blame Girard for the boy's death, but it was time to send out letters, to call in favors, to pester the generals, and start tracking the French pestilence down.

"Then don't visit the graves now," the countess said, her expression more puzzled than disapproving. And yet, she seemed to expect something from him, something in the nature of an apology or explanation.

So be it.

"I joined up to get away from Helene, and she was pleased to see me go."

The admission was out, made mostly to the toes of Christian's riding boots—his loose riding boots. He willed himself to get the devil off the bench, but his tired ducal arse stayed right where it was.

"She was a difficult wife, I take it."

Helene had been a difficult cousin too, based on the countess's dry tone.

"Helene was vain, spoiled, selfish, and mean," Christian said. "At times. She was also gorgeous, generous, scatterbrained, and capable of kindness, but we did not suit, and we were both growing to accept that."

Though accepting Helene's penchant for flirting

had been beyond him, and that was what had eventually driven him onto Wellington's staff.

His duchess had been faithful, so far as he knew, but in the curious manner of troubled marriages, Christian had the sense if he'd remained underfoot, his presence would have goaded her to cross even that line.

"Did you go to war to get yourself killed? Over a woman? I cannot picture the Duke of Mercia being so romantic."

Neither could he, thank God. "I did not go off to get killed. I went off to serve King and Country, and if I might point out, I succeeded." The notion was no comfort whatsoever, but torture did that too—put a man beyond any comfort.

"You succeeded spectacularly."

The small woman beside him worried her upper lip with her teeth, probably biting back more words. She had a healthy sense of self-preservation, did the countess.

And a way with a silence.

"I wanted more children," Christian said, giving up the struggle to maintain any dignity in this conversation. "A spare seemed a prudent undertaking. She said she'd gut me in my sleep did I attempt it. I thought time apart would help. It did not. It had not as of the last leave I took."

"She owed you a spare," the countess said, her tone stern. "We talked about this before we married, Helene and I. She pitied me because Greendale was my lot, but I was prepared to present him with children."

She was blushing, which restored his spirits, if not

his dignity. The touch of color looked well on her, as did a color other than black. The lady was, viewed in a certain soft morning light, attractive. Certainly attractive enough to remarry.

"You would have loved any children you bore old Greendale." This truth was the closest he could come to consoling her.

Though for what? Childlessness? For being married to an old martinet who was jealous of his flower gardens? For having to serve as Helene's most recent confidante?

And how did they get onto this indelicate and personal topic?

"I am to meet my steward directly after breakfast," he said. "Shall I walk you back to the house?"

"Please." She extended her hand, he drew her to her feet, and this time, it was Christian who was ambushed.

She gave him another of those kisses to the mouth, rose up off the bench and kept coming, a one-woman, fragrant, soft cavalry charge of pleasure and comfort. After she'd brushed her lips across his, she also gave him a more intriguing gift.

She rested against him, fully, gave him her weight for a moment, let his greater height and what strength he had hold her upright. The sensations were exquisite.

Her hair tickling his chin.

Her breasts, unapologetically soft and full against his chest.

Peppermint—from her tooth powder?—lingering on her lips.

His reactions were slow, and she seemed to understand they would be, for she remained against him long enough that he could loop his arms around her waist, rest his chin against her temple, and let the peace of the embrace settle over him.

Girard deserved to die, slowly and painfully, but of all the things Girard had destroyed in Christian's life, he had not, nor would he ever, destroy this moment.

"I wanted the graves to be tidy for you, too," she said. "For all of us, the graves should be tidy."

The countess was protective of those she cared about, and in her admission, Christian found proof that she cared about *him*. She hadn't assured him she'd remain for her entire year of mourning—the most he could ask of her, for now—but she'd given him a morsel of her trust.

He turned her under his arm and walked her back to the house without allowing her to leave his side.

Eight

"WHY NOT A HACK ABOUT THE PARK ONE DAY SOON?" Mercia asked his daughter. He had the knack of pausing long enough to invite the child to answer, but not so long as to create expectations. Gilly wondered where he'd learned such interrogatory skill, or if he simply had a gift.

"Hearing no objection," he went on, "I'll invite the countess to ride with us."

"I haven't a proper habit, but I will make one up, now that I know the stables are open to guests."

Something nonplussed then a trifle aggravated flickered in Mercia's eyes.

"We'll choose her ladyship a mount, shall we?" He put the question to his daughter and extended a hand to the child. "One must indulge in some anticipatory spoiling if one is to form an alliance with a horse or a member of the opposite sex. You are not to repeat that to your governess, Lucy."

As if she'd repeat anything to anybody.

Mercia took his daughter from stall to stall, eventually lifting her onto his hip, something the girl was old enough to object to, and wise enough to enjoy. She was content to wander from one velvety equine nose to another, her head resting on her father's shoulder.

And the picture they made, two blond heads nestled together, the duke occasionally murmuring quietly to his daughter, gave Gilly an odd pang for Helene. This was lost to Helene, this simple outing to the stables with father and daughter, lost forever. Watering the flowers in the library, surreptitiously watching His Grace scratch out letters to his old army connections— many of them still on the Continent—that was lost too.

Peeling his oranges.

Kissing him. Reveling in the sandalwood scent of him. Feeling his heart beat with the firm, steady rhythm of a trotting horse.

"Come, Countess, there's a lady asking to make your acquaintance," the duke said. "I presented this one to Helene on the occasion of Evan's birth."

Gilly caught up to His Grace and peered over an open half door at a dainty golden mare with four white socks, a white blaze, and a flaxen mane and tail.

Gilly stretched out a hand to the horse. "She is darling. It's a shame she's not being ridden."

"The lads no doubt dice for the privilege of taking her out," Mercia said. "But she's the right size for you. Helene disdained her because of her modest size."

He said it casually, as if having such a generous lying-in gift disdained wasn't of any moment, but Gilly had begun to wonder if anything Helene had said about her husband was true. Perhaps a sojourn in the army had done him good, or perhaps Helene's judgment had been less than objective.

The duke was not grim; he was serious, as a mature man might be serious.

He was not selfish; he was disciplined.

He was not a great brute, but rather a tall, handsome—if lean—man, whose kisses were the opposite of brutish.

And if he was a ravening lecher, Gilly saw no evidence of it. Helene had claimed he'd kept mistresses and conducted several liaisons simultaneously. Gilly hadn't questioned where such lurid information came from, but had prayed Greendale might do likewise and leave her in peace.

"Child, your hour of liberty has flown," the duke said, easing Lucy to her feet. "Will you join me here tomorrow? Perhaps we'll put you on a leading rein, and let you have a turn on Damsel while the countess cheers you on."

Lucy's little face lit up, and she clapped her hands together as she nodded emphatically.

"We've an assignation, then, so be off with you." The duke turned her by her shoulders and gave her a gentle shove. "Mind you go straight to the nursery, and don't get your pinafore dirty on the way, lest Nanny and the countess be wroth with me." He shook a playful finger at her, then blew the child a kiss.

Grim?

The girl scampered off, turning to wave at them from the barn door, then cutting a line across the gardens toward the house.

"She's more animated for having you about," Gilly said. "The entire staff is elated to have you home again."

"Oh, quite. Risen from the dead and all that. Would you walk with me, Countess?"

He wrapped her hand over his arm, the ease of it giving Gilly a private pleasure. On those occasions when it had been necessary to walk with Greendale, he'd spent the entire promenade hissing criticism at her, while presenting a bland countenance to the world. Strolling on Mercia's arm felt...peaceful.

And protected, the opposite of Greendale's carping and threats.

"You're silent. This makes a man nervous, Lady Greendale."

"We're sharing a roof, Your Grace, and we have been cousins by marriage. Might you call me Gillian? Nobody does anymore." Not that Greendale had. His names for her had been...not worth recalling. Gilly leaned closer to her escort.

"Gilly is a pretty name."

In his less vile moods, Greendale had called it a peasant name. "How long do you suppose you'll stay, Your Grace?"

"Stay?" The duke snapped off a red damask rose, took a whiff, then passed it to her. "This reminds me of you."

Another compliment?

"Stay here at Severn," Gilly said, wanting to touch the rose to her nose, but finding the impulse oddly intimate. "Before you leave."

"I've quite sold out, Countess, and the only reason I'd set foot on the Continent would be if old army matters required it of me, and they well might."

"But you've estates elsewhere. Business in Town,

matters that will take you from Severn." Part of her wanted him to travel on, lest she cross the line from kisses given out of friendship and comfort to kisses of a different nature.

"Are you asking if I have a mistress in Town, languishing for lack of my company? That would have been fast work, my dear. Should I be flattered or insulted that you suspect such a thing of me?"

My dear? Was he teasing? She recalled him shaking his finger at his daughter in mock sternness. "You should be quiet. I would never ask such a thing."

Though she might suspect it.

"Helene did." He disentangled their arms and took her by the wrist instead, leading her to a shaded bench. "At great, vociferous, and tiresome length, she accused me of being quite the blade on the town."

Good heavens. It was one thing to complain to a cousin, quite another to rip up at one's husband. "You cut a dash. Greendale remarked it."

"Greendale was still wearing powder and patches. He'd criticize the angel Gabriel for flying. I was faithful to my vows, Countess. My parents were a love match, and I married Helene hoping to esteem her greatly."

He fell silent while Gilly cast about for a change in topic—Helene had hoped *to be esteemed* greatly, and apparently she had been. The duke went on, his tone thoughtful.

"I often suspected Helene had a wandering eye and couldn't quite admit it to herself, so she must see the fault in me."

To his list of attributes, Gilly added astuteness, which was not a great blessing under some circumstances.

"She very much enjoyed being Duchess of Mercia," Gilly said, relieved that it was the truth.

"She did. I take consolation from that."

"Will you observe mourning for her and Evan?"

"That depends in part on the guidance I receive from Vicar, but I am inclined to take up second mourning, as Helene will soon have been gone for a year."

"And Evan, too."

The duke's lips twisted in an expression Gilly recognized not as distaste so much as impatience.

"What?"

"I feel as much guilt as grief where the child is concerned," he said. "For various reasons, but in part because the little fellow needed me more than my duchess did—the best person to show the next duke how to go on is the present version. And yet, my presence in the nursery was barely tolerated, and the army seemed like a good use of an extraneous duke."

He was confiding in her, and Gilly was equally dismayed and touched. Damn Helene for her selfishness anyway, and English dukes numbered only several dozen in a good year. How could even one be extraneous?

"You are not extraneous, Your Grace. Not to Lucy, not to your tenants and staff."

"What about to you, Countess?" Despite the gravity of the question, his blue eyes held humor, and maybe something else—curiosity?

"You are not extraneous to me, either. I am the one imposing on your household."

"You will disabuse yourself of that notion." He rose and drew Gilly to her feet. "When Vicar comes to call, you will pour. When Lucy needs her first habit, you will supervise the creation of it. When the tweeny steals the underbutler's attentions from the first parlor maid, you will intervene, or civilization throughout the shire will cease."

"While you do what?"

"Wait for my daughter to speak and try to address what needs addressing regarding my past."

He gave her a little bow, touched his finger to the flower Gilly still held, and took himself back up toward the house.

Leaving Gilly to wonder, if in his questions and confidences the duke might—without any conscious intent to do so—have been flirting with her, just a little.

❦

To Christian's great pleasure, in response to inquiries regarding Girard and Anduvoir, a letter arrived from Devlin St. Just. Out of the pile of otherwise trivial social correspondence, that one was saved back, to be read in the solitude of the library at the end of the day.

The volume of good wishes from Christian's peers and neighbors quite honestly surprised him. Each day brought more letters, some from people he'd never met, congratulating him on his safe journey home, thanking him for his service to the realm "above and beyond the call of duty," wishing him well in light of his "noble sacrifices."

Platitudes, all of them, and they made Christian at once furious and humble—though nobody had any word regarding Girard.

"Will I disturb you?" The countess in her dark bedclothes stood in the doorway, her hair a golden rope braided over one shoulder.

"Of course not." Christian rose, for she was a lady. An increasingly kissable, holdable lady. "Sleep eludes you?"

"I'm hoping not." She advanced into the room and closed the door to keep in the fire's heat. "I've brought your volume of Blake back, lest it find its way to some trunk or portmanteau of mine."

She was doing it again, hinting at her departure, and all the conflicted emotion he'd felt contemplating his mail transferred itself to the lady in bare feet before him.

Long feet, with high arches and pink, fetching toes. Surely, composing odes to a widow's feet indicated inchoate loss of reason?

"Shall you choose another volume? And what can you be thinking, my dear, to wander about unshod?" He hoped she was *home*, where such lapses were not a privilege but a right.

"I wasn't thinking." But she smiled, that same wan smile that he often saw her turn on Lucy. He suspected that smile signaled a lack of children in her life to love, which lack she ought to lay squarely on Greendale's no doubt tidy grave. "A want of regular, rational processes is my besetting sin, according to my late spouse."

"Whom you have the sense not to mourn over-much. Come here by the fire, then, and be warm, despite your lack of forethought. I'll choose another book for you."

"Kind of you." She advanced to the hearth and took a seat on the bricks. "You've had the fire going all day. The bricks are warm."

"I want one room in the house where the constant chill in my bones must do battle with a decent fire. I know it's summer, but…"

Before he could bluster his way into some ducally appropriate explanation, she stroked a hand over the bricks.

"The warmth helps," she said. "Someone should make it a rule that spouses die only in spring, so the warmth of the summer is available in first mourning to provide the simplest comfort of all."

And to think Greendale had tried repeatedly to call her stupid.

Christian brought her another volume of poetry. "An anthology, perfect for browsing at the end of the day."

He sat on the hearth beside her uninvited, because he hadn't wanted to give her a pretext for popping off to her widow's bed. "Thank you for protecting me from Vicar and his wife. I'd forgotten he has four girls to fire off."

"He was subtle about it, but a new roof for the nave must take precedence, I'm sure." She hugged her robe more tightly around her, despite the fire hissing and popping softly behind them.

"Is the church in such bad shape as all that?" And shouldn't Christian take Lucy—and the countess—to services some fine Sunday morning?

"I don't know. When I visited here, Helene wasn't inclined to attend services."

"We neither of us were. I used to go occasionally, show the flag, admire a few babies. Vain of me, playing the duke."

"And was your faith much help when you were captured?"

"No," he said, the question taking him too much by surprise for him to make the proper polite noises. "Not in the sense you mean. The Old Testament, perhaps, where simple justice is endorsed, but certainly not that tripe about turning the other cheek and forgiving them, for they know not what they do. They knew damned good and well what they did, delighted in it."

Though Girard had seemed sincerely regretful too, which Christian desperately wanted to attribute to malignant genius. And yet, an echo of the blond guard's final apology—"I'm sorry for it… Girard is sorry for it, too"—rose up from memory. Did the devil apologize for his own wickedness?

"It's frightening," her ladyship said, hugging her knees, "to think such evil is truly walking among us, probably going to services, admiring babies, even as you once did."

Did she regard her late spouse, fencing her away from the roses, denigrating her intelligence, as an exponent of such evil?

"I was morally asleep," Christian said. "I wish to God I had remained in such a state of innocence."

She turned her head, her cheek pillowed on her knees. "You don't sleep well now, do you? I can find you down here most nights up until all hours. You ride out at first light, and you look…unrested."

"You are in an observant mood tonight, my lady."

Except she could always be counted upon to harpoon him with the occasional pithy observation, the periodic disconcerting question. He wasn't sure he liked her for it, but he liked her for the courage it suggested.

And for bearing such a sweet, restful fragrance.

"One worries about you," she said, huddling down more closely to her knees. "You are almost as quiet as your daughter, Mercia, and when one thinks the company of your military fellows might be useful to you, you're stuck here in the country, partly at my insistence."

"You did insist, didn't you?"

"You let me."

That smile again, sweet, a little sad, a little self-mocking. He got up—the hearthstones were damned hard under his backside—and went to his desk, opening the bottom drawer.

"I have something of yours," he said, crossing back to the hearth. He resumed his place beside her, there on the hard, warm bricks, and unfolded her black silk shawl, letting the slippery pleasure of it run through his fingers, warm now, not cool.

"Here." He looped it over her shoulders and used it to draw her close, holding the gathered hem with its delicate, extravagant embroidery in one hand, and bringing his free arm across her shoulders.

Such slender bones she had, and so sturdy.

"You're cold. Despite the fire, your bare feet have made you cold."

Or maybe she was merely lonely, but beside him, right beside him, the tension gradually seeped out of her.

Like the sands in an hourglass sinking from one chamber to the other, Christian felt loneliness trickling from her into him. Or maybe what filled him was his awareness of being set apart by his experiences, the way a widow is set apart by her grief. The distance was always there, but with activity, chronic fatigue, and determination, he could ignore it.

She burrowed closer, and it relieved something in him, that she wasn't put off by that distance he carried inside him. His simple, animal warmth could draw her closer.

"Tell me you'll stay." The words were out, unbidden. He was foolish for having to speak them aloud, and desperate for her answer. "Countess…" He closed his eyes, but this was no help, because it made him more aware of her warm, rosy female scent. "Gillian." He leaned closer, thinking to say more, right into her ear, but his lips grazed her temple.

"Say you'll stay with us." He whispered the words, hoping his voice reached her over the soft roar of the fire.

He gave in to the impulse welling up over the loneliness, and kissed her temple, then her cheek, letting his lips linger, then drawing away.

Those kisses had not been erotic, but neither had they been exactly cousinly—not to him. She should slap him, she should bolt, she should politely tell him she would depart at week's end…

She slipped an arm around his waist. "For now. I'll stay for now."

They stayed huddled like that—cuddled—until the clock chimed midnight, when the countess lifted her head and gave a yawn.

"We must to our beds, Your Grace. My riding habit is finished, and tomorrow I'd like to ride out with you and Lucy."

"I'll look forward to it." Though in a small corner of his soul, the part that felt ambushed by this impulse to put his mouth on her, he also dreaded their next encounter.

She soothed, beguiled, and healed some aspect of him, brought him down off the high, cold misery of the French mountainside, and yet…revenge would be closer if he stayed on those ramparts, alone save for rage, scars, and memories.

He escorted her up to her bed, and she allowed it, another small satisfaction he'd castigate himself for in the morning—maybe. At her door, he tarried, wanting to say something, to hear something from his voluble countess.

"Sleep well," he said, leaning down to touch his lips again to her forehead. She was standing, he didn't have to twist his neck, and it was the easiest thing in the world to touch those lips again to her cheek as well.

"And you," she said, lifting a hand to brush back the hair that had come loose from his queue. "Try to rest."

He both wanted and dreaded her kiss, but she only ran her hand over his hair again, turned, and disappeared into her bedroom.

Leaving him alone in the cold, dark corridor, relieved, bewildered, and telling himself all that mattered was that she'd said she'd stay. Even if he spent time in London, off on the other estates, or tracking down and killing Robert Girard, she'd stay.

"With all due respect, General, you should investigate why nobody searched any harder for Mercia when he went missing."

Devlin St. Just kept his tone casual, but no less than three generals had invited him—a mere colonel—into this late-night hand of cards. The purpose as revealed after adequate portions of brandy was to harass him into extracting a report from the Lost Duke.

Who was found, and probably still lost. God knew, Devlin often was.

"We're happy to nose around a bit," General Baldridge said, newly up from the South. "But it's a delicate business when a duke goes and gets himself captured out of uniform and there's a war on. How much effort is enough?"

General Tipton, arrow straight, sober as a Methodist preacher, eyebrows like a tangled gray hedge, took up the reins of the conversation.

"All we're suggesting, St. Just, is that you look in on the man. Reminisce over a few brandies. He seemed to take to you."

"And your dear papa wouldn't mind if you were given some leave, eh?" General Porter added.

Dear Papa being the Duke of Moreland, who happened to be married to the Duchess of Moreland, who would deliver a harangue worthy of a gunnery sergeant on the topic of wasted ammunition if she learned Devlin had been offered leave and declined it.

But going home meant dealing with Devlin's family…and feeling keenly the absence of his brother

Bartholomew, and the fading presence of his brother
Victor, slowly dying of consumption.

War seemed a cheerier prospect, but the Corsican,
buttoned up on his island in the Mediterranean, was
no longer obliging.

"I've my own men to see to," St. Just said, but he
understood army politics too. "Perhaps in a few weeks."

Baldridge beamed an avuncular smile. "A few weeks,
then. Word is Girard held Mercia for nearly a year, and
Girard is the devil's spawn even in the estimation of his
own superiors. Damned man has turned somebody up
sweet at the War Office, though—who'd have thought
he came from English stock? We would give a lot to
know how a soldier born to every privilege withstood
Girard's treatment, St. Just. Quite a lot."

A promotion then, and promotions would be hard
to come by in peacetime. At the very least, Devlin
would have the pick of the commands available—if he
could get a decent report from Mercia.

The generals wanted to know how Mercia had
been abused, in detail, what torments, in what order,
and how he'd withstood them. What injuries had he
suffered, how had those been dealt with, or had his
wounds been departures for further abuse?

St. Just knocked back two fingers of fine French
brandy—he'd sent his papa a case the previous week—
and excused himself from the next round of cards.

And as wearying as the prospect of dealing with his
family might be, they loved him. He had no doubt of
that. The alternative—shipping out for a wilderness
garrison amid the Canadian winters—had no appeal
whatsoever, not even in peacetime.

So he'd be the next to torture Christian Severn, this time into reliving months of hell the duke was no doubt desperately trying to forget.

❧

The countess with the spine of steel, who'd so casually allowed Christian a scrap of passing affection last night, was disobeying his orders.

His requests, rather. Christian stepped down from Chessie's back and leaned on the stone wall surrounding the family plot.

"I told you to leave this to the gardeners, my lady."

"Good morning, Your Grace." The countess—Gillian—sat on her heels and drew the back of her hand across her cheek, leaving a smudge of dirt. "I don't recall you forbidding me to tend these plots, though you asked me not to bring Lucy here."

Christian sensed about thirteen separate rebukes in those two sentences. For failing to greet her properly, for using the imperative, for accusing her of ignoring his wishes, for not bringing Lucy to her mother's grave, for not visiting that grave himself, and little Evan's grave, and on and on.

She made her words count, did Lady Greendale. He resigned himself to summary court martial, tied up Chessie's reins, and sent him off toward the stable.

And again, the sight of the horse trotting away tickled some vague recollection in the back of Christian's mind, the very elusiveness of the memory adding to his bad mood.

"Won't the lads worry about you? Fear you've come to harm?" her ladyship asked.

"Not unless I can tie up my reins as I tumble into a ditch."

He scrambled over the wall. A year ago, he would have vaulted it cleanly, but he didn't trust himself to pull that off, and got up a little resentment of the countess as a result.

"What exactly are you doing?" He dropped to the blanket she'd spread under her knees. "I employ an army of gardeners, and they're well paid to keep the entire estate in good trim."

"I'm transplanting violets and lily of the valley. Here, make yourself useful."

She passed him a clump of earth with some violets sticking out of one end, slender white roots dangling from the other. He stared at those roots, so pale and vulnerable and yet necessary to the plant for life and stability.

"I have a general notion which end goes down and which goes up, but what had you in mind for these, Countess?"

She spared him a glance, and she might have been smiling—not at him, of course, for he was out of her favor over something.

Kissing her last night?

Not kissing her last night?

"Put them in there," she said, pointing with a hand trowel. "Along Evan's grave."

"Aren't we supposed to greet the dead, say prayers as we work? Maybe sing a hymn or two?" He scratched at the dirt with some implement she passed him. The tool was like a metal claw and bit into the soft soil easily, though he hadn't the knack of using it with his right hand.

He switched it to his left. The two fingernails Girard's fellows had appropriated had almost grown back to a normal length, the wound to the smallest finger was nearly healed, and by virtue of riding, he'd developed some grip strength as well.

"You are disrespectful of the dead," she said, hacking at her patch of ground with the trowel.

"You are disrespectful of me, regularly. Of all in your path. God above, those smell good." He took her gloved hand in his and brought some lily of the valley to his nose. "Why did you choose these?"

"They manage well in partial shade, and you have them in abundance along your walks. Give those back."

She'd dropped her hand, leaving him sniffing the little white flowers, their dirt trailing over his riding breeches. He passed them to her at nose height.

"Stop teasing." She took the flowers and smacked his hand. "If you must tarry here, at least plant something over your son's grave."

He'd spent half the evening at his son's grave, telling the boy all about his sister, about Cousin Gilly, and Chessie. Happy things, mostly, so the sorrow could wash through him all the more cleanly.

And yet, on this pretty morning, the countess's tone was sharp, too sharp.

"What's amiss, my dear?" He patted his violets into the ground as she did violence to the earth with her trowel. "Tell me, hmm?"

Maybe she'd felt coerced into staying here at Severn, and needed to dress him down for that cozy scene by the hearth last night. To think she had regrets over it made him sad, for if she had regrets, he'd have to muster some too.

He truly didn't want to distress her.

He put his gloved hand over hers. "Countess, desist. You are vexed, and I would not have it so."

"How can you not care about them?" she wailed softly. "They were your family, and you don't even care…"

"Not care?" He sat back, setting his claw-toothed tool aside. "You conclude I didn't care for my family because I am indifferent about the ground where their remains lie? Is that it?"

"You're…almost jolly, and they're d-dead."

She was crying. Hell and the devil, the Countess of Starch and Disruption was crying. To shut her up—to make those damned tears stop—he stood, put distance between them, and spoke over his shoulder.

"Would you have me crying, Countess? I haven't seen you crying over your departed husband. You have rejoiced in his death, rather, and told me you are happy he's gone."

"You cannot be happy Evan is gone." She glared up at him, her face dirty and tear streaked and furious. "You cannot."

"Why not? He cost me access to my duchess's intimate favors, did he not?"

Christian had no idea where those ugly words had come from, but he knew they weren't true. He'd loved his son, loved his wife, even, though not in the manner he'd wanted to. And he hated himself—not Girard, or not only Girard—because he, the husband, the papa, hadn't been here when they'd needed him so desperately.

He braced himself on the wall, back to her, as a pair of arms slid around his waist from behind.

"You don't mean that, Christian Severn."

She held him fiercely, her female shape undeniable, as if she would impress the words on his very flesh. "You cannot mean that. Helene said you doted on the boy. She wrote me thus as well. And you always treated Helene with respect. She gloated over that to me regularly."

He nodded, hoping to shut the woman up. She was fearless in her willingness to put into words what ought to remain unspoken. He turned, thinking she'd step back, but she instead attacked him from the front, leaning into him, wrapping him in her arms, pushing her nose against his throat.

He surrendered to the moment and brought both arms around her. She was little and sturdy, and very obviously female, and holding her was a pleasure and a…relief.

"I'm sorry. I do not mourn my husband properly, and I am nobody to tell you what you ought to feel."

Still, she didn't move. Christian used his teeth to tug off one glove, his left, and stroked his damaged hand over her hair. He wanted to comfort her, but she sought words from him, not caresses and silent wishes.

"You worry nobody will tend your grave," he said. "It's real, that worry."

She moved against him, getting closer when he'd thought she would pull away. She ought to be pulling away, ought to be running back to Town or Greendale Hall, or anywhere to get quit of a place where she was made to cry.

"When you are imprisoned," he went on, "you suffer bodily. War is hard enough on the soldier in service to his country. Prisoners cannot be spared a great deal of charity, else who would fight to the death to avoid capture? The physical deprivation is not so hard to understand, but inside your mind... Your captors assure you that your people have forgotten you, that nobody came to find you, that you were allowed to fade immediately from memory, and you..."

She was crying still, making miserable little noises against his chest, but he forced himself to find more words. For her.

"You are told and shown and shown again that you do not matter, and you never mattered. Not to your captors, which is only fair, but not to the mates you fought beside, not to your King, not to your own family. They tell you that until it makes sense, and you cast aside whatever you believed that doesn't fit with that truth. But, Countess, I promise you, your grave will be tended when God calls you home, and you will be mourned."

He had not comforted her with those words, for she shuddered against him, her tears the more profound for being so quiet.

He didn't know what else to do but to hold her, stroke her hair, and wonder at this capacity for sorrow. Her grief felt as if she cried not for Helene and Evan, not even for herself, but for him.

"I'm s-sorry," she said, sighing like an overwrought child against his chest. "I'm so sorry."

He did not ask her for what or whom she was sorry, and neither did he let her go.

Nine

Gilly stood in the door to the nursery suite, arrested by the scene before her.

"This…this vermin is not to be brought into my house, is that clear?"

The duke spoke softly, with a lethal edge, while an orange kitten mewled piteously from its place in his gloved hand. He wasn't squashing the thing, but his tone of voice alone would terrify it.

"Very clear, Your Grace." Harris bobbed a curtsy. "Very clear."

But Lucy stretched up a hand toward the kitten, wiggling her fingers in a silent plea for the little cat. The duke held the beast higher, the epitome of the school yard bully as he glared down at his daughter.

"You brought it in without asking, Lucy, and it's bad enough they lurk in the stables and granary, hang about the hay mows, and haunt the dairy. I'll not have such as this bedamned, benighted, spawn of the devil under my roof, and you are not to bring another into the house."

Lucy stamped her foot, crossed her arms over her

chest, and glared right back at him, while Harris looked on in dumbstruck horror.

"Excuse me," Gilly said, crossing into the room. "Lucy and Harris can see to returning this little fellow from whence he came."

She lifted the kitten from the duke's palm, passed it to a startled Harris, and spared Lucy a warning look. Lucy took Harris by the hand and towed her from the room.

"You're excused," the duke said, his expression still thunderous.

Gilly waited until the child and her governess were gone, closed the door, and considered a duke far more upset than the situation called for.

"You never sneaked a kitten into your rooms as a child, Your Grace?"

"I did not." He was the picture of paternal pique, and over a kitten. *A kitten?*

"A puppy then? A frog? You didn't put a butterfly in a jar or some minnows from the swimming hole in a watering can and hide them in your closet until you should have been abed, only to take them out and examine them by the light of a single pilfered candle?"

He ran a hand through his hair and turned his back on her.

"The child does not need your fits of temper, Mercia."

"She damned well doesn't need that flea-infested bag of mischief under her covers either."

"Many people dislike cats." But *kittens*? Who could dislike a kitten?

"I loathe them."

He turned to face her, his expression...ducally unreadable. "I suppose you expect me to apologize to Lucy?"

"For what?" She crossed her arms as Lucy had done. "You are lord and master here, and she did not have permission that I know of to bring the cat indoors even to play with."

He stalked past her. "I have not the manners necessary to spar with you over this. I bid you good day."

And then he was gone, temper and all, leaving Gilly to take up a rocking chair near the windows and watch as three stories below, Harris and Lucy made their way through the gardens to the stable. His Grace had been dressed for riding, which meant he'd probably cross paths with Lucy in a few minutes.

And he might apologize for the way he spoke, but not for ordering the cat out of the house. He'd been near panicked to find the kitten in the nursery, and God help Cook's big, fat mousers if His Grace ever dropped in on the kitchens unannounced.

❧

Christian was enough of a horseman not to take out his temper on Chessie, but he needed to gallop, to charge headlong over his fields and fences, not trot sedately within the limits of his imperfect stamina.

The cat...that blasted little orange ball of fluff dashing across his boots...

He rode for miles, knowing he'd pay for his exertions, only gradually able to notice the terrain he covered. Severn tenant farms, a corner of the home wood, the gently rolling hills leading to the Downs, bridle paths he'd learned as a boy, streams he'd first crossed on his pony behind his papa on the way to the local meets.

His, and if he wasn't careful, Easterbrook would be administering the lot of it while the Duke of Mercia occupied a tidy suite of rooms at Bedlam.

His estate was in disarray, his daughter gone mute, his household likely in no better condition than the land but for the countess's efforts to take it in hand, and the Duke of Mercia was completely undone by the unexpected sight of a stupid, fluffy little cat. How was he to pursue Girard, track the man down, and administer justice if the sight of a *kitten* nigh parted him from his reason?

His upset had cooled to mere irritation—at himself, his daughter, and still, at the bloody cat—by the time he walked across the back terrace, intent on ordering some decent sustenance.

He would be bone tired from overexerting himself, but for the present, he was pleased to be ravenous. He couldn't recall being ravenous at any point in the past year, and he considered it something of an accomplishment.

"What the hell are these?"

He put the question to a passing footman, who scooted back two steps before answering.

"Her ladyship's trunks, Your Grace, for her trip into Town tomorrow."

Four large trunks, stacked two and two, sat along the hallway nearest the porte cochere.

"Take them back up to her room, and please ask the countess to join me in the library." He stomped off, the heels of his riding boots signaling his ire to all in his path.

Thought she'd leave him, would she? Thought she'd champion the rights of cats and naughty little girls over those of a man in his own home? Thought she'd abandon him and Lucy over a single display of temper? He'd show her temper, by God…

"Good afternoon, Mercia."

Serene, smiling, her ladyship came into the room, though she moved with more dispatch than grace. She wasn't a swanning sort of countess, which was good. Easier to read her the Riot Act that way.

"Where the hell do you think you're going?" he asked, taking the offensive. "I saw your trunks. Up and leaving without a word? How do you think Lucy will like that, hmm? She's only a child, and clearly attached to you, and here you are, haring off at the first sign of minor discord in the household."

She stopped and opened her mouth, but wasn't fast enough, given his mood.

"Nothing to say, Countess? For once I catch you without a glib reply? Come, does a little display of ducal authority honestly offend your sensibilities all that much?"

He paused, and it was a mistake, for she advanced on him, her blue eyes promising a stinging return volley.

"That wasn't a display of ducal authority, Your *Grace*. That was a tantrum, unprovoked and undeserved, and you'll have that child sneaking all manner of creatures up to the nursery simply to watch you cursing and stomping about the room."

"I did not curse."

"Bedamned," she said very clearly, the language all the more foul for the disdain she applied to it. "Benighted, spawn of the devil…perhaps not taking the Lord's name in vain, but certainly intemperate language unsuited to the nursery."

"I will not be made to apologize for objecting to that beast's presence in my daughter's rooms." He'd nearly shouted, likely surprising himself more than he'd surprised her.

And over a *kitten*.

"Then don't apologize." She took a leaf from Christian's own book and turned her back on him. Her posture was worthy of a seasoned officer on parade march, and it was a relief not to have to meet her eyes. "Perhaps you will explain your antipathy toward kittens."

She didn't make it a question, merely tossed a verbal gauntlet over her shoulder while she fussed a bouquet of white roses. Christian couldn't see exactly what she'd done, but the bouquet was taller by the time she took up a seat on the sofa.

"First, my lady, explain why your trunks were packed."

"Please have a seat, Your Grace."

Order him about, would she? But wandering around the room would only make him look as agitated as he felt. He dropped down beside her. "I'm sitting. I hope you're pleased."

The footmen arrived bearing a substantial tray, complete with the tea service, sandwiches, and tea cakes. The ubiquitous peeled orange sat divided into sections on a silver plate, a blossom of healthy citrus, and Christian wanted to hurl the damned thing against the wall.

She was leaving, and he was growling when he ought to be groveling.

No, not groveling. He was constitutionally incapable of that—*thank you, Robert Girard*—but apologizing at least.

And not explaining. Another constitutional incapability, for he wasn't sure himself exactly what had got into him.

"I received a letter from my barrister," Lady Greendale said.

"You're involved in a lawsuit?" Lawsuits were never good. They invariably ended in scandal, expense, and wasted years. "Against whom?"

"I am not involved in any lawsuits, but I retained Mr. Stoneleigh to advise me regarding the inquest following Greendale's death. He was invaluable in that capacity, and has now asked me to attend him in Town."

"And you drop everything and take off like a hound on the scent when the lawyer snaps his fingers? That, I can tell you, is not how one deals with men of the law, Countess."

"Does keeping your lawyers waiting for you improve their service or the outcomes of your legal matters?"

"I'm a damned…dashed duke." Who was afraid of kittens. "Their service had best be impeccable whenever I'm so unfortunate as to need it."

"Yes, well…" She passed him a cup, and he took an unthinking sip.

"God in heaven…" He put the cup down,

swallowing cautiously. She'd served him real tea, not the infantile combination of milk, hot water, and sugar he'd been forcing down for the past two months. Christian waited for his stomach to rebel, to clench in miserable, acid rebellion, but the pleasurable taste in his mouth wasn't obliterated by any other bodily response.

"I'm sorry," the countess said. "I forgot, honestly. Let me fix you up…"

"No. I'll manage. The tea isn't very strong yet, and you've added plenty of cream."

"I fixed it as if for myself. You have me flustered."

He took another sip of tea, pleased to be able to, but determined to stop at half a cup.

And flustered was gratifying. She didn't look flustered, but the lady was quiet, and she'd bungled his tea.

"Flustered, my dear? Perhaps it's your lawsuit that has you unnerved."

"The matter is something to do with Greendale's will," she said, stirring her tea. "Stoneleigh would only say there's no cause for worry, only cause to consult."

"Haven't you a solicitor to deal with something like a will?" Christian had an entire cricket team of them, though offering the countess the use of one didn't seem to be what the moment called for.

"I'm more comfortable meeting with Mr. Stoneleigh, who will direct me to a solicitor if one is needed."

Matters usually went the other way around, with the solicitor directing business to the barrister, but the countess hadn't yet taken a sip of her tea.

"Tell me what's afoot," Christian said, trying to make it a helpful suggestion rather than a ducal mandate—and mostly failing. "And drink your tea before it gets cold."

She gave him another puzzled look, but took a sip then set her cup down. "Orange, Your Grace?"

He wanted her to call him by name. Nobody referred to a duke by name—Helene certainly hadn't, not even when he'd come to bed of a night—but all this Your Gracing…

Even Girard had referred to him by his title.

"No oranges, thank you, and quit dithering about. If you have a legal worry, you are under my roof, and I will relieve you of it, do you deign to allow me."

He'd fallen a bit short of making a helpful suggestion, though the woman was smiling at her tea.

"The trunks are empty. I'm traveling to Town by way of Greendale and retrieving more of my belongings."

Abruptly, the tea tasted ambrosial. The trunks were not a sign of her impending departure; to the contrary, they were for collecting more of her effects and bringing them to Severn.

Where she now…resided.

"Will four trunks be enough?" He popped a section of orange into his mouth. They could spare her a farm wagon, should she need it. He'd drive the thing himself.

"Four will be plenty. I'll gather up only my personal belongings from Greendale and send them here, if you'll allow it."

"Of course I'll allow it." He'd like to see her try to send them elsewhere.

"Greendale told me repeatedly that upon his death, I would receive the bare minimum required by the settlements, a dower portion of the unentailed estate, though I assume he organized his finances so that sum is paltry."

"What about a dower property?" Because if she ever were wroth with him, she ought to have a dower residence to retreat to.

"Greendale has a dower house," she said, helping herself to a section of orange. "His lordship did not spend a single farthing on its upkeep during the eight years of our marriage."

"Has the dry rot or creeping damp, then?" He tried not to sound pleased about this, but if he were lucky, the roof leaked as well.

"Likely has bats. I'm sure Easterbrook would allow me to stay in the main house until the dower house is marginally habitable, but he'll be finding himself a bride, and I can't look forward to sharing the table with her."

"He is obligated…" Christian began, but she stopped him by holding up a section of orange. He took it with his teeth, as she'd no doubt intended.

"How is it men cannot see themselves ever tolerating charity, but women are supposed to meekly, even gratefully, accept it?"

"A dower house isn't charity. It's your due for putting up with that old besom for eight years of days… and nights."

She shuddered, confirming Christian's sense the marriage had been a trial. He was pleased about that too, also displeased for her sake. He held out his cup for a refill, the first having helped settle him rather than agitate him further.

She poured out, her movements graceful and relaxed, not those of a lady prevaricating about her plans.

"I am loath to return to Greendale with the dower house in its present state. I am also not looking forward to haggling with Easterbrook's bride over which objects were part of my trousseau and thus mine to keep, and which were part of Greendale's family collection. You truly don't mind if I send some things here?"

"I am not keen on you undertaking this mission without my escort, but you may send anything you like here for safekeeping."

"Mission? As if I'm one of your cavalry officers?"

"You would have buttoned old Soult up in a trice. Boney would have fallen shortly thereafter."

She smiled at his prediction, the real, private, sweet smile, and something in his vitals eased. If she was smiling, maybe she really did intend to return to him.

To them.

"Was Lucy very upset over that cat?" he asked, surprised to see he'd finished his second cup of tea as well.

And damn, it had been good. A hot, sweet cup of good black tea, served by a proper English hostess under his own roof.

"Not very. She knew she'd been caught transgressing. Are you truly upset with her?"

"I certainly acted upset." He'd been furious, and the anger had been both appropriate—wonderfully, marvelously, bracingly appropriate—and all wrong.

The countess passed him half the remaining

orange sections, and took half for herself. "You were on your dignity."

They munched oranges in prosaic silence—his teeth and gums were much improved—while he tried to muster his courage. She scooted closer to top off his tea, then stayed right there beside him, adding her rosy scent to the fragrance of the orange.

"Have a tea cake," she said, putting one on his plate. "I certainly intend to have some."

They were adults. They should have begun their meal with sandwiches and a serving of small talk, but consuming oranges together had somehow become a ritual uniquely *theirs*.

"I was…upset, over the cat."

She held up a tea cake. He took it from her hand and dutifully had a bite. The confection was rich and sweet with a dash of nutmeg. Now that he was trying to talk to the woman, she crammed his maw with delicacies.

"We'll spoil our dinners," he said, though how long had it been since he'd had a tea cake?

"We're adults. Spoiling dinner is one of few prerogatives thereof. You were saying?"

"About?"

"The kitten."

She watched him with those big blue eyes, but they weren't judging, they were solemn, patient, and kind.

"Cats…" He had to look elsewhere, at the porcelain service adorned with birds the same color as her eyes. "Cats toy with their prey. They delight in toying with their prey, and teach their young to do likewise."

"The French?"

He nodded. "The Château had an abundance of cats." Miserable, hungry wretches who had had the freedom to leave but remained, like rats skulking about the foundation of a ruin, only meaner and more deadly.

She slid her arm around his waist and hugged him. "We must put you back on your mettle. Have another cake."

He had five.

❦

The trip to Town was providentially well timed, for conflicting emotions besieged Gilly.

She was developing tender feelings for the duke, and that would not do, because she was determined never again to be under a man's thumb. Not by action of marriage, not by action of her foolish, lonely heart.

Maybe a little in love would be acceptable, except Mercia wasn't a little-in-love sort of man. He was mad, dark passion, sweeping emotion, and complete loss of reason, with his gaunt male beauty, his wealth and power, and his haunted past. He also needed another bride, preferably a sweet young thing with pots of money, a fertile womb, and not a thought in her head save the pleasure of wearing a tiara.

What sensible widow crowding close on twenty-six years on earth wanted to watch a man she was even a little in love with pursued by that sort of competition?

But where else was she to go?

Mercia would be offended when—not if—she took herself off to dwell elsewhere, even if Lucy were managing better by then. His Grace honestly regarded

Gilly as a relation deserving of his protection, and he was determined to provide it.

Maybe he needed to.

As Gilly prowled the sitting room that served as antechamber to Mr. Stoneleigh's offices, her musings were interrupted by a tidy young man sporting a deal of Macassar oil.

"Mr. Stoneleigh will see you now, your ladyship."

He ushered her into a baronial inner sanctum, one graced with thick Turkey rugs, a huge marble fireplace, and a massive dark desk, behind which, like a tall, dark-haired captain on his poop deck, stood Mr. Gervaise Stoneleigh.

"Countess." He came around the desk and offered her a bow. "You are in good looks, my lady. My apologies for asking you to travel while your loss is so fresh."

"Nonsense, Mr. Stoneleigh. Location does not lessen or enhance grief, particularly when I feel anything but bereaved."

He looked peevish, or perhaps nonplussed at her honesty.

"Come now," Gilly said, handing him her black jacket. "You told me I may speak freely with you, did you not?"

"I did." He looked at the jacket as if he hadn't a clue where it had come from, then deposited it on a hook on the back of the door. "Please have a seat, and assure me you're going on well since last we met."

His solicitude was offered in such punctilious tones Gilly wasn't sure it was genuine, but then she caught him looking at her, dark eyes focused with peculiar intensity.

"I am in good health and enjoying the hospitality of

the Duke of Mercia, a cousin by marriage through his late duchess. He's asked me to assist him in putting his household to rights at the family seat, and to take an interest in my niece, which is hardly an imposition."

"You've retrieved your belongings from Greendale?"

"I have, though you didn't tell me what the urgency is."

"I'm not sure there is any, but I've received word Easterbrook may take up residence there sooner than later. He's mustering out."

Thank goodness she'd retrieved her belongings, though she and Marcus had always rubbed along civilly. "Leaving the army? I thought he loved it."

"Napoleon is at long last vanquished, and the options for those who want to remain in service are far flung, and not likely to offer as much action. Many of the officers are happy to return to home shores."

"And the Army can hardly afford to keep them on when there's no war to fight." Though men did so love to commit slaughter in the name of patriotism, didn't they?

Some men. She couldn't see Mercia ever again setting foot on the field of battle, thank heavens.

Stoneleigh's lips twitched, probably his version of a fit of hilarity.

"Let us sit, Mr. Stoneleigh, and let us be direct with each other. You may speak freely, and I assure you I will not quote you."

He led her to a conversational grouping near the yawning fireplace—no fire for the man of law, not on a pleasant summer day.

"You truly are in good looks," he said, his tone puzzled. "Was marriage to Greendale as bad as all that?"

Her marriage had been a hell beyond the worst imaginings of the seventeen-year-old innocent she'd been. She suspected even Stoneleigh would have found the circumstances daunting, and he was far from innocent.

"Marriage to Greendale was worse than I'd wish on the Corsican himself."

He let the comment pass and took a seat in a wing chair at a right angle to Gilly's place on a gorgeous blue brocade sofa.

"I'll be direct at your invitation: Are you with child, Lady Greendale?"

"Heavens, no."

"You're sure?" He was absolutely serious in his inquiry.

"Not unless the Second Coming is imminent, and I the unworthy vessel chosen for the Almighty's arrival."

"You might want to take measures to alter your status in this regard," Stoneleigh said, once again the brusque barrister. "I've had a look at Greendale's will, and you benefit greatly if you can produce a posthumous child, your ladyship."

"Greendale regaled me at many turns with the terms of his will, Mr. Stoneleigh, and I assure you, he intended to leave me penniless."

"He wasn't entirely forthcoming, then, because he wrote a codicil about a year ago, and left the unentailed sum of his estate, less your dower portion, to any child of your body born within a year of his death."

"He was giving me permission to get with child practically at his graveside? What an odd notion."

"No, he was conforming his will to the common law, which attributes paternity of a child to the mother's husband, up to one year into her widow-hood. This is in part why mourning lasts a year."

The common law needed to consult with a competent midwife. "Not even horses carry for a year in the normal course, Mr. Stoneleigh."

"Common law predates modern science, and even nature allows for some variability."

He looked very prim, defending his silly common law, but Gilly would have liked him for it if she didn't already firmly approve of him.

"Well, this is all very interesting, but hardly relevant to me. I am not with child, I cannot be with child, and I doubt I could accomplish it even if I tried. Was there more?"

He crossed his legs and settled back in his chair, studying her as if she were a rare legal volume on loan from another barrister. Maybe the cool, capable Mr. Stoneleigh had expected some other reaction from her.

Perhaps she was to proposition him to accommodate her quest for a child, reducing the hourly rate for his services in light of her bereavement. Of course in the process, she'd catch a chill, what with being in intimate proximity to *him*. She was smiling at her thoughts when he fell silent.

"I'm sorry, you were saying, Mr. Stoneleigh?"

"I've seen what funds you gave me into the keeping of Mr. Worth Kettering, the man of business I use myself. He is particularly careful dealing with a widow's mite, and has had good success with his investments. He will expect you to call on him, and you will receive quarterly statements describing the progress of your funds. But a word of advice, my lady?"

Stoneleigh's advice had prevented Gilly from being charged with murder.

"I am not in any great hurry, Mr. Stoneleigh." Only a small hurry, because she could not countenance Mercia being anxious over her absence.

"If Mercia is inclined to settle a competence on you, you'd be well advised to see the thing done." Stoneleigh was being oblique, possibly insinuating something nasty.

"I assure you, Mr. Stoneleigh, His Grace is recovering well from his ordeal. His faculties are sound, and we need not worry about his imminent decline or demise."

Gilly was fiercely proud of her duke, that she could offer these assurances, and with such confidence. Mercia was emerging from captivity stronger than he'd been, stronger than any duke had ever been, and Wellington had nothing to say to it.

"His recovery might well be part of the problem."

Stoneleigh was not unkind, but subtlety was not his forte, and Gilly did not want to endure tea and crumpets with him until he meandered around to whatever plagued him.

"How could healing from all manner of abuse be a bad thing, Mr. Stoneleigh? His Grace lost his wife and son while he was in France. A lesser man would not have the resilience to cope with that much grief."

"He copes by plotting revenge, my lady. The word at the clubs is Mercia intends to confront his captors and see them pay for their transgressions. He's begun gathering information, laying his traps, some say."

In his way, Stoneleigh was trying to be kind— and failing.

"Imagine, Mr. Stoneleigh, having no privacy about your bodily functions for months. Imagine having your fingernails forcibly extracted. Imagine beating after beating. Imagine your body decorated with so many scars, you resemble a walking piece of appliqué. Imagine your sleep always interrupted, your ability to digest food ruined…"

She was nearly shaking at this litany, and Stoneleigh was none too happy with her for imposing it upon him.

Gilly rose, unwilling to allot more time to Stoneleigh's gossip.

"Of course, His Grace will remain informed regarding the whereabouts of the demons who tormented him. We are at peace, however, and his succession hangs by a slender thread. He will not jeopardize the Severn family holdings for petty quests for revenge. If ever a mortal has learned the folly of violence, it is Mercia."

And what an intimate, unlikely lesson for Gilly to share with a young, healthy duke of the realm, a man in his prime.

Stoneleigh's eyes were expressive, something he likely worked to hide. He wanted to tell her to get that competence in writing, though. Gilly could see that much as plain as the gold pin in his cravat.

Stoneleigh turned the topic to Lucy, to the victory celebrations and their reported expense, and was soon draping Gilly's jacket around her shoulders. The movement put Gilly in mind of Mercia, who'd used her shawl to draw her close…

"Lady Greendale, you will keep me apprised of how you fare, won't you?" He was giving her his Concerned Barrister's look again, hooded, intense, and compelling. "You'll call on me if I can be of any service whatsoever, my lady? I'll have your promise on this."

Gilly pulled on black gloves. "You are being dramatic, Mr. Stoneleigh, and I must say it's endearing, so yes, I'll give you my promise."

He bowed low over her hand and escorted her to the door, all starch and propriety. Behind his calculating lawyer's mind and brusque manner, there beat the heart of a knight errant willing to tilt at windmills on behalf of a damsel in distress—or the common law.

Gilly sent Mercia a note letting him know her business with Stoneleigh was satisfactorily concluded, and lingered in Town a few days, seeing to her wardrobe. She made use of Mercia's town house, hoping the duke used her absence to grow closer to his daughter.

His Grace loved little Lucy, he loved his land, and he grieved for his departed family. Gilly knew he did, despite the absence of tears or words to that effect. Silence could be more articulate and profound than all the words in the language.

And as for revenge, she would not believe it of the man who'd wrapped her shawl about her and held her so tenderly only a few nights past. Mercia was healing, as Gilly was, and violence had no place in the process. Not for her.

And not for him. She was almost sure of it.

❧

Christian missed his countess and thought Lucy did too. The child was less animated, less enthusiastic when he went up to the nursery after the countess's departure.

"She will be back, you know," he said as they walked out to the stables. Lucy was in a miniature riding habit, one that Gillian—he used her name, a small weapon to combat her absence—must have fashioned for the child, because the hems were shorter than they would be on an adult's clothing.

"You could put some embroidery on this fetching little outfit," he said as they approached the barn. "I'm sure her ladyship would help you design something for it."

Lucy gave a halfhearted nod, suggesting the countess's absence might not be the only reason for the child's blue devils.

"Are you pining for your kitten, princess?"

She glanced up at him, her gaze guarded, then dropped her eyes. He'd guessed correctly, at least in part.

"Your kitten will grow up to be a sleek, fat-headed tomcat, ever interested in the ladies and in the hunt," Christian said, thinking this description might fit many a lordling too. "He will stay up until all hours, yodeling pathetically when he's in love, which will be most nights outside the month of December, and one can hardly look forward to having that around the house, can one?"

Lucy's lips twitched, and she shook her head. A start.

"And when he's of a mind to mark his territory, he'll sneer at the chamber pot and mess all over the curtains and rugs, leaving a stench that lingers for days. You don't want him anointing your drapes, do you, princess?"

Another shake of her head, a little broader smile.

"And when he becomes dyspeptic, he'll present his last three meals right at your feet after he's partially digested them, including such bones and hair as will not allow of proper alimentation. We don't want that going on in the house, do we?"

She grinned at him, and his heart gave up a burden laid there not only by his foul language in the nursery, but by some half-starved French cats and the predators among whom they abided.

"Well, then, no more cats in the nursery. Agreed?"

She stuck out her hand for him to shake. He did, then swung her up onto the ladies' mounting block. The grooms led Chessie over, Christian climbed aboard, then hauled Lucy up before him.

They had a perfectly lovely ride, with Lucy pointing and bouncing in the saddle when she wanted to direct his attention to something—a late lamb stotting around his mama in the high summer grass, hedge apples in bloom, a swan on the small lake.

He let Chessie wander under low-hanging tree limbs, so he had an excuse to bend close and cadge a soapy whiff of his daughter's clean, silky hair.

"You know, princess, I would keep your secrets, did you want to whisper them to me. You need not speak aloud, but merely whisper a word or two in my ear someday, should you no longer desire to be so alone in your silence."

She went still before him, and he wished he could see her expression.

"But your silence is precious as well. I'll tell you a secret, if you like."

She nodded, cautiously.

"I had pets, in…France. You'll think me foolish—*I* think me foolish, for that matter, but they were my only friends. Do you know of whom I speak? Little fellows with no weapons, no big teeth or fierce claws, helpless little beasts who wanted only a morsel to eat, and to live out their days in peace. Can you guess who they were?"

What was he doing, telling this to a child?

But she was listening; he knew she was listening.

"They were very quiet, like you, quiet as mice, for they were mice. They came around looking for crumbs, hiding from the castle cats, and I let them eat what fell from my plate. We became great friends, the mice and I. We endured our privations together."

But the mice had never become tame, had never quite given up their wariness, no matter how cold or hungry they were. He'd admired those small, soft, helpless creatures, and as miserable as his rations had been, he'd never begrudged the mice their crumbs.

Lucy said nothing, but she relaxed back against her papa.

She no doubt thought he was teasing, but he was damn near tears, and finished the ride as silent as his little princess.

Lucy must have picked up on his mood—she was a bright child, after all—because when he went to swing her down off the high mounting block used by the ladies, she clung to him for a moment, her arms lashed around his neck, her face buried against his shoulder.

A hug, for the man who'd had no friends save the mice, from the daughter who could not tell him she loved him.

Ten

CHRISTIAN TRIED NOT TO SPEND HIS DAYS LOOKING down the drive, anticipating Gillian's return from Town. She'd sent a note along telling him she was detained by sartorial matters and would not be back until week's end.

So he stayed busy, which wasn't difficult.

The land steward, Hancock, was happy to ride out with him as the weather permitted; the tenants were pleased to have his lordship "drop by" on a schedule Hancock carefully arranged. Vicar came to call again, a fifteen-minute ordeal without Gillian smiling and chattering over the tea service.

Christian had nightmares, of course, worse for Gillian's absence, or for something, but it helped— some—that he was gradually adding activity to his day.

Having word of Girard's whereabouts would have helped more.

St. Just had warned Christian about others held prisoner, fellows who'd taken months to regain enough health to rejoin their regiments. Christian's body wasn't taking months. He was putting on muscle, his teeth and gums were restored to reliable use, but his mind wasn't coming along at such a spanking pace.

The nightmares were to be expected, but at least once every day, he'd hear a door slam and his heart would pound for no reason.

Candlelight glinting off a paring knife could make his lungs seize.

He'd attempt some simple task with his left hand—tying a cravat—and fail so miserably he wanted to destroy all in his reach.

This last problem was particularly vexing. His left hand was growing stronger, but its dexterity was limited. The right hand was strong enough, but was still clumsy. Hands were such an obvious, integral part of bodily competence that Christian became determined to address his manual limitations.

But every day that Gillian lingered in Town, the demons rose higher in his mind: What was the point of learning to shave himself right-handed—not that he'd suffer a valet to come near him with a razor, of course. What was the point of coaxing Lucy to speak again? What was the point of continuing to draw breath? The world had thought him dead once before, and gone on turning quite handily without him.

And then he'd hear Girard's silky voice in his ear.

"Shall I kill you today, *mon ange*? Would you like that? To leave me here in this miserable pile of rocks all alone, hoping the Corsican can recover not only from the drubbing of your armies, but also from the Russian winter? Shall I give you permanent silence, and victory with it? I would envy you too badly, did

I commend you to the angels, so me, I think no death
for you today…"

Girard's regard for him had been disturbingly
convincing. Girard had kept Christian alive, in part
through those backhanded recitations of France's
losses and tribulations, though Christian would be
damned if he'd ever thank the bastard for it. And to
complicate matters, Girard was apparently the son of
an Englishman. What conflicted loyalties lay behind
Girard's stratagems, and had the colonel truly longed
for death himself?

A clock chimed, midnight.

*Put in your mind a picture of what you can look
forward to and…add details to it, one by one, until the
picture is very accurate and the urge to do something
untoward has passed.*

Christian fell asleep, finally, as he had for the previous six nights, telling himself Gillian was better off
putting some distance between herself and the Severn
household. He wanted her under his roof—under his
protection—but he had little to offer her other than
that—at least until he'd dispatched Girard.

But as sleep claimed him, he pictured her, small,
golden-haired, bustling about, her voice a lullaby to
calm the most tortured soul.

❧

Gilly woke knowing the time had come to quit daw-
dling and get herself back to Mercia.

To *Severn*. To Severn, the house, the household,
the little girl who would not speak, and yes, to the
man trying to find his footing with all of it. Mercia

was part of what Gilly returned to; he could not be the whole of it.

"Safe journey, your ladyship."

Meems offered his good wishes, such as they were, from the front steps as the traveling coach came around the corner from the mews.

"My thanks. You may be assured I will report to His Grace that I was graciously received by his staff in his absence."

Meems looked pained, but offered her a nod, and then stepped back so a footman could hand her up.

She took out her anthology of poetry and tried to read, but the exercise was useless. The day was overcast, the light quite dim, and her mind darted about like a caged finch. The coach rolled on, until Gilly came abruptly awake somewhere among the fields and farms of Surrey.

The coachman's voice came to her, low and soothing, but with a panicked note under the words. The horses cantered over a rare smooth stretch of road, and still, the coachy urged them to slow.

"Ho up, lads. Easy…easy… There we go, boys. That's it…"

A sharp crack, and the team tried to bolt, while the coach bobbed crazily behind them.

Gilly fetched up hard against the wall, grabbed the leather strap above her head, and started praying while the coachman resumed his crooning and pleading.

"Now, laddies, ho ye, ho and ho and that's it… Good boys you are, good boys you be…"

The coach came to a stop, swaying on its springs.

A white-faced groom peered in the door. "Yer ladyship's right enow, then? That were a rum go there for a bit. 'Is Grace will 'ave our arses—our 'eads if ye've suffered 'arm."

Eight years of marriage came to the aid of her composure. "I'm fine. What happened?"

"Wheel come loose. Lost it a good mile back, but we've a good team, and they came right, didn't they?"

He was as pale as death, suggesting they'd had a very close call. The coach listed heavily, but was held somewhat upright on the three remaining wheels and the web of harness. The wheelers shifted restively at the unaccustomed distribution of weight, while the coachy kept up his spoken lullaby.

"Perhaps I'd best stretch my legs a bit," she said, and the door was open before she'd collected her reticule.

"Perkins is 'olding the leaders, yer ladyship." The groom's voice still held a quaver that suggested danger had been only narrowly averted.

"I'm sure all will soon be in order," she said, offering him a smile. Smiling was a skill, and Gilly had learned to apply it in all manner of difficult situations. "John Coachman," she called up to the box, "your passenger is unharmed. Shall we get out the muzzle bags and send a groom for the wheel?"

"Muzzle bags?" The man blinked down at her, his complexion every bit as ashen as the groom's. "Oh, aye, for the 'orses. Dunston, be about it, then fetch that blasted wheel."

Gilly assessed the sullen sky, saw rain wasn't an immediate concern, and fetched her book from the coach. She stuffed the poetry in her reticule, and over the slow pounding of her heart, sorted through the situation to find the next necessary task.

There wasn't one, except to offer a familiar prayer for her continued existence.

She marched to a nearby stile, perched upon it, took out her embroidery, and began to stitch.

By the time she'd finished three tidy inches of hem on a handkerchief for Lucy, Dunston was pushing the wheel up the track like a large, ungainly hoop. The wheel was intact, which was a relief, because there wasn't a farmhouse or smallholding to be seen.

"The going will be slow," the coachman said, "but once we bang the wheel back on, we'll get ye on your way, your ladyship. From His Grace's grandda's time, we've carried spare pins and such in the boot of the traveling coaches, otherwise you'd have to walk to the next village."

"How far would that be?"

"A good half league, and it do be threatening rain."

Another inch of hem and Gilly had the handkerchief done, the wheel was on, and the horses were trotting sedately on to the village.

"I tell you," Perkins was saying up on the box, "it ain't natural. A normal woman woulda had the vapors and been a-shriekin' and a-carrying on."

"Normal woman?" John Coachman paused to speak soothingly to his leaders. "There's women been following the drum all over Spain for years, women raising children in Seven Dials. Courage don't limit itself to men."

"Not this man." Perkins heaved a mighty, mighty sigh. "I seen that wheel come loose, I about shit myself."

"I about pissed myself," Dunston said from the roof behind them. A pause suggested medicinal spirits produced from the well-stocked boot were making the rounds.

"And if I'd had a free hand," John said quietly, "I would have crossed myself, like my old Irish granny did."

"While 'er ladyship does her tatting," Perkins said. "It ain't right. I tell ye, it just ain't right."

Because the coach was moving slowly, and Gilly had the slot open to the box, she heard their conversation. She'd heard its like before—the help muttering that her ladyship lacked the delicacy her position demanded—particularly early in her marriage.

What her ladyship had lacked was proper discernment about choosing a husband.

When the men fell silent, she took out the book of poetry, embroidery in a moving coach being more than even she undertook with any success.

❧

Christian stood naked from the waist up before a small mirror propped on a windowsill in his sitting room. A bowl of steaming water sat at his elbow, his shaving kit laid out in gleaming order beside it. Bright afternoon sunshine was intended to make his task easier, though it didn't. Nothing could make his task easier.

The staff had orders to leave him in peace until teatime. He was not home to callers.

He'd trimmed the damned beard close to his face without cutting himself, save the once, a nick bleeding sluggishly down his neck into the hair sprinkled over his chest.

He'd been shaving for nearly half his life, and

scraping the razor along his throat should be no great matter. The blade was sharpened to a fine edge, a sharp blade being safer than a dull one.

But which hand to use? The damaged left, the awkward right? And what did it matter, for they both shook.

How long he stood, razor in his hand, blood oozing gently down his scarred chest, he did not know. When he thought of bringing the sharp edge to his skin, his guts knotted up, his ears roared, and his vision dimmed at the edges.

His heart pounded so hard, it must surely be trying to escape his chest.

And even as he knew his reactions, while not rational, were to be expected, another part of him was inexorably parting ways with his reason. The longer he stood, shifting the razor from hand to hand, a bearded stranger staring back at him with wild blue eyes, the harder it was to breathe slowly, to think.

Why was he doing this?

Where was Girard?

Would Christian welcome the burning kiss of the razor if his hand slipped? Welcome it like a long-lost friend?

"Your Grace."

The countess quietly closed the door behind her, but Christian was so far gone in his memories and fears, he merely watched her. He knew who she was; he didn't want her to see him like this—again—but he could not form the words to chase her away.

"You were lost in thought," she said, crossing the room sedately. "You did not hear me knock." Still she didn't look at the brutality mapped on his chest, arms, and torso, didn't look anywhere but into his eyes. "I should have knocked louder, I'm sure."

She stood before him, a little green bottle in one hand, and reached up a finger to his collarbone.

"You're bleeding, you wretched man. Why…?" But as she dropped her gaze, she took in the accoutrements of his task.

"You were seeing to your toilette," she said, relief in her eyes. "You'll let me help you."

Her voice pushed back the worst of the shadows in his mind. He passed her the razor, relieved when she took it from his hand.

"Shall you sit, Mercia? You are too tall for me to attend you properly when you stand." She brought a dressing stool over to the window and stood back, arms crossed as if his height were a minor transgression for which sitting was the prescribed penance.

"Lock the door." He'd managed the words, a growled order, not a polite request.

She set the razor aside, locked the door, then turned him gently by the shoulders to face the afternoon sun. "This won't take long."

It took forever, the slow, soft slide of the razor on his throat, over his cheeks and jaw, all around the contours of his mouth and above his lips. Gillian had a deft touch, soaping, scraping, scraping again, and she talked to him as she worked.

"I had to make my obeisance to the shops while I was in Town, though I kept my blacks on all the while. In summer's heat, going about with a veil on isn't practical, but people will surely talk if one doesn't.

Chin up, Mercia. Almost done, and I've brought you some scent that put me in mind of you."

And then the ordeal was over too quickly, and Christian missed the feel of her hands, confident, gentle, sure and easy as she turned his jaw, slid the razor over his skin, and brushed his hair back from his face.

He clung to her voice while she patted something that smelled pleasantly of ginger and lemon onto his cheeks.

"You're quite a handsome man under your plumage, you know. Helene used to lord it over me, which was her right, of course. Though your cheeks are pale, thanks to your beard."

She brushed her hand over his cheeks, then down his neck, to his shoulders. Her touch was light, but in no wise tentative. She was…petting him, the way he'd pet Chessie, for his pleasure and for the horse's.

"Look at yourself," she said, turning him by the shoulders to face the mirror. "A ducal countenance, if ever I beheld one."

She kept a hand on the middle of his bare back, and he mentally shuddered to think of the skin beneath her fingers. Ridged with a bizarre pattern of scars, Girard's idea of a joke, to make living embroidery on his prisoner, hemming along bone and muscle in little pink puckered ridges that would fade but never leave Christian's body or his awareness.

And yet, his countess touched him, casually, easily, proud of her handiwork with his whiskers.

"You're still lean," she said, "but coming along nicely. No wonder Helene was such a braggart, having a swain like you for her own."

The hand on his back radiated warmth, steadied, supported, and reassured, as it brought life and heat to places inside him long lost to light.

To be touched with such kindness...

"I missed a spot," she said, taking her hand away and reaching for the damp towel on the windowsill. She went after blood dried on the slope of his chest, a brown streak that came away easily enough and soiled the towel.

As she scrubbed at him, the sunlight caught all manner of highlights in her hair, from red to bronze to flax to...

He put his finger under her chin and turned her face up to the light.

"Gillian, how in the bloody hell did you get such a goddamned ugly bruise?"

⤙⤚

His Grace was breathtakingly handsome, more so than when he'd been a younger man, more so than when Gilly had first confronted him up in London a few weeks ago. Without his beard she could see he'd lost the worst of his gaunt edge, put on some weight, and some...confidence. Maybe a lot of confidence.

But he was glaring at her ferociously, for all his finger traced her hairline gently.

"I bumped my head when we lost a wheel about two hours from here." She stood close to him, and his body heat, clean and scented with the ginger and lemon aftershave, threatened to swamp her wits.

"You put ice on this?" His touch moved over her forehead slowly, then he sank all four fingers into her hair and feathered the pad of his thumb over her bruise.

She could not move, did not want to move. "Ice wasn't on hand. We were in open country, and I would rather have spent the time completing our journey than pestering each coaching inn for some unlikely ice."

He set his lips to her bruise. Gilly's insides rose up and sighed when his arms slipped around her, for when, when had anybody *ever*, kissed a hurt of hers better?

"John Coachman will rue the day," he said.

The duke brought her against him so Gilly's cheek was pressed against the scarred flesh of his chest. They'd shared embraces before, but nothing like this. His fingers massaged her nape, his flat male nipple was directly in her line of sight, and she felt empty and hungry and mortified all at once.

But oh, *feathers*, he was holding her snug and secure against the warm, muscular planes of his body, with his freshly shaved scent teasing her nose, and the rise and fall of his breathing a lullaby to her common sense.

She opened her mouth and turned her face to his chest. Not a kiss, certainly not a nibble. She inhaled, trying to get nearer to his essence, and bundled in, closing her eyes to the half-naked sight of him. She'd been terrified in that coach, and she was terrified in a different way in Christian Severn's embrace.

Later, she'd think. Now, all she wanted was to *feel*. Feel him, feel them together, feel her body coming to life with all the terror and determination of a spirit first emerging into the world.

"Gillian?"

She felt his voice as much as heard it, and understood he was putting a question to her. Before she could lose her nerve, she framed his newly smooth jaw with her hands. He could turn his face aside, thwart what her body insisted she needed, but he only pressed his mouth to the heel of her hands, left and right.

Then she found him with her lips. Went up on her toes, and sealed her mouth to his, having no plan beyond that.

His arms came around her, as snug as an anchor's chains around their capstan, giving her purchase and balance, and most of all, giving her relief from the fear he'd pull away and turn from her.

He stroked a hand over her hair, slowly, and Gilly's desperation eased. She needn't gobble him up; he'd allow a little savoring.

She followed his lead, trailing her fingers through his golden hair, glorying in the silky abundance of it, shaping his skull, tracing his nape, learning him in each bodily detail.

To touch...*to caress*, to surrender to tenderness and desire and the fierce, awful longing.

He lifted his mouth from hers and traced his lips along her temple, then down, over her jaw, and Gilly understood: he wanted to touch as well, and she would glory in that too. She stood still for him as he inhaled through his nose, his breath breezing warmly past her ear. He nuzzled her neck and made her shiver with the pleasure of it, then teased the corner of her mouth with a half kiss.

She dimly perceived he was withdrawing though, easing her down, and her disappointment was tempered only by the knowledge he abandoned her reluctantly. When he'd mapped each of her features thoroughly with his mouth, when his hands had traced each knob and bump in her spine, he came to rest, his chin on her crown, his arms securely around her.

"Countess, you must forgive me."

Countess, not Gillian. He didn't let her go, and Gilly hid her face against him. Goddamn him, he sounded genuinely remorseful when she ought to be the one mustering regret.

"We have committed no wrong requiring forgiveness."

"You are widowed and alone, under my protection if you're under anybody's, and I have taken advantage of your grief."

His hand moved over her hair, cradling her head to him as if to emphasize his role of protector, but was simple protection ever a matter of such gentle handling?

"I am not grieving. I am *celebrating*."

She tore herself from his arms and stomped into his bedroom. When she passed him a dressing gown, he took it.

"I am sorry," he said again. "No woman, much less a lady, much less *you*, should see me thus." He shrugged into the dressing gown, and Gilly wanted to weep for the loss of the sight of him, even as she knew that blue velvet garment was all that remained between her dignity and utter wantonness.

"Your modesty becomes you, Mercia, but if you think I find you anything but appallingly beautiful, you are an idiot."

Idiot? Had that word come from her mouth, and directed at him?

He knotted the belt. Slowly, slowly one corner of his mouth kicked up, then the other. Only to settle back almost immediately.

"You were married to an old man," he said, expression shuttering. "Perhaps compared to him, even I fare tolerably."

He found a brush on the windowsill and used his reflection in the shaving mirror to bring some order to his hair, but didn't queue it back.

"You torment me, leaving it loose." She snatched up a black hair ribbon and marched over to him. He stood still while she bound his hair back.

"Countess…"

"Gillian, I should think. I've shaved you and dressed your hair."

The smile again, even more fleeting, as if he hadn't the stamina for it. "And kissed me."

"I wasn't the only one doing the kissing, Your Grace."

She clung to that. She'd interested him at least a kiss or two worth.

"To my confoundment and delight, I did kiss you. And enjoyed it thoroughly, but, my lady…I cannot allow myself to take such advantage again."

"Whyever not? I'm a blessed, benighted widow. I've finally reached the point in life where advantage may be taken."

"No, it may not," he said, a little of the duke infusing his voice. "You bestow favors where you will, with discretion, but you shall not be taken advantage of."

"We are at an impasse," she said, trying to fathom

what he wasn't saying. Some issue or insight lurked in this ducal posturing, something he was talking around. "I would have us kiss again. You are telling me you enjoyed what just passed between us, but will deny me in future out of concern for what or whom? Me?"

She thumped down on his sofa, sure in her bones the Almighty had put men on earth to drive women barmy. "I can assure you I'd consider it the greater regard did you indulge my foolish impulses, Your Grace."

Admitting that caused a blush to rise and made her determined to keep her yammering mouth shut, lest she lose her self-control entirely and beg him for more kisses, more caresses.

He sat beside her and took her left hand in his right.

She wanted to snatch her hand away, but also to climb into his lap and resume kissing him. He traced her knuckles with his left hand while she felt him marshaling arguments, preparing to ease her down gently again.

"I can barely tie back my own hair," he said. "After several clumsy attempts, I manage something like a queue, but it's tedious, and inclines me to go about like a half-groomed barbarian instead."

"Most unmarried men of any station have a valet—"

He shook his head. "I cannot abide to have another man tend me." He wasn't proud of that; the humiliation was in his voice.

"You allow me to tend you."

"I could toss you across the room with my bad hand. And you are not a man."

Yes, he could toss her across the room with one hand. He was both taller and, at least recently, more fit than Greendale had ever been, and Gilly had never been bothered by that, which was…interesting.

"You did notice my gender. I'm encouraged, Your Grace."

"You don't want to hear my explanations and apologies. I can only apologize for that as well."

"Your excuses."

"You are asking me, in essence, to compromise you." He did not sound angry, so much as amused—drat and blast him. "Whether with ill-timed kisses, or indiscretions of a more passionate nature. You would regret it, you would hate me, and while I do not deny you'd find pleasure in it—I would insist on pleasure for you—your eventual distaste I could not abide. Not all of my scars have been revealed to you, my lady."

He stared straight ahead, as if puzzling out the honor of it for himself.

And Gilly puzzled out a few things too, holding his hand as the late-afternoon sun cast the room in a mellow light.

He needed her to think well of him.

He held her reputation in significant regard.

He thought her attraction to him was a function of grief or abstinence, not unique to him, not something out of the ordinary for her.

And he desired her. In his touch, in what he said, in what he did not say, the Duke of Mercia desired her.

And most important of all, something Gilly had no doubt divined on an intuitive level but had needed to hear, too: he'd promised her that if they were intimate, she would find the experience pleasurable.

He'd said he'd insist on that, and she believed him.

❧

"Oh, aye, it were a bad, bad moment."

John Coachman banged his tankard in a signal for a refill, which the gentleman sharing the snug with him would no doubt pay for. The gentleman was buying, said his uncle had been a coachman, and the gent always stood a coachman to a drink when traveling from Town.

John was ever fond of good English ale, and the Lion and Cock served some of the best summer ale in Surrey. The day had been long and hot, mostly spent loading up Lady Greendale's things from the old earl's place and piling them high on the wagon. The return trip to Severn would be a thirsty undertaking, indeed.

"We'd been making good time from Town," John said, "for her ladyship were keen to get back to Severn."

"Fancies running the duke's household, does she?"

John blinked at his ale, because the comment bordered on impertinent, and come to that, the fellow talked a bit toplofty to be a coachman's nephew. Might even be some Frog or some American in his accent.

"She fancies her wee niece," he said. "Devoted to the girl, used to come over regular when Her Grace were alive. She's a widow to boot. Where else can she go but to family?"

"Where else, indeed?"

The gentleman took a sip of his ale, and John had the passing thought he looked out of place with his Town clothes, his Town gig, and his Town airs. The Lion and Cock was a posting inn, true, but the humblest variety of the species.

"So there we were," John said, "the team a-cantering along, and I look down and see the front wheel wobblin' on its pins."

"But nobody came to any harm. *Quel dommage.*"

John caught the impatience in the man's voice. Town fellows weren't likely to appreciate a well-told story.

"Thanks be to Almighty God." John banged his tankard for emphasis. "An' out come her ladyship, calm as you please. Told me to send a groom for the wheel, and to put the feed bags on my team."

"A cool head, then, for a lady."

This didn't seem to please the gentleman either, but ale wasn't a gentleman's drink, so John forgave him his mood.

"You have that aright. But beg pardon, sir. What did you say your name was?"

Eleven

FIVE DAYS.

Five days since Christian had held his countess against his naked chest, tasted her sweet kisses, and felt her hands moving over his body with desire. He could hardly credit the memory.

Helene had never touched him like that, not when he was whole and hale and his mind free of shadows and memories. Not when he was blessed with a younger man's exuberant erotic responses, not when he was newly wed and honestly trying to forge some sort of friendship with his duchess.

Before his marriage, there had been women, of course there had been, and he'd enjoyed them and regarded it as his most enjoyable obligation to see that they enjoyed him as well.

But those had been professionals or bored wives who'd long since met any marital obligations, experienced ladies of the world. They'd liked bedding a lusty young duke, liked being seen on his arm, liked dancing the supper waltz with him.

He'd been a...sexual trophy, just as for Girard, he'd

been a trophy of war. The whole notion made him want to retch.

"Be there some reason we're stopping back at Timwood's so soon, Yer Grace?"

Hancock's homely face was a study in impassivity, and Christian couldn't recall a previous occasion when Hancock had questioned his employer's directives.

"I have a reason," Christian said, putting thoughts of his countess aside. "Timwood breeds those enormous dogs."

"Mastiffs," Hancock said. "As his da and grandda did before him. Best in the shire for tracking, and a fair dog for work too."

"And nigh big as ponies. I want one, possibly two."

"Two be a mighty lot of dog."

"Severn is a lot of house." While the ladies in that house were diminutive.

Mrs. Timwood was so overcome at a second visit from "the dook" in two weeks she about quivered herself into an apoplexy. Mr. Timwood, when he understood His Grace was interested in a puppy, lost his deferential air.

"David, Jenny, go dust up the whelping box and let Duchess know she's to have visitors."

Christian was being announced to a dog. He rather liked the idea. "Your bitch answers to Duchess?"

Timwood grinned. "Me da named her, and a right duchess she is too. Excellent bloodlines all around, but a sweet nature, for all she's protective of those pups. Eight of them, there are, four and four, dogs and bitches. Not a fault in the bunch."

"To which sire did you breed her?"

Christian had asked the right question, for Mr. Timwood launched into a diatribe laced with more begats and out-ofs than could be found in a book of the Old Testament. By the time the three men were assailed with the pungent scent of the kennel, Christian was certain the bitch's lineage went back at least to the Conqueror's dog, if not to some pup Jesus had played with as a boy.

"That 'un be the runt," Timwood said, though the thing wasn't any smaller than its siblings, that Christian could see. "He'll be big enough, but he hangs back, see. He's smarter than the rest, mayhap, waitin' and seein' rather than scrabbling away to get to the tit. There's always another tit, ain't there, fella? But he'll not get the attention, the way he is."

Timwood scratched the little beast's ear, then went on to regale Christian with the virtues of the other seven puppies. They were. geniuses, according to Timwood, ready to learn to fetch His Grace's slippers, light his pipe, saddle his horse, and hunt up his dinner. They'd offer protection, companionship, and cut a dash on the street in Town...

And all the while the runt curled up by himself at the side of Duchess's roomy whelping box.

"Who plays with the runt?" Christian asked.

"This 'un." Timwood picked up a wriggling ball of puppy. "The dimwit. He's too good-natured. He'll work his heart out for ye, but don't be trusting him to guard the chickens. He'll cadge a nap when Renard comes by for a visit."

The dog hung in Timwood's big hands, panting happily, looking every bit as stupid as his breeder suggested.

"I'll take the runt and the dimwit."

A look passed between Hancock and Timwood, the visual manifestation of, "Oh, the Quality!" Christian allowed them their silent communication and scratched a silky puppy ear.

"Come week's end, this one would have gone into the rain barrel," Timwood said, holding up the runt. "And now he's gone for a dook's dog. God looks after fools, drunks, and strays, aye? To drown the pup woulda hurt me heart—Missus usually sees to such things—but he'll have a big mouth to feed once he's weaned. He's good-lookin' enough, though. He'll do for ya, Dook."

Christian accepted the dog, narrowly avoiding having his face bathed by a curious pink tongue.

"And this one. Stone stupid, he is, but yer not buyin' him for his brains." He passed the dimwit to Hancock, who suffered the dog to lick his chin.

"You're sure they're ready to be weaned?" Christian distracted the puppy by letting it sniff his riding glove.

"We've been feedin' them from the dish for the past week. Duchess is looking a mite peaked, according to the missus. Milk and gravy to start, some juicy bones for their puppy teeth, and soon, any table scraps ye got."

Chessie sniffed the puppy, then looked away, as if to indicate he cared not one whit for such a small excuse for a beast. Christian aborted his original plan, which had been to transport the pups in his saddlebags. He settled for holding the thing in one hand and guiding the horse with the other, while Hancock managed similarly.

"Can't say as I've ever ridden with a dog," Hancock observed.

"Nor have I. Pay him more than he asks."

"Beg pardon?"

"He'll try to gouge us on general principles, but if he makes a fine profit on the runt and the dimwit from this litter, he might try harder to sell the next runt and dimwit to some preening earl's son. I might be able to connect him with a London factor for that express purpose."

Hancock dodged more chin-licking. "May I ask what you intend to use these beasts for, sir?"

"Leverage."

Thankfully, it was beyond Hancock's ability to ask His Grace what on earth he meant.

❧

"Come, princess."

Christian held out his hand to his daughter. They had a routine now. Late morning, after he'd ridden out, after he'd spent several hours with his stewards and his correspondence—and his grooming and penmanship—he went up to the nursery and sprang Lucy from her studies.

They strolled the garden, examining the flowers now rioting in abundance. They rode out, with Damsel on a leading line, or Lucy up before her papa on Chessie. Twice they'd taken a rod and tackle to the estate's nearest fishing hole and dropped a line.

Today, Christian had other plans.

The best part of these outings was that Lucy insisted Gillian join them, and this spared Christian having to hunt the lady down.

She'd become a ghost, sending her regrets at meal times, no longer drifting down to the library with her books at night, barely sparing him two words when they passed in the corridors.

And it killed something in him to see her diminished in any way. She was putting distance between them, salvaging her dignity in the face of what she could only regard as his rejection. So he opened his campaign to preserve their friendship with the most effective weapons he could muster.

"Come along, Countess." He held out his left hand to her, while Lucy kited around on his right. "Lucy and I must inspect the stables, lest the lads think they can laze away a pretty summer day."

"You two run along. I've a few things to see to."

"They can wait, right, Lucy?"

His unwitting conspirator let go of his hand, crossed to the countess, and dragged her by the wrist over to Christian. He seized the lady's hand in his own.

"My princess has spoken, as it were. Go gracefully to your fate."

Gillian's blue eyes reflected exasperation, but also something he hadn't expected to see: hurt. She tried to mask it, but it caused his smile to falter.

"Please, Countess. I've been shut up with the ledgers all morning, and I would have this respite with the fair ladies of my household."

She slipped her fingers through his. "Very well, but we mustn't linger too long. Lucy has sums to do, and I have correspondence of my own."

"Who commands your letters?" he asked as Lucy took his free hand and fell in step beside him.

"Marcus Easterbrook," she said, her tone gratifyingly impatient. "I can report to him that my things are removed from Greendale." Her usually confident stride hitched. "*He* is Greendale, now. How...odd."

"It is odd," Christian said, resisting the urge to carry Lucy, because that would mean dropping the countess's hand. "You finally get comfortable with your courtesy title, assure yourself the real title holder will live forever, and then—poof!—he's gone, and you're the duke, or the earl, and everybody calls you something you don't answer to, and looks to you for decisions you've no idea how to make."

"I don't think Easterbrook—Marcus—will be quite so at sea," the countess said. "He's waited an age to succeed to the title, though he and the old earl were hardly close."

"They were uncle and nephew?" Though Christian didn't care for the topic particularly, he was glad they were having some sort of conversation—while they held hands.

"Great-nephew, the title being one preserved through the female line. Their visits were mostly a matter of Marcus putting up with his lordship's condescension. Marcus came to Greendale when on leave, but was always relieved to be on his way to Severn when proprieties had been observed."

"He came by in my absence?"

"He was dutiful, and your heir."

"Not once Evan was born." Lucy tugged on Christian's hand, dragging him over to a bed of roses, and forcing him to give up his connection to the countess. "You know, princess, when you don't speak to me, it means you communicate more often with your touch. You pull me about, turn my head, touch my arm… I'm not sure I miss your words as much as I'd miss this."

Out of the corner of his eye, he saw the countess was listening to him. Good. She thought he would not compromise her, but it was more a matter of he *could* not, despite wanting to.

But neither would he let her slip into indifference when they could be friends—good friends.

"Maybe you should not encourage Lucy to remain silent," she said as he knelt to sniff a rose. "Maybe we should all stop speaking until she relents."

He rose, pleased to feel the motion fluid and no particular strain on his thighs or knees. "Then perhaps I should have to touch you more, Countess, and you would have to touch me, hmm?"

He took her hand again, she didn't fight him, and they managed to reach the stables without trading any more salvos. Even sparring with her was a pleasure though, and Christian kept his powder dry mostly out of deference to his daughter.

"Princess, I was out with Hancock yesterday," he said as they ambled down the barn aisle. "I came across a little fellow who demanded to make your acquaintance. He doesn't speak much, not so a duke could understand him, but he managed to insist that you befriend him."

Lucy cocked her head, her expression solemn and puzzled. The countess was pretending to pet Chessie, but she was listening too. He knew it by the angle of her head, and the slight tension in her shoulders.

"Where is he, this stray fellow demanding to be your friend? Come, I'll show you."

He drew Lucy farther down the aisle, while the countess trailed them. When he opened the half door to an empty stall, Lucy peered around her papa's side into the gloom.

"He's resting," Christian said. "No doubt exhausted from chewing old boots, cadging treats, and tripping up the lads."

Lucy dashed around him to kneel before two puppies dozing on an old horse blanket. The puppies blinked at her sleepily, yawned, and let her pet them. She held a hand up to her father, two fingers raised.

"Yes, there are two." Mostly because carrying eight puppies home on horseback would not have been practical.

The countess came up beside him. "Oh, *my*. Christian, what have you done?" She brushed past him to kneel in the straw next to Lucy. "Lucy, just look at them. Look at those paws, and their ears, such silky precious ears, and those handsome eyes…"

Lucy cocked her head, asking the question the countess would not.

"This one…" Christian stroked a hand over the runt, who appeared to have grown in less than twenty-four hours, "is for my dearest Lucy." He handed his daughter her puppy, as its sibling struggled to his paws. "And this one is for my dearest Gillian. He has no sense, I'm told, but he's much in need of a friend, lest he stumble into a rain barrel and come to harm. You're good at befriending strays, my dear. I had to commend him into your keeping."

"I'm good at…" She cradled the dog to her cheek. "You wretched, awful, odious, low-down… *Oh, Christian.*" Then the dog was licking Christian's ear, for the countess had leaned in to hug him as tightly as she could with a wiggling puppy between them. Christian wrapped an arm around the lady, gave her a squeeze, then forced himself to lean away.

"I gather you like your pets, ladies?"

Lucy nodded emphatically, the dog cradled in her embrace.

"What shall you name him, Lucy?"

She pointed without hesitation, and Christian followed the line of her finger.

"Rake?"

She nodded.

"Interesting choice for the fellow who wasn't the most outgoing of the lot," Christian said. "You may call him Rake, while I shall call him Runt. This one was Dimwit, but the countess may choose another *nom de maison* for him."

The French came out easily, naturally, the way any English aristocrat normally peppered his speech with French—and without even a frisson of nausea.

Interesting. He had the disconcerting thought that Girard would have been proud of him.

Christian assisted Gillian to her feet, keeping an arm around her waist. "Let's introduce them to the gardens, shall we?"

Lucy put her puppy on the ground, while the countess kept hers in her arms until they reached the garden. Christian strolled along, treasuring the feel of Gillian at his side, silently promising the dog years at

the hearth if he continued to provoke such a senti-
mental mood from the countess.

In captivity, Christian had never been touched in
friendship, never known tenderness or kindness at the
hands of another. If he was forced to accept a bath, the
service was rendered with disrespect. If he was tended
by a doctor, it was without anesthetic or palliative, the
care given hurriedly, even fearfully.

And Girard's hands on him had been businesslike
and fleeting—thank a merciful Deity.

Lady Greendale had renewed a certain appetite
in him, one he hadn't realized he'd possessed—for
sweet touches, for care and tenderness and tactile
loving kindness. She had it in her very nature to offer
such touches, and she'd have him believe she even
desired him.

He could not atone for that, but neither would he
part with her physical presence in his life. If he had
to buy her dogs, give her horses, and keep his own
animal nature to himself to do it, he would.

By God, he would.

❧

The puppies were effective diplomatic overtures. Gilly
understood them clearly for the olive branch they
were intended to be. She wasn't sure what Christian's
motives were with respect to Lucy, but the child
adored her pet.

Not Christian. *Mercia.*

"We're to have a guest."

"You startled me, Your Grace." Gilly put down her
embroidery hoop as he took the seat beside her on a

bench amid his mother's rose gardens. Yards away, Lucy tossed a ball to the pups, who grew larger by the day, like creatures from some fairy tale.

"I don't know who plays harder," Mercia said, "the child or the dogs, but it's too quiet, that scene. She should be shrieking with laughter, calling directions to them. Every night, I go to bed telling myself we're one day closer to when she speaks to us again, but it grows difficult to keep that faith."

Oh, and wouldn't he offer just such a confidence, a glimpse of paternal insecurity more dear to Gilly than all his ducal swaggering about the estate with Hancock.

"I have the sense," he went on, "this silence of hers has a purpose."

"What sort of purpose?"

"I don't know. What are you embroidering now?"

She held up a silk shawl, sized for a child, the hems decorated with dragons tumbling along one side, unicorns leaping across another. She'd made sure the creatures were a bit chubby and that every one of them grinned its way across the fabric.

"For Lucy?"

"I can make one for you, Your Grace."

"And wouldn't that be lovely? His Grace dressing in lady's clothing. See how long I'd stay out of Bedlam when that got out."

"You are the last person who will find himself in Bedlam." She hoped her tone put this observation in the realm of fact rather than opinion. "Who is your guest?"

"*Our* guest."

She let that go by, a harmless dart in their ongoing

struggle to…what? In her case, it was a struggle to not fall in love with a man who was determined to be decent to her when what she sought was indulgence of her wanton nature.

Her recently discovered, very frustrated wanton nature, damn him. Greendale was probably laughing at her from the grave.

As she fell asleep at night, try though she might to pray her way to the arms of Morpheus, Gilly found herself calling to mind the lovely heat of Christian's naked skin, the taste of his mouth on hers, the silky texture of his hair, and the pleasure—the utter, soul-deep relief, and the pleasure—of being held securely in his arms.

While Christian seemed equally determined to entice her into some sort of friendship.

He wasn't exactly charming, though he was attentive, seeking her out several times a day, always with some question: Was the lavender ready for harvest? Did she fancy goat cheese or only cow cheese? Had Lucy enough books to keep her occupied?

And now, *they* were to have a guest.

"Who is this guest?"

"Colonel Devlin St. Just. The Duke of Moreland's oldest, though born on the wrong side of the blanket. I traveled with him in France."

How to ask: Before or after the ordeal of captivity?

He was rubbing his thumb over a hem of Gilly's shawl, the black silk she wore around the property except on the warmest days.

"Are you looking forward to this company?"

"You called me Christian."

"I did no such thing."

"When you saw Dimwit," he said, his fingers slowing as they moved over the fabric. "You said, 'Oh, Christian.'"

She'd hoped he had not noticed. "I beg your pardon then, it was an oversight."

"My name is not an oversight. I used yours, too."

He'd called her his dearest Gillian, and she'd had to hide her eyes against a silky, panting puppy. And now, the dratted man was going somewhere conversationally. Somewhere Gilly did not want him to go.

"If you used my name, sir, you overstepped."

"You invited me to use it, my dear." He was smiling now, faintly, his gaze on the shawl, and that didn't bode well at all. "Because you've shaved me and dressed my hair."

And she'd kissed him. *Merciful feathered saints.*

"How are you managing?" she asked reluctantly, though she had wondered—incessantly. "You've remained clean shaven."

"I was uneasy regarding the proximity of a razor to my throat." The smile was gone as if it had never existed, a seedling unable to sprout roots or leaves. "If I don't think of the blade, if I concentrate on the scraping away of my whiskers, not on having them scraped, I manage. Does that make sense?"

"You stay outside the business," she said, knowing all too well what he meant. "You watch yourself being shaved, as if you were the man in the mirror, not the one whom the razor touches."

"Yes." A telltale crease appeared between his golden brows. He was puzzling something out, possibly about *her.* She spoke to distract him.

"Tell me about this Colonel St. Just."

The duke blew out a considering breath. "He is both canny and kind, probably a soldier poet beneath all his Irish charm and ducal bluster. I traveled north with him when I left Toulouse. He's the oldest of ten, and it informs his style of command."

"Interesting. Aren't most officers younger sons?"

"Many are. I think you will like him, and I know he will like you."

"What are you insinuating?"

"Nothing," he said, reaching over to pat her hand. "Not one thing."

And then he fell silent, watching his silent daughter, and Gilly could do nothing but sit silently beside him, wondering what it meant when a man recalled a lady's every word but refused to kiss her again.

❧

"You are charming my countess," Christian said, passing a brandy to St. Just. In civilian clothes, the colonel was handsomer than ever, and Christian was curiously glad to see him.

"Lady Greendale is charming me," St. Just said, pausing before a pistol crossbow, the smallest in the Severn family collection. "My thanks for the libation. This little darling has to be quite venerable."

He held his drink as he studied the weapon, a man who knew to savor the finer things, when another officer on leave might have tossed back his brandy at one go.

"That weapon is two hundred years old, at least." And it still looked lethal as hell. "Her ladyship charms all in her ambit, including my daughter." Though what had been amiss with the late earl of Greendale, that Gillian apparently hadn't charmed him?

Christian poured himself a drink from the tray some thoughtful countess had sent up to the armory, half the amount he'd given St. Just.

St. Just turned his attention to a longbow, a weapon nearly as tall as the men who would have used it.

"If Lady Greendale is the reason your hands don't shake, you've put on two stone of muscle, and your eyes no longer look like you recently took tea in hell's family parlor, then I must consider her a friend."

"She's part of it." Two stone? Well, perhaps one. One and a half. "A big part. She has the gift of domesticity, of creating a comforting sort of tranquillity."

"My five sisters do that for me. Her Grace is not my mother, though for reasons known only to her, she loves me as if I were one of her own. The girls, though…they scold and hug and laugh and watch a fellow all the while, catching him at the odd moment and prying confidences from him."

"And you love them for it?"

He moved on to another longbow, this one Welsh and supposedly a veteran of the Battle of Agincourt. Christian's father had let him shoot it once, on his fifteenth birthday. His forearm had sported a fierce bruise for weeks.

"How can I not love such sisters?" St. Just asked. "You saw what I saw on the Peninsula. The officers' wives, the laundresses, the cooks. They put up with the same deprivations the soldiers did, and complained a good deal less."

Both men fell silent, while St. Just was polite enough to appear to savor his drink and Christian wondered why generations of Severns had kept these weapons in this high-ceilinged, carpeted stronghold, as if they were treasures rather than instruments of death.

"I dread going home, too, though," St. Just said, apropos of nothing save perhaps his drink, the lateness of the hour, and the battered suit of armor standing guard in a corner.

"You do," Christian said, "because you think the effort of holding the war inside you, and your family outside you, will defeat your reason. When you were campaigning, it was exactly the opposite. You carried your family in your heart, and the fighting went on around you. It's…difficult, being a soldier, and also somebody's son, somebody's dear older brother."

Somebody's papa.

The proceeds from a sale of this old lot of death and destruction would feed a deal of puppies.

Or old soldiers.

"And as carefully as they teach us to shoot," St. Just said, sighting down the stock of a cavalry crossbow, "as punctiliously as we look after our mounts and our gear and our weapons, they don't teach us what to do with that difficulty of being two men housed in one body. I suspect it's half the motivation for the battlefield heroics we saw time after time."

Christian took the cranequin from him and replaced it on its brass wall hooks. "A wish to die rather than hold those two men in one body?"

"A deadly confusion, in any case, a fatal inability to suffer both peace and war in the same human being."

St. Just had no visible scars, but watching him balance an ivory-handled dagger on his finger, carefully indifferent to the weapon's nature, while minutely attentive to its craftsmanship, Christian endured an abrupt need to drag his guest from the armory.

"Be glad, St. Just, you don't have to add to a soldier's confusion the burden of a ducal succession."

St. Just put the knife down beside its mates on a bed of blue velvet. "What can be confusing about that? Surely even the French couldn't spoil your recall of those activities."

No fire had been laid in the armory. It was summer, after all, and who in their right mind lingered here?

St. Just held his drink up to a branch of candles, as if light had never done anything more fascinating than shine through an inch of brandy. "What aren't you saying, Mercia? You're no damned eunuch."

Damned, perhaps, nonetheless.

"I am not whole." The words were out, four little prosaic words, but Christian's throat promptly closed up, as if to stop any more prosaic words from escaping and mortifying him further. The small crossbow occupied his line of vision; a compulsion to smash it suffused his hands.

Both of his hands.

"You are not…" St. Just's mouth screwed up in consternation. "I've seen your scars, but otherwise…"

In for a penny… St. Just wouldn't pretend he'd misheard, wouldn't brush such a disclosure aside, and maybe Christian had known he wouldn't.

"Girard enjoyed decorating me with scars," he said, blowing out a breath. "You've seen the symmetry of them, front and back, side to side. I bloom with delicate, pink scars, as if I wore a bouquet. At first, it nigh cost me my reason, to know every time his superior officer came around, Girard would cut on me again, slice at my flesh, murmuring sympathy the whole time…"

St. Just swore with soft, Anglo-Saxon intensity.

"But then it became almost a relief, not a pain but a…consolation. His knife was always sharp and clean, and it stung, but it also… I could manage it in silence, without fail, I could manage those messy, interminable sessions in silence. He never cut deeply, never. I soon realized Girard cutting on me was for show, and Girard comprehended my grasp of his agenda."

Christian's words were swaddled in the quiet of a big old house late at night, and what was a guest supposed to say to such a disclosure, anyhow?

"I've heard the like," St. Just said, so very calmly. "One of the laundresses had scars."

Christian had not *heard the like*, though it was rumored the Regent was far too willing to open a vein, even when the physicians told him he'd been bled enough.

"A woman with scars?"

"On her arms, well above her wrists," St. Just said, rearranging the knives so they formed not a fan but a circle on their blue velvet. "She wasn't trying to end her existence, and the other women said she'd long had the habit."

Christian had not taken a sip of his drink, and neither had St. Just.

The brandy was, after all, French.

And yet, Christian wanted to finish the topic, though it would probably mean he never saw St. Just again.

"Girard sensed his little torment was no longer doing much mental damage to me, if any, but cutting is bloody, dramatic, and impressive to those who witness it. Anduvoir in particular seemed to enjoy those sessions with the knife."

"Then may Girard and Anduvoir both die a slow, painful, bloody death." St. Just lifted his glass, a toast to the eventual demise of two Frenchmen who'd been no credit to their nation.

"And roast honestly in hell," Christian said. "I understand spies are tortured if they're taken captive out of uniform, but Anduvoir's interest in me was beyond the natural perversions of war, if there are such things."

"One understands your meaning."

St. Just wouldn't pry. Christian would have to make this confession on main strength.

"Girard occasionally traveled to Toulouse to meet with his superiors. The first time he was gone, the guards thought to extract a confession of treason from me, and damaged my hand in his absence. He was wroth with them for overstepping, to the point that I remained safe in his absence thereafter."

"No, you did not." And neither did St. Just look away, play with his drink, or study the ancient, priceless weaponry.

"Girard went on leave again, I know not where, and his immediate superior dropped in on the Château. If Girard was sick, Anduvoir was sicker. He was jealous of the prisoners sent to Girard, but lacked the skill Girard had for keeping us alive while flaying our souls. With not half Girard's skill with a knife, Anduvoir rendered me...as a Hebrew."

A few beats of silence, then St. Just's rapidly indrawn breath. "Almighty, everlasting, merciful, bleeding Christ. He *circumcised* you?"

Christian nodded, memory abruptly flooding his mind with the scent of his own blood, the horrific burning, the uncertainty...

"I took days to get up the courage to assess the damage, because Anduvoir went about inflicting his mischief piecemeal over the course of what felt like hours... The pain was bearable, but the not knowing exactly where he'd stop, if he'd stop, how to live if he'd gelded me. Girard must have caught wind of what was going on—the entire garrison lived in fear of Girard—because he arrived in a temper and put a stop to matters before Anduvoir could do lasting injury of a more than cosmetic nature."

Christian had formed the words..."if he gelded me," but he'd lived the question for the balance of his captivity. Girard had said nothing upon his return, but had sent a physician to ensure the wounds were clean.

And he'd not taken any more leave. What did it say, that Christian had been reassured to know Girard had remained with him, behind the cold stone walls of the Château?

"When I had healed, Girard told me we'd had our last session with the knife. He promised me, no more cutting after that day, and I foolishly felt relief because he'd spared my face. I'd worried about that, which seems nigh hilarious in hindsight. The jailer lied, the corporals lied, Anduvoir habitually lied, but Girard was, in his diabolical way, honest. And why in God's name am I telling you this?"

St. Just's scowl was ferocious, but not…not frightening, not *frightened*, and not disgusted either.

"You're telling me, so at least one other person on the face of the earth knows what you went through, so you're not quite as alone in your nightmares and waking terrors. I respect your confidences."

His hand tightened around his glass, and Christian expected him to stalk from the room. Instead, he muttered gratifyingly vulgar curses involving French commanders and a male donkey.

Then, "I respect *you*, Mercia. *God*, do I respect you."

He finished his drink in a swallow, flicked his gaze over Christian—a fulminating, assessing glance—then hurled his glass directly at a Severn family shield mounted high up on the opposite wall.

Brandy fragrance perfumed the air, and the dregs trickled down the surface of the shield, putting Christian in mind of the blood that had trickled down his legs until the stones beneath his bare feet had been slick with it.

"I'm selling the lot of this," Christian said, passing his glass to St. Just. "Every knife, bolt, and bow. I want it out of my house."

"Good," St. Just said, nodding once, fiercely, then hurling Christian's glass into the corner of the room with such force, the knight in battered armor went clattering to the carpet.

Twelve

"I WISH YOU COULD STAY LONGER," GILLY SAID. SHE walked with St. Just in the rose garden while Christian—*His Grace*—and Lucy gamboled ahead with the puppies.

"My family would not understand did they get wind I was tarrying in Surrey," St. Just said, "though your household here is a wonderful excuse for tarrying."

"His Grace has been more animated for having another fellow to racket about with, like the two puppies are more active than one would be. I thought he'd never stop plaguing you last night about your stud farm."

"As much land as he controls, he's smart to gather knowledge where he may," St. Just said, "and support." He put an emphasis on the last two words, confirming Gilly's suspicion that the dark-haired colonel had a fine grasp of the subtleties.

"What need has the Duke of Mercia for support?" Gilly paused to pick a nearly blown damask rose, forgetting until she'd pricked herself that what they boasted in scent, the damasks matched in thorns.

"Allow me." St. Just produced a folding knife with startling ease, sliced her off a half-dozen pink flowers, and wrapped them in a monogrammed white silk handkerchief. "You know what need he has for support."

St. Just was a handsome man, in a large, soldierly sort of way, with laughing green eyes many a debutante would envy, though his perception was in excellent working order. Gilly accepted the flowers from his hand, handkerchief and all.

"Mercia is doing much better," she said. "He's a great deal stronger, gained flesh, resumed his duties…he's…"

"Lonely," St. Just said. "He's a soldier home from war, and he's lonely and wondering if he endured all that suffering merely to balance ledgers, count lambs, and swill tea with the parson. I think, Countess, you might be lonely too."

His words held an unspoken suggestion, and Gilly was abruptly not sorry at all the man was leaving. Yes, he'd distracted Christian from his preoccupation with her, but the cost was apparently these pithy insights from their—His Grace's—guest.

"Is Lucy lonely as well, do you think?" Gilly put flippancy into the question.

"I have five younger sisters, so I will say yes, I think the child is also lonely, though less so with you and Mercia and the dogs underfoot. You will accept my thanks for your kind hospitality, my lady, and my sincere wishes that your loneliness will soon abate, for you are entitled to your supporters too."

He bowed over her hand and sauntered off, calling to Lucy to demand a parting boon of her. He scooped the child up, whispered something in her ear, and had her dimpling and smiling the most coy smile Gilly could recall the girl producing.

Being the oldest of ten had indeed informed St. Just's approach to command.

By the time St. Just put Lucy down, the grooms had brought around his horse, a big roan gelding with a coarse head and a sweet eye. St. Just and Christian walked off a few paces, speaking quietly, while Gilly tried to distract the puppies from sniffing about the horse's feet.

The men ambled back, St. Just pulling on his gloves, while Christian sent the puppies off in the direction of the folly near the center of the garden. St. Just checked over his saddle and bridle, then grabbed his host in a hug and pounded him twice, hard, on the back.

Christian's expression was momentarily perplexed, then…bashful, before he returned the blows, and St. Just let him go.

"You know, Mercia," St. Just said, swinging onto his horse, "the world boasts plenty of Hebrew children, and has for thousands of years."

This peculiar comment had His Grace's lips turning up.

"Get ye to Kent," Christian said, "where your sisters can spank you for such impertinence. If you're posting back to France by way of Portsmouth, then drop in on us again, please, and mind my letters, Colonel."

"I will stay in touch. You have my direction. See that you do likewise."

When St. Just had cantered off, Christian slipped his arm through Gilly's, and she let him, because saying good-bye to a friend was never easy.

"We're at peace," she reminded him. "You'll see him again."

"You might be right," he said, his smile fading.

"What was that comment about Hebrew children?"

The smile came back, brilliant as summer sunshine on the lakes beside the drive.

"It was the truth," he said, sneaking a kiss to her cheek. "Nothing less than the blessed, simple truth."

❧

St. Just's visit bore two kinds of fruit, each, in Christian's view, positive.

First, Christian found his internal view of his captivity shifting. He'd been considering Anduvoir's work with the knife a shame to be privately borne— proof of capture, of failure—and that was at least half of what prevented him from allowing another to look upon his scars and disfigurements.

In France, St. Just's reaction to Christian's limitations had been to polish his weapons, to offer protection to a fellow soldier, not revulsion or judgment.

And in England...St. Just had aimed his revulsion squarely at the French.

Where it should be aimed.

As St. Just had destroyed elegant crystal tumblers, Christian had barely stifled a shout in affirmation of the violence. For with St. Just's destructiveness came not only the certainty that Christian had been deeply violated, but also a renewed desire for revenge.

Christian should never have doubted either the violation or the entitlement to revenge, but the captive allows himself to be taken, after all—and doubt thus gains the only toehold it needs to assault the prisoner's self-worth.

And somewhere in these shifts and awakenings came a hope—the thing Christian had become deaf and blind to while a prisoner—that the Countess of Greendale hadn't been momentarily accessible to him merely out of grief and bodily deprivations.

She'd seen his scars, told him quite baldly he was desirable to her, and acted like a woman susceptible to a man's advances. Despite the scars she hadn't yet seen, he could build on that. Encouraging her interest would take time, stealth, and more charm than he'd ever laid claim to, but he could build on it.

His first opportunity came several days after St. Just's departure, several rainy days of mundane discussions with the countess over breakfast and dinner, unremarkable encounters in the quiet of the nursery, and long evenings lying in wait for her in the library—in vain.

When the sun came out, Christian accosted his quarry as she emerged from the back steps, a piece of paper in her hands.

"Might I hope you're coming to discuss menus with me?" Christian asked. "It's Monday, and we last had this discussion a week ago, if memory serves."

She looked...prim, tidy, and disgruntled, but forcing her to share household decisions was part of his strategy.

"Perhaps if I leave these menus with you—"

He plucked the paper from her hand. "No such luck. I'll not be chasing you all over the house to suggest we substitute green beans for the braised carrots on Wednesday. Come along." He tugged her by the wrist—oh, what a pleasure to put his hands on her—and towed her into the library.

"You do favor the garden," he said, perusing the menus.

"It's summer, of course I favor the garden, particularly when what Cook prepares is served in the nursery as well."

"I didn't know that. I thought children were supposed to be fed only bland foods, bread, pudding, soup, and more pudding."

"That is old-fashioned thinking, Mercia." She meandered, spinning the globe, flipping over the pages of the atlas, taking down a book only to put it back.

"You have made a study of child-rearing practices?" For Helene had found the topic of little interest.

"Child-rearing is becoming a popular topic among those with more experience and education than I." She stopped by a window that had been cracked to let in the scent of the roses bedded beneath it.

"You are restless, my dear. Let's be truant this afternoon and go for a ride." He could see by the longing in her eyes she was tempted. "You want to, I want to. The horses want to. Nip into your habit, and I'll meet you in the stables."

"Lucy will be jealous if she sees us."

"Lucy is a child who must serve out her sentence in the schoolroom. Besides, she commanded your exclusive attention for half the morning, while I toiled in solitude over my ledgers."

Yes, he tracked her schedule, through observation, through the maids, through the footmen, and he thought they all rather abetted him too. He saw the countess's lips firm in inchoate mulishness, and turned her by the shoulders.

"Shoo," he said, nudging her between the shoulders. "It's a beautiful day, and you've earned an outing."

She went, casting him a curious glance over her shoulder.

Curious was good; it was a start.

As she cantered along beside him on the little mare thirty minutes later, Christian concluded that at some point in her life, Gillian had been a very competent rider. She cued the mare subtly and moved easily with her horse.

"Would you like to hop a few stiles, or stay on the flat today?" he asked.

"This is an ambitious hack for me," she said, patting the mare. "We usually have Lucy with us, demanding we idle along, unless she's up before you."

"I first felt a horse in flight from my perch up before my papa," Christian said. "The feeling was wonderfully secure, in the saddle with him, but flying over a log. To me, we were topping the hedges at Newmarket, though I'm sure the obstacle wasn't twelve inches."

"You have good memories of your childhood?"

"Wonderful, for the most part. You?" He brought Chessie down to the walk, realizing the horse was winded before he was—lovely horse.

Lovely day.

"Not wonderful, not awful. My mother had some mischief in her, but Papa was stern. He contracted marriage for me with Greendale, and that should tell the tale."

She spoke as if contracting marriage was akin to contracting plague.

"You gained the title Countess of Greendale. Some would call that a successful union." Though even ten years ago, Christian would not have.

Annoyance, plain as day, crossed her face. "I gained years in the household of a nasty old man. But for his cronies in the Lords, he had no joys, no passions, no light in him. My papa condemned me to darkness. When I came crying home to my mother six weeks after the nuptials, Papa denied me more than a second cup of tea before I was summarily bundled back into my coach, my bags not even unloaded from the boot."

Her words were bitter, making Christian regret the topic. "When next you choose a husband, you can select a livelier fellow of fewer years."

"Why would I select another gaoler?" Her expression was still unhappy. "I have my little portion, a place to live for the nonce, and my freedom. You cannot know what that means to me."

A place to live "for the nonce"? He "could not know" the value of freedom?

Christian brought Chessie to a halt, crossed his wrists over the pommel, and gave her the entire weight of his stare.

"I'm sorry," she said, fiddling with her reins. "You do know about losing your freedom, I didn't mean that you didn't…but that was war, and marriage comes with the sanctity of a sacrament, and…oh, bother. I didn't mean it the way it sounded."

"No matter. Not all men are like your late spouse."

He nudged the horse forward and let her stew. A

change in topic was in order, but it was her turn to offer something.

"You're regaining your passion," she said, nearly startling him out of the saddle. "You aren't simply trying to recover your wind, or intent on addressing the neglect of the estate. You're out here because you wanted to sit astride that horse."

"And that is a passion?"

"You rode everywhere before you joined up," she said. "Helene said you were a natural for the cavalry, though she hated that you bought your colors."

"She neglected to tell me she hated it." And Helene had not been a woman given to keeping her own counsel.

Unlike Lady Greendale. Worse yet, the countess was riding to the left, as most women did if they had only one sidesaddle, and Chessie was on Damsel's right, so the countess's face was visible only in profile.

"Helene said she wanted you to resign your commission, but knew you wouldn't abide by her wishes if she asked."

"She knew that, did she?"

And if Helene *had* asked him? Would he have come home, tried again, swallowed his pride? Would they have become friends in truth, forged some sort of meaningful truce? To think maybe they would have was reassuring, to think they both might finally have matured enough to become something of a family.

Except that now, Helene was gone, Evan was gone.

"Must I apologize again?" the countess asked. "I did not mean to turn the topic so melancholy."

"Thoughtful, not melancholy."

She nodded, accepting his absolution. Before Christian could think of another conversational gambit, her lips turned up in a positively wicked smile.

"I'll race you to the bridge."

The mare shot forward before Christian could decide whether accepting such a challenge was gentlemanly. Chessie, however, considered it his equine duty to stick with the mare, so off they went. The larger gelding quickly came up on the mare's flank, and Christian caught a glimpse of a grinning countess, bending low to whisper encouragement to the mare.

And then she wasn't smiling.

"Christian!"

Over the pounding of hooves, Christian perceived the fear in Gilly's cry. Her seat slipped a hair to the left, and he caught sight of the foregirth banging loose against the mare's side.

He urged Chessie next to the mare, snaked an arm around Gilly's waist, and hiked her out of the saddle just as it tipped sideways, then slid down to hang under the galloping mare's belly. The bias girth kept the saddle on the horse, inspiring the beast to a flat-out run in her efforts to escape the nuisance beneath her.

"You're safe. I've got you." And he did, had her firmly around the waist as he hauled Chessie to a halt. "Merciful God, Gilly." He dropped the reins from his right hand and tightened his arms around her. "Merciful, everlasting... That might have been the end of you."

She leaned into him, her arms around his neck. "It wasn't. I'm fine, I'm just..."

She shuddered, then let out a great sigh and stayed in his arms atop the horse, clinging to him while he clung to her.

"I can walk," she said at length.

"Nonsense." He hiked himself over the cantle then slid to the ground over Chessie's rump. "Your mare has regained her senses by the bridge. You stay right where you are while I fetch her."

They returned to the stables with Christian riding the mare bareback, her saddle left behind for the grooms to retrieve, while Gillian remained awkwardly perched on Chessie. When Christian assisted the lady from his horse, he paused, arms around her again, this time in full view of the lads and the house.

"Christian?" Her voice as she burrowed against his chest was tentative. "Your Grace?"

"Hush, you've had a fright. I'm reassuring you."

"Quite." Her tone held humor, enough to suggest she was as reassured as she would permit herself to be.

"I think a medicinal tot is in order," he said, not stepping back but turning her under his arm and starting her off toward the house.

"For my nerves?" The woman seemed utterly composed but for the slight dishevelment of her hair.

"Yes, damn it, for your nerves."

"That's what I mean, about regaining your passions."

"I beg your pardon?" She was going on about his passions, when less than thirty minutes ago, that damned saddle...

"When I met you in London, earlier this summer, you would not have sworn at me. You were too controlled."

He could not grasp her point, and it was all he

could do to refrain from grasping *her*. "I wasn't swearing at you. I was swearing at the situation."

"Well, you wouldn't have. Might we adopt a bit more decorous pace, Your Grace? I will soon grow winded."

He slowed down, hadn't even realized he was hustling her along. "You regard my colorful language as a positive development?"

"I do. Maybe you're getting adequate rest and proper nutrition, maybe you're healing in more subtle regards, but you're making great strides."

They'd reached the back terrace, and when she tried to march out from under his arm, he let her get a few paces off.

"I want to kill Girard," he said, having no earthly idea where the words came from. "I could get passionate about that, about choking the man to death with my bare hands. Slowly. Lethally passionately."

Her expression didn't change, save for a slight raising of her eyebrows. "Such thoughts are to be expected."

He laid an arm across her shoulders and resumed a more sedate progress across the terrace. "I lie awake at night, and instead of reliving the torture, I think now of putting Girard where I was and watching impassively while what was done to me is done to him. What I want to do to Anduvoir ought to shame me. This is not a fit topic for a lady, particularly not for a lady who nearly came to harm in my care. You will please give me your opinion of the roses."

She shrugged against his arm and brought them to a stop. "Bother the roses. In all likelihood, I would have come to no harm save for a few bruises. I've come off my share of horses, and I tend to heal quickly. You were about to fetch me a brandy."

She took him by the wrist and steered him toward the French doors that led into the library.

"God, yes, a drink."

She was hauling him along barehanded, she'd called his name from the back of her horse, and she hadn't turned a hair when he'd mentioned his most recent and bloody version of a lullaby.

Of course he needed a drink, preferably several.

&

His Grace downed a finger of brandy in a single swallow. Gilly, by contrast, took a cautious sip of her drink and let the heat slide over her throat. Why, when heat in quantity galloped through her veins, was she imbibing spirits?

His Grace was regaining his equilibrium and not merely regarding the mishap with the saddle.

While Gilly was losing hers.

"If you actually imbibe the drink, the benefits are more apparent, though even the feel of the glass in one's hand can be steadying too," he said.

He imbued his words with more force, his step with more energy. On the occasion of St. Just's parting, His Grace had smiled. By the week, if not by the day, he was less the man who'd survived torture and captivity and more the man…

Whom Helene had termed "aggravatingly virile."

Oh, Helene.

A tap on the door spared Gilly further scrutiny from the duke, though she wasn't expecting a footman to come in bearing her sidesaddle.

"How old is your saddle, my lady?" Mercia asked. He took it from the footman, dismissed him, and hefted the whole business onto a reading table.

"Less than ten years. I brought it with me when I married, so I took it when I decamped from Greendale."

"Does Lucy use it?"

"No, Your Grace. Sidesaddles are usually built to a lady's particular measurements, and the horn wouldn't be placed properly for Lucy."

He gave her a look that meant he—a decorated cavalry officer—regarded the information as suspect simply because it hadn't crossed his notice previously.

Aggravatingly virile, indeed.

He peered at the girth and waggled the fingers of his left hand at her in a beckoning gesture. "Come here."

"You might at least append a palliative question mark to your commands," she said, but she went to him and set her drink aside.

"Look at this." He pointed to the billets that held the girth's buckles. "You see the stitching here and here is in perfectly good repair, but it broke here, or was cut."

"Cut?"

"The leather's not stressed, and we see no unusual wear on the greater area, no rub marks. Believe me, my lady, the night before a battle, a cavalryman inspects his gear and puts it in as near perfect working order as he can. Your saddle was tampered with."

A feeling went through Gilly, like the shock when her coziest socks scuffed over a thick rug. The sensation startled, like a bad scare, and made her insides tangle uncomfortably. She recognized the sensations as first occurring on her wedding night, a condensed and physical form of dismay with not a little panic thrown in.

"I don't believe you."

"Who knew when you were traveling down from Town?"

"You think somebody loosened the coach wheel?" She picked up her drink and took a preoccupied swallow, only to take too much. As she set the glass back down and tried to keep the coughing ladylike—and how did one do that?—His Grace patted her back.

"You need water," he said, drawing her closer to the sideboard.

"I'm *fine*," she countered, dragging her feet on general principles. "Stop towing me about like so much cargo, and the wheel was not tampered with, and my girth just…just broke."

"You're trying to be brave."

Gilly might have hit him, but he was passing her a glass of water. She made herself take a deep breath and let it out, lest she grab the glass and dash the contents in his face.

Except he looked so…concerned, and she knew he was right: she was trying to be brave or rational or something. Trying to cope when she thought the worst of her coping days were behind her.

"Just a sip." He scolded like a mother hen, as if he expected her to do exactly as he said even though she was no longer coughing.

She took one sip, set the glass aside, took two steps closer to the duke, went up on her toes, and kissed him.

Her actions hadn't been the result of any mental process identifiable as a decision, and thus made no sense to her mind, but to her body…oh, to her body, kissing was the logical reaction to any and all situations involving proximity to Christian Severn, much less a situation that had left her frightened and flustered.

She'd meant this kiss like a slap, an abrupt, riveting departure from expected behavior. A means of disconcerting a fellow who showed every sign of assuming command without Gilly's consent.

But his arms came around her slowly, carefully, and his tongue traced her lips as he groaned a sort of sigh, and his embrace alone was enough to have her clinging back, tucking herself closer to him to feel how their bodies pressed together.

"Kiss me." His voice was low, just above a whisper, and his mouth tasted of the sweet brandy when he opened it over Gilly's.

His tongue came gently exploring, and Gilly's insides collapsed in on themselves, like a house of emotional cards disintegrating when a window bangs open in a stiff breeze. Had she not been gripping him tightly, her knees might have given up the job of holding her upright.

And then she was scooped up, hoisted against the duke's chest, and carried to the sofa, where he laid her down, her head propped on the brocade pillows.

She wanted to protest the loss of his warmth—of his mouth—but he was back, perched at her hip and leaning down close enough she could see the variations in the blue of his eyes. This was much better. Prone, she needn't worry about standing; she need only concern herself with pulling him closer, getting his hair loose from its queue, and fusing her mouth to his as he invited her to do exploring of her own.

"Gilly, we have to stop."

She blinked; his forehead was pressed to hers. "Why?"

"Because the door is unlocked."

Well, that was plain enough. Gilly thought about sitting up, but that would precipitate an awkward discussion and mean she couldn't lie there, inhaling ginger-and-lemon aftershave while her fingers stroked over silky golden hair and her heart thudded against her ribs.

He left her to lock the door and came back to sit at her hip. "You started it, my lady."

Must he look so pleased?

And yet, he was so *dear* when he was pleased.

"No denying that," she said, hoping he'd think the flush was from the brandy—not the kiss. And it wasn't a blush. Was. Not. "But you were hovering."

"I shall hover more often."

"I do apologize."

"There's no need for that," he said, and she hoped that was the start of a smile in his eyes, except it was a fairly fierce expression for it to be a smile. "Can you explain, at least?"

"I wanted to stop your hovering."

"Interesting strategy. Has it worked?"

"Well…no. Here you are again."

"Let me propose another theory to explain your rash actions." He traced a finger over her brows, a gentle, even sweet gesture Gilly felt in her vitals. "You fancy me."

"I fancy…?" She blew her hair off her forehead, intending to blow his hand away. He repeated the caress instead, further threatening her composure. "I've never heard such a taradiddle." She fancied him the way some women fancied shoes, bonnets, and chocolate. She fancied him like sunlight and water, like air, like—

And that would not do.

"You fancy me, you were overset by the topic under discussion and by the events of the day, and you sought my arms as a result."

"I wasn't kissing your arms." She muttered the words as she struggled to sit with her back against the armrest, and knew a little consternation. He sounded entirely too calm, given the content of his words.

And the idea that he could possibly have put a ducal finger on a small truth…

Oh, *feathers*. Oh, damn and blast, a real truth.

"There's no fancying involved," she said, swiping at a lock of hair that insisted on dangling against her nose. "You're good-looking enough, and underfoot. I'm a widow. Widows are allowed queer starts. You mustn't feel the need to start blathering on about honor and poor relations."

She'd hit him if he gave her that speech again. The smile he directed at her was so gentle, she knew he wasn't fooled. He scooted closer and took her in his arms.

"Calm yourself, Gilly. I fancy you too."

Gilly. How she loved to hear him say her name, to verbally caress a part of her Greendale had found plebeian and unimpressive.

And Christian fancied her. She let the pleasure of

that admission wash over her for a moment, the way she'd enjoy sinking into a hot bath before tending to her ablutions.

"Are you about to launch into homilies on the topic of my hating you for compromising me, and grief and honor and more masculine rot?"

"No." He pulled back a few inches too, which created for Gilly the disadvantage of being studied when she'd rather do the studying. "I ought to, but I've had a shift in perspective regarding certain matters, or I think I have. Besides, some fairly tame kissing does not a lady compromise."

That was fairly tame?

"I'm capable of discretion," she said. "And I'm sensible of my duty to Lucy."

He frowned, as if her words were somehow complicated and layered with meaning when they weren't.

"I'm not sure I'm capable of discretion," he replied, his expression disgruntled. "Not where you're concerned. And if you wanted to distract me from the fact that somebody has tried twice now to cause you serious harm, that will take even more than your considerable charms, my lady."

"You fancy me." She could not believe she'd said it aloud, and not in reply to his very stern tone of voice, but it caused him to gift her again with that gentle, wicked smile.

"I fancy you, my dear. Alive and whole is a particularly fetching combination. You'll humor me if I insist on some measures intended to keep you safe."

"I'm not going back to Greendale." With each passing day, Gilly became more determined on that.

"The memories are not cheering, and I would not crowd Easterbrook—Marcus—as he's trying to establish his household."

"No, you're not going back to Greendale. You're staying here, where I can keep you safe from all save my own mischief."

She liked the sound of that, though she shouldn't. A more prudent woman, even a prudent widow, would be appalled, and lecture him sternly about overreacting to minor accidents, suffering paranoia, and turning up ducal on her over nothing, but she didn't.

She leaned into his embrace and was silent.

Thirteen

Torture bore an intimacy, similar to that of a bad marriage. Only the tormenter and his victim knew the exact, awful course of the misery suffered. Those two participated in the dark duet of pain and manipulation to the exclusion of any spectators or seconds.

Though to be fair, Girard had eschewed physical pain as his preferred means of extracting information from Christian. With scientific precision, Girard tried to induce compliance by alternating pain and pleasure, abuse and care, setting himself up as the god of both dungeon and daylight.

More than anything, Christian had feared coming to love his captor. In a calculus known only to the captive, such a thing was possible, even inevitable. The bonds formed outside captivity faded to improbable memories, leaving only the relationship based on deprivation and hurt, balanced with an equally insidious appearance of mercy and generosity.

The prisoner, in an effort to maintain his sanity, lost his connection with a universe created by a just and loving God, where questions had rational answers, and pain was expected to be productive of some end. He existed, cast out of all light, all reason, save what kept breath soughing in and out of a battered body and a despairing spirit.

Girard had offered women at various points, and Christian had been relieved to his bones to feel no reaction. Not to the vacant-eyed slatterns recruited from the French army camp, not to the apple-cheeked dairymaids, and not—thank a merciful Deity—to the rare women taken prisoner and thrust into the dungeon to share Christian's fate.

Early in his captivity, he'd noted the occasional morning salute resulting from a need to heed nature's call. Even those responses had been reassuring, initially, but then they'd faded, and indifference to everything—sexual functioning included—had become a necessity.

And then, the circumcision as St. Just so baldly pronounced it, a surgical Latin term for what Christian privately regarded as intimate mutilation.

Anduvoir's wielding of the knife had felt like the mutilation of Christian's soul, but in an odd way had given him back his life. Thereafter, he'd truly stopped caring, truly stopped wanting to speak, to scream, to rail against his fate. He'd become stronger for the absence of any emotion save the will to live, and even that...

The countess shifted in his arms, making a sound that suggested she was descending into sleep as she cuddled against him on the sofa.

He let her drift away.

Napping had been one means by which he'd coped with the long, uncomfortable nights, and just at that moment, he needed to hold her. He'd been convinced until recently he could not be an adequate husband to her. If his scars didn't scare her witless—and apparently they did not—then there had been the continuing lack of animal stirrings from his base urges.

Until recently.

And then he'd discounted what he felt as mere biological habit, not enough to sustain a wedding night, until St. Just, with a soldier's blunt kindness, had made his little comment about a full complement of Hebrew children throughout history.

The man was right. Disfigured did not necessarily equate with dysfunctional.

And if this last kiss had proven anything to Christian, it had given him incontrovertible evidence that his heart was not the only part of him once again taking an interest in life.

❧

Gilly awoke to the novel and lovely sense of being held in a man's arms, and realized Christian had shifted her as she'd dozed. She was cradled in his lap, supported by his arms, Christian's chin against her temple.

"Sleeping Beauty awakens."

His tone was bemused and teasing, and she felt the words in low down, unmentionable places. A prudent woman, even a prudent widow, would have scrambled off that sofa.

She nuzzled his arm, catching scents of soap and linen from the sleeve of his shirt. "I must look a fright."

The silliest words a female ever uttered, though usually, she uttered them while patting a perfectly intact coiffure. Gilly blew the stray curl off her cheek and tried to find her common sense.

"You look delectable, if a tad pleasantly disheveled. We're about to talk though, so you'd best get comfortable."

"Yes, Your Grace." She closed her eyes and snuggled down, letting her use of his title serve to chide him. That same tone had never failed to make Greendale—

She would not think of Greendale.

"Will you still be Your-Gracing me when I'm inside you, Gilly? Will you call me Mercia when passion overcomes your reason and you cry out in pleasure?"

She opened her eyes, and what she saw in his expression did have her scrambling off his lap. He wasn't teasing; he was genuinely looking forward to learning the answer to those questions.

Perishing *feathers*. *Now* he called her Gilly, her very name a seduction. That was what came of impetuous kisses.

She retrieved her glass of water, relieved he'd let her put even that much distance between them. From the look in his blue eyes, he considered enticing her to dally in the same vein as he did stalking particularly juicy—and doomed—prey. She took a sip and sat on the hard bricks of the hearth, across a low table from the duke lounging on the sofa.

When had he become such a well-muscled specimen, and how was she to look him in the eye now that she'd attacked him not once but twice?

"You must allow, two accidents befalling you in a span of days is at least a dangerous coincidence." He took a sip from the water glass she'd placed on the table.

The dratted man watched her over the rim of the glass the whole time, drinking from the same spot she had, and Gilly felt panic welling up at the implications of such a simple action.

Such drama, and over a few kisses.

Except—this awareness thumped into her mind, rather like a blow—he hadn't meant the two incidents of kissing as the accidents he'd referred to. Something had shifted in Christian's regard for her, and not because the girth on her saddle had broken.

"I will allow those mishaps are unsettling accidents, but only that. Coaches lose wheels, riders take the occasional tumble. Those are everyday occurrences."

"In the eight years of your marriage to Greendale, did either occur to you even once?"

"No," she said, trying to focus mentally on the topic of her safety. This was difficult, when her body had developed an acute and inconvenient physical awareness of the duke. *When I am inside you…*

"Then you will indulge me, my lady, when I ask you not to leave the house without either my escort or that of at least two footmen?"

She mentally reviewed the words independent of his leonine stare.

"You'd make me a virtual prisoner of the house." Indignation gave her some purchase against the fog in her brain and the lassitude in her limbs. "I spent eight years bowing and scraping to Greendale, denied my liberty. I shall not exchange his domineering possessiveness for another man's, not ever."

That sounded convincingly clearheaded, and was even true.

"I seek to keep you alive," he countered, running his finger around the rim of her glass. He had her drink cradled in his lap, resting against his falls. She looked away as he continued to speak.

"You agreed to join this household, so you should consider yourself bound by my dictates. I'm not suggesting we lock you in a tower for the rest of your days, only that you exercise some reasonable caution for the nonce."

Reason was not her friend, and never had been. *But you'll be a countess, Gillian. A countess...*

"You make it sound so simple, to be again attended everywhere as if I were a child of Lucy's years."

"You make it sound so awful, to have the company of brawny fellows—or me—dedicated to your welfare when you're out-of-doors. Can you detest me so much as all that?"

His lips quirked, as if he'd made a jest, but those eyes of his were watchful and serious, and Gilly realized abruptly she'd swum into even deeper waters than she'd feared.

"You are good-looking," she said, her tone resentful. "Too good-looking and good-smelling and good-sounding, *and* now you've become nigh brawny yourself. I cannot think straight when you're giving orders and duking about, and when you turn up charming and reasonable, I am even more befuddled."

"Is to duke a verb now?"

"Don't distract me, and yes, when you're underfoot, there's duking going on."

"And some countessing too, I suspect." His finger stopped moving round and round on the glass. "For the next little while, indulge me, Gilly. Let me give you my arm when we're out of doors, let the footmen carry your basket when you're in the garden. I'll assign you the handsomest of the lot, my only aim to keep you safe from harm."

She nibbled her lip, hating him for being so believable.

"Please, love…I wasn't here to keep Helene safe. I wasn't here to look after my own son when he fell ill. Let me protect you."

And listening to him, listening to the low, utterly serious words, it was easy to forget how closely protection could resemble possession. He believed what he was saying, and he had a point: Gilly was under his roof. Her choices were to leave, or to obey him.

She could leave later, when Lucy was in better spirits; when memories of captivity didn't have the duke seeing threats in every shadow.

For now—only for now—she'd obey him, and only in this matter of permitting an escort out of doors.

Only for now.

❦

The countess was not a sedentary detainee, but Christian had hardly expected she would be. He would come in from his morning ride to find her dragging two bleary-eyed footmen all over the gardens, even as the sun was peeping over the Downs. By late morning, she was on his arm as they made their outing with Lucy. She spent the afternoons on the back terraces or again in the gardens, embroidering, reading, tatting lace, or working at the social correspondence Christian delegated to her in such volume.

He decided to take pity on his footmen and joined her as she once again headed for an afternoon out-of-doors.

She set her basket at her feet and crossed her arms. "I thought George and John were to assist me."

"Alas for you, you'll have to make do with a mere duke," he said, picking up her basket. "What are we about today, Gilly? Gardening, I see." He winged his arm, and a martial gleam came into her eyes.

"I'm tending the graves." She took his arm, looking pleased with her strategy.

"More transplanting, then?"

"Yes, though it's too late for the lily of the valley to bloom."

"There's always next year." Her tactics wouldn't deter him. Graves were part of a soldier's life, after all.

She marched along beside him in silence, but it was a beautiful summer day, and Christian was content simply to bear her company. He'd grown accustomed to looking out his window and seeing her in the gardens, to listening for her footsteps coming to fetch him to the nursery, to seeing her across the candlelight at the evening meal.

"Is somebody tending Greendale's grave?" he asked.

"That is not my concern. He would not allow me to garden while married to him. I'm not about to turn my skill in that regard to his benefit in death."

She wasn't an unkind woman—far from it—but her antipathy toward her late spouse was intense to the point of puzzling Christian.

"By rights, you should have hated Helene," he said, hoping to turn the subject. "She had much that might have been yours."

"A tiara?" She stopped while Christian opened the gate to the family plots. "I had my title, little good it did me."

"Helene had a young man for a husband, one who sought to indulge her at least initially, and who left her in peace when the marriage foundered. She had children, a boy and a girl each, she had many friends and gallants, she had tremendous wealth, and staff to wait on her hand and foot... She had every reason to live."

His countess preceded him through the gate, and he was relieved she didn't respond to his last observation, or to the puzzlement in his tone.

"I'll take the blanket," she said, holding out a hand. He passed it to her from the top of the basket and watched while she spread it out, not near the headstones, but near the wall, where a bed of irises was going dormant after blooming profusely earlier in the year. Their scent had comforted him on more than one long, quiet evening.

"We're to separate those?"

"It's early," she said, "but yes. They'll do better for setting down some roots before winter comes, and in autumn, the Holland bulbs will demand lifting and separating. You needn't bother to help."

"I brought riding gloves." He dropped to the blanket beside her and passed her one of his gloves, then put up his left hand. She held out the glove, though he'd developed the knack of putting on his own over the past few weeks.

"Your hand looks better," she said, working the glove over his fingers. "The nails are growing in, the fingers not so bent."

"The hand wants use. It hurts to use it, it hurts if I don't use it, but at least then it has some strength and flexibility." He got his right glove on by himself, because she was regarding him with an entirely too thoughtful frown.

Her ladyship gestured with a hand spade. "You start on that end. I'll start on this one. They're likely choked most tightly up against the wall."

He had a momentary vision of bloody bodies all jumbled together at the base of some Spanish town's siege walls while a hot wind whipped across an arid plain and flies buzzed in a malevolent cloud.

The Forlorn Hope they'd been called, the volunteers who had led the charge when the guns had breached the walls. For those who survived, it was a good chance at a field promotion, which meant a raise in pay, but it was near-certain death as well.

Still, volunteers had never been in short supply, and they'd broken every siege Wellington had put them to.

"Christian?"

He stared down at the hand spade she held out to him. "Woolgathering."

"Go gently. The roots are tender."

He knelt up, the better to get at the tangled roots and leaves, and started working back against the old stone wall surrounding the family plots. The roots erupted from the ground, a twisted, gnarled puzzle that seemed to him in want of a few good swats with the sharp side of a shovel.

"You have to be patient," she said. "Think of them as ailing, in need of tender care."

He sat back, rows and rows of stretchers in his mind's

eye, the groaning of the dying in his ears alongside the silence of the dead and nearly dead. And the stench…

Why today? Why the hell did these ghosts have to walk today?

"Was Helene truly prostrate with grief?" The question was out, a means of keeping his morbid imagination from dwelling on battle horrors.

"I was here," the countess said, setting a dirty white root aside and using her gloved fingers to pry at another. "She'd brought herself nearly to exhaustion fretting over Evan. Easterbrook was very concerned for her."

"She nursed Evan herself?"

While Christian battled an ache in his fingers, Gilly tugged the root from the choke hold of its neighbors. "She hadn't the patience, but she fretted nonetheless, looked in on him constantly, spent a great deal of time trying to write to you and ask you to come home."

"I would have come." He would have, had he not already been taken captive. Odd, how life could time tragedies for the most exquisite complement of sorrow.

"You would have," the countess said, setting the second root aside. "Even Greendale didn't grouse when I told him I was going to her. She didn't know what to do, didn't know how to cope."

"Life hadn't asked much of Helene to that point," he said, seeing for the first time that Helene had been closer to childhood than adulthood when he'd married her. Not a woman with a great deal of personal fortitude, certainly not prepared to be a duchess.

And it wasn't her fault, any more than captivity had been his.

"Helene excelled at being pampered and indulged, a disservice often inflicted on a young woman with abundant beauty." The countess bent over the flower bed to get a better angle with her hand spade. "But when Evan didn't rally, Helene blamed herself. In her mind, if she hadn't sent you away, God would not have punished her by taking her child."

"Remarkable, isn't it, how we manufacture guilt to fit most any occasion? Everybody dies."

She peered up at him over her shoulder. "You blame yourself." She sat up and took off her gloves. "Oh, Christian…"

He stared straight ahead, seeing the dank, dark walls of the dungeon where he'd been held all those months.

"Girard explained my situation as a choice." His own voice sounded far away, detached. "I could spare the lives of countless men by keeping my silence, but he promised assassins would see to the death of my wife and my heir did I keep my peace. He could describe the English countryside as if he'd ridden it himself, as if…" Christian frowned down at the tool in his hand. What was he supposed to do with it?

"And if you had told him what he wanted to know?"

"My men would die, and many others with them. Thousands."

She made a sound of muted horror and wrapped an arm around his waist.

"My family was innocent," he said. "I did not kill them. Girard's threats were merely an obscene coincidence, and he stopped making them early in my captivity—they were simply one taunt among his arsenal of torments. I know that, but I should have been here. If I'd been here, Evan would not have taken a chill, or fallen ill, and Helene would not have done what she did."

He recited his conclusion woodenly. He'd fashioned it in his mind weeks ago, when Easterbrook had first explained that both the duchess and the heir had died, and in Christian's mind, the *mea culpa* had sounded smooth, like a catechism. Spoken aloud on a pretty summer day, the words had no sense, but were still somehow compelling.

"Helene was liberal in her use of laudanum," Gilly said. "You know this. Think back, Your Grace. She threatened to use it on her wedding night."

He regarded the unearthed irises in a growing pile on the countess's blanket. Helene *had* used a little of the poppy on their wedding night, and been a relaxed bride as a result. He'd wondered why all nervous brides didn't use the same trick.

"But if I had been here, I would have watched over the boy," he said, and this was the demon that plagued him the worst. An adult woman could be trusted to look after her own interests, her own health, not so a toddling infant.

"You said yourself you were banished from the nursery." Gilly rubbed the center of his back, where a cold tightness dwelled regardless of the pretty day. "The weather was not bitter, or even particularly damp. Evan was a healthy child, and his illness started with a simple sniffle."

"Was he bled?"

"Helene said you disapproved of the practice, so no."

That was something. Helene had respected his wishes and spared the child at least that horror. "And he was gone in a week?"

"One week, and Helene was wild in her grief, or perhaps her guilt, then she got word you'd been reported missing."

"Only missing, not dead?" This mattered, though to a grieving mother, the distinction had likely been lost.

"Only missing. Marcus had leave to tell her in person, and he assured her every effort was being made to find you."

"Then why in the bloody hell would she be so careless with her sleeping draughts? Why cast her life away like that?"

"You aren't indifferent."

She said it so solemnly, he had to turn his head and risk looking at her.

"Good *God*, of course I'm not indifferent! She was my wife, I loved her in my fashion, and while her death was ruled accidental, she herself committed the accidental misuse of the drug that took her life. That is nigh suicide, Gilly, recorded as accident only out of deference to her title, or perhaps to her daughter's memory of her, and had I been here, *it would not have happened.*"

"Don't do this." She leaned into him, pressed her face to his arm, even as she kept her hand on his back. "Helene blamed herself for the child's death, blamed herself for sending you away when there was no spare in the nursery. She howled with the anguish of it like a wounded animal, and it was no more her fault than it is yours. You said it yourself: everyone dies. Everyone. Instead of cursing yourself for being taken captive, you must celebrate that you yet live."

She shook him by his arm; then she rose to her knees and wrapped both arms around his shoulders.

"Helene had choices," she went on, "and if she chose to take her life, there is nothing anybody can do about it. You have a daughter, you will have more children, you will laugh and love and live. You will."

"Do you think she killed herself?"

The countess sat back down on her heels, and Christian was both relieved to be free of her embrace and disoriented, like those irises, dug up, cut loose, all their tender parts exposed to the sunlight.

"Only Helene knows what her intentions were, but she said nothing to me about wanting to die. It's easy, with one dose taken, to become confused about how much was consumed and when. By low light, many drops can look like a few, days blend, memories blend. Laudanum deaths are legion among the ill."

"If she did...take her own life..." Christian set his hand spade down. "I was missing, soon to be presumed dead, her son was gone... If she did, I cannot blame her."

Dirt was everywhere—on his gloves, his breeches, on Gilly's blanket, and the same dirt that grew flowers provided a final resting place for the mortal remains of people who had been loved while they'd walked the earth.

"You must not blame yourself, either, Christian. Never once did Helene express any sentiment reproaching you for being taken captive. Never."

They sat in silence for long minutes before the countess yanked up one more root, tossed it on the pile, and sat back again. "I owe you an apology," she said.

"For?"

"Thinking you were indifferent to your losses."

"You have your own guilt to manage in that regard," he said, but he felt too hollow to explain what he meant. Hollow and curiously light. "We all grieve differently."

She nodded and passed him the little spade, and it seemed to Christian the roots came up more easily after that.

⁂

Gilly forced herself to focus on the gardening, but her insides were in an angry, disbelieving uproar.

What kind of mind would make a man choose between his family on the one hand and his comrades in arms on the other? Between home and hearth, and the men under his command?

And it was no credit to this Girard person that he'd ceased his taunts early in Christian's captivity. The seed of self-castigation had been planted in fertile soil and allowed to flourish at the expense of Christian's sanity.

Watching Christian tear at the hapless irises, Gilly realized the duke had tried to take his own life, or at least contemplated it. She'd had her concerns, particularly when she'd walked in on him with a razor in his hand, a wild look in his blue eyes.

God.

God.

Or the devil. She'd long ago given up trying to comprehend how the Deity could command loyalty when so many of His creations were left in abject, blameless misery. Only a cruel God could strike down small children with wasting diseases, or make the elderly suffer lonely years waiting for death after the passing of a mate.

She silently gave thanks—again—for her widowed state.

"Have you anything to drink in that basket, Lady Greendale?"

She wanted him to call her Gilly, never that other name.

"Cold tea. Help yourself. You've made fine progress." Far more than she had, but then, he was far stronger.

"I probably traumatized the ones in the ground as much as the ones in your basket." He sat back on his heels and drew his forearm over his brow. At some point, he'd turned back his cuffs and opened the throat of his shirt.

"These are not cuts," she said, running a finger over the skin in the bend of his elbow. He set the jug of cold tea aside, allowing her to trace a series of round, red scars that looked all too familiar.

"Cheroot burns. They hurt like hell but heal fairly quickly."

"That…that…Girard was his name?" She covered the scars with her palm. "He was a devil. You're right to want him dead, but better to make him live with the memory of the crimes he perpetrated."

"Interesting theory, though those particular scars

were courtesy of his ever-helpful superior. Girard considered burns messy, crude, and prone to infection—infection is particularly noisome, according to Girard."

"One hopes he drew that conclusion on the basis of firsthand experience, for burns are also painful, and Girard of all people deserves to suffer."

His Grace looked at her oddly, as if he wanted to smile but didn't dare. "You're very fierce, Countess. Are you also thirsty?"

"No, thank you. How can you explain torture to me in one breath and offer me a drink with the next?"

"Because you might be thirsty. I'm nearly grateful for the scars."

Gilly swiped at her temple with her glove, and succeeded in sprinkling dirt on her bodice. "You talk nonsense, Your Grace."

"I've been demoted to Your Grace again." He sat on his rump, extending one leg and drawing up the other knee. "The scars reassure me I was indeed taken prisoner. I didn't make it all up. When you're the only one to vouch for your memories, they become...suspect."

He was in the strangest mood, and Gilly was so angry at this Girard person, she could nearly countenance a violent end for him. Nearly. Thank God the duke had been able to move beyond such petty reactions.

"Take your shirt off, Mercia."

"I beg your pardon." But he didn't sit up, didn't poker up. "It's a pretty day, why would you want to see me unclothed, Countess?"

As if the weather were deserving of consideration?

"You shall tell me," she said as he lay back and closed his eyes. "You shall tell me about each damned scar and what you recall of it."

"No."

She crawled over to him and began unbuttoning his shirt. "Yes."

"Gilly…" He put a hand over hers. "It's my cross to bear."

As if she'd steal his memories of torment? "And you will bear it, whether you show me this or not. I've seen you. It's just flesh."

She unbuttoned his shirt, expecting him to get to his feet and stride off at any moment. She pushed the shirt aside and frankly stared at the expanse of disfigured flesh before her. Studying it had seemed gauche and thoughtless before.

It felt necessary now.

"Here," she said, tracing her finger over his sternum, which sported a thick welt along its length. "Tell me about this one."

A sigh, which made his chest rise and fall, but still he didn't get up.

"Girard said he'd cut out my heart. He was losing patience that day. It's easy to forget the war went badly for France, too."

Gilly kept moving her fingers over the scar. "What else did he say?"

"He said…" The duke raised his head and met her eyes, his expression disgruntled, or resigned. "He said he'd cut out my heart and feed it to the officers guarding me, my heart being as tough as the meager rations they'd been reduced to. They all had a good laugh over that, while I silently delighted to think Girard had let slip that his garrison was nearly starving."

Gilly did not laugh, nor did His Grace. He paused, stilled her hand over his heart, and then resumed the tale. When the sun was low and the shadows were long, and the duke had swilled most of the cold tea, Gilly helped him get his shirt back on. They folded up the blanket but left the basket for the footmen to bring in, and walked back to the house hand in hand.

Fourteen

CHRISTIAN'S SLEEP WAS SO ROUTINELY UNSETTLED THAT he took a good while to realize he wasn't having the sort of waking nightmare that seemed more real than a dream.

He was *sick*. Heaving-his-guts-up, head-poundingly, bone-achingly sick.

And behind at least one locked door.

The first order of business was to retch into the chamber pot, which was thankfully otherwise empty.

And the second, and the third, until he wasn't bringing up the tea anymore, but suffering dry heaves.

He tried to gain his feet, only to feel the floor tilting. The clock over the mantel read about an hour shy of dark, which led him to recall coming up to change before dinner and succumbing to sleep.

How long had he been unconscious?

He tried again to stand and didn't make it past his knees.

So he crawled.

He'd crawled out of the Château. He didn't dwell on that memory, but he'd been weak and had been tied tightly to the cot. His extremities wouldn't do as he'd bid them, and he'd been desperate to regain his liberty.

The door seemed to recede, but by slow degrees, he closed in on his quarry. The mechanism of the lock was devilishly stubborn, particularly because Christian's hands sported eight and ten fingers apiece as he stared at them. He fell into his sitting room and lay on the floor, swallowing back more dry heaves.

When he could open his eyes, he saw the sitting-room door to the corridor was ajar by a few inches, and he determined he'd shout for help.

He croaked, and the sound of what passed for his voice both scared him and puzzled him. He was afflicted by the notion that because he'd chosen not to speak to another human soul for months, his voice would abandon him when he needed it most.

The fear and fancy in that thought had him mustering his resolve. He organized himself up onto all fours, sat back, and bellowed.

"Gillian!"

She slept across the hall from him—he'd become acutely aware of that lately—in the best of the family bedrooms. They'd argued about it, a room in the family wing as opposed to the guest wing.

"Gillian!"

He would crawl across the room, crawl across the hall...

And then his door flew open, and she pelted into the room in a black dressing gown sporting embroidery that seemed to dance along its hems.

"Your Grace? *Christian?*" She was beside him in a

dizzying instant, the very scent of her easing Christian's suffering. "What's amiss?" Her hands ran over his face. "You're ill. Let me fetch the footmen to get you…"

He shook his head. "No footmen."

"But I can't lift you."

"Help…me." He extended one arm but that destroyed his balance, so he almost fell off his knees.

"Close your eyes," she said. "You're vertiginous, which means perhaps your ears are ailing as well."

With Gilly's aid, he staggered to his feet, then across the bedroom.

"Steps up to the bed," she warned. His arm was across her shoulders, but he was using her to remain upright, not simply to steady his balance. It took two tries, and he ended up falling facedown onto the bed, but he made it.

"You lost the tea you drank outside. This must be some sort of summer influenza."

"Gillian, lock the door."

She sat at his hip, for he'd managed to get himself onto his back.

"Lock the damned door."

The stench of his own vomit was threatening to start him heaving again, and he knew a profound mortification that she should see him thus.

"You want me to lock the door?"

"Nobody else…" He swallowed and felt the room spinning even as he lay flat on his back in a bed that likely hadn't moved for two hundred years. "Poison."

All three of her faces registered the last word. Christian saw that she comprehended what he'd said, and then he promptly lost consciousness.

✑

Gilly refused to let the duke die. For hours, she bathed every inch of him when he was fevered, wrapped him in blankets when he shivered, held the basin while he suffered dry heaves, and let him nigh break the bones of her hand while he cramped and groaned and shook and cursed.

In his lucid intervals, he made her swear not to open the door to anyone, not to allow another to see him in his weakened state. So she sent their excuses down to the kitchen for dinner, locked the door behind her, and prepared to lay siege to his illness.

"I'm not sick," he rasped shortly after midnight. "This is poison, I tell you."

"You aren't fevered anymore," she said, laying the back of one hand against his forehead. "You haven't had the heaves for more than an hour. Whatever it is, it's subsiding."

"Pray God you speak the truth. And don't you dare drink that water."

"I'm thirsty, for feathers' sake!" But she put the glass down without sipping. "What if I fetch the carafe from my room?"

"Did you drink from it earlier?"

"I did," she said, thinking back. "Immediately before you fell ill, and I have no symptoms."

"Then fetch it, but be quick and quiet."

"Dawn is still several hours off, Christian. Who's to see me?" She retied the sash of her night robe and did a tired version of flouncing out of the room, again locking the door behind her.

What if Christian were right, and he'd been

poisoned? What if somebody resented the Lost Duke being found and had taken measures to return him to the land of the dead?

Or what if he'd caught some dread malady while in captivity, and it was only now manifesting?

She hurried across the hall, careful not to wake the footman dozing at his post at the end of the corridor. When she returned to the ducal suite, Christian was sitting up on his bed, wearing only his knee-length drawers.

"Either you're feeling better, or you're in want of a scolding."

"Maybe both." He pushed to his feet, keeping a hand on the bedpost. She remained silent while he doddered along the perimeter of the room to the privacy screen. "I feel like old Wellie marched his entire infantry through my mouth in the middle of high summer."

"You'll want some water." She set the carafe on a vanity that held his shaving kit, hairbrush, comb, and a hand mirror, then left him to his own devices.

"I'll want my tooth powder." At a careful totter, he disappeared behind the screen, leaving Gilly to survey the bed.

"I'm changing your sheets." Something garbled came back that sounded like assent, which was fortunate. The linens needed changing. She opened the French doors leading to his balcony to let in the night breeze, and set the covered chamber pot in the next room.

He emerged from his ablutions looking pale but tidier, his hair caught back in its queue, his face scrubbed. He grabbed one side of the sheet and helped her strip the bed, a skill any public-school boy—or soldier—would have acquired.

"You don't think it was poison," he said.

"I don't know what to think. I was accused of poisoning my late spouse. I would hate to be accused of poisoning you."

He balled up the rumpled sheets and tossed them over the screen while Gilly retrieved fresh ones from the chest at the foot of the bed.

"We eat most of our meals together," she said, unfurling the sheet over the mattress. "You're the only one with symptoms."

"The only one in the entire household?" He caught a corner of the sheet and tucked it under the mattress while Gilly did likewise on the opposite side of the bed.

"Yes, in the entire house, and in the neighborhood, as far as George knew."

"You trust George?"

"He's one of the footmen you set to guarding me, so yes. Moreover, he's a young man who hopes you'll look on him favorably when your house steward retires this fall. I doubt George is trying to do you in."

Across from her, the duke stared at the half-made-up bed as if it were a chessboard and the game well advanced. "Not me. They were trying to do you in."

"Not this again. I'm in fine fettle." And too tired to humor His Grace's queer starts.

"Did we trade oranges today?" He sat and patted the mattress, but a cozy chat was not in the offing.

"I haven't eaten any oranges today." She settled beside him, trying to recall everything she'd eaten or drunk, everything he'd eaten or drunk.

"The tea." They said it at the same time.

"That tea was intended for you," he said. "I chased off the footmen at the last minute on impulse, because I was sick to death of ledgers and I'd missed you."

She looked away, not sure that was a helpful admission under the circumstances.

Under *any* circumstances…

"I guzzled down most of your cold tea. Do you usually consume the whole of it during an afternoon's gardening?"

"Yes, if it's a hot day, like today," Gilly said, feeling abruptly chilled as the plausibility of Christian's conclusion sank in. "You didn't drink it all."

"But you had none, and I had half the jug. I'm nigh twice your weight, Gilly. Someone means for you to die."

He put his arms around her, and she scooted as close to him as she could get.

❧

Having an enemy under Christian's own roof galvanized the military officer in him, and Christian rejoiced to have that part of himself back. For too long, he'd been nothing but a captive, and by God, *by God*, he was ready to fight again.

Revenge was a fine notion to sustain a man while he regained his strength, but engaged battle was the surest sign of a full recovery.

"Whoever means you harm, Gilly, they'll have to

go through me to get to you, and I'm more trouble than they can possibly imagine."

"But who would want me dead? I'm nobody. I'm nothing, a plain little impoverished widow whose best years are behind her." She sounded so bewildered, as if she honestly believed that assessment.

"You are a titled lady, a member of this household, and the woman who wouldn't let me die only hours ago. You also have to be exhausted."

"How can I sleep when you tell me somebody wants me dead?" She rested her forehead against his shoulder, and his rage spiked. She was small, a quiet, diminutive woman who'd known enough grief and misery in her life. Only a fiend would prey on her.

And while Girard was a fiend, he'd had a Gallic gallantry where women were concerned, and no tolerance for soldiers who abused the whores and laundresses.

"You're staying here with me, madam. We both need rest, and I won't be able to close my eyes if you're intent on sleeping elsewhere."

She was apparently so rattled she didn't protest, didn't come at him with eleven reasons why he was wrong, misguided, and a fool. He hurt for her, that she should be so daunted.

"You were right," she said miserably. "You were right about the coach wheel and Damsel's girth. You're right about the tea."

He wished to God he'd been wrong. "There's nothing to be done about it until morning."

"And then?"

"We'll make plans when I'm not recovering from poison, and you're not exhausted from combating its effects on me." And he'd find out where the hell Girard had gone to ground, for despite a back-handed chivalry toward the women at the garrison, who else would have the wits to cause Christian such diabolical mischief?

Gilly sat beside him, staring at her hands folded in her lap, and he wanted to howl. His countess at a loss was a daunting sight. Old Greendale hadn't been able to blight her spirit, but someone else was certainly trying to.

They'd fail spectacularly. He'd make sure of it. "Come to bed."

"I can't." She sat up straighter, a ghost of her spirit manifesting. "The staff will never stop gossiping."

"They never do stop gossiping, but you're a widow. If you want consolation from me in your grief, it's your business, as you yourself reminded me."

"Your tune has changed, Your Grace."

"So has yours. If we're to share a bed, you will please use my name."

She squared her shoulders, a gesture that boded ill for a man who wanted a few hours sleep before join-ing battle in the morning.

Drastic measures were called for, or one of them would soon be in strong hysterics.

"Oh, fine, then," he groused. "Get yourself killed and leave a man to grieve all over again when he's hardly getting his bearings." He sat back against the headboard and folded his arms behind his head. "Leave his only surviving child utterly bereft, cast adrift by a cousin too cavalier to accept the protection lying immediately to hand."

He raised his gaze toward the shadows flickering on the ceiling. "Go ahead and thwart my authority as head of the family, head of the household, *and* the local magistrate."

Gilly crawled across the mattress, which was roughly the dimensions of a foaling stall.

"Leave me to drown in guilt and helpless rage," he went on. "To waste my remaining years in fervent prayer for your immortal and entirely too stubborn and misguided soul. Strong drink will be necessary in quantity, I'm sure, and given the bodily ordeals I've been subjected—"

"Hush." She looped his arm across her shoulders and curled down against him. "I'll stay here for now, but you must hush."

He rolled up on his side, pulled the sheet up over them, kissed her shoulder, anchored his arm around her middle, and hauled her against his body.

And then did as she'd commanded.

❧

Gilly woke to two sensations, the first easy to identify: warmth. She was half on her side, half prone, and Christian lay along her back, a ducal blanket, his leg snugged up to her bottom and insinuated between her calves. His naked, muscular, hairy male leg.

The second impression was harder to classify, and not strictly of the body: she was safe. He held her securely with an arm about her waist, and he'd put himself between her and the door. She faced the windows, faced the pure blackness of that hour between moonset and sunrise, and knew a sense of peace that surpassed anything she'd experienced since her wedding.

And then his hand, his damaged left hand, moved. He shaped her breast gently, and Gilly both felt and heard him sigh. His breath whispered over her nape, and she hoped he'd merely been moving in his sleep, reliving a minor marital pleasure.

Except to her, it wasn't minor.

And they weren't married.

His hand moved again, with more purpose, and more heat spread through Gilly, from low in her belly and between her thighs. She put her hand over his to stop him from further caresses.

"I thought you were awake." His voice was a rumble in the darkness, right behind her ear. "I'll stop if you wish it, Gilly, but only if you wish it. This is where fancying a fellow can lead, for a widow with the courage to indulge her pleasures, and I'm almost sure you do fancy me."

He opened his mouth over that place where her shoulder and neck joined, while Gilly tried to think.

And failed. She wanted him; he desired her as well. They were of age, neither one was married, and he was no longer nattering on about his honor, or hers, or—

He set his teeth on her and scraped a slow slide out to her shoulder. She closed her eyes and savored the feel of Christian holding her close, savored his heat and the strange sensations—part need, part desolation—that must be inchoate desire.

The desire she would examine soon, but first, Gilly gave herself a moment to enjoy the pleasure of revenge.

Greendale might have been a decent husband.

Gilly hadn't been his first wife, he'd been experienced, and he might have relied on that experience to show her consideration.

He'd shown her shame, misery, and mishandling, and now—now—Gilly was in bed with a man who knew how to cherish, how to go slowly, how to *pleasure*. She hoped the knowledge had Greendale spinning in his grave and trying to claw his way out of hell.

Christian shifted, and the loss of him along her back and side was physical and emotional both, and then he was back, nudging her flat onto her back and shifting his weight over hers.

"Spread your legs, love. Make a place for me, or tell me to sleep on the balcony."

"Don't go." She was sure of that much, sure she didn't want to be alone in this big bed, but as for the rest... She was wicked to want it, to want him, but also...right. Right that they join, though he wasn't speaking of marriage.

Nor was she ready to raise the topic with him.

"Stop thinking, my lady." He hitched up on his forearms, so his body caged hers, and evidence of his arousal, hard and warm, lay against her belly.

"I can't..." She couldn't see him, couldn't read his features in the darkness. "Don't rush me."

He might have laughed silently. His belly bounced against hers, they were so very, very close.

"Haste is the last thing on my mind." His lips brushed against her temple, then her eyes, her brows, her chin, and occasionally, as if it were just another feature, her mouth.

"You like this darkness. You like learning me by feel." He would also like having his scars invisible to her, which Gilly understood better than he knew. Feeling very bold indeed, she nuzzled at him until she found his mouth with her own. "I like it too."

She sensed endless patience in him, and so she learned at the age of almost twenty-six how to kiss a lover. Such kisses involved tongues, lips, taste, feel, and soft, needy noises that had her pressing up into his body, into his arousal, and wanting to consume him with her hands and her mouth.

"Now who rushes whom?" he asked.

Was he laughing at her? "If you can manage ducal grammar, I'm doing it wrong, aren't I? I thought so. Tell me then what I must do. I'll do as you ask, as you say."

Please don't leave me.

She hadn't been able to get free of her husband's attentions fast enough, had dreaded the man's every touch, his every visit to her bed. With Christian, she wanted to surrender herself to an eternal night.

"A biddable countess is an alarming prospect," he said, closing his teeth over her earlobe. "Though I'm entirely your slave as well, as it should be in a shared bed. You, for example, might ask me to attend your very sensitive breasts."

He dipped his head and ran his nose over her nipple. Her fingers sank into his hair—she'd long since destroyed his queue.

"You want to take off your nightgown, don't you, Gilly?"

Oh, she did. She wanted to badly, entirely, immediately. He shifted up to straddle her, and between them, the garment was gone, tossed off into the darkness.

"Better, hmm?" He settled down, but lower,

resting his cheek against the slope of her naked breast. "Better for me, but for you too, I think." And then he turned his face and nuzzled her again, but this time without the interference of fabric.

"Mercia...Christian." She arched up, wanting his mouth. Needing it more than she needed her very dignity. "Please."

"I live to bring you pleasure."

Such a declaration ought to have sounded mocking or at least ironic, the sophisticated aside of a man happily at ease with bedsport, but to Gilly, his words rang like a vow. He closed his mouth over her nipple and drew on her with a slow, wet heat, making her back arch and her breath hitch.

"You like that, or am I mistaken?" He rested against her again, his tone pleased.

"It's...almost too much."

"Too pleasurable, or too intimate?"

"What a thing to ask me." She tried to sort the answer out in her mind, except he'd switched breasts, and Gilly felt as if he were drawing the tide of desire up through her body with his mouth. Too pleasurable *and* too intimate, both. Intimate because he knew the havoc he created inside her.

"If you were bored, or perhaps looking for diversion," he said, "you might use your hands on me."

Her hands? Where were...? They rested on his shoulders. She winnowed them back from his temples, indulging a long-suppressed desire to tangle her fingers in the abundance of his hair, not simply brush a hand over it. She caught a rosy scent, but not quite the soap she preferred herself.

"You smell of roses." She brought a silky lock to her nose and caressed his cheek with it.

"To remind me of you." He left off using his tongue on her nipple, and shifted as if he'd similarly torment her belly.

Her belly?

"Where are you going?" She held him motionless by a fistful of hair. "I can't kiss you if you disappear under the sheets."

He stopped, and a considering silence ensued before he shifted again, back up over her. "Your wish is my most sincere desire."

Holy, everlasting *feathers*, the man must be unloosing on her a year's worth of very skilled kisses. His tongue flirted, teased, appeased, and flirted again. He tasted her, he coaxed her into exploring his mouth, he offered her his tongue and she took it, and all the while, Gilly grew more and more tense, more needy.

"Your…Christian…" She wrapped her legs around his flanks. He let out a groan, mostly humor and something else that suggested his patience was at least tried, though by no means exhausted.

He braced an arm under Gilly's neck, which left him a hand free to torment her breasts. If his mouth was skilled, his fingers ought to be declared illegal by act of Parliament.

"You have to tell me if you want more," he said, his mouth near her ear. "Tell me, Gilly."

She nodded against the pillow, arched her back to thrust her breast into his hand, and realized the wretch wanted to hear her speak the words, too. "I want…"

"You want me? You want what all this entails?"

He flexed his spine, and the rigid length of his cock slid over the top of her sex, and up her belly, then subsided.

"I want you," she said, trying to turn his head with her hands so she could get her mouth back on his.

"You shall have me then."

He was a cavalry officer, Gilly reminded herself. He understood strategy, and he was applying it. His hand shaped her breast, not quite as gently, and his touch made her desire leap. His fingers knew how much more was perfect, his kisses grew hotter, wetter, and even Gilly's sense of balance threatened to abandon her.

"Christian...Christian...please. I don't know how..."

"I know," he said. "Trust me, Gilly. Do you trust me?" He moved again, his cock sliding over her sex, gliding wetly up, then down. She strained against him, frustrated and gratified and more frustrated still.

"You have to tell me, Gilly. Say yes."

"Y-yes..."

Above her, he slowed, his thrusts became languid, and Gilly wanted to scream and pound on his back with her fists.

"You're saying yes," he whispered. "Yes, Christian."

"Yes, Christian, but please God, *now*."

She tried to flex her hips when he retreated, to change the angle so he'd cease this maddening *rubbing* and join their bodies. That had to be what she sought, though there was no way to know anything for certain, not when she was so befuddled and overwrought.

"Oh, sweet, merciful feathers...*Christian*."

He came into her body slowly, and she was glad

now for the dampness easing his way, because his proportions challenged her to the point of near-pain.

"Relax, love. Take a breath, let it out. I won't move until I feel you relax."

But she wanted him to move, needed him to. She did as he bid, breathing in, then slowly easing the breath from her body.

"Again."

He remained exactly as he was, poised above her, but his hand brushed a caress over her brow, then came to rest around the back of her head so her face was cradled against his shoulder. He did it again, more slowly, and the sheer *tenderness* of his touch had Gilly sighing.

He pushed in deeper, and she sighed again until he set up a shallow rhythm.

"You can move with me, or not. I'll last longer if you don't, but not much."

She wanted to ask what he meant, but he'd settled his mouth over hers, his kisses again lazy, and then… not so lazy.

Something in Gilly's vitals began to hum, to heat up and spread out and take over her limbs and her mind. She lifted up to meet his thrusts, and tried to grip him when he'd recede from her.

"Ye gods…" he whispered against her neck. "Just holy… Ah, Gilly."

His tempo picked up, but more than that, he stopped being so delicate with her, and Gilly's body began to sing.

"More." She meant to whisper in his ear, but the single word must have conveyed desperation, because Christian cast off any semblance of politesse and possessed her in fierce, carnal abandon.

She came undone, utterly, completely, unexpectedly. Somewhere between *what on earth* and *oh, God, Christian* Gilly's body became a ravening, mindless creature of pleasure, surprise, and more and more pleasure. She keened into his neck, clung, shook, clawed at him, and started all over again when she felt the damp heat of his seed deep inside her body.

When the storm passed, he went back to petting her hair, and she experienced for the first time the postcoital intimacy of breathing in counterpoint to a lover.

"I had no idea," she said, smoothing his hair back. "No earthly clue…"

"Ah, Gilly. You unman me all over again."

He shifted to his side and pulled her into his arms, which caused his cock to slip from her body, and the sensation brought her pleasure, even as Gilly endured a sense of loss at Christian's absence.

"Shall you weep now?" He held her close, his chin on her temple, and the very snugness of his embrace was reason enough to weep.

"Is it expected?"

"How does a man answer such a thing? From what I recall of my distant, misspent youth—you will note my tact—some women do, some of the time. I understand it now better than I used to."

"You want to weep?" She cuddled closer, listening for his heartbeat. She couldn't see anything of his expression in the dark, but she was newly wise to the nuances of his words and to the ability of her body to listen to his.

"Maybe I will weep a little, for joy." He reached away from her. "Spread your legs." She lifted a leg, awkwardly, and he tucked a flannel against her sex.

"Lest my seed be so rude as to leave your body and mess the clean sheets, when it might be about putting my babe in your belly."

He rubbed at himself with another cloth, and Gilly marveled that she should feel no lapse of dignity between them.

"You would weep for joy," she said, nuzzling his chest with her cheek. "One understands this."

"Does one?" His tone was dry, indulgent too. "You can't possibly. Give me your hand."

He took her hand, removed it from where she was caressing his chest, and put it over his softening length.

"Do you feel anything different, Gilly?"

"Of course it's different. Men don't stay...aroused but for a few moments, and then...it's supposed to be like this, isn't it?"

Had Greendale lied to her? He'd filled her head with all manner of nasty comments, but she'd regarded those as his opinions, to which he was entitled. He'd had his opinions regarding marital relations, too, but in those, she'd been so terribly at his mercy.

"I'm supposed to be soft, yes," he said, kissing her brow, "because I am so thoroughly satisfied, but here..." He brought her fingers to the end of his shaft. "I have no foreskin."

This was of some moment to him, she sensed that, but Gilly hardly knew what she was supposed to say. She wouldn't have known if he'd had three foreskins, whatever a foreskin was.

"Your functioning doesn't seem impaired. You were..."

"Yes?"

"A revelation, Christian. You were a wonderful revelation to me."

He was silent while she explored him in the darkness, traced his length, shaped his stones and sifted through the nest of hair at the base of his shaft. His hand fell away, and he lay quietly while she learned him, until he grew aroused again.

"Was it the French?" She asked the question now, while she still could, while it was pitch dark and she could plead she didn't know any better, though she'd known the answer the moment she'd conceived the question.

"Yes. The French."

She moved over him, straddled him and curled down onto his chest as if she'd protect him bodily from the memories. He framed her face and held her still while he kissed her, and then he nudged at her sex with his cock.

"I can touch you like this," she said, tracing her fingernails over his nipples. He drew in an audible breath, then settled a palm over each of her breasts.

"And I can touch you."

They teased each other in lazy wonder, until Christian went still beneath her. "Gilly?"

"Hmm?" She let him find her then, let him ease that first glorious, sweet, tantalizing inch into her body.

"You are a revelation to me too."

Fifteen

His Gilly counterpointed passion with a touch-ing modesty. She had her nightgown back on before Christian had finished using the tooth powder, even as the first gray lights of dawn stole around the curtains.

"I should get back to my own bedchamber," she said, shrugging into her black dressing gown, which sported more fantastical embroidery than Christian had seen on any one garment.

He picked up a sleeve and peered at the green, gold, and purple patterns chasing around the cuff. "Does this qualify as mourning attire?"

She belted it snugly. "It's black, and who's to see me?"

He put his hands on her shoulders, and she waited while he lifted her hair out of her nightclothes. "I've destroyed your braid, Countess."

"And you're proud of this," she said, sounding proud too, as well she should.

"Sit you," he said, guiding her by the shoulders to the chest at the foot of the bed. "We need to talk."

Her expression went carefully blank, and he had to wonder what was going through her female brain.

"We'll have the first of the banns cried this Sunday," he said, hoping to allay any silly doubts she entertained.

She shot to her feet so fast she nearly knocked him on his arse. "*We* will do no such thing."

She turned around to glare at him, her arms crossed over her chest, her hair streaming down her back like some Valkyrie of old, but diminutive, and all the more formidable because of it.

"What did you think I was asking you, not two hours ago under the covers, Gilly?"

"I thought you were asking to bed me, of course." Her jaw snapped shut, and he saw he had blundered. She wasn't angry, she was *hurt*. He could not stand the thought he'd hurt her, not over something as important to a woman as this.

He got down on one knee and took her hand in both of his.

"Gillian, Lady Greendale, my countess and friend, will you do me the very great honor of becoming my duchess?"

That ought to do it. He stayed genuflected before her in his dressing gown, feeling ridiculous as he waited for her soft, special smile.

She scowled, the sight of it enough to curse him with a brand of uncertainty he hadn't felt since the last time Anduvoir had come sauntering into his cell, the stench of his cigar preceding him.

"What do you take me for, Mercia? Get up, and we'll have a rational argument, which you will lose."

He rose, careful not to let his bewilderment show, though referring to him as Mercia was a discouraging sign. "At least have a seat while we argue."

She sat upon the carved chest with all the dignity of the aging queen, and swished the skirts of her night rail closed over her knees.

"You think to keep me safe by offering marriage. That is entirely unnecessary, though gallant of you." Her weapon of choice was logic, which boded ill in a woman just come from her new lover's bed.

"I can keep you safe more easily if we're married. That isn't why I offered." A disconcerting realization, that.

"Guilty conscience then, or grief, or male urges. Thank you, but no. Marriage to me on that basis will not do."

"Will not do for me?" He sought refuge by rummaging in the wardrobe, though he had an entire dressing room in which he might have hidden— except he didn't want to give her a chance to bolt.

"Of course not. I was married to Greendale for eight years, Your Grace, and I could not bear him a child. You need heirs, and I cannot provide them, though I am sorry to have to bring up such a tender subject."

This was a feint, a not quite convincing one. Christian discarded a pair of silk stockings necessary for court attire, searching instead for the wool variety he'd been happy to own in quantity in Spain.

"I've done some nosing about," he said, when he'd laid hands on a clean pair of stockings. "Greendale had had four countesses, each of them coming to the marriage in the blush of young womanhood, and none of them conceived. I have no doubt where the blame lies for a lack of direct descendants."

He knelt before her and brushed her night robe aside to reveal her bare, elegant feet.

"The present Lord Greendale is my heir," Christian said. "And some second or third cousins in Dorset or Hampshire after that, jolly squires grown fat off their sheep. We correspond twice a year. I need not marry a broodmare out of duty."

"But you ought," she wailed softly. "You are Mercia, and the next duke should be raised by you. Where did you learn to do this?"

"Argue with you? Natural talent, I suppose."

Her lips quirked up before compressing into a severe line. "Where did you learn to put stockings on a lady's feet?"

"Early in the marriage, I used to put my stockings on Helene's feet, lest she catch her death. She had perpetually cold hands and feet." Also a cold nose, of all things. The recollection pleased him, for only a noticing husband would have perceived it.

"I cannot marry you now. I'm still in mourning."

This approached clutching at straws, and included the gratifying qualification that she could not marry Christian *now*. "You loathed the old besom."

"I owe my own reputation proper decorum, nonetheless."

"So marry me this time next year," he said. "We'll get a start on the intimacies betimes, and we're already perfecting our ability to disagree civilly." He tucked the other sock onto her second foot and remained kneeling before her, lest she go haring off clear to Greendale.

She twitched the collar of his dressing gown then smoothed it flat. "What we did in this bed was ill-advised, though I cannot regret it."

"Ill-advised?" He did not like that term. He very much liked her lack of regret.

"Imprudent. Below stairs, there will be talk."

"I was ill," he said. "Were you to allow me to die or to suffer mortal agonies when you are the logical source of care for me?"

"Why me?"

"You are a widow, and you nursed your ailing husband for weeks before he succumbed. You were here when Evan fell ill. Who else would know as much as you about caring for an invalid?"

She closed her eyes, as if seeking patience. "I must return to my room."

Retreat, which suggested he'd routed her, albeit temporarily. "In a moment."

He kissed her, tasting surprise, curiosity, and capitulation in her return fire. Time to put his guns down, or at least pause to reload.

"I have surprised you with my proposal," he said, his forehead leaning on hers. He'd surprised her with his ardor, and she'd more than surprised him. "I'm sorry you feel ambushed. Badly done of me. I want to marry you, Gilly, but you have a point: we've some matters to sort out that rather take precedence over setting a date."

"I have *not* said—"

He kissed her again, but she was on to his tricks and merely endured the visit of his mouth upon hers.

"You needn't *say*. Greendale was an awful old curmudgeon, I understand that. So you take your time, look me over thoroughly. Count my teeth, put me through my paces."

Her hand smoothed his hair back. "You're not a horse."

"I'm a horse's arse. You were harried into marriage once before, and that ended badly. Am I right?"

She shifted so her forehead rested on his shoulder, and Christian scooted in closer, as if he'd protect her from her own past.

"Yes. Too right. One day I was memorizing my fifth declension nouns, and the next, my mama was taking me shopping for a trousseau. When I met Greendale, I had to excuse myself with a megrim so I could sit in the carriage and cry all the way home. He was on his best, most jovial behavior when courting me. He did not improve with time."

"I will. I'll bring you more puppies, I'll read poetry to you, even that stupid Blake, and I'll—"

She lifted away, but the fight had gone out of her. "Groveling becomes you ill, Mercia."

"I've amused you. Your smile is worth the affront to my dignity." What little dignity he still had. Christian traced her hair back from her face. "You won't run off? Somebody means you harm, my dear. I would much rather you stay here and castigate me for my impetuous ardor. If you leave…"

He'd come after her and fetch her home. He didn't say that, because it smacked of taking her captive, which he could not do.

"I care for you," she said, the words a grudging admission. "I did not choose my first husband well, and in that you're right. I will not be rushed into marriage again."

He waited, because she wasn't finished, and because

talking like this was something he and Helene had never learned to do, a realization that in itself gave him regret and…hope.

"I'm sorry. I did not mean to rush you." He'd meant to marry her, though, and still did.

"I also…" She gathered her dressing gown at the throat and glanced over at the window, where another lovely summer day was gaining its wings. "I don't want to take advantage of you."

"Of *me*? I'm a duke, I'm wealthy, I'm twenty-seventh in line for the damned throne, I'm—"

She put soft, rose-scented fingers to his lips, the ghost of a smile playing around her mouth.

"So modest, Mercia." The smile faded, and her hand cradled his jaw. "You are grieving so much, healing from so much, and your instinct to protect overwhelms your sense. I will remain at Severn, and we will talk later of marriage."

She urged him against her so he could pillow his cheek on the silk covering her thigh. Yes, his protective instincts had overwhelmed his sense, and so they would continue to do until he'd identified her malefactor.

As her hands settled in his hair, another insight struck: Gilly's protective instincts had overwhelmed *her* too, and when Christian had those instincts of hers settled down, he'd make the lady his next duchess.

⤢

Gilly had spent the night in Christian's bed and slept wonderfully, despite the events of the previous day, and now she was…

She ran her hands over the soft abundance of his unbound hair.

Now she was so befuddled, by passion, by fatigue, by fear, by *him*. Christian nestled against her, knelt at her feet like a tired child, and he was no doubt fatigued, but he was also canny as hell.

"Perhaps you should send me away."

He raised his head up, his hair in disarray from her attentions. "Perhaps I should take you away."

"Where would we go?" She should not have asked that question. If she went away with him, she'd have no choice but to marry him.

"I have property in a dozen counties. You choose." He rose and took her hand to assist her to her feet, then stood frowning down at her in the gathering morning light. "After our first night of loving, I don't want to part from you."

Their first, because he was confident they'd share others, and so—may heaven help her—was Gilly.

"I'm traveling clear across the hallway, Your Grace."

He smiled crookedly at her form of address and put one of his hands on each of her shoulders.

"For last night, thank you, my lady. I wasn't…" He tucked her closer, and Gilly allowed it because some things need not be said staring a woman directly in the eye.

And he'd already delivered her a lengthy lecture about the poison, and not eating or drinking anything unless he was with her.

"You doubted yourself," Gilly said. "Doubted your manhood over that business with the French and their perishing knives, may they rot in hell."

Along with Greendale. Gilly hadn't thought she could *be* any more enraged at her late spouse, but the morning brought that revelation too.

"I doubted myself, yes." Christian brought her fingers to his lips. "I have doubted myself for months, but a man doesn't sort out such things easily on his own."

"You're sorted out now," she said, smiling up at him, because this, too, was a scar they shared. "I am a bit sorted out as well."

Not entirely, of course. She might never be entirely sorted out. She'd been married to Greendale for 3,147 nights—she'd done the math the day he'd died—and each one had been awful.

No wonder she was hesitant to accept Christian's proposal, even though every single particle of her heart, mind, soul, and strength craved to become his wife.

❧

In the days that followed, Gilly felt as if her true grieving were getting under way. Christian came to her room each night, scooped her up, and bore her away to his bed. At first, he was careful with her, his attentions always tender and sweet and limited to one coupling per night. By degrees, he became bolder.

Gilly had the sense it wasn't his confidence that was increasing, it was hers.

And therein lay some of the grief. As Greendale's wife, she'd quickly grasped that her marriage was a sad caricature of what a marriage should be. With Christian's example to compare it to, though, she realized her marriage hadn't been merely sad.

Her union with Greendale had been tragic, a murder of a marriage. Thank God that Christian was a man who understood the futility of violence in any form.

May-December pairings were common enough, particularly among titled men who had the wealth and position to take their pick of the debutantes on the market each year. Gilly had known some of those couples among Greendale's cronies, and even their marriages could be characterized by affection and respect.

She'd never been more relieved than when Theo Martin had told her Greendale was unlikely to recover. Her husband had taught her how to hate, how to loathe and abhor another human being. How to endure a nightmare with a fixed smile.

With Christian, she was learning how to cherish and esteem, and no matter how she chided him for his presumption or made noises each morning about him overstepping, each night, she clung to him and gave him her body and another piece of her heart.

"You're quiet," Christian said. How long he'd been standing in the doorway to her sitting room, she did not know. "You've made this place your own nest. I like it."

He liked her, and Christian Severn's liking was a precious rarity.

Gilly had appropriated pillowcases and slipcovers from her trousseau, such that embroidered flowers and designs from her wildest imagination were creeping over the couches and chairs.

"You'll be after my curtains next," he said. "And you've started Lucy on this habit of decorating every fabric in sight."

"Greendale allowed it," she said. "He thought a woman with her head bowed over her hoop was a pleasing sight." To take what her late husband had permitted and make it an excess had been a form of revenge.

Sharing herself with Christian was more of that same revenge, at least in part, and Gilly hated herself for that.

Christian crossed his arms.

She rose and drew him forward by the wrist. "Whatever it is, say it."

"I'd prefer you were bowed over my sated and prostrate form." He pulled the door shut behind him and let her tug him into the room.

"We shall not be indiscreet here in the broad light of day," she said, but she'd left a question in the words when she'd intended a stern admonition.

He smiled down at her. "Someday, Gillian, I will have you writhing and moaning in the broad light of day. Outdoors even."

"You'd get leaves in my hair." She could afford the humor, because he was behaving.

"Among other places, but then I'd help you remove them."

"You are so naughty."

"Do you mind?" He kissed her ear and rested his chin on her crown.

"You cannot spend your entire day seeing to my safety. I ought to leave," she said, genuinely sorry to bring this up again when his mood was so winsome.

"Not without me. We've had no word of the girl who prepared your lunch basket with the poisoned tea, and inquiries at the Lion and Cock yield only the information that she began to work there last winter and hailed from the West Riding."

"If she could get to my food, anybody can." Or they could get to his.

"No, they can't." His eyes were very sober, his hands on her shoulders steady. "I've sent everybody from the house staff whom I can't vouch for personally off to visit family, which is common enough between haying and harvest. Your footmen or I attend you wherever you go, and the entire staff has been warned to watch for strangers."

"They've been…protective," Gilly said. "Discreet, but protective."

"You're surprised?"

"I left my slippers in your bedroom that first night."

"So?"

The great lout was genuinely perplexed. "Below stairs, they know."

"That we share a bed? If you say so."

"I don't like that they know." She hated that they knew, hated that they might think her guilty of every weak, wanton behavior Greendale had accused her of.

Christian's gaze narrowed, more closely approximating the ducal sphinx Gilly had barged in on weeks ago in London. "Will you pretend you don't like what we do?"

She would have moved out from under his hands, but he only let her turn, and wrapped his arms around her from behind. "The question is sincere, my lady. I would not for the world impose on you."

The wretch, saying such things out loud.

"I like what we do."

"Then is it me? Perhaps you'd rather disport with a different partner?"

And behind the arrogance of the question, Gilly heard a hint, a well-hidden, ducally disregarded hint of vulnerability. She turned in his arms and pressed her face against his chest. She had licked, kissed, and nuzzled her way over most of this chest and had found it delicious.

"I will never disport thus with another. I promise myself every morning I will not disport thus with *you* again, at least not until matters are settled between us."

His hold on her loosened. "I do not understand your dilemma. I have determined you need time to sort it out yourself, and this sits ill with me, but as a measure of my regard for you, I do not force the matter."

"Oh, no, you do not force the argument, you merely—"

"Yes?" He slipped his hands down and cupped her bottom, which meant she took notice of his male flesh growing hard between them.

"Even arguing arouses you."

"Everything about you arouses me." And oh, he sounded so smug, so pleased. "Though sometimes to protectiveness or humor or admiration in addition to desire."

"Lust, simple lust from too many months soldiering."

"You are an intelligent woman," he said, the smugness turning to perplexity. "Frightfully so, in fact. Why do you delude yourself with such patent tripe?"

"Stop." He was about to launch into his I-care-for-you/Greendale-is-holding-your-future-hostage speech, one he'd come up with by their second night together. "None of your campaigning. It's entirely possible I have brought danger to your household, and marrying me is the last thing you should do."

He enfolded her in his arms, using his most devastating tactic, meeting her protestations and common sense with this endless, boundless, *silent* affection. He was affectionate in and out of bed, as if all those months in France he'd been storing up a need to touch, to tease, to be tender, and now it poured out of him at the sight of her. His affection dizzied her and broke her heart and made untangling her wants from his best interests so much harder.

"You are not safe on your own," he said. "Lucy needs you, and I need you. Recite your reasons and arguments, Gilly, but please don't go. Before I'll let you leave me, I will take myself off, though I will despise doing it. In my absence, the staff will watch your every move and taste everything you eat or drink before you touch it."

"I am not banishing the Duke of Mercia from his own family seat."

"Not yet," he said, though his tone suggested he was willing to be banished if it would please her. "Now let us put aside this bickering you insist on. The morning is advanced, and Lucy will be wroth if we neglect her."

Gilly conceded the point, because she did bicker, and the contention reassured her of her position for form's sake, but it did nothing to put her resolve into action.

Each night, she grew closer to Christian; each night he asked for and won more of her trust until Gilly herself had to admit that her reservations were crumbling and her fate becoming inevitable—provided she had the courage to seize it.

❧

They'd had their argument for the morning, which brought the total for the day to two, because they must also have an argument upon rising, sometimes even while Christian was making love to his Gilly.

Delicate and spicy business that, arguing with a woman while plundering her treasures. It left Christian off balance, and yet Gilly was passion itself in his arms.

Another tiff would ensue over tea, and the end of the day would include sleepy mutterings. And all the while, Gilly stole his heart, tied him in knots, and tossed his most tender sentiments aside so she could find her benighted embroidery hoop.

In some peculiar way, sparring with her and making love with her both honed the craving for revenge Christian nursed to more thriving health by the day. Odd, that loving a woman and pursuing violent resolution of the threats to a shared future with her should entwine thus.

"Your girth is repaired," Christian said as he and his lady reached the second-floor landing. "We might go for another ride one of these fine summer days."

"Autumn will soon be here. Will you go up to Town for the next session of the Lords?"

Ghastly thought, though his letters had finally yielded some interesting rumors regarding the whereabouts of one Robert Girard, weasel at large.

Half-English weasel, of all things, and successor to a baronial title, which was doomed, alas, to die out with him. Prinny would likely even shed a tear or two before seizing the weasel's assets.

Did Girard have any vestiges of Englishness left that could regret the lapse of a title? Christian shied off the notion, for such sentiments would give him something in common with his tormentor—his soon to be late tormenter.

"Would you like me to take you and Lucy up to Town?" Not that he'd allow his womenfolk anywhere near Girard or his reported whereabouts.

Gilly marched up the stairs toward the third floor. "Lucy might enjoy such a visit, for she needs her papa, but you need not drag me up there."

"You don't think the Town staff as loyal as the Severn staff?" Christian asked as he followed. "You don't think I will need a hostess in Town? You have to know anybody in my employ who disparages you will be turned off without a character."

She paused at the top of the steps, her skirts swishing about her half boots. "If somebody repeats the truth, they aren't disparaging my character."

"I weary of this topic, Gillian. You will either make an honest duke of me and accept my suit or content yourself with my affections on terms more acceptable to you. Those are your options, my lady."

She fell silent, her eyes pained despite her serene expression. His next tactics were reconnaissance and subterfuge—the distasteful and ungentlemanly business of spying—to determine what, exactly, made marriage to him so repugnant to her.

He stopped her headlong march in the middle of the empty third-floor corridor.

"Do you fear I would treat you as Greendale did? Deny you the gardens, expect you to embroider my stockings, head bent by the hour?"

"You're weary of the topic, if you'll recall." She fired off that retort, and he let her, because his question had been at least close to the mark. Gilly's marriage had left her afraid, though of exactly whom and what, Christian could not fathom—yet.

He was loath to admit his instincts as an interrogator owed something to Girard's example.

Six steps in the direction of the nursery suite, Gilly stopped again abruptly.

"What?"

She put a finger to her lips, and Christian fell silent. A sound drifted down the corridor, one he hadn't heard for some time: a child singing.

"That's Lucy," Gilly said, steps quickening. "Oh, thank God, that's our Lucy, and if she can sing, she can..."

Our Lucy. And she was his Gilly, whether she knew it or not. Christian gently hauled her back by the wrist. "The child will fall silent as soon as she senses we're here."

"You can't be sure of that," Gilly said, wrenching from his grasp.

"She talks in her sleep."

They conducted this exchange in fierce whispers. "How do you know that?"

Gilly had her routine for the end of the day, and he had his. A patrol of the garrison, so to speak. Before she could argue with him further, Christian addressed her again, loudly enough to be heard in all directions.

"You may not embroider my handkerchiefs with

flowers, Countess. Anything other than the family crest or my initials would be unfitting to the dignity of a duke."

The singing stopped, and Gilly's eyes, so full of hope, filled with tears.

"None of that," he said softly. "She can't know we were eavesdropping. Argue with me, Gilly. You excel at it."

She blinked back the tears and stood inches taller. "I will decorate where I please, as I please, Your Grace. Even my own papa allowed embroidery on his handkerchiefs, and he was every bit as high in the instep as you."

"I'm not high in the instep, I'm a duke. You will note the difference."

"And being a duke is somehow the better of the two?"

He winked at her and let the question go unanswered as they reached the nursery door.

"Good day, Harris," he said. "Is Lucy free to entertain callers?"

"She finished her sums early today, Your Grace. You should have passed her. She's down the corridor, in the small playroom with the dogs."

"Countess, you'll join me?" He winged his arm at Gilly, and she took it. When they were alone, she hissed and arched her back, and spat and carried on verbally, but she never under any circumstances denied him the opportunity to touch her, and for that, among many other traits, he treasured her.

"Good day, Lucy." Christian bowed to his daughter to make her smile and saw the countess suck in a breath. Gilly wanted to force the issue of the singing, and he didn't blame her. "Shall you stroll with us in the garden, Lucy, and bring those two reprobates whom you have ensorcelled here in your tower?"

Her brows twitched down.

Gillian took Lucy's hand. "He means you charm those dogs into doing your bidding when they ignore everybody else."

Lucy's smile grew broader.

"I know," Christian said, taking her other hand. "You play with them, and thus are endeared to them. I donate my favorite pair of slippers to their evil ends, and yet they ignore me unless I threaten them with death by rolled-up newspaper."

He went on in that fashion, teasing, grousing, being more papa than duke, because the gruffness was needed to keep Gilly from bawling, and the teasing was needed to charm his daughter.

And both—Gilly and Lucy—were somehow becoming necessary to him if his life was to have any meaning at all. That he would have to leave them for a time to dispatch Girard did not sit well, particularly not with Gilly having so nearly come to harm.

And yet, Girard—canny bastard—was likely the author of that harm, intending that it force a reckoning between them.

He and Gilly played with Lucy and the dogs, visited the stables, and returned the child to her nursery. The afternoon stretched before them long and lazy, and Christian spun mental strategies about how he'd put the hours to their best use with his countess.

"I am a trifle fatigued," she said, and Christian's mood improved to hear it.

"You haven't been sleeping well of late. I delight in comforting you in your restless slumbers."

"Maybe you're the cause of my restless slumbers."

"You don't like it when I rub your back, Countess? When I make those circles on your nape, slower and slower until the arms of Morpheus beckon?" *He* delighted in that ritual, for it relaxed him and pleased him to be of service to her.

She kept her powder dry until they were approaching the house. "I really do need a nap, Christian."

Christian. Her version of wheedling, and damnably effective. "Then so do I."

"No, you do not. You need to ride out. You've foregone that pleasure to tarry with me for the past few mornings, and dear Chessie will pine for you."

"The way he pined while I was in the hands of the French? The brute was eating out of Easterbrook's hand by the time I stumbled back to life."

The observation held genuine annoyance, because the familiar mental tickle was back. Something to do with the horse.

"I'm sure in his way, Chesterton was praying for your safe return. Now, shoo."

"I'll walk you upstairs, Gilly."

She huffed out a breath. "Christian…"

Even in that sniffy, huffy tone, he loved to hear her say his name. "Either you take my arm, or it's George and John."

She took his arm, and they progressed through the house in silence. When they reached her door, she tried to close the thing in his face, but he slipped through and turned her by the shoulders.

"None of that," she said.

"You are ever eager to relieve me of my clothes, Gilly, but you've yet to allow me the same pleasure."

"And I'm not about to allow it now."

"So modest." He wrapped his arms around her from behind, because when they were married, surely, she'd trust him with her nudity. "Will you dream of me?"

"I cannot know such a thing."

"I *know* you have nightmares."

She walked out of his embrace and sat at her vanity, removing pins from her hair as if they—or something—had been irritating her.

"I know," he went on, letting her put some distance between them. "I have them too, and you soothe and comfort me. I'm aware of your kindnesses, Gilly. I'm grateful for them."

"You say I have nightmares too."

He watched her, watched the nervous twitching of her fingers, and knew he was probing close to her wounds. "Your nightmares pass. I hold you, speak a few words, and you become quiet."

"I don't…" She regarded herself in the mirror, her expression wary as a thick blond braid came unraveled down her back. "I don't talk in my sleep?"

"You do not." Though if she did, it would clearly bother her tremendously. "But you know, Gilly, if you have some dire secret, I would keep it for you. If you put a period to old Greendale's existence, the man would probably thank you himself were he able. From what I've gleaned, at the end, he wasn't able to chew his food or tend to his bodily functions. An old codger like that would likely rather be dead than so helpless."

He kept his eyes on her, watching for any sign he'd guessed a truth.

His Gilly, taking another life? He could not picture it, not even in kindness, not even if Greendale had ordered her to do it. She'd probably object to Christian exterminating even the likes of Girard.

The thought gave him pause—uncomfortable pause.

Gilly twitched a few more pins from her hair. "You wouldn't be nervous to think I killed my husband? Wouldn't retract your proposal lest you end up in the family plot? You'd endorse such violence despite all biblical admonitions to the contrary?"

"Gilly…" He shifted to stand behind her and put his hands on her shoulders, which revealed her to be as tense as a fiddle string. He spoke quietly near her ear.

"In France, I went a little mad, sometimes more than a little. I sustained myself on fantasies of the havoc I could wreak when I got free, the blood I would spill, the tortures I would devise for Girard and his corporals and lieutenants and superiors."

"They wanted you driven mad." She kissed his forearm where it lay along her collarbone. "They did not succeed."

"Of course they did. I saw things that weren't there, Gilly. I had no idea if I was dreaming or waking most days. I prayed to any god who might hear me." He dropped his voice even more. "I tamed the mice so I wasn't so alone in my cell. I pretended they brought me news. I named them. We had conversations, the mice and I. Sometimes when I was sure I was alone in the darkness, I whispered to them."

He dropped his forehead to her nape, the nape he loved to stroke and kiss.

"You befriended the mice, so you forgive me the murder of my husband?"

"It isn't for me to forgive or judge or anything," he said, relieved she wasn't questioning him about the mice. "It's for me to protect you, cherish you, and keep your confidences."

As she protected him, cherished him, and kept his confidences—kept his very heart.

She had no immediate reply, so he held her, his body bowed over hers, while common everyday English sunshine beamed in the windows and a pleasant summer breeze fluttered the lacy curtains.

"Find out who owns that château now," she said, laying her cheek on his arm.

"In God's name why?"

"So you can blow the damned thing up and erect a monument to old Wellie on the site, or to good King George, *or to the mice.*"

"And you wonder why I must make you my duchess."

Sixteen

GILLY WAS LOSING GROUND TO CHRISTIAN DAILY, nightly. No matter how she picked fights, argued, resisted, and flounced off, Christian showed her tolerance she didn't deserve. He'd learned this endless forbearance in France—from that dratted Girard fellow—when Gilly's dithering should have turned him into a violent lunatic.

Thank a merciful deity, it had not. She could not have fallen in love with another man prone to violence.

Her courses arrived, and she was honestly grateful—though a failure to conceive gave her no cause for rejoicing. She'd hoped an indisposed female might be unattractive to Christian, but no. He brought her to his bed, the same as any other night.

"Put me down," she said before he'd left her bedroom. "I am indisposed."

"By ill humor? This is no impediment to what I have planned for you. For us."

"Christian, no."

He peered down at her, looking so dear, so

bewildered and ducal at the same time, she took pity on him. "I am…enduring a feminine indisposition."

"For pity's sake…" He sat with her on her bed. "No wonder you've been such a shrew lately. Poor lamb." He kissed her temple, and she wanted to smack him.

"I have not been a shrew."

"No, dearest." He kissed her again, trying not to smile. "Of course you haven't."

She turned her face to his shoulder. "I am not your dearest."

"That is rather for me to say. Are you uncomfortable?"

"You are incorrigible."

"Also very understanding of female complaints." He picked her up and headed for the door. "Will you need anything in particular? A tot of the poppy?"

"I refuse to answer such questions." Her face was flaming, but she should have known he'd be like this: forthright, concerned for her, cheerfully willing to demolish anything between them as inconsequential as her privacy or her dignity.

She'd developed the habit of looking forward to her courses because it meant a week free of her husband's company. He'd called it a filthy female tendency, a noisome blight resulting from a woman's failure to conceive and submit to her God-given duty.

How she had treasured the filthy, noisome blight for eight years.

"Seriously, love." Christian bumped his bedroom door closed with his hip. "You must tell me if you're uncomfortable." He set her on the bed and crossed the room to lock the door, disappearing momentarily to lock the sitting-room door as well. He came back and set his hands on his hips, studying her.

"Are you concerned you'll be untidy on the ducal sheets?"

"*Must* you?"

"My father warned me about this," he said, advancing on her. "He said women need special understanding at such a time, for they fall prey to odd notions."

"*Women* get odd notions? You steal me from my bed every night, provoke me to nightmares, and you say women get odd notions?"

"I return you to where you belong," he said, prowling up to the bed. "To where you want to be, and yes, women get odd notions. You fret that you're unlovely now."

She had to look away. Some misguided female had admitted such a thing to him; he had no other way of gaining such an insight, though Helene would not have had the courage to express such a vulnerable sentiment.

"You resent the untidiness and wish you were coping with a pregnancy instead," he went on, sympathy in every syllable. "Carrying a child, for all it leaves you ungainly and puts your life in danger, seems to agree with you ladies. Many of my comrades in arms remarked such a thing."

"You talked about childbearing as you waged war?"

He wasn't to be diverted. He untied the bows of her dressing gown.

"Scoot over to your side of the bed," he said, peeling her out of her robe. "When you are indisposed, comforting you is my privilege."

He tossed his dressing gown to the foot of the bed, and, of course, he would comfort her while he wore not one stitch, the way he usually slept. That he would trust her so easily with the sight of his nudity still moved her to ferocious tenderness, and to envy of his confidence.

"Over." He waited while she crawled to the middle of the bed, then climbed in after her and spooned himself around her. He propped his chin on her shoulder. "Shall I fetch you a hot-water bottle?"

He'd soon have her in tears. "And inform the kitchen staff what you're about?" But he'd do it, and not many men would.

"You don't want me to leave you here alone in this bed," he said. "Not until the covers are all toasty." His hand settled low on her stomach, resting there until the warmth of it eased Gilly's ache.

"Helene said you were a considerate husband. You can move your hand lower." She showed him.

"Helene said I was considerate?"

"She said for all you were a great strapping brute with too good an opinion of yourself, you were considerate in the ways a husband ought to be. Still, she worried about conceiving."

"Because our children would be great strapping brutes?" His kissed her nape, the same as he always did. "Helene was not petite—and we won't speak of her now if it bothers you."

Perhaps it bothered him? Gilly laced her fingers with his, because Helene should have been the one to let him know his considerations had been appreciated.

"Because her mother had very difficult lying-ins,

Christian, and did not recover from the birth of Helene's youngest brother."

His hand went still. "She never said. In damned near a decade of marriage, she never mentioned this. Bloody hell, my own wife, and she was afraid for her life."

Gilly set his hand away and went up on her elbow to peer at him. The night was cool, so a fire had been lit, and the coals gave off enough light that she could see his face.

"She knew her duty," she said. "We talked about it. The family was originally considering offering you me, recall, because I was younger than Helene, and marriage would mean nobody had to pay for my come out. I offered to take you on, before Greendale had put his plans for me to the solicitors, but Helene wanted to be your duchess."

"She wanted to be *a* duchess, anybody's duchess. All the little girls want to be duchesses." He was disgruntled, upset even. "Helene gave birth easily, the physician and the midwife assured me of that, both times."

Gilly pushed him to his side, which meant pushing at him until he divined her purpose and complied on his own initiative. She hiked herself up higher on the pillows and spooned herself around him, throwing a leg over his hips and tucking an arm around his waist.

He took her hand, kissed her knuckles, then flattened her palm over his heart. "Did you want to be my duchess, Gilly, my love?"

The question was wistful, the endearment devastating.

"Go to sleep, Christian. You have an appointment with Chesterton shortly after dawn."

He rolled onto his back, his expression serious.

"Marry me, Gillian. Please." He stroked his hand down the side of her face. "I talk to you, and were you my duchess, you would not suffer in silence over something as frightening as childbed. I'm…not as young as I was when Helene got her hands on me, but I'm not as stupid, either."

Young, his euphemism for whole of mind, body, and spirit, innocent of the evils men could perpetrate on each other, ignorant of war, murder, and torture.

I talk to you…

"Rub my back for a bit?"

He held his palm against her jaw and looked like he might for once pick a fight with her instead of the other way round. Then his lips quirked up.

"If you're asking for comfort from me, then you must be abjectly miserable, poor thing." He rolled to his side and tucked her into the curve of his body, his hand making slow, easy caresses low on her back.

And despite how his touch eased her aches and relaxed her closer to sleep, Gilly was indeed abjectly, utterly miserable too. He might talk to her, but by no means was she doing a proper job of talking to him.

✧

Christian's countess fell asleep easily, which was reassuring. She admitted by night that they should be together bodily, but resisted by day what he was coming to conclude was the only course: they must marry.

He loved her, though how and why this had come about, he could not exactly pinpoint. Something to do with peeled oranges, soft kisses, black silk, and a rather ruthless approach to gardening. He sensed, though, that announcing his feelings would drive Gilly away, hurt her, or maybe frighten her.

He talked to her, and she listened. She did not talk to him, not about what mattered.

Not about her marriage.

Not about how desperately she wanted children.

Not about her feelings for him.

Something haunted her blue eyes; something kept her willingness to trust under tight rein and thwarted Christian's efforts to woo her.

So he loved her instead, with his body, with his patience, with his consideration, and with his mind.

When she woke before dawn, he let her slip out of bed. She didn't leave his room, but rather, went behind the privacy screen, made use of his tooth powder, and came back to join him in the bed thereafter.

"I know you're awake, Mercia. Your expression is too angelic."

"I am your angel," he said, not opening his eyes. "Get over here and let me keep you warm."

"When did you acquire such an affectionate nature?"

He flipped the covers up for her and considered her question. "In France, maybe. Maybe it was always latent and wanted only the right countess to come along and bring it out."

"You're affectionate with Lucy, too, and with your horse and those puppies."

"They won't be puppies for long. I'm glad you allow me to be affectionate, Countess. Have I told you that?"

"You tell me, though not with words."

He liked that reply, liked that she didn't make it a

point of honor to chide him for it, or to pretend she merely tolerated his attentions. She curled up against him easily, their bodies having grown familiar with each other.

"How do you feel this morning?" he asked, sliding a hand over her tummy.

"Somewhat rested. What have you planned for this day?"

"I was considering riding over to Greendale," he said, rubbing his chin over her crown. "Marcus has been in residence for some weeks, and I've yet to pay a call."

"He's your heir, shouldn't he call on you?"

Did she fear Christian's absence, even for a day? "We've corresponded. Your departed spouse left his estate in disarray, so unwilling was he to part with coin before the last needful moment."

"He was a cheese-paring, nip-farthing old penny-pincher." She never used one insult when three would do for her late husband. Had a bit of the gunnery sergeant about her, did his Gilly.

"Thus Marcus is up to his ears in squabbling tenants, sagging fences, and weedy crops. One wonders why the man didn't put his foot down with the old earl prior to this."

"Because the old earl had a wicked temper," Gilly said, trailing off into a yawn. "He was not beyond leaving all his personal wealth to charity should Marcus defy him or cross him or disrespect him."

"In which case, Marcus would not have been able to sell his commission, but would have become an absentee landlord to a neglected estate, thus ensuring the misery of all. Tell me again you didn't poison your spouse."

"I did not poison my spouse."

He laid his cheek against her breast. "You thought of it."

"Many, many times."

"I do understand, you know."

"You couldn't possibly."

Her hand drifted in his hair, and he closed his eyes, for having his scalp rubbed was a guilty pleasure. Gilly was astute about how he liked to be touched, or maybe he craved any contact with her on any terms.

"Marry me, Gillian. Please."

"Stop it." She left off petting his hair and struggled toward the edge of the bed. "Your constant importuning is not attractive, Your Grace, and I am considering your offer as seriously as I can."

"Referring to me as Your Grace is also not attractive, not from you, not when we're private. Come back to bed."

That merited not even a glance. She flounced about the room—petite women had a way with a flounce—looking for the wool stockings he insisted she borrow, no doubt intent as always on leaving him before the chambermaids came to poke up the fire and bring the morning tea.

"They're under the vanity."

A halfhearted glare, and she went down on her hands and knees to retrieve the errant stockings. Christian worked himself to the edge of the bed, enjoying the show and trying not to think of ways he might enjoy *her* in such a pose.

Gilly was modest, even in bed, always keeping her

nightgown on until the candles were out. Though he'd shown her a variety of sexual positions, she'd balked at getting on her knees before him, claiming it wanted dignity.

As if…

"Ouch." She muttered it and went still, half under the vanity, half not, and then she moved, and the fine linen of her nightgown ripped.

"Don't move, love. You've probably caught the thing on a nail, for which somebody will pay."

"Don't…" She backed out, stockings in hand, but succeeded only in tearing her nightgown the length of her back and starting a thin red welt up near one shoulder.

"Let me help you up, Countess, lest I get naughty ideas while you linger in a very fetching position." He ambled over to her and couldn't help peering at the strip of pale flesh revealed from her shoulder blade to the small of her back. In all their lovemaking and disporting, he'd yet to see her—

"Gillian?" He stared at her back, and she quickly sat up on her heels.

"Don't look." She tried to gather the nightgown closed around her throat, which only had the effect of parting it farther where it had torn at the back. He looked more closely even as she continued speaking. "You mustn't…Christian, please. Don't look."

Scars writhed over her skin, thin white lines, some pink, a few of a brighter hue. They grew denser closer to her buttocks.

"Gilly," he kept his voice steady with effort, "love, what happened to you?"

"Don't look!" She scrambled to her feet, but he man-acled her wrist in his hand when she would have bolted from the room. "You must not…please…you must not."

He wrapped his arms around her, rather than distress her with further inspection. "Who did this to you?"

She shook her head, her face pressed to his bare chest, her mouth open as her body began to shake.

"You've been hiding this," he said, cradling her against him. "You've been careful, haven't you, to keep me from seeing you?"

A soft sob escaped.

He marveled that his voice even functioned, because he wanted to scream, to do violence in her name, to whip somebody as hard and as often as they'd gone after her, and then harder still.

"Was it your father? You said he was stern."

She shook her head, crying audibly now, the sound terrible and raw.

"Tell me." He gathered her close, his hands tracing the disfigured patterns on her flesh. "Please, love, you must say who did this."

"My husband. My husband did this to me."

❧

Christian's hands stilled on her back, and Gilly wished she could retrieve the words. For years, she'd held her head up on the strength of the knowledge that her situation had been between her and Greendale only. The servants had likely guessed—Gilly had needed some time to learn to fight Greendale in silence—but they hadn't *known*.

Her parents had known, but they'd chosen denial as the better course, leaving her at the age of seventeen in the hands of a monster.

Helene had suspected, and welcomed Gilly as a frequent visitor in recent years as a result, but Helene hadn't known either, not for a certainty.

"Stay here." Christian's arms dropped away, and he grabbed up his dressing gown and left the room. In his absence, Gilly found her night rail and donned it over the ruined nightgown.

Would she ever see this bedroom again? Duchesses were not an old man's widowed whipping post.

As minutes ticked by, it occurred to her she didn't have to do as Christian said.

Not ever, because he wasn't to become her husband, and yet, she sat exactly where he'd left her.

When Christian returned, he carried a large tray.

"Come," he said, setting the tray down on a low table. He dragged two chairs close to the fire and stood behind one, his expression unreadable. "We shall talk, Gillian, Lady Greendale. You shall talk to me, and I shall listen."

Lady Greendale. Even hearing her title hurt. "Why?"

"Because you didn't even have bloody, bedamned, tame, fucking mice."

Whatever she'd expected him to say, it wasn't that. She crossed the room as much on her dignity as she could manage and took the indicated chair.

He took the other, poured for them both, and added cream and sugar to hers.

"Drink it. Don't just hold it and expect you can

wait me out." His expression was so fierce, Gilly did
as he said, and to her surprise, the tea was good.

Strong and bracing, like the man giving her such a
broody perusal.

"He was doting at first," she said, without intending
to say anything, "or as doting as a pompous old man
can be. I did not know what to expect on my wedding night, except for my mother's admonition that if
I submitted quietly, it would be over quickly, and it
would hurt only the first time."

He clearly didn't like what he heard; neither did he
interrupt her.

"It hurt rather a lot, and I cried and begged him to
stop. He slapped me for it. Repeatedly." She paused
and took a sip of her tea, wanting to recite rather than
remember. "I did not at first comprehend what he
was about."

"Your pain and humiliation aroused him."

Six words, but they were so astonishingly accurate
Gilly left off staring at her tea.

"Yes. I did not understand on my wedding night,
and not for a long while thereafter, but he couldn't…he
couldn't finish, and when I cried, and he could become
violent, it allowed him to achieve…to reach…"

"To spend."

"Yes, to spend inside my body, or in his own hand.
If that happened, he'd beat me for it, say I caused him
to waste his seed."

"And you put up with this for eight years?"

"The last few years he wasn't as apt to try," she
said. "I think the ignominy of not being able to per-
form even when he raised his hand to me overcame

the pleasure he took from the beatings. And he was never…he wasn't like you."

Dark brows drew down fiercely. "In what regard?"

"He wasn't…firm. He was soft, until he started whacking at me, and then he'd grow a little firmer, but not like you." She took another sip of tea and dared glance at Christian again. "I never inspected him closely, if that's what you're wondering. I have no idea what his male parts looked like. I didn't want to know."

And yet, she was glad to know what Christian looked like, felt like, tasted like, smelled like.

"Bloody hell." He scrubbed a hand over his face and turned a scowling regard on her. His hair was in disarray around his shoulders, his face dark with an inchoate beard, and she could not guess at his reaction. "Didn't the servants hear you? He must have taken a riding crop to you."

"A driving whip, usually, a riding crop sometimes. Greendale chose his moments for the servants' half days, and the late nights when all were abed. He'd accost me at other times and ask me to speak to him privately."

"He'd wake you up from a deep sleep when it pleased him to?"

She nodded, once. How could Christian know that?

"And he'd turn up sweet at odd times too," Christian said, his grip on his teacup appearing perilously tight. "And you'd begin to hope, to think maybe the horror was behind you and things could be different."

"Only for the first year or so."

"Eight years." He made the scrubbing motion with his hand again, as if something were getting in his eyes. Then his head came up, and he regarded her with a piercing, blue-eyed stare. "And the servants never heard you, not once?"

"They did not," she said, finding her tea was finished. She set the cup on its saucer. "But they guessed. I could hardly move some days for the way he hurt me. He was full of casual tricks too. He'd accidentally step on my slipper when in his riding boots, then apologize for an old man's clumsiness. He'd kiss my hand and beg my forgiveness."

"I am going to be sick." Christian glanced around the chamber, as if genuinely searching out the chamber pot; then his eyes came back to her. "Your hand, the little finger. Did he do that to you?"

"My hand?" She brought her left hand up, with the slightly crooked little finger. "I was playing my flute, and he took exception to the noise. Usually, he was careful not to risk injury where an evening gown might reveal it, but he took my hand and held it to the hearthstones, then started beating at it with his cane. He was particularly angry that time, and I wasn't fast enough."

"The tea? You didn't spill it on yourself, did you?"

"He spilled it on me, and again apologized very prettily while the footmen looked on."

Christian grew silent, his hand propped on his chin, and Gillian felt something inside her going cold with dread. And then when he did speak, his voice was very hard. "You blame yourself for what befell you."

"Of course not." She lifted the teacup to her lips,

only to recall it was empty. "Of course I didn't blame myself. I am not an imbecile."

"You were seventeen, and your parents were powerless to help you, so they ignored what they'd done to you for the sake of gaining a title to boast of. By sacrificing you, they kept the familial coffers sufficiently lined that your cousin could snabble a tiara. From *me*. You were the only one who could have stopped your wedding to Greendale, and you didn't."

He spoke quietly, the same voice she'd heard from him when he was newly back from France, unable to take much sustenance and jumping at any loud noise.

"You are spouting nonsense, and it isn't very nice of you, Christian. More tea, if you please." She passed him the cup and saucer, hoping he'd ignore the way her hand shook.

He watched the cup and saucer trembling in her hand for a pointed moment, then fixed her a second cup.

"Then when it was obvious the marriage could not be undone," he went on as if there'd been no pause, "you were the only one who could have orchestrated your own escape, and you failed to do that as well."

"And what purpose would that have served?" she said, staring at her tea. "Anybody I sought aid from would have been bound to return me to Greendale's care or suffer the King's justice. My own father, my uncles, they would not help, Helene could not, Marcus could not, not openly. Greendale was careful to ensure I made no friends, and never allowed even the vicar to call on me privately. Greendale read my correspondence, controlled my money—"

She had to set the teacup down lest she shatter it, and the last thing, the very, very last thing she sought was to indulge in the violence her husband had delighted in.

"And still, you think you should have found a way," Christian went on. "Passage to America, a life following the drum, a lady's companion on some remote Scottish island. You never stopped blaming yourself, and belittling yourself, until you began to believe the things he said about you."

She gave up wondering why Christian, of all people, would say such mean things to her, for he spoke only the truth. By the second year, her marriage had become precisely as he'd described it.

"I came to believe I wasn't conceiving because I dreaded the prospect," she said. "To imagine bringing a helpless child into that man's household. The housekeeper was the one to tell me I was his fourth countess, every one of them as petite as I am, and they'd all despaired of having children too. Something my parents had carefully neglected to tell me."

She made herself tell him the rest of it. "The housekeeper's admission must have been overheard, for Greendale fired her without a character the next week."

"So you stopped even looking for allies," Christian said, staring at the fire. "You no longer even talked to the mice."

What was he going on about with his blessed mice?

"I prayed for his death. I did not kill him."

"You think I'd blame you?" He flicked a glance over her. "Men like Greendale need killing, badly. That his evil will have no representation in the next generation is divine justice, and did you kill him, I'd toast you for it in the streets of London."

"And get me hanged by the neck until dead."

Because violence begets violence, as surely as cats had kittens and horses foals.

Her logic silenced him, for of all men, Christian could understand her reasoning.

She sat in her torn nightgown and robe, trying not to feel chilled, trying not to feel *anything*, while the stubborn wish that he'd take her in his arms again plagued her badly.

"You cannot marry me because of what Greendale did to you," he said at length, something in his tone both angry and weary. "Not yet."

"I want to marry you, but I did not want you to see…to *know*. I contemplated death with affection, Christian, rather than face more years like that, blaming myself. And yet, I did not surrender my power on this earth. My power, my dignity were wrested from me and smashed to bits, while my family and all of Society went merrily on their way and the law applauded. One grew…bewildered."

"I understand."

She feared those two words were his way of initiating their good-byes, because her bewilderment had come between them, and who knew when she might resolve it?

Then he did something odd. He slid out of his chair and knelt beside hers. She braced herself, not sure what to expect, for the moment did not call for the dramatics of a *parfit gentil knight*.

He slipped his arms around her waist and laid his head in her lap.

"Your Grace?" He'd done this once before, when he'd first started proposing to her. He burrowed in closer and nuzzled her thigh.

"Christian?"

"Hush, love. We can argue more later, but for now, hush. You mustn't fret, but I cannot leave you alone right now. You have humbled me in ways I never conceived a man could be humbled."

"I've *humbled* you?" The useless lump was back in her throat, along with useless, stupid tears. He liked it when she stroked his head, so she did that, over and over again, while the tea grew cold and her heart broke.

Over and over again.

Seventeen

THANKS TO A MERCIFUL GOD, THE DAY OF GILLY'S awful revelations saw a surprise visit from Devlin St. Just, who was in the neighborhood on a horse-buying mission.

"I wanted to smash the damned teapot, but she looked so broken," Christian said. They'd ridden far and wide on Severn property, the day cool enough that the horses were frisky. Christian shared his confidences between brisk canters and gallops over the stiles.

"Her experience puts your situation in perspective. What will you do?"

His situation. He was a war hero for silently enduring a few months of Girard's intermittent abuse, while Gilly remained emotionally imprisoned after eight years of silent torture, for which the law and Society both had guaranteed her tormenter impunity.

"I will give her time." He'd give her his hands, his sight, anything, if it would help her regain her sense of worth and joy.

"You want to give her the rest of your life and all your wealth and consequence," St. Just said. "She may never get back on the marital horse, so to speak, and you have no sons."

"I don't need sons. I need Gilly."

"Have you told her that?"

"In the King's English."

"Not have you said the words, but have you communicated your need for her?"

Christian frowned at his friend—for surely, one in whom such confidences could be reposed was a friend—but St. Just wasn't finished.

"You're a duke, wealthy, powerful, reasonably good-looking when you make the effort, and a decorated war hero. She's a penniless victim of an abusive spouse. What can she possibly have that you need?"

"Everything."

"Gracious, you are smitten. I'm impressed."

"With the lady's charms?"

"With your courage. You were broken too, and for you to care like this…" St. Just fell silent while his horse danced around some droppings in the road. "You have found the best revenge, my friend."

"I was damaged. I was never broken. Girard reminded me of that frequently." And he'd relished those incessant reminders, though he was sure they'd been intended as taunts. "Gilly has sorted me out and put me back to rights."

St. Just looked pained and pointed off toward the village steeple. "Race you."

Christian put his spurs to Chessie's sides and thought he'd have an advantage because he knew the territory. St. Just had ridden dispatch though, and beat him by a length.

"Your heart wasn't in the steeplechase," St. Just said charitably. "And my mount is in better condition than yours. I was planning to head closer to Town before the sun sets, but invite me to spend the night."

"So invited," Christian said, relieved somebody would join him and Gilly for dinner—and St. Just's mount *was* a splendid beast. "We'll dine informally and find you something of mine to wear, though I warn you, embroidery is showing up on my attire in unlikely places."

St. Just looked intrigued, necessitating a change in topic. Christian stroked a gloved hand over Chessie's neck, for the old boy was still heaving a bit. "We caught Lucy singing to her puppies."

"Is there a but coming?"

"But she's still silent when she knows anybody can hear. Gilly thinks we ought to confront her. I cannot agree."

"Why not?"

"She knows how to speak. She writes great convoluted stories using vocabulary far beyond her years. Her life is made lonely and awkward by her silence, therefore I conclude she does not speak because she cannot."

"You didn't speak. Perhaps she knows this."

Why hadn't this occurred to him? "Just so, I did not speak because it became the only means of remaining alive. Gilly kept a silence of her own, finding it the only refuge for her dignity and self-respect. Some silences we are compelled to keep."

St. Just, who likely had a few silences to his name, didn't argue the point. "She seems a happy child, your

Lucy, but I asked Her Grace if she'd ever heard of such a thing, and she hadn't."

"Your stepmother?"

"She has raised ten children and was unfashionably involved in the process, as was Moreland."

"If you learned your sister were married to an abusive old man, would you have left her to the situation?"

This time, St. Just's gelding shied at a rabbit scampering across the path, though the rider barely took notice of the creature. "My sister would be on a boat for Denmark or Philadelphia before sunset, with substantial coin in her pocket and papers indicating she was the wife of some late yeoman."

How quickly he answered. How blessed his sisters were. "What about the scriptural exhortations?"

"As far as I know, St. Paul had no wife, nor did the Lord himself."

"Interesting viewpoint."

"My father's insight, oddly enough. I wanted to pass along some news to you, though."

"We approach the stables, so say on."

"I've heard rumors in Town regarding Girard."

Abruptly, the moment stood out from all the moments of the day, all the moments since leaving that wretched French mountainside. The angle of the afternoon sunlight on the lake, the chestnut draft team standing nose-to-tail in the nearest paddock, the tune some stableboy whistled as he ambled along a fence row toward the far pastures—they dropped onto Christian's awareness like ink onto a pure white sheet of vellum.

"You've heard rumors about Robert Girard?" He

did not refer to the man as "my" Robert Girard, but with the entitlement of one bent on revenge, Girard belonged to no other.

"Yes, Robert Girard, late of the garrison at Château de Solvigny." St. Just leaned over to pat his mount on the neck, fussing the beast's mane rather than studying Christian's expression. "He's supposedly larking about London in anticipation of taking up the management of the St. Clair barony. Of all things, he's come into an English title. The government's official position is clemency for veterans of any nationality."

Christian halted his horse, as St. Just's words were growing dim over the roaring in his ears and the pounding in his chest.

"I thought you'd want to know."

"What I want…" Christian spoke again, less softly. "What I *need* is to kill him."

Chessie moved forward without Christian asking it of him.

St. Just's expression remained calm. He had, after all, led cavalry charges against the French. "Dueling is considered murder. Given your title and your history, not a magistrate in the realm would prosecute you."

Which made no difference whatsoever. Girard was moving about freely in England, not three hours' ride to the north. His proximity underscored his ability to bring harm to Gilly. "You'd serve as second?"

"And I've at least two brothers who'd do likewise on short notice, if need be, and their discretion is without fault."

"Marcus might be offended if I didn't ask him. He

served with us." And yet, Marcus was best situated to keep Gilly and Lucy safe, too.

"That is entirely your decision. You have adequate equipment?"

Christian didn't see the stable yard, he saw the stone walls of the Château, usually damp, always malodorous. He saw a cat, lying in wait at the base of those walls.

"You don't ask if I have adequate skill," Christian said, satisfaction and anticipation twining through him in a peculiar combination of glee and dread, much like the sentiments of Wellington's infantry when approaching the end of a siege.

"Girard was not reputed to have any skill with a sword," St. Just said, "and the French pride themselves on such things. He'll choose pistols, likely, and you have time to perfect your aim, though you were accounted an excellent shot."

"I was good," Christian said, drawing Chessie to a halt. "I was quite good before Girard's men mangled my better hand."

"So practice. I will leave you my various directions as I travel about."

Neither man moved to dismount, and the stable-boys must have sensed something of the discussion, for they lingered nearby without intruding. "You're not settled at the Moreland family seat?"

"I stay in the country, mostly, but make my obeisance before the family as needed. Moreland wreaks havoc in the lives of his legitimate offspring, and torments his heir incessantly regarding the succession. How Westhaven deals with it is beyond me."

"You're always welcome here."

St. Just swung off his horse, ran up the left stirrup, and loosened the beast's girth. "One anticipated such graciousness, hence the present imposition."

Christian dismounted as well, prepared to get particulars from St. Just regarding the source of his rumor, when a thought intruded.

"You haven't badgered me about my report." And St. Just had barely mentioned it on his last visit, though Christian had every sense St. Just's superiors wanted the document badly—nosy blighters.

"Nor shall I badger you."

"I've written it. I haven't parted with it."

They fell silent until the stableboys led the horses away.

"You will," St. Just said, "when you're ready. If you do go up to Town, you need to know you've acquired a *nom de guerre* or two. They're calling you the unbreakable duke and the silent duke, also the quiet duke."

"I appreciate the warnings." All of the warnings. He turned toward the house, where his unbreakable, silent, and quiet Gilly waited. "And those appellations are rather an improvement over being the lost duke."

Gilly was grateful to Devlin St. Just for keeping Christian occupied for the afternoon, grateful to him for providing most of the conversation at dinner, and yet still more grateful that the colonel offered to take his host off for a brandy in the library.

"Gilly, are you headed upstairs?" Christian addressed her as Gilly, not Countess, which should have been some reassurance, but she hadn't been able to get her bearings with him all day.

"I thought to make an early night of it."

His gaze moved over her, and she wished he didn't have such intimate knowledge of her bodily cycles.

Or her past.

Or her heart.

"St. Just, you will pour me a drink while I light the lady up to her chamber."

St. Just, the wretch, merely offered her a good-night bow.

Christian waited until they'd reached the first landing to start his interrogation, though of course a simple question would have been too direct.

"You look tired, Gillian, but then you did not sleep well last night."

"Perhaps I'd better remain in my own bed tonight."

The words were out, unplanned, but she didn't want him to be the one to make the awkward excuses. Her disclosures had changed things, allowed doubts and despairs to break free that she'd spent months walling up, brick by brick.

"Do you forget somebody has tried three times to kill you?" Christian moved along at her side, his voice holding a thread of steel.

"I've been thinking about that," Gilly said. "I've concluded it was merely a batch of meadow tea gone wrong. Somebody thought they were picking mint and pulled up a noxious weed. And as for the other, wheels come loose, leather breaks."

"Meadow tea is not served in my household above stairs," Christian said with painful gentleness. "And it did not taste like meadow tea. That was a strong black tea, the household blend, Gilly, sweetened no doubt to cover the taste of poison."

She'd known he'd say that, but hearing the words put her anxiety that much closer to out of control. At least in Greendale's household, she'd known exactly who her enemy was, and that his malevolence had predated her marriage to him.

"I would ask you to use my bed," he said, "and have done with this farce we endure nightly, carting you about from room to room, but you will not oblige me."

"So you'll let me have some solitude tonight?"

"You crave solitude?"

She craved him, and she craved an innocence so far lost to her, nothing would resurrect it. "I am tired."

"Then, my love, you must find your bed." He stopped outside her door, pushed it open, and peered in to see the candles and the fire had been lit. He stepped aside to let her pass then followed her in.

And that was a relief, that he'd still presume to that degree.

He sat on the bed while Gilly went to the vanity and began to take down her hair.

"No matter what I say to you right now," he mused, "it won't come out right."

"Say it anyway," she rejoined, using the mirror to appreciate the picture he made at ease on her bed. "You talk to me, remember?" And how she loved him for that.

He lounged back on his elbows, a great, lean, ducal beast of a man with far too much patience.

"You think things have changed between us because I know what a hell your marriage was, and you're right: things have changed. I can't view you the same way."

She bent her head, as if to locate her brush, but all she really wanted was to hide her eyes and weep, for with his changed view, her own view of herself dimmed too.

"I never wanted you to know. I never wanted anybody to know. That was my one victory, you see."

"You wanted to keep your silence, because you believe your experiences have disfigured you on the inside as Greendale tried to on the outside."

Greendale had tried and succeeded.

Gilly stared at boar bristles and wood, the same hairbrush she'd taken with her from the schoolroom to her marriage, for Greendale begrudged her even so small a thing as a brush.

"I can't stand the sight of a buggy whip or a riding crop, and can't use them myself. I'm always nervous serving tea to guests, afraid somebody will be burned. I hate the smell of burning tobacco, and I can't abide the thought of sleeping with the bedroom door unlocked."

His expression in the shadows behind her was tired and thoughtful.

"Go to sleep," he said. "You've trusted me with only the start of a very long list of transgressions Greendale perpetrated during your marriage. If St. Just were not here, I'd be brushing your hair, did you allow it, while you told me more of the abominations you'd rather not acknowledge."

"I'd allow it."

She offered the words as an olive branch, a small reassurance that though things between them might be changing, her regard for him was constant.

"You should know of my plans," he said, picking up the candle from the mantel. "I might have to go up to Town in the next weeks, though not for any great length of time. If I do go, I'll ask Marcus to bide here temporarily."

She nodded, because he was right: the chances of meadow tea poisoning a large man nigh to death were miniscule, and Marcus was a battle-hardened officer, the same as Christian.

"Lucy will be glad of a visitor," she said, "and I haven't seen Marcus myself since his last leave."

Christian held the candle low, so his features were cast in flickering shadow. "You know I care for you, Gillian."

He made no move to approach her, to kiss her good night, to take her in his arms. Gilly sat at her vanity and pulled pins from her hair, when she wanted to pitch herself against him and cling to him with everything in her.

"And I care for you." She could say it now, now when his proposal was no longer under discussion.

He left, and Gilly was crying even as she fastened the lock on the door latch. She did as he'd suggested and took herself to bed, cuddling up to the pillow on the side of the bed he'd vacated.

৵৽

Christian saw his guest to bed late, because they'd started comparing notes and reminiscing about various battles and generals they'd both served under. Eventually, he realized that St. Just had as much trouble sleeping as the next veteran of the Peninsula.

Then too, Christian was procrastinating. He had no intention of sleeping alone, not tonight of all nights, not with Gilly's disclosures so fresh in his mind and her behavior so dauntingly distant.

But he thought back to his first weeks and months after leaving French hands. He'd been barely human, and he'd suffered no more than she. Physically, Girard's tortures hadn't been the worst humanity had devised, nor had they been applied all that frequently.

The worst brutality had been mental, the uncertainty from day to day regarding his fate, the tantalizing hints of hope and decent treatment followed by days of neglect or worse. Then too, the sense of having been so easily forgotten by his fellows had demoralized him. But what was that compared to Gilly's situation, which her own parents had fashioned for her and the law declared her legally bound fate?

Having been only recently freed from her marriage, still she'd bestirred herself to bring Lucy's situation to Christian's attention, to demand that he be responsible toward his daughter.

He checked on Lucy and found her sleeping peacefully, two growing puppies snuggled in beside her, then repaired to his own room where he peeled out of his clothes, washed away the dust of the day, and turned down the bed. Wearing only a dressing gown, he crossed the hallway, unlocked Gilly's door the same as he had every night, and lifted her into his arms.

"Christian?"

"Of course it's Christian. If St. Just has taken to poaching, I'll meet him over the weapon of his choice."

She blinked up at him then closed her eyes. "My indisposition is yet upon me, and you will not even jest about wreaking violence on a fellow soldier."

Had she been fully awake, she'd have kept more of that chilly distance. Half-asleep, she had some trust in him, and that was encouraging—also sweet.

"I sleep better when I'm certain you're safe."

That was the extent of their discussion, and he was grateful for the silence. Better that she get her rest than that they waste their breath arguing. In sleep, she curled up against him easily and rubbed her cheek against his chest.

In sleep, she let him hold her and laced her fingers through his. She let him comfort her when the nightmares came.

He prayed it was only a matter of time before she allowed him to face her waking dragons with her as well.

❦

"Of course I'll stay an extra day," St. Just said, keeping his voice down, though he and Christian stood outside the breakfast parlor. "Is it wise to abandon your lady now, given recent developments?"

"I'm not abandoning her," Christian said. "I'm following her example."

"Which would be?"

"Let's eat while we talk. We'll have more privacy."

Christian waved the footmen off, served himself and his guest, and took his place at the head of the table.

"You were off your feed when first we met," St. Just said. "Matters seem to have righted themselves."

Christian's plate bore thick slabs of fragrant, crispy bacon, a mountain of eggs, and two pieces of toast lacking crusts.

"I am on the mend largely thanks to the countess." Who was still abed in the ducal chamber, because Christian hadn't had the heart to return her to her own rooms in the cold, gray predawn light. "When I was in such bad shape, her approach was to insist on a normal routine. She made me sleep at night and face the days, made me deal with my daughter, made me eat what I could. She brought me back to life."

"You brought yourself back to life," St. Just said, tucking into his eggs. "These are good. You don't spare the cream."

"Cook personally prepares anything coming to the table now. Not only are we safer, we eat like royalty. You'll want butter on that toast." Christian slid the butter dish over to his guest, because whatever St. Just did not put on his toast, Christian would put on his.

The prospect of dealing with Girard hummed through Christian with a violent joy, sharpened his every sense, and gave the day an edge of anticipation. And yet, a part of him also fretted over Gilly and wished he'd been free to tarry with her above stairs.

"Have you made any progress determining who the countess's malefactor could be?"

"In my nightmares, I imagine the French are behind this danger to Gilly. Girard could describe the land around here as if he'd walked it himself." Though preying upon a noncombatant departed from the curious code of honor Girard had held himself to throughout Christian's captivity.

St. Just used exactly half the butter on his toast then nudged the remainder closer to Christian's elbow. "Would Girard have failed on three consecutive attempts?"

The question inspired a pause. Christian's knife, holding a fat dollop of butter, poised over his toast.

"He would not, though Anduvoir might. Do we know where Anduvoir is?"

"I can find out." St. Just's tone suggested Anduvoir had best be halfway to Russia.

"The theory that Girard is harassing me through Gilly has another problem," Christian said, resenting the demands of logic when the pleasure of violence called loudly.

St. Just made a circle with his fork while he chewed a mouthful of ham.

"Girard was canny. One wants to attribute to the enemy every fault ever exhibited by humankind— stupidity, vulgarity, mendacity—and yet, he was none of those things. We are at long last at peace, and Girard would have no motive for antagonizing me now, particularly if, as you say, he's turned up with an English barony around his neck."

St. Just poured himself more tea and topped off Christian's cup, as if they'd been in the officers' mess sharing their daily ration of beef, potatoes, and gossip.

"Given how many English peers Girard has mistreated, that barony will likely have the same result as a target on his back," St. Just observed. "Girard might live longer if he found his way to Cathay, but not by much."

Abruptly, Christian's hearty, satisfying English breakfast lost its appeal. St. Just implied somebody

would call Girard out before Christian had the chance.
He pushed a forkful of eggs around on his plate, eggs
that would have made him weep had he been served
them in France.

"I have reason enough to wish Girard biding in
hell, but with respect to Gilly's troubles, the kitchen
maid we suspect of poisoning the tea hailed from over
near Greendale and had worked at the local posting
inn there. Gilly has suggested the woman was one of
Greendale's castoffs. He was not at all faithful to his
vows, and he let Gilly know it."

St. Just took a tactful sip of his tea. "So you're off to
pay your condolences to Greendale's heir?"

"My heir too," Christian said. "At least for a time.
Easterbrook has his hands full, what with the condition Greendale was left in."

"The manse is falling down about his ears?"

"The house itself is in fine shape, but every outbuild-
ing and tenant farm is in precarious condition. Gilly was
willing to stay with Lucy and me initially because the
Greendale dower house is in such poor repair."

"Will Easterbr—Greendale set it to rights?"

"I doubt it, not for some time. And I'll lock the
woman in a tower before I let her leave my protection."

"Make a captive of her, will you?" St. Just reached
for his tea as Christian's balled-up serviette flew across
the table at him.

"Not subtle, St. Just."

"Subtlety has never been my strong suit. Too
many years soldiering. Too many younger siblings.
Too many imbroglios with dear Papa, His Grace, the
Duke of Stubbornness, and his bride, the Duchess of

Now See Here, Young Man. How do you get the butter so light?"

"It's a mystery. Cook is fifteen stone if she's an ounce, but she has the best hand with the cream. Then too, she knows we've your company again. She's likely smitten with you or your appetites."

"Get you to your horse, Mercia, before I'm forced to improve your manners with a round of fisticuffs."

"You aren't riding out with him?" Gilly stood in the doorway, looking freshly scrubbed and braided, also tired. She'd had a restless night, seeming to need Christian's arms around her to sleep at all.

"Good morning, Countess." St. Just was on his feet before she'd taken a step.

"My lady." Christian rose to hold her customary chair at his left. "Good morning. I'm off to pay a call, and St. Just has agreed to bear you company for the day."

She visually assessed the colonel, not with any warmth. "Don't feel you must stay with me. I can make do with George and John."

Oh, delightful. They would start the day quarreling. Though her pugnacity was, in its way, reassuring—probably to them both.

"Would you like your usual fare, Countess?" Christian stood by the sideboard, an empty plate in his hand.

"Please, and I'd like to know where you're off to if Colonel St. Just must be left with my care."

"To Greendale. Marcus has been in residence for several weeks, we've traded the requisite correspondence, it's time to pay a call, and St. Just's presence means you need not come with me—unless you'd like to? We can have the coach brought around for you."

He kept his tone casual and busied himself preparing her plate, but he wanted her to choose his company over another day at Severn, particularly a day in St. Just's handsome and charming company.

Which was exactly how a man felt when he was badly, sorely, and completely smitten. Gilly would no more want to spend time at Greendale than Christian would enjoy a return visit to the Château.

"I'll bide here," she said, tucking her serviette on her lap. "Lucy will pine if we both leave, and Greendale has no positive associations for me. Colonel, what shall we find to do with ourselves?"

She ignored Christian as politely as company would allow, and he let her. Maybe she was peeved because he was leaving for the day, but the call really should not be put off when St. Just's presence made leaving the property easier.

Maybe Gilly was cranky from a restless night or from being taken from her own bed when she had halfway asked to have a night to herself. Maybe she resented having to entertain company.

And maybe she would simply take her sweet time coming to terms with the fact that everybody needs an orange peeled for them, from time to time.

❧

Gilly dabbed her toast with jam—the table boasted no butter—and ignored two large, worried men who likely did not know what to do with a grenade of female emotions lobbed into their midst, her fuse lit and burning down.

Tossing and turning in Christian's arms—always

in his arms—Gilly had come to the mortifying conclusion that Christian had been right: marriage to
Greendale had left her ashamed of herself. Exactly as
Christian had said—had accused—she blamed herself
for her marriage and for not finding a way out of it.

Greendale had been depraved but not brilliant.
Gilly could have absconded with the silver from her
trousseau, taken a coach for Scotland, and made some
sort of living with her needle.

She might have fought back, revealed her scars to
Polite Society, arranged a visit to Helene but instead
taken ship for South America. By the hour, she had
listed the plans and schemes she might have, should
have, and *did not* attempt.

She also blamed herself for revealing the whole business to Christian, who had put all the violence he'd suffered behind him and focused on building a life around
the daughter he loved and his ducal responsibilities.

And Gilly blamed herself for being rude over breakfast to the man she loved, though as awkward as things
had grown between them, she didn't like the idea of
him traveling to Greendale without her.

She couldn't say why the idea rankled, but it did.

And thus, she was on the drive after breakfast, ready
to bid Christian farewell on more cordial terms than
she'd shown him earlier.

"Good of you to see me off." Christian settled on
the lady's mounting block next to where Gilly stood.
"You were less than charming over breakfast, except
to St. Just."

"I am yet tired," she said, though those words
weren't what she wanted to convey to him.

He stood and took the step necessary to close the distance between them.

"It won't work." He put a hand on each of her shoulders and brought her against him. "Paw and snort all you like, Gilly. Dodge, duck, and dawdle, but your temper won't chase me off. I'm tending to a duty, but I'm also giving you some peace and quiet."

She put her arms around his waist and let herself have the comfort of his embrace for a moment. "Don't let Easterbrook make you smoke any of his smelly cigars."

And that had nothing to do with anything either.

"Gilly, the only sleep you found was when I held you. I want to always be there to hold you."

She held on to him, trying to believe what he was telling her. Christian's mistreatment by the French made him only more dear to her. Her mind trusted that Greendale's abuse did not sully her in Christian's eyes, did not make her less worthy of Christian's regard.

Her heart was more wary.

"I didn't want you to know." An orphan's cry for her mama might have been more forlorn, barely. "I didn't want you to know I'd let somebody treat me like that. A shame is less wounding if it's private."

He was silent, simply holding her, and Gilly took it as a measure of her upset that she let him embrace her more or less in public. A quick hug between cousins-by-marriage might be excused, but not this.

"I cannot know the experiences you've survived, Gilly, except what you tell me of them." His hand stroked across her back, as if he would remind her of what he'd seen and that her scars did not frighten him. "I will tell you what somebody told me: I respect you all the more for what you've confided, both because of what you survived and because you don't pretend it never happened. The shame wounds you, but it belongs entirely to Greendale."

If Christian did not get on his horse soon, she'd be telling him every last, awful detail. "I wanted it all to die with him."

"The mistreatment died with him, but you, my love, did not, for which I will ever give thanks. You'll be decent to St. Just?"

"I'll flirt my eyebrows off with him."

This earned her a chuckle. "He's a cavalry officer. He won't scare easily."

Christian kissed her forehead, and Gilly couldn't help holding him tighter.

"I'll stay if you ask me to," he said softly, right near her ear, "but I owe Marcus a show of support."

"Go then." She stepped back quickly, before she started begging. "Give him my regards, and tell him…"

She never wanted to see Marcus Easterbrook again, never wanted to see Greendale again.

And never wanted to say another good-bye to Christian Severn.

Gilly made a decision. She made her decision based on the way Chessie nuzzled at Christian's pockets, the way Christian had held her right here in the stable yard, the way a man he'd befriended stood a few yards off, pretending to play with the puppies while standing guard over Christian and Gilly both.

"Tell Marcus to blow the dower house to kindling. It has the creeping damp, and I cannot see myself inhabiting such a sorry dwelling, ever."

"I'll tell him no such thing." Christian smiled as he kissed her cheek, which both gratified and annoyed her, for she'd been deadly serious and trying to convey something besides the proper fate of a neglected heap.

Then he was up on his horse, a groom handing him his crop. He lifted it as if to flourish it in a salute, but caught Gilly's eye.

In her heart, *Don't go* warred with *Take me with you.* She blew him a kiss and tried to smile. He touched his hat brim with his riding crop and still didn't nudge Chessie off down the drive.

"Gilly?"

She shaded her eyes to meet his gaze.

"Keep this for me—or destroy it." He tossed her the crop, and she caught it, the first time she'd touched such a thing willingly in years.

"Until this evening," he said, and then he and Chessie were clattering over the cobblestones and cantering down the curving driveway until they were out of sight.

Gilly held the riding crop without looking at it and waited for the familiar pounding to begin in her chest.

And waited, while the puppies gamboled, the morning breeze rippled the surface of the lake, and Gilly's heart...went about its job, as if she held a stick to throw for the puppies, or a flower.

Christian had entrusted her with a simple riding crop, a wooden handle covered in cowhide, the braided leather ending in a short lash. She'd seen hundreds in her lifetime, held a few dozen, and swatted the occasional lazy horse with one, though never in anger.

She was still drying her tears a few minutes later when St. Just ambled over, passed her a plain cream silk handkerchief that smelled slightly of horse, and proposed she give him a tour of the gardens.

Eighteen

OF ALL THE INCONVENIENCES PLAGUING MARCUS Easterbrook, Christian Severn, eighth Duke of Mercia—and ironically, heir to the Greendale ancestral pile—figured as the most prominent. Even the damned weather cooperated in His Grace's bloody social whims, for it was a perfect summer day. Sunny, dry, and pleasant without being hot, and the duke's note had said he'd join his cousin for a midday meal.

Bad enough the man was unbreakable, and unkillable, but he was also likely to be punctual, so Marcus put the kitchen on notice that a proper feast had best be forthcoming at the one o'clock hour.

The staff would not disappoint. One result of inheriting from old Greendale was a staff who knew how to take orders from their betters.

And if Marcus were lucky, his dear former-step-aunt-the-countess would accompany Mercia on this call between relatives. Her ladyship had to be getting restless, what with being in mourning, and Mercia observing half mourning for the fair Helene.

Marcus wandered down to the stable, seeking a

distraction from thoughts of Helene. Of the many bothersome results of Mercia's return to the living, losing the use of Aragon—Chesterton, to the duke— was one of the worst. The beast had been handsome, faultlessly trained, and possessed of beautiful gaits.

The sound of hooves in the stable yard signaled Mercia's arrival. Marcus put on his best charming smile, squared his shoulders, and prepared to greet a man who lacked the common decency to die when the opportunity presented itself, or even to lose his reason so a trustee—in the person of a devoted cousin—might have been appointed to oversee the ducal assets.

"Good morning, Your Grace." Marcus extended a hand to Mercia. "A beautiful day for a ride. Hullo, horse. He looks to be thriving in your care."

"As he did in yours." The duke slapped Marcus hard on the back then looked around as a groom led the beast away. "The stables are not falling down. You exaggerated shamelessly."

Mercia's handshake was firm, his voice hearty, his dismount lithe. Marcus wanted to punch His Grace in his smiling face.

"Compared to Severn, this place is a disgrace. And I wish I could say I've found a great stash of the King's coin hoarded up during all the years of neglect, but Greendale spent it on his entertainments and keeping the house up."

Mercia's smile turned disgustingly sympathetic. "You can always marry an heiress. In the alternative, rent out the house to some rich cit, fix yourself up a bachelor's paradise in the gatehouse for a few years, diversify your incomes, and come visit me often. I promise to break out the best the cellars have to offer, and listen to all your woes."

Goddamned hail-fellow-well-met.

"Sounds like good advice, particularly if I want to look in on my uncle's widow from time to time."

"She offered to take Lucy in hand." The words put shadows in the renowned Severn blue eyes, and this was a relief, because Marcus had lost his only spy in the ranks of Severn servants.

"The poor girl still hasn't found her tongue?"

"No, and I lose hope she ever will. If seeing one's dear papa rise from the dead, and commanding the daily care and company of the countess hasn't wrought a miracle for Lucy, I'm not sure what will."

Thank God. "She doesn't lack wits," Marcus said, leading his guest through the extravagance of the Greendale gardens. "Perhaps you might send her north to one of those establishments that deal specifically with hysterical females."

Marcus, having done some research, could name a few that would treat the girl with admirable attention to discipline.

"The physicians offer their tuppence worth of guesses, but that's all they are, guesses. You're good to ask after her."

"The best cousin you'll ever have, and I've promised decent food and drink, because God knows Greendale took care of his cellars. Come, and we'll wash the dust of the road from your throat. How is the countess, by the way?"

Mercia paused by a bed of mostly blown roses that

had likely cost more than the mount Marcus made do with in Aragon's absence. "Lady Greendale is struggling, Marcus."

"Mourning is a difficult time." What could make Gillian, Lady Greendale, struggle now, if eight years before the mast with the old man hadn't done it?

"Mourning is difficult for us all. Helene was your friend."

For God's sake…after months of silence among the bloody French, Mercia had to turn up fearlessly blunt now. Marcus made a study of the roses, though if this variety had a scent, he could not detect it.

"Helene was your duchess, but these are gloomy thoughts on a beautiful day. Come up to the house, and we'll enjoy some fine brandy before you interrogate me over lunch."

He watched a strange look cross His Grace's features at the use of the word interrogate, and knew a little satisfaction to think in some small way he could make his famous, unbreakable, quiet, ducal cousin squirm.

It wasn't enough, but it was something.

St. Just's gaze traveled from the vines twining up the curtains, to the pansies blooming on the pillowcases and slipcovers, and the intricate geometric designs on the runner gracing the coffee table in Gilly's sitting room.

"You really do embroider everything in sight," he said.

"And I embroider some things out of sight," Gilly replied then realized from the smile on St. Just's face that his imagination wasn't conjuring images of handkerchiefs.

"Mercia warned me to lock up my stockings," St. Just said, sauntering into the little parlor. He was a good-looking man, less refined than Christian, but blessed with a pair of green eyes sporting long dark lashes and winging dark brows. All in all, an imposing man, but somehow, less of a man to Gilly than Christian.

St. Just had never been taken captive, never known torture, never been moved nigh to violence at the sight of an unexpected kitten. These facts ought to diminish Christian, but in her eyes, they gilded his courage and made him all the more remarkable.

"If you keep looking at the clock, my lady, the hands will advance, and your duke will return, but a visit to the back terrace might be in order if you're not to entirely waste this beautiful day."

"You've been very patient with me," she said, rising. "Another turn through the park might serve."

He offered his arm and matched her pace as they made their way to the terrace. He'd been a cheerful if ruthless companion when she gardened, pulling weeds beside her with a sort of barbaric enthusiasm. She'd asked him about his horses, though, and his gaze had softened considerably.

Over lunch, he'd told her amusing stories about his siblings and about that august personage, his father, the Duke of Moreland. Then he'd let George and John stand guard outside the study door while she caught up on correspondence, but here he was, again taking escort duty.

"Do you miss your siblings, Colonel?" she asked as they descended from the back terrace.

"A challenging question, to which a man not decorated for bravery would say, of course."

"But you are a brave man, so…?"

"I miss them, and I dread them," he said, and rather than tour the roses—which were past their prime—St. Just escorted Gilly in the direction of the stables. "We've been at peace for months now, and I expect to wake up one day and say to myself, 'Well, now, things are back to normal, and isn't that a great relief?'"

"Except?"

"Except I keep waking up prepared to tell my men we're moving on to another town, farther to the north and east, pushing our way across the entire Iberian Peninsula to crawl up Bonaparte's back. I expect to hear we're besieging yet another bloody walled city, and I do mean sanguinary, with all the same carnage and misery the last siege provoked."

The charming officer had gone, leaving a career soldier in his place, and Gilly liked this fellow even more than that officer.

"You miss war?" Gilly asked, because she missed nothing, not one thing, about her marriage to Greendale.

A curiously happy thought.

"I grew used to it," he said. "I knew who my enemies were, who was under my command, and what our objective was when we marched out. I had specific tasks: get this report to that general, count the number of horses in the following towns, and so forth. This is not a fit topic for a lady."

"The interesting topics never are. So you do miss it."

The gardens were past their peak, and the fall flowers hadn't yet started to bloom. St. Just knelt to snap off a sprig of lavender and held it under his nose.

"I miss having a purpose as compelling as life and

death, King and Country. I miss being something besides Moreland's oldest by-blow."

My goodness, no wonder Christian considered this man a friend. "Moreland has more than one?"

"I have a half sister similarly situated, and in many ways, her lot is more difficult than mine."

Gilly did not ask what could be more difficult than war; she didn't need to.

And St. Just wouldn't say more, wouldn't prose off into a description of his siblings again. Though it might have been the easier course for them both, Gilly didn't want him to.

"I've heard rumors," St. Just said, crumpling the lavender in his fist. "Rumors the Corsican is trying to escape from his island, rumors the French would march with him again if he did. The poor devils have forgotten how to go on in peacetime, and Napoleon left them little enough to go on with."

The scent of lavender wafted on the summer air when St. Just opened his fist.

"And you're ready to fight him again if he does." Gilly didn't make it a question. St. Just looked so unhappy, so bewildered, she realized she'd hit the mark. "Why?"

He tossed the mangled lavender aside and was quiet for a moment, gazing out over the back gardens, then one corner of his mouth kicked up.

"Damned if I know. Pardon the language."

Gilly remained beside him in the fading afternoon light and realized if Christian were there, he might have an answer. He might have the wisdom and the courage to understand why a man, a good man, was choosing war and death over a life of peace and plenty.

"Your brother is ill, isn't he?" Gilly asked.

"I will have to admonish your duke that unpleasant confidences spilled over the brandy aren't for a pretty lady's ears."

She led him to a bench, the topic being a sitting-down sort of subject.

"I keep you in my prayers, Colonel, and Christian considers you a friend. You needn't worry I'll spread gossip." To the vicar? Who was concerned only about his leaky roof and launching four daughters?

"I would never accuse you of gossiping. Victor puts a brave face on his illness for the sake of my parents. We all know he's consumptive, but my father acts as if Victor malingers, and we must drag him to the sea and the quacks and the countryside all in aid of denying his approaching death."

"Once death becomes a friend, much becomes easier. Easier for the one dying, but perhaps harder for those left to grieve."

St. Just sat beside her, a man comfortable in his skin if not entirely comfortable with peacetime. "You've recently buried a spouse. I am remiss to bring up such a dolorous topic when you're in mourning."

Gilly had been the one to bring it up, not the colonel.

"I am in mourning," Gilly said, "but not, I think, for my late husband. Shall we walk farther, Colonel? The sun will soon set, and the light is so pretty."

He winged his arm at her, and Gilly tried to enjoy his silent company. He was charming enough and all that was considerate, like Christian. He bore a pleasant scent and was of a height with Christian too.

But it wasn't the right scent; it wasn't ginger and

lemon with an undercurrent of rose. St. Just was a
hair too tall, a tad too thickly muscled, his eyes green
not blue.

He was a good man; he wasn't the right man. He
sought a return to war, for which Gilly did not blame
him, but part of why she was in love with Christian
was that despite his past, he'd turned his sights to peace
and to a future free of violence and destruction.

As Gilly could.

As she had, and this notion, too, was a wonderfully
happy thought.

⊷⊷

The duke's appetite was in good repair, and to Marcus,
that was depressing enough. His Grace laughed heartily at some joke Marcus's ancient steward told, flirted
with the tenants' daughters, and generally comported
himself with more bloody charm than a regiment of
officers on leave. This Mercia had been easy to forget,
the hearty, healthy man in great good spirits.

When Mercia had left London, he'd still been
swilling hot water instead of tea, downing oranges
to address inchoate scurvy, jumping at shadows, and
barely capable of riding on his own through the park.
He'd received not one caller, though dozens of calling
cards from the best families had been left at his door.

Marcus's spies might have been lying, but chambermaids were usually too stupid to know when they
were being pumped for information, particularly if
they were being swived silly at the same time.

"What emerges as your first priority as you put
Greendale back on solid footing?" His Grace asked.

They were walking their horses to the stables after spending much of the afternoon ambling around the Greendale property. They'd toured only the tenant farms in the best repair, Marcus being unwilling to reveal the full depth of the estate's problems to anybody save his man of business.

"I cringe to say it, but probably liquidating what isn't entailed, though that has become complicated."

"Complicated how?"

Life had been so much easier when one's enemies could be murdered outright.

"I must wait to get my hands on the personal estate until the lawyers have done with their fussing."

"They should be able to turn loose enough money to maintain the estate," Mercia said. "Bloody vultures. If you need funds, you have only to say."

"Good of you."

The words cost him, but Marcus fiddled with his horse's mane in an effort to appear appropriately self-conscious.

"I can put in a word at the law offices for you if like. I might be going up to Town in the next few weeks, in any case."

This was news. "For the opening session of the Lords?"

"Personal business. If I do go, I'd appreciate your spending some time at Severn in my absence."

"Particularly if it's during that exercise in manual labor, frustration, and sweat known as harvest, I can accommodate you. Does this have to do with our struggling countess?"

For whom Marcus did, in fact, have a few stirrings of genuine pity.

For the first time in that entire day, Mercia's eyes looked bleak, lost even.

"Some misfortune has befallen her since Greendale's death," he said.

Delightful. "I heard the inquest grew unnecessarily nasty. Unfortunate, but it's behind her now. If I'd been on hand, things might have gone differently."

Very differently.

"I don't believe she was ever truly under suspicion." Mercia drew his horse up in the stable yard, and neither man nor beast looked the least bit fatigued, whereas Marcus had been spurring his gelding for the last three miles. "She's had a string of accidents that haven't struck me as accidents."

What were cousins for, if not to confide in? "Somebody means her harm?"

"Somebody means her dead."

In terse words, he recounted a coach wheel coming loose, a cut girth, and a near miss with poison, any one of which should have been adequate to end the countess's life.

But they hadn't been.

"I rather hope Gillian's characterization of events is the accurate one," Marcus said. "Accidents, or a jealous mistress cut out of Greendale's will."

"In which case, having run off the kitchen maid, Gilly is safe enough at Severn."

Gilly?

"Where she can dote on Lady Lucille," Marcus said, though anybody doting on the girl was not a sanguine thought. "Send word, and I will be only too happy to enjoy your hospitality for as long as you need me." The words sounded sincere, because they were sincere. Perhaps the first sincere thing he'd said all day.

"I appreciate it." The duke crossed his wrists over the pommel. "I meant what I said about a loan, Marcus. We're family, you looked in on my family for me, looked after my horse, held the reins while I was rotting away on a French mountainside. I owe you."

Marcus swung out of the saddle and handed the tired gelding off to a stableboy. Mercia's thanks should have gratified, but they only enraged. "Guarding your back was my privilege, and a loan won't be necessary."

"Be stubborn then, it's a family virtue."

"Or a vice," Marcus said, particularly when exhibited by a captive of the French. "Stubbornness can definitely be a vice."

Mercia smiled and cantered off, looking handsome, happy, and too goddamned healthy for words. Stubbornness might be a vice, but it was one they shared. Marcus took himself up to the house and bellowed for his secretary. That worthy came scurrying up from the kitchen and bowed to his master.

"I need to write a letter to Robert Girard, St. Clair House, on Ambrose Court in Mayfair. Have it couriered, and you're to forget every bloody word of it before you leave this room."

The secretary was used to such commands. He'd served under the old earl and written many a note to the fair Helene for Marcus on various visits at Greendale. She'd never written back, but that hardly mattered now.

Maybe having Mercia meet up with brigands on his homeward journey would have been easier, but the silent duke enjoyed too much popular interest now. His death would be investigated, and the first question asked would be: "Who benefits from his passing?"

So let it be this way, with Girard serving as the instrument of Mercia's death. No code of law or code of honor would protect Girard from the consequences of killing such a well-regarded nobleman, regardless that it was murder on the so-called field of honor. Girard at the very least would be hounded from the country, and not a soul would protest his absence.

No man whose body—whose hand—had been that badly treated could expect to prevail in personal combat, not even the unbreakable duke.

◈

"Did you miss me, Gilly love?"

A great warm weight settled along Gilly's back and shifted the mattress behind her.

"Did you lock my door?" Sleep hadn't been elusive, it had been entirely absent, and only a portion of Gilly's wakefulness had been on her own account.

"Of course I locked the door. What do you take me for? The maids know to leave my chambers alone come morning, but I'd be completely undone did they walk in on me here. I like this bed, it's cozier than mine."

"Smaller, you mean." She flopped over onto her back, trying to see him by the moonlight streaming in the window. "And you won't be here in the morning."

"Will too. Budge over. Cozy means I don't want to be hanging off the mattress all night."

She shifted to the far side of the bed, realizing he'd

once again put himself between her and the door, something she'd never had to ask him to do. "How was Marcus?"

"Too much the officer for me," Christian said. "Stop frowning at me, love, and cuddle up. The nights grow chilly, and we can't have your favorite duke taking an ague."

"Heaven forfend." She curled down against his side, tucked her head on his shoulder, and slid a knee across his thighs, for he was her favorite duke. Also her favorite man. "Better?"

"You are all that is accommodating. I ran into St. Just saying good night to his horse. He said he had a thoroughly agreeable day, and why I haven't married you defies reason."

"You won't allow me to find sleep," Gilly said on a sigh. "You must badger me for good measure, haunt my dreams, and threaten to scandalize the maids in the morning to see me flustered."

"You're still indisposed, aren't you?" He twisted his head to kiss her brow. "Poor dear. Your biology makes you cranky—has anyone ever told you that?"

"I'm going to sleep now."

"Now that I'm here, of course you are." He drew circles on her nape with his thumb, lazy caresses that drained all the nameless worry out of her.

"What do you mean, Marcus was too much the officer?"

His fingers on her neck slowed. "He was all bonhomie and good show. He's facing near ruin at Greendale but wouldn't let me lend a hand."

The estate was another victim of Greendale's legacy,

and in some ways, one bearing the more difficult wounds to overcome. "How could you tell?"

His hand shifted to knead her shoulders, and Gilly let loose a soft groan. "My countess sounds like Chessie after a good roll."

"My duke has a few talents that might endear him after all."

"You got the important part right," he said. "I am your duke, but back to the matter at hand. Marcus was careful to take me around to his best farms, but still, the fences are sagging, the land is tired, the herds are adequate, but the beasts are runty enough to suggest years of inbreeding. The servants scurry around like whipped dogs, and Marcus claims the solicitors won't turn loose of any of the estate monies because of legal restrictions."

"Greendale had coin," Gilly said. "Or he acted like he did." She stifled a yawn and shifted her leg to a more comfortable position on Christian's thighs.

"Move your leg like that again at your peril."

Her eyes flew open. "I'm not...I'm still indisposed."

He patted her bum through her nightgown. "That doesn't preclude me from wanting you, or you from wanting me."

Would anything? "It most certainly should."

"Gilly, dearest lady, you likely treasured your indisposition because it meant old Greendale stayed at a distance. He's dead. If you want your pleasure of me, I'm not put off by a little untidiness. Copulation is messy. That's part of its charm."

"You are entirely lacking in delicacy." And yet, his honesty, his simply lusty directness was as precious to her as the feel of his fingers circling gently on her neck.

"I am entirely lacking in subterfuge when it comes to my countess. Give me your hand." He followed her arm down and took her hand in his. "Feel this."

He put her fingers around his engorged shaft then took his hand away.

"You get into this state merely from *talking* to me?"

"And from missing you, and touching your sweet flesh, and feeling your leg brushing against my thighs in an unintentionally provocative manner."

He fell silent, and Gilly trailed her fingers over his length—intentionally. He was quite aroused, so aroused she considered risking the sheets. And her dignity.

"You can bring me off, love, touching me like that."

"I can…?" She stroked him again, though repeating such vulgar language was beyond her—taking her nightgown off before him had once been beyond her too.

"Take you about two minutes, and you'd have a very grateful duke in your bed, did you try it."

"A very chatty duke…" she muttered as she sleeved him with her fingers, a light grip, and stroked over the length of him while he flexed his hips.

"That's it," he said, setting up a rhythm. "And you could come here and give a lonesome duke some kisses to linger over lest he rush his fences."

The hand on her nape slid up into her hair and guided her head so he could get his mouth on hers, but she pulled back.

"I'm glad you're home." Foolish words, but she wanted to give him something, because in his blatant desire for her, even in her indisposition and crankiness and fatigue, he gave her a precious gift.

"I'm glad to be home." His mouth was still smiling when he set his lips against hers.

He kissed her with easy languor, letting her take the lead until the end, when his hand closed over hers and he demanded more than a light grip. He shoved the sheets aside, bowed up, and cradled her against him tightly, while a wet warmth spilled over their hands and his breath seized in his chest. When he lay back on a sigh, he still didn't let her hand go.

"We'll need a handkerchief, Your Grace, or a flannel or a—"

"Hush." He stroked her hair. "Give me a minute to hold you, and then an hour to thank you. You now have a favor to call in, Gilly, the best kind of favor."

He was so cheerful about the whole business, so easy with it, while Gilly felt an inconvenient urge to weep. She withdrew her hand, grabbed a handkerchief from the night table, and tossed it onto his chest.

"You'll have to do the honors, love. You've shot my horse right out from under me."

"I'm to...use this?" She dangled the small white cloth before his nose.

"Somebody had better. I'm missing in action. Felled by sniper fire, *non compos mentis...*"

"Do shut up." She dabbed at him. Then used one hand to hold his softening member and the other to scrub with the monogrammed linen. She finished up rubbing briskly at his belly and resumed her place curled against his side. His passion had a scent, musky, male, and not unpleasant, but...different.

"How much longer are you indisposed?"

"Weeks."

His belly bounced with suppressed humor, and Gilly smiled despite the ache in her throat.

"I'd wait weeks for you, Countess."

"Provided I occasionally shot your horse out from under you?"

"Two can play at that, you know. Not only lonely dukes are susceptible to pleasure."

"Hush, now." She kissed his nose and tucked herself beside him.

Christian was playful, but if anything ever happened to him, Gilly would not survive his loss. Thank God, Christian was resuming the bucolic life of an English duke; thank God he'd offered to resume it with her.

He was quiet for long minutes while his hand wandered around her neck and shoulders. Shot his horse, indeed. She closed her eyes, pleased with herself, and with him too.

⚜

"I don't want Marcus babysitting me."

Gilly's displeasure was evident in her tone and in the way she planted her hands on her hips. The stable lads found somewhere else to be, but Christian wasn't fooled. The lazy blighters were all within earshot, and they'd soon let him know what they thought of the man who riled their favorite little countess so early in the day.

"I told you I wouldn't leave you unprotected when I had to go to Town," he said, keeping his tone reasonable with effort.

"Send St. Just to tend me, or content yourself that I'm not in any danger. They were mishaps and accidents."

"They were not." He was sure of it. He did not know why he was sure of it, but he was. Soldier's instinct, maybe, or the conviction of a man who'd had too much bad luck in recent years. "I don't even know that I'll be traveling to Town soon, I merely wanted to remind you of the possibility in case I need tend to anything for you while I'm there. Shall I call upon Mr. Stoneleigh? Check on your funds? Find you more shawls to embroider?"

"Do not patronize me, Christian."

Her use of his name ought to have gratified him, but given her tone, it was…chilling, like the metal-on-metal sound of iron bars locking into position.

"I'm trying to communicate with you," he said, advancing on her. Before she could flounce away, he laid an arm across her shoulders. "St. Just will be down from the house any minute. I promise I'll argue with you the livelong day, but might we have a short cease-fire to see our guest off?"

Our guest. She appeared to ponder taking issue with that then gave him a terse nod. "We can."

"I do mean it. If it makes you feel better to fight with me, Gilly, I'll be your sparring partner." Because he knew well the gratuitous urge to hit something—anything—when the proper object of a vengeful impulse was beyond reach.

"Until you run off to London."

She was doing her best to show the colors, but Christian heard the undercurrent of worry in her words, worry for him, but also worry about how she'd fare in his absence.

"I'm not running off to London. I'm tending to business, the same as you did earlier this summer. You can send me long, nasty letters criticizing every aspect of my personality while I'm gone. You can draw Lucy aside and explain to her the failings of the common man, and the worse failings of her own papa. You can convert Chessie to your cause, because you've already turned my entire staff against me."

"They love you," she said, drawing away to look at him.

"They love you more, Gilly dear." As he loved her more each day. "You looked after Lucy when I could not, and if the staff at Greendale knew something of the state of your marriage, they very likely gossiped with our staff as well."

She paused in their progress down the barn aisle. "They should have a disgust of me."

"You have an undeserved disgust of yourself, which you should turn on your late spouse and leave there, but here comes the colonel, looking entirely too pleased to leave us."

"We need to talk, Christian." She spoke quietly, all the fight gone out of her.

"You're not leaving me." He hadn't meant to say that, hadn't meant to make a pronouncement to a woman who was entitled to a permanent dislike of men and their dictates.

"Christian Severn," she said, smoothing his hair back gently. "I do not want to leave you. You are my favorite duke."

St. Just chose now to come strutting across the gardens, saddlebags over his shoulder. He whistled a nimble, jaunty version of "God Save the King," as if he knew his timing was awful.

"We will talk, Gillian," Christian said, leaning closer and cadging a kiss to her cheek despite St. Just's approach.

"I see you, Mercia, behaving like a naughty schoolboy and trying the countess's patience," St. Just said. "I can only thank your staff my horse hasn't been exposed to such a puerile display."

"His Grace is feeling frisky this morning," Gilly said. "Autumn approaches, and he's suffering the fidgets. Makes him prone to mischief."

"Don't listen to her," Christian said as St. Just's horse was led out. Christian took the saddlebags from his guest's shoulder and tied them up behind the cantle.

"See to my mount, Duke, while I see to your countess." St. Just winged an arm at Gilly and tossed out one of his charming smiles while Christian busied himself with checking over the fit of the bridle and girth. This display of caution was idle, for St. Just would repeat the inspection before mounting, but Gilly liked the colonel and deserved a moment with an ally.

They walked off toward the garden, leaving Christian to pet the beast, a big, solid bay gelding, not the same one as the last time St. Just had come through, for this one was more elegant with a more refined head.

"Cozening my horse, Mercia?" St. Just asked a few moments later.

"Cozening my countess, St. Just?"

"Stop it, you two." Gilly sounded half-serious in her scold. "The colonel has places to be, and he'd best get to them. Cook says her knees are acting up, and that means rain by nightfall."

"I'm off to Town, then," St. Just said. "Mercia, I'll be in touch. Countess." He bussed her cheek and whispered something in her ear, meriting him a terse nod. Christian drew Gilly back and slid an arm around her waist.

"Come by any time, St. Just," Christian said. "Cook will miss you."

"I'll be back," he said, swinging onto his horse. "I want to see when Lady Lucy's dogs are pulling a pony cart around with His Grace at the ribbons." He blew Gilly a kiss and cantered off, the personification of elegance in the saddle.

"How did I travel the length of France with our guest and never realize he's a devilish good-looking man with a penchant for kissing other people's countesses?"

"His papa is a duke," Gilly said, sliding away from his side. "That can explain a lot about a man's penchants."

"You are my hostess, if you'll recall," he said, letting her put some distance between them. "And I am your duke."

She wandered away, into the garden, but he kept her in sight, and not only because he and the lady had some significant matters to sort out. She might tell herself she was the victim of accidents and mishaps, or that a jealous kitchen maid was capable of orchestrating the malfunction of a coach wheel or the sabotage of a saddle.

Christian knew differently.

Nineteen

CHRISTIAN WAS THE SOUL OF PATIENCE, SO MUCH SO that Gilly wondered if he'd had second thoughts about proposing to her.

His lovemaking was patient too—tender, lyrical, sweet, and silent. Gilly had fallen asleep in his arms, when her best intention had been to talk to him.

Truly talk.

She wanted to accept his proposal, wanted to embark on the joys and challenges of being a wife to Christian Severn. Not duchess to the Duke of Mercia, the Lost Duke, or the Silent Duke—that wretch was welcome to dwell in the past, along with the unfortunate Lady Greendale—but finding the right moment to talk of the future was difficult.

They were shooting at targets a week after St. Just's departure, a pastime Gilly had taken to with relish. When Christian had first suggested it, she'd cringed at the noise and destructiveness of it, but the first time she'd hit her target, she'd felt such a thrill she'd joined him every day since.

She'd need years to catch up to him, though. He

shot flying targets out of the air, hit his mark from great distances, and could manage clean shots from peculiar angles while he himself was in motion. Whatever had been done to his left hand, it hadn't affected his ability to fire a weapon at all.

"You had to shoot from the saddle, I take it," she said when he'd shown her a maneuver involving shooting on the run, dropping, rolling, and discharging his second barrel.

"From the saddle, from the ground, from the trees. I was once posted as lookout in a church steeple, and fired a warning shot to my men by hitting the bell hanging from the town hall across the square. That didn't sit well, but it was the only way to gain enough height for decent reconnaissance."

"Do you ever miss the army?"

"No, I do not." He passed her a loaded pistol. "Why would I?"

"St. Just said something about the Corsican making plans to escape," she said, taking the gun. "Another man might be consumed with hunting down his captors and putting an end to them. I thank God you are not. I've dealt with enough violence to last a lifetime, and I could not endure it casting a shadow over the future."

She'd worded her sentiment carefully—*the* future, not *our* future.

The pistol was small, as guns went, the barrel only four inches, which meant it hadn't much aim over distances. Despite a mortal loathing for violence, Gilly liked knowing that, liked understanding why it was so. Christian had explained it to her, just as he'd made her learn how to clean her gun, how its mechanism worked, and how to handle it when it was loaded.

"The Corsican has nothing else to do but make his little plans," Christian said, scanning the hedgerow and looking very ducal indeed. "Try for the twig about six feet up on that oak."

Being short, Gilly had to train herself to aim a little higher than she thought she should, to let her hand follow her eye. Christian moved to stand behind her. She took aim and clipped the thing neatly.

"I do like it when the bullet does what I tell it to."

"You like it when everything does as you say." He took the gun from her hand. "More shooting, or have you had enough?" His teasing had a small edge to it, or maybe Gilly was the one on edge. He hadn't said anything more about going up to Town, but dukes invariably spent time in London.

"Enough practice. The air reeks of our efforts."

"I used to hate the stench of sulfur," he said, sounding a bit puzzled.

Ah, another quagmire, which Gilly understood well. "Just as you hated cats and the sound of the French language on a man's lips and sudden noises and loud noises... What?"

"We're to be disturbed," he said, purposely setting the gun aside so a footman could approach them. "What is it, George?"

"Beg pardon, Your Grace, a letter came from Town by messenger."

Christian held out his hand, and Gilly felt a sense of foreboding. Perhaps St. Just was planning another visit, except the man knew he need not send warning, and certainly not by courier. Christian tore the missive open and scanned its contents, his expression betraying nothing.

"I will be nipping up to Town after all."

Feathers. Damned, perishing feathers. "St. Just summons you?"

"Something like that. Shall we see if all this racket has disturbed Lucy's lessons?"

She let him get away with that, let him dangle the obvious distraction before her, and let him saunter along beside her through the gardens. All the while, Gilly felt a growing silent tumult.

Christian was still settling in, still recovering. He wasn't supposed to hare off on business—he was a duke, for pity's sake, his business came to him with a snap of his elegant fingers.

"I'll send a note over to Marcus," Christian was saying. "He'll be more than happy to have a respite from the challenges at Greendale."

"I don't want him here," Gilly retorted, knowing her reply was irrational, knowing her voice held a note of panic.

"Gilly…" He paused at the French doors leading to the library. "He's family, and he's agreed to do this for me. I'm hopeful if I ask a favor of him, he'll let me provide some assistance with Greendale in return. It's a sop to masculine pride, I know…"

She stomped off a few paces and turned her back to him.

"Gillian?" He walked up behind her and stood near enough that she could catch a hint of lemon and ginger, but he didn't touch her. "Talk to me."

Now he wanted to talk, while Gilly wanted to weep and wasn't exactly sure why. "He smokes horrid cigars."

A patient, considering silence greeted that pronouncement, then, "Make sense to me, Gilly. You are a wonderfully sensible woman. Explain to me your reservations, because I *must* go, and I must know you are safe when I do. Am I being unreasonable?"

No, but neither was Gilly.

She whirled on him, prepared to beg. "Marcus knew, Christian. He *knew* exactly what Greendale was about, and he did nothing. Kissed my hand and went on his way to call on Helene or scamper back to Spain or up to Town, there to drink the winter away with his fellow officers on leave."

Christian's arms came around her, promising security and more of his patient reason. "Did Greendale raise his hand to you before others?"

"His voice, occasionally, before the servants, not his hand."

"Then Marcus likely suspected you suffered nothing worse than a tongue lashing."

"That is balderdash," she said. "I have uncles. I know how men are. You gather around the port or the brandy and you talk of women, and you have no privacy from one another regarding your bodily pleasures."

"Some men," he said. "But Greendale was arrogant. He would not boast of having trouble consummating his vows."

"He would boast of bringing his rebellious wife to heel, like some hound prone to running riot."

"You are so very angry," he said quietly. He held

her tighter, and Gilly wanted to rage and break things and cry, not because he didn't understand—but because very possibly he did, and he was leaving anyway.

She stepped away instead and did not take Christian's arm. They went up to the nursery in silence, a distance growing between them that Gilly both needed and hated.

Why didn't Christian invite her to go with him to Town?

Why couldn't St. Just be recruited to serve as her nanny again?

What had been in that damned note?

And why, despite all his importuning Gilly to talk with him, had Christian grown in some way, once again, silent?

"How is my scholar doing today?" Christian asked.

Lucy held up her copybook for him to inspect.

"You have the prettiest hand," he said. "You get that from me. Your dear mama's scribbling was nigh incomprehensible, but she told the best stories over tea and had a marvelous sense of fun."

Lucy pantomimed shooting with a gun by cocking her thumb and forefinger.

"Yes, we were shooting, the countess and I. When you are twelve, I will show you how to shoot as well, if you like. You may start with the bow and arrow when you are ten, if you'd enjoy that?"

She nodded vigorously, and Gilly was struck as she often was by how badly Lucy must want to communicate with her father. Christian had the knack of carrying on conversations with the child better than the nurse, the governess, or even Gilly herself. His skill with the child was gratifying and maddening, both.

"I must beg your company at tea today," he said, "because I'm off for a few days to Town. I have business the stewards cannot resolve."

What *business*?

Lucy put her forefingers to her temples and trotted in a little circle.

"No, I will not take Chessie. I'll make better time with the curricle. You can take Chessie out for me in my absence, can't you? At least bring him some treats so the old fellow won't mope."

Lucy grinned and swung her father's hand.

"I'll miss you too, princess, and I will miss our countess, and Chessie, but I will not miss those two." He nodded at the puppies—already showing the promise of great size—slumbering on a rug. "They will be as big as ponies ere I return, but with only half the wit. I am glad horses do not bark, else we'd have no stables."

He nattered on, about how interested he'd be to see Lucy's drawings when he returned, and he might stop by the shops while he was in Town to pick up some pretty hair ribbons for his pretty daughter. Gilly went to a window seat and watched while father and daughter charmed each other.

"You won't have time to miss me," Christian said, "and Cousin Marcus will come stay at Severn while I'm gone. I'm sure it has been an age since he's seen you, and he'll be very impressed with how much you've grown."

The transformation in the child was so swift and radical, Gilly would not have known it was the same little girl. Lucy drew back, crossed her arms over her chest, and shook her head vigorously side to side. Her expression was a small thundercloud as she glared up at her father.

"You don't want me to go," Christian said. "I'm sorry, dear heart, but go I must, though not for long."

She seized his hand, and the shake of her head became frantic.

No, no, no, *no.*

Her mouth worked, and Gilly prayed this tantrum might be a backhanded means of compelling the child to speak, but Lucy merely formed the word "No" silently, repeatedly. Then, "Stay. Please, stay."

"Lucy…" Christian knelt at eye level with the girl. "Enough of this. I am not off to war. I am merely trotting up to Town, and I have provided for company in my absence. The countess will visit you daily, at least. You have promised to look in on Chessie for me, and I will not indulge the antics of a toddler in my grown-up girl."

He ran his hand down the side of her face, just as Lucy's tears began to fall in awful, wrenching silence.

Something was wrong; something was more wrong with the child than usual. Christian picked Lucy up and settled her in his lap while he took a rocking chair near the window.

"Don't cry, child. I'll be back, and all will be well, you'll see."

Tell him, Gilly thought as her throat constricted. *Tell him what's wrong, and he will bend his whole being to repairing it, but you have to tell him. You must tell him what you want, in words he can hear and understand.*

She left them their privacy but did not know if she admonished the child or herself.

❧

"You think to leave me." Christian waited until he had Gilly in bed to make his accusation. "Why, Gilly?"

Though he knew why. In some intuitive, female corner of her soul, Gillian apparently suspected her favorite duke was plotting a murder, the first of several, and calling it pressing business.

Why else would he leave his distraught and teary daughter in the nursery with a sanctimonious lecture about growing up and making Papa proud?

"Why are *you* leaving *us*, Christian?"

A woman whose very life had depended on vigilant study of her husband would not be put off by platitudes. She'd trust her instincts, as Christian had learned to trust his.

"Us?" He shifted over her and ran his nose along her temple, taking in a whiff of roses and Gillian.

"Me and Lucy. I have never seen anything more heart wrenching than a child who will only cry silently on her papa's shoulder."

Neither had Christian, and yet, if Girard had plotted to end Gilly's life, he was not above taking the child, even harming the child, for ends Christian could not fathom.

"She's concerned I'll go off to war again and be captured by another mad Frenchman, which is understandable." He kissed the smooth warmth of Gilly's brow, as if he might kiss away her doubts.

"She's not concerned, she's wildly upset."

As was Gilly.

As was, truth be known, Christian. In his headlong glee to put a period to Girard's existence, he had failed utterly to account for Gillian's dim view of men and their violent behaviors.

Of *all* men who indulged in violent behaviors, and her reaction was entirely reasonable, while for Christian, backing down from the opportunity to dispatch Girard was unthinkable.

Lying to Gillian was beyond unthinkable. And yet, what did Christian say to her, the woman who'd saved his soul if not his body?

Nothing of any consequence, that's what.

"You and Lucy can miss me together."

Silence, the most trenchant, impenetrable silence Christian had encountered. He remained poised over the woman he loved, and quite honestly babbled, because he admitted the possibility—slim, but more than theoretical—that Gilly and Lucy could have a lifetime to miss him.

"The sad truth is, Lucy will never learn to trust that I'm always coming back to her if I don't occasionally depart for a few days." His lips, all of their own volition, wandered to Gilly's mouth.

And she accepted his kisses, which was a mercy, because it occurred to him only now—now when he was once again doing business with death—that these might be the last kisses he'd ever give her.

"Shall I love you like this, my lady?"

She brought her knees up on either side of his flanks, as close to an invitation as he could hope for from her.

"I think I shall." He dug deep and found reserves of patience sufficient to pleasure her more slowly than he had before. She became pliant in his arms and gradually began to move under him. When her kisses turned voracious, he pressed himself into her, slowly, slowly.

"Say you'll miss me, Gilly." He went still inside her, though restraint tormented him sorely.

"Don't go. It isn't right that you go, not this time. You won't talk to me, Christian, and I need you to talk to me."

He'd lose her if he admitted the violence of his errand, if he admitted to any characteristic in common with her late, vicious husband. He'd lose her if she learned he'd been untruthful.

"Are you afraid I won't come back to you?" He brushed a lock of hair off her forehead. "Afraid I'll be distracted by the noise and frivolity of Town?"

She closed her eyes and snugged her body closer to his. "You're up to something, Christian. I can feel it. I'm worried for you, and you won't tell—"

"Feel this." He pressed forward by excruciating degrees, then withdrew at the same tempo almost to the point of leaving her body.

"Tell me…why you…must…" she said, but he advanced again, and her voice trailed off.

He wanted to confide in her, wanted to have no secrets, no silences between them, ever, but some truths were too costly.

"I will tell you I love you," he said, lacing his fingers with hers on the pillow and setting up a gloriously languorous rhythm. "I love you as I've never loved another, as I never will love another."

"Oh, God…Christian." She bowed up, her face against his shoulder, and control slipped from her grasp. He wasn't expecting passion to overtake her so soon, and he lost the battle to draw out his own pleasure. As he went over the edge with her, all he could think was: *I love you. I love you. I will always love you.*

He didn't know he'd made that declaration aloud until silence fell in the aftermath of their loving. Then he realized that come morning, he was the one who'd be leaving, but tonight, Gilly might be the one making her farewell.

❧

The day unfolded as His Grace had predicted, which ought not to have surprised or disappointed Gilly, though it did both. They rose and parted as they always did, despite her sense that he would have made love to her again if she'd shown the least receptivity.

The duke had devastated her the previous night with his soft, repeated declarations—and with his silence. He'd known exactly what he was about, too, embracing her when they were both spent and whispering vague apologies as if he regretted his infernal business.

Christian had once told her that his captor, the thrice-damned Girard, had also offered apologies.

"Good morning, my dear." He kissed her cheek as he made his way to the sideboard in the breakfast parlor. "Were you waiting for me?"

"Enjoying my first cup of tea in peace and quiet."

"You may enjoy it more now for having delightful company." He paused, plate in hand. "Shall I dish you up some eggs?"

"Toast will do, thank you."

He passed her a plate bearing four toast points, then helped himself to at least six eggs' worth of omelet, two pieces of toast, and a half-dozen strips of bacon.

A far cry from half a buttered scone and nursery tea.

"When will you leave?" Gilly tried to put the question evenly, but her voice caught.

"I expect Marcus here by midmorning," he said, flourishing his white linen serviette. "I should not be gone outside of a few days, a week at most. The drama you and Lucy have subjected me to would be flattering were it not so inconvenient."

She buttered her toast, wondering if he'd consider a bullet hole in his boot inconvenient. Her own reactions made no sense to her. She wanted him to stay, and she wanted to quit Severn herself, to be free of the kindness and patience in his eyes, the *pity*. He'd turned a deaf ear on her pleas regarding Marcus, and he'd all but lied about his reasons for going up to Town.

"I will keep a close eye on Lucy," she said. "I swear the girl was almost upset enough to speak yesterday, but then it occurred to me Marcus was here on leave when Evan was so ill and Helene died."

The realization made her toast stick in her throat, because what might the *sight* of Marcus do to Lucy, who'd ceased speaking from the time of the man's last visit?

Christian's expression went from pained to resolute. "Perhaps the sight of me returning from Town will move her to speak. Would you like more tea?"

She let him top up her cup, let him blather away about the weather and the coming harvest and about the team he'd have hitched up for the trip to Town.

He was doing the ducal equivalent of chattering, as she used to chatter at him, except his effort was the more effective distraction when she could not ignore even the sound of his voice.

Marcus arrived on schedule, declaring himself glad to be useful to his nearest family, and Gilly's sense of disquiet rose higher.

Marcus might have been *useful* to Gilly on any number of occasions—by inviting Greendale up to Town, by finding a moment alone to ask her if she was moving so stiffly for a reason, by insisting the dower house at least have a decent roof.

None of which explained her current unease. Had she grown so dependent on Christian that she was afraid to part from him? This boded ill, because she could not marry a man who kept secrets from the woman he professed to love.

"Marcus," Christian said, perhaps knowing Gilly didn't want to hear even the Greendale title, "I will leave you to the comforts of the library while the countess sees me to the stables. I have instructions for her regarding Lucy's studies in my absence."

Marcus sketched Gilly a bow. "I will spare myself the tedium. Studies were never of much appeal to me."

He departed, boot heels ringing on the polished floors in a way that set Gilly's teeth on edge because the cadence reminded her too strongly of Greendale.

Leaving Gilly to accept Christian's proffered arm. Before Marcus, Christian had been punctiliously polite with her, a bit of argument by demonstration.

Christian would treat her that well, were she his duchess. He'd never remonstrate with her before others, never fail to show her the utmost courtesy, never allow her to suffer insult from another.

But she'd have to marry him to be his duchess.

"You are quiet, my dear," he said as they made their way through the gardens. "This does not bode well for the King's peace."

"For yours, you mean? What is there to say, Christian? You are off on this mysterious errand, which you refer to as simply business, but I believe nothing about it is simple. Have you been summoned back to Carlton House? Or is it a command performance at the Horse Guards?"

"Neither. This business is of a personal nature, affecting only me. You must not concern yourself."

"Must I not?"

They reached the stable yard, and Christian signaled the grooms that he was ready for his curricle.

"I meant what I said at the house." He slipped his arms around her waist. "Please take extra care with Lucy while I'm gone. She will fret and worry and need your common sense and cheerful company."

"She'll have it."

"And I need to know you won't decamp in my absence."

His arm tightened fractionally, or Gilly would have withdrawn at least far enough to see his face. In profile, he looked more stern than usual, which only increased Gilly's sense of anxiety.

"You think I'd leave Lucy alone when she was so adamant she did not want Marcus here?"

"She was adamant I not go away," Christian said, peering at her.

"She was happy to discuss your trip with you in her fashion until you mentioned that Cousin Marcus would be coming to stay in your absence. Then *and only then* did she become cross…and disconsolate. This morning she was withdrawn again, barely acknowledging our visit."

"Helene was prone to the same moodiness," he said, stepping away and tugging on his driving gloves. "Lucy will be gamboling with her puppies before I'm gone an hour. Now, this has been an enlightening digression, Countess, but I asked for specific reassurances from you, and I've yet to hear them."

He rested his hands on her shoulders. "Promise me you won't leave in my absence. I want to hear the words, Gilly, and you will look me in the eye when you say them."

If Christian was this worried that she'd leave him, he must be up to something very bad, indeed. "Damn you, sir. I was waiting for your next proposal."

He smiled a crooked, sad, and slightly smug smile. "I'm waiting for your promise."

"I will not depart in your absence unless for some dire emergency, and then I will leave my direction with Harris and Nanny."

"A fit of pique is not a dire emergency. Can we agree on that?"

"We can, else you'll stand here the livelong day badgering me."

She wanted to pick yet another fight, and he was *leaving* at a time when only something dire ought to take him away. She stepped closer, putting her arms around him for all the stableboys to see—again.

"You will propose again, won't you?" she asked now that the moment of parting was upon them. "You needn't repeat the bended knee part. When whatever is haunting you that requires you to charge off to London is put to rest, I would like to hear another proposal very much."

His arms closed around her, and his chin came to rest on her crown.

"This little business will pass, Gilly, while my feelings for you are constant. You are testing us both and grieving in your fashion and wondering what will become of you now that your enemy is in the ground. The generals always had the worst time controlling their troops when a siege broke and the city had fallen. That's when the real mayhem ensued, and you and I are no different."

"I'm not some pillaging infantryman to express my frustrations with gun and bayonet." Of that, she was certain.

"You know a great deal about being besieged, though."

He spoke gently and too quietly for anyone else to hear. The words were easy to understand on the surface, but the sense of them went much deeper. She took a breath and let herself feel his arms around her, let her cheek rest against his muscled chest.

"I'm about to cry."

"I know of nobody who has greater justification for tears."

She heard the curricle being brought around, and the sound of the wheels rattling against the cobbles struck at her. Christian was truly leaving, and now, *now*, she clung to him.

"I want to be angry with you. Angry enough to push away from you."

Still, he didn't turn her loose. "You have every reason to be angry, love."

"But not with you."

"And I have no excuse for being wroth with every cat I see, but if I find one in my house, I will still be tempted to toss it out the nearest window. That is a small price to pay for walking in the sunshine and being free to love you."

"Don't." She pressed her fingers to his lips and felt his mouth curve in a smile.

"We are talking, my love. This is a vast improvement over bickering and silence."

"It is, and now you'll spoil the mood by leaving."

"I will be back, and we will resume this discussion. I am aware difficulties lie ahead, Gilly, but I am determined we shall face them together."

"By leaving me here and keeping your infernal silence."

His smile faded, and she realized not only were they talking, he was *listening*. This heartened her— and frightened her—more than all of his smiles and promises together.

"I will be here when you come home, Christian. I can make that promise, but no others."

"I'll sustain myself on that much." He looked like he wanted to say more, but the leader of his matched team of blacks chose then to stamp a hoof. "I'm off. See to Lucy for me, and I'll bring her some storybooks from the shops in Town."

"Bring yourself." Gilly kissed him on the mouth

and should have known better. His arms closed around her tightly, and what was meant as her parting shot became his closing argument.

"Be off with you," she said, settling back on her heels. "Your horses grow impatient."

He stepped into his vehicle, took up the reins, saluted with his whip, and tooled the team out of the yard.

All before Gilly could find the nerve to tell him she loved him too.

⁓

The proprieties were observed easily, with Christian tracking Girard to one of the newer clubs that very evening. All it took was slapping a sweaty leather riding glove across Girard's face before many witnesses, including St. Just, who would serve as Christian's second. Contrary to best practices, the blow carried some force and left the corner of Girard's mouth bleeding.

And Christian enjoyed that, making Girard bleed all over his linen while others looked on. He would enjoy killing the man even more, despite the fact that Girard now styled himself Sebastian St. Clair—Sebastian Robert Girard St. Clair—Baron St. Clair.

"A challenge, then?" Girard rose, pressing his handkerchief to his mouth. "A duel to the death?" He looked Christian up and down. "As you wish, *mon duc*, and I look forward to matching myself against you now that you've had time to recover from your ordeal. War takes such a toll, does it not?"

Girard was gaunt, and his Gallic panache seemed

labored—which wasn't as gratifying as it ought to have been. Christian wanted to best a worthy and deserving opponent, not put down an ailing dog.

"Name your second, Girard, and St. Just will call upon him."

"My man, Michael Brodie, who dwells with me on Ambrose Court, shall second me. The choice of weapons will be communicated to you. Now, you have interrupted my reading, Your Grace, though your business was understandably pressing. If you will forgive me, I will resume my amusements."

Girard turned his back with the virtuosic rudeness of the French, and won points from the onlookers for his sangfroid.

"Cold bugger," St. Just muttered as he and Christian gained the street. "One would think he expected you, he left such a clear trail."

"He's thinner," Christian said. "He's aged since last I saw him." And yet, Girard was the same too, dark hair worn fashionably long, green eyes that could convey humor, indifference, and even respect without a word, and a coldness beneath every gesture and word that suggested no human soul had ever inhabited that big, lean body.

St. Just kicked a loose chip of cobblestone into the gutter. "Now is not an easy time to be a former French army officer. What does Lady Greendale make of all this?"

"You think I'd tell her about a duel, for pity's sake? Gillian does not look favorably on male flights of violence." And if she'd loathed Greendale's vile temper, what would she think of murder?

Premeditated, *scheduled* murder, conducted while sober witnesses stood by, ensuring the rules of ritual homicide were punctiliously observed?

"You and the lady seemed close," St. Just said, finding another pebble to send skittering to the gutter. "I'm often surprised at what Moreland tells his duchess behind closed doors."

"Gilly has enough on her plate, and she is a lady."

St. Just held his thoughts until Christian settled beside him in the privacy of the ducal town coach, but only until then.

"You withheld your plans from the countess to spare her sensibilities, of course, but you also anticipated she would disapprove of you taking another's life."

"Not exactly, but close. She would disapprove, she would worry, and she's fragile right now."

"Interesting word coming from a man who couldn't find an hour's respite from his nightmares."

"Silence, St. Just. Girard needs to die, and there's an end to it."

St. Just said nothing more on the subject, and really, what more was there to say?

The next day, when the colonel took himself off to Ambrose Court, Christian traveled to the City to pay a call on one Gervaise Stoneleigh.

"Your Grace, this is an unexpected pleasure," Stoneleigh said after offering a perfectly correct bow.

"Unexpected, I will believe. You will make some time for me regardless?"

"Lady Greendale would require it of me."

"Direct," Christian said when he'd been shown into a surprisingly elegant office. Potted violets grew on the windowsill, and one wall held framed sketches of a smiling lady with two small, chubby children. "Bluntness saves time, I suppose, but one always expects lawyers to prevaricate on general principles."

Stoneleigh nudged a clay pot an inch to the left, so the small, tender green plant sat in direct sunlight.

"As one expects the nobility to be arrogant on general principles. Please have a seat, Your Grace."

"I can see why Gillian hired you," Christian said, taking one of two opulently cushioned armchairs.

"That would be the Countess of Greendale."

Stoneleigh did not make his comment a question, though neither was it *quite* a scold, and he did not ask permission to sit in his own offices. Christian was pleased for Gilly that this dark, unsmiling man had her custom.

"She is Gillian to me, and she, alone among all others, calls me by my given name."

Stoneleigh's brows rose then settled, surely the lawyer's equivalent of an exclamation of surprise.

"Shall I ring for tea, Your Grace, or would you like something stronger?"

One could tell a lot about a man by the drink he served. "Something stronger, if it's not too much bother."

When they'd enjoyed fine libation indeed, Christian withdrew a sealed letter from his pocket and passed it to his host. "I will transact some business in the next several days that might result in my death or legal incapacity. That epistle is for the countess in the event of such an outcome."

Stoneleigh set the letter aside without even glancing at it. "The rumors are true, then? The clubs were all a-chatter last night because you'd challenged the man responsible for your ordeal after being taken captive."

Such delicacy. "*I* was responsible for being taken by the French," Christian said. "At the direction of his superiors, Girard exploited the technicality of finding me out of uniform and treated me to months of torture."

"Ah, so we're now killing soldiers who follow their generals' orders," Stoneleigh remarked, topping up Christian's drink. "And *were* you out of uniform, Your Grace?"

Any officer captured out of uniform was presumed to be a spy, and spies were regarded by gentlemen and scoundrels alike as beneath contempt.

Stoneleigh's willingness to lawyer that point now was not helpful.

"I was naked, Stoneleigh, bathing in the same river the soldiers on both sides used to water their horses and wash their clothes. My uniform was in sight, spread on nearby bushes to dry, had the French bothered to look, and the ducal signet ring graced my finger."

"So you were out of uniform."

"What is your point?"

"In the next day or two, you will get yourself killed or do premeditated murder," Stoneleigh said, his air patient, as if he were instructing a dim junior clerk. "One seeks to understand how exactly your honor was slighted, that one might explain it to the countess when your death adds to the misery that has already befallen her. I assume that is what this letter is for?"

When Christian remained silent, Stoneleigh flicked a glance at the missive Christian had spent hours composing.

"A maudlin exercise in futility, to be visited on the woman in the event of your death?"

A barrister knight errant. Tedious, but at least Stoneleigh was Gilly's barrister knight errant.

"That letter includes a substantial bank draft, made out to her, along with a few lines of apology and encouragement."

I love you. I will always love you.

Stoneleigh steepled his fingers and said nothing. He didn't have to speechify further, for Christian already understood that anybody who considered himself Gilly's henchman could not approve of this duel.

"I will pass along the letter should I hear of your death," Stoneleigh said, "and return it to you if you prevail. You're confident of prevailing?"

"I'd be a fool to call myself confident against a man of Girard's cunning. I'll do well enough with pistols. If he chooses swords, a few prayers for my soul might be in order."

"Your Frenchman isn't stupid. A stupid man might have tried to hide."

"He's not stupid, but he's arrogant and given to histrionic displays and—unless I miss my guess—weary to his soul."

If a soul he indeed possessed.

Stoneleigh rose and busied himself moving pots of violets around so the most flowers benefited from the sunlight pouring in the window. "You've chosen your seconds?"

"We have."

"Well, then, I have nothing more to say except best of luck. Where is the match to take place?" He lifted one blue ceramic pot sporting a cluster of deep purple flowers and sniffed.

Gilly had been denied even the pleasure of the gardens. Would she tend Christian's burial plot if Girard should prevail? She'd probably plant nettles over Christian's grave and water them frequently.

"St. Just will offer three locations in reverse order of my preference." He went on to describe them, two being in London's environs, one in a secluded corner of Hyde Park, and all surrounded by dense woods to ensure privacy. When Christian left an hour later, he was confident that Stoneleigh would deliver the missive to Gilly if the need arose, and keep his mouth shut about the business generally.

When Christian returned to St. Just's town house, St. Just's mouth was busy swearing heartily in what Christian suspected was Gaelic.

"Calm down," Christian said, closing the door to a surprisingly well-stocked library. "You met with the second, and the details are resolved. If you can recall the King's English, you might consider sharing those details with me."

A volume of Blake sat near a reading chair, opened to the very same damned poem Christian had quoted for Gilly. She'd known much more about being mocked in captivity than he'd understood.

"He's chosen foils," St. Just spat. "The bloody Frog wants foils."

Well, of course. "To the death? Hard to kill a man with a foil."

"Not hard," St. Just said. "Time-consuming, for you must pink him over and over, or try for a lunge to the heart or lungs or windpipe—some damned organ that will shut him down. Messy business, foils, and not the done thing."

An odd notion flitted through Christian's head as he shoved Blake into a desk drawer: captivity came in many forms. A marriage being one, a dungeon being another, *a quest for vengeance another*, though far preferable to the variety Girard had traded in.

"Perhaps among the French, foils are the done thing."

St. Just left off pacing long enough to move a carved white pawn on a large chessboard that sat under a tall, curtained widow. The set was marble and had to have cost a decent sum.

"If you'd like to spar, Mercia, I can accompany you to Angelo's."

"Generous of you, but if I did not acquit myself well, my confidence would suffer, and if I bested you, I might become overconfident."

"Tell me you've at least been practicing," St. Just said, walking around the chessboard and fingering a bishop, as if he'd oppose himself.

"I've been practicing."

"With a *sword*?"

"You fret over details," Christian said. "I must meet the man, St. Just. For the sake of my own sanity, I must meet him, and the outcome is in God's hands. If I best him, he's dead. If he kills me, he will be tried for murder and executed. Either way, a just God will see a period put to the man's existence."

"Not God," St. Just said, shifting the black bishop half the width of the board. "Don't bring the Almighty into it. That good fellow thought twenty years of mayhem at the hands of the Corsican was merely entertaining. Half a million men dead in the 1812 campaign to Moscow alone, and you want God to determine the outcome of this duel?"

"St. Just, must I get you drunk?"

"Tonight, yes," he said, scowling at the board once again from the white perspective. "You're to meet your man the day after tomorrow, at daybreak in the copse a quarter mile distant from the Sheffield Arms. We've arranged for two surgeons, as the choice of weapons was—Blessed Virgin preserve us—foils."

"St. Just, calm yourself. All will be well."

"Forgive me. My mother was a Papist. She was a fallen woman, but a fallen Papist woman—they are the most pious of all." He shifted a white knight, so the blighter was imperiled but closing in on check. "All will be well once you get me roaring bloody drunk."

Seeing no alternative, Christian proceeded to do just that.

༄

Two nights without Christian in her bed had left Gilly unrested and unsettled. She told herself they'd parted on a positive note, they'd made progress, but progress toward what, she could not say.

She couldn't bring herself to garden, she couldn't embroider, she couldn't wander the house for fear of running into Marcus. He'd been polite enough over dinner the previous evening, but he'd *watched* her, and Gilly was afraid did she remain in his company, she'd start blurting out questions.

Did he *know*?

How much did he know?

Had it ever occurred to him to assist her?

Had Greendale threatened him?

Had Greendale ever raised a hand to his heir? A buggy whip? A riding crop?

They might have said a great deal to each other, but considering Gilly could barely endure what Christian knew of her past, the less she saw of Marcus—and the less she smelled of his wretched cigars—the better.

By contrast, she was specifically charged with spending time with Lucy, who'd grown listless indeed, so although the hour was early, Gilly left her sitting room intent on heading for the nursery. She was surprised to find both George and John waiting for her in the corridor.

"Good morning, gentlemen."

"Milady."

"Did Lord Greendale set you to following me?"

"Nay, milady," George answered. "'Twere the dook. Said we was to stick to you like flies to honey, and it would be worth our Christmas pudding to do as he bid."

"Then we're for the nursery," she said, relieved it was Christian spying on her and not Marcus. "And possibly a stroll in the gardens."

They looked resigned—the gardens again—as they fell in step directly behind her. She was half thinking of a nooning picnic with Lucy when she paused at a faint whiff of tobacco in the third-floor corridor, where it had no business being. The playroom door was a few inches ajar, and Marcus's voice came from behind it.

"Even your nurse and your governess haven't heard you speak," he said, his tone musing. "I must applaud your diligence, child. When I said you must not speak one word of what you'd overheard, I hardly thought you'd take me so literally. Your mama is gone now, and no one would believe it did you accuse me of trying to persuade her to leave your papa."

A pause ensued, the length of time it took a man to puff on a cigar.

"As for the rest, your papa is about to meet his demise on the field of honor at the hands of the very Frenchie who was delegated the matter more than a year past. Justice delayed is justice denied, eh? Justice for me—and expensive justice, too, I can tell you."

Silence, while Gilly's blood ran cold and the scent of a burning cigar threatened to upend her breakfast. She put her finger to her lips and shook her head, lest John and George fall prey to heroic notions. Without making a sound, she motioned for them to follow her back down the stairs and into her parlor.

"He's a scheming bounder," George hissed. "Beggin' your ladyship's pardon, but what Greendale was sayin'…"

"Hush, George. I need to think."

George and John exchanged a look while Gilly's mind whirled.

Marcus had conspired with that awful Frenchman? *Marcus* had tried to woo Helene from Christian's side? *Marcus* had threatened Lucy into complete silence?

Marcus, who now had her and Lucy right under his paw.

"Gentlemen, I need your attention, and I need

to get word to the stable to put my sidesaddle on Chesterton, and to saddle Damsel for Lucy. We'll need a groom, too, and your greatest discretion." She gave them instructions and prayed luck would be with her and with Christian.

For they would both need it.

Twenty

GERVAISE STONELEIGH EYED THE MISSIVE SITTING ON his mantel and wondered, not for the first time, if Mercia knew what he was about. A man facing a duel must make his arrangements, that was part of the common sense of the process, but most men facing duels hadn't had their hands—their bodies, their minds—mangled by their opponent.

Which might give Mercia a tactical advantage, or it might put him at a practical disadvantage.

Or both.

A knock on the door of his library disturbed Stoneleigh's evening solitude. "Enter."

"Beg pardon, sir, but a female has come to the door, and she has a child with her. She says she's a client." The butler's face betrayed nothing, not curiosity, disapproval, concern—nothing. Stoneleigh paid him handsome wages to say nothing as well.

"Bring them in."

Gillian, Lady Greendale, followed the butler in, holding the hand of a golden-haired girl Stoneleigh would guess was about seven or eight years old.

"Hanscomb, a tray with both tea and chocolate, and close the door behind you. Lady Greendale, an unexpected pleasure."

Another unexpected pleasure.

"I am sorry to impose," she said, still clutching the child's hand. "We've come up from Severn today, and I couldn't find the colonel, and His Grace isn't residing at the ducal town house, but Girard is going to kill him if we don't warn him."

A silence ensued while the countess caught her breath and Gervaise puzzled out the sense of her words.

"Perhaps the child might enjoy her chocolate in the kitchen?" Bad enough he was about to discuss a duel with a grown woman. In the child's presence, such a thing could never be mentioned.

"Lucy stays with me."

"I can talk," the girl said. "I'm staying with Cousin Gilly."

The silent child, then, the one Lady Greendale had despaired of, but silent no more.

"I am to host two damsels in distress," Stoneleigh said. "Your duke is safe enough as we speak. I know this, for His Grace called on me, and I have some familiarity with his schedule. He will come to no harm tonight."

He gave the lady a pointed look, and she nodded.

The tale that emerged over sandwiches and tea cakes would give Mercia nightmares for years, provided he lived to hear it, and provided His Grace's other nightmares didn't absorb his every sleeping hour. Lady Greendale tried to convey some of the story in adult code, only to be thwarted by the girl.

"Cousin Marcus loved my mama," Lady Lucy volunteered at one point. "But Mama said he was an amusement to her. She told me that, but when she told Cousin Marcus he grew very angry and said he'd risked everything he had so they could be together. Mama laughed at him, and I crept away."

"You did the smart thing, then," Stoneleigh said. "Have another tea cake. They promote sound sleep."

Lady Greendale's eyebrows rose, but she nonetheless selected a small raspberry-flavored cake for the girl. Her ladyship was tired, with shadows under her blue eyes and a drawn quality about her mouth. Haring up from Surrey with a child in tow and a would-be murderer likely in pursuit wouldn't improve a lady's appearance.

"I wasn't smart enough," the girl said, munching her tea cake. "Cousin Marcus knew I was there, and he said if I told one word—even one word—of what I knew, then terrible things would happen. Evan died, then Mama died, and then Papa didn't come back. What could be more terrible than that?"

"What indeed?" Stoneleigh murmured. "I know something terrible, though not as terrible as your cousin's mischief. Desperately needing a decent night's rest and not getting it is terrible."

The child looked skeptical, the expression showing her resemblance to her father.

"My ladies, I can send you to my sister's, or you can flaunt all propriety and stay here with me. My staff is most discreet. In the alternative, I can escort you to Mercia's town house."

"Marcus will look for us there, and I would not want to involve your sister."

The general populace regarded the practice of law as an exercise in tedium, when in fact, Drury Lane could offer no more riveting drama.

"Then you shall be my guests."

He waited for Lady Greendale to tuck the child in, then sent the maid to bring the countess back to his study, because a judicious scolding was in order.

"Lady Greendale, your duke would not want you interfering." He passed her a finger of brandy, it being a canon of unwritten law that counsel keep the medicinal tot on hand for the occasional distraught client.

"My duke has no idea what he's up against. Girard won't offer a fair fight, and no one can warn him but me."

"I can go."

She shook her head. "I would not burden you with the details of Marcus's perfidy. This is a family matter, truly."

His curiosity was piqued, though he allowed her a moment to sip the brandy. "Another drop?"

"No, thank you." Lady Greendale was distressed—sorely distressed—but composed. Greendale had no doubt taught her that trick, may the old blighter be cavorting in hell. "Please tell me what you know, Mr. Stoneleigh. I suspect a duel has been planned?"

He told her what he knew: that a contest of honor had been scheduled for the very next morning, though its exact location was as yet uncertain.

❧

Unique among his peers, Christian had never met another on the field of honor. Dueling struck him as a chancy way to settle a matter of pride—honor usually didn't enter into it—particularly for a duke with an obligation to a titular succession.

So he knew not how he should feel when he contemplated single mortal combat with a personal enemy. The exchange with Stoneleigh had put doubts in his mind, and doubts were a liability.

Technically, Girard had played by the rules of war, such as war had rules, but only technically.

Did that matter? To Gilly, it would matter a great deal.

Girard had tormented, but he had also protected. He'd seen to Christian's welfare, and ultimately, spared Christian's life—after holding him captive for months.

And he would delight in knowing Christian was afflicted with last-minute doubts.

St. Just sauntered into the breakfast parlor, impeccably turned out for five in the morning.

"You've been up all night?" Christian asked, for he'd turned in early and left a morose St. Just to the company of some excellent brandy.

"Nearly. Ran into my father, by the way, who'll happily have Girard arrested and deported if you'll let him know the location of this morning's meeting. Said it has to do with courtesy among dukes."

"Please give Moreland my thanks if I'm unable, but deportation won't be necessary." Nor would it be easily accomplished, if Girard indeed had an English patrimony.

"I doubt Girard would survive deportation. Word of this duel alone will mean his death, do you not see to the matter for him."

"Girard might welcome death." Could life itself

be a form of captivity? Gilly had nearly reached such an impasse. "His emperor is taken prisoner, he has no cause to fight for, and all his machinations were in vain. Now he finds an English barony hung around his neck, if rumor is to be believed, while any number of British officers will relish his death. This is a failed life by any standard."

And the notion of accommodating Girard with a tidy, quiet death did not appeal.

"A challenging life. My coach awaits."

"Thoughtful of you."

St. Just's unmarked coach assured privacy—and convenience in the event a body needed transport back to Town. Christian put that thought aside and followed his second out into the predawn gloom.

The journey to the Sheffield Arms passed in silence, and like most mornings as autumn approached, saw a layer of ground fog in the low-lying areas of the terrain.

"The air is still," St. Just said. "A mercy."

"With swords, the wind hardly matters as it would have with pistols."

St. Just scrubbed a hand over his face. "Bloody damned farce, swords."

"My friend, we are soldiers. We did not sit at the ancestral pile like spiders in our webs and dally with our prey. We fought. As officers, we led the charge. We set the example. We gained the victory."

St. Just stared at the shadowy hills and fields. "But this charge is not for King and Country. This is a bloody damned duel, and I do not trust that Frenchman to acquit himself honorably."

"He will." Of this Christian was certain. "His arrogance and whatever idiosyncrasy passes for his conscience ensure he will behave honorably."

St. Just said nothing, and the coach rolled into the yard of the Sheffield Arms. Christian climbed out as the sun was nearly peeking over the horizon, and made his way through the trees to the appointed location. Girard had arrived before him, a pair of foils in an elegant case open on a folding table under the trees.

"Good morning, Your Grace."

"Girard. Or do we address you now as Lord St. Clair?"

The Frenchman looked pained, but Christian no longer had to hear every piece of drivel the man spouted, so he turned his back and waited for St. Just to join them.

The seconds conferred, and the principles limbered up with their weapons, but the surgeons were not yet on the scene.

"You can start without the surgeons," St. Just said. "I don't advise it."

"Another five minutes then," Christian replied.

As a soldier, he'd seen many sunrises that might have been his last. As a prisoner, he'd gone for weeks without sight of the sun, only to find it too painfully bright when he had been given liberty from his dungeon.

A soldier accepts the possibility of his death, particularly when he's in captivity.

But Christian was a soldier no longer. He was Mercia, with a responsibility to his people and to his title. He had a daughter who'd seen far too much loss and confusion in her short life.

And he had Gilly.

She was the still place inside of him, the utter conviction that he could not fail. She was the bright light of reason, the warmth of hope, the promise of wisdom sufficient for all the troubles a lifetime could present.

And from her perspective, what Christian undertook with Girard was a betrayal of her.

Quite possibly from Christian's perspective as well.

"The surgeons are here," St. Just said. "You can still apologize."

"Remind me of that again, and I will challenge you, St. Just."

"See if I'll volunteer to be your second twice."

St. Just conferred with his counterpart, a tall, broad-shouldered blond whom Christian recognized as the jailer, the last person to see Christian in captivity.

The man who had, on Girard's orders, freed the lost duke.

Christian exchanged a nod with the fellow, the jailer looking better fed and better dressed, but as twitchy as ever—and not particularly apologetic.

Upon the signal of Girard's second, Christian took a position opposite Girard, saluted with his weapon, accepted Girard's answering civility, and gathered his focus for the moment when St. Just would give them leave—

"Wait!" A female voice broke the morning stillness, and four male heads swiveled back toward the Sheffield Arms. "For the love of God, you must not proceed."

"Thank Jesus and all the holy angels," St. Just said. "Your countess has come to rescue you."

✑

Christian, looking composed, tidy, and very much
alive, shot his opponent a pointed look. The dark
brute who must be Girard saluted with his foil and
passed it to a blond fellow hovering near St. Just.

"Countess, good morning." For a man about to
fight for his life, His Grace sounded perishingly steady.

"This is not a good morning," she said, advancing on him. "What can you be thinking?" She shot
a venomous look at Girard. "And you, you do not
deserve to die. You deserve to live with the agony
of what you tried to do and the fact that you failed
utterly to do it."

"Did I fail?"

Gilly had not one instant to spare for such a creature, or for his Gallic irony. "You cannot kill him like
this, Your Grace."

"Do you mean I am not capable of it, or I should not?"

This distinction mattered to him, Gilly could see that,
and she forced herself to pause and choose her words.

"Of course you would dispatch him handily," she
said, her hands fisted on her hips. "But you cannot
do murder. You are not some violent beast, a thing
without a conscience to kill on a whim or for your
own passing pleasure."

Greendale could have behaved thus, but not her
Christian.

Christian shot a look at the Frenchman, who was
rolling down his cuffs, not a care in the world.

"I cannot countenance a world with Girard in it,
Countess, much less him strolling the English countryside like some squire with his hounds."

"He will die," Gilly said. "But not by your hand. You must not. You tried to explain this to me."

"What on earth are you talking about?" Christian was very still, very quiet, and very unhappy with her.

Her heart, already racing, thumped against her ribs.

"You tried to show me," she said. "You tried to convey to me, that after years of fighting against a bitter enemy, you can lose yourself in the belief that it's enough merely to *be* his enemy, even when the hostilities are over. But if you sustain yourself on that bitterness, your foe wins twice, for you are as much his slave as if you were still chained in his dungeon."

Christian was listening, so Gilly pushed the next words out. "I am no longer Greendale's drudge, no longer his marital whipping post. You tried to tell me the wars are over. I could not hear you, but you must listen to me now."

Girard heaved a sigh when Gilly wished an apoplexy would befall him, and still Christian stared at her, as if trying to decipher words in a foreign language.

"Listen to the lady, *mon duc*," Girard said in a voice as aggravatingly reasonable as it was damnably attractive. "I am not the one you need to kill, for the war *is* over, and I am among those who lost. We fight with swords so I might have the time to explain this as you drew my blood, and I perhaps drew a bit of yours."

Girard's voice was the essence of civility, the French accent soft, the tension in the words razor sharp. "Ask yourself, Your Grace, how Anduvoir knew exactly when and where to capture you. Who knew what you were about, who had something—a great deal—to gain by your death?"

"Listen to him, Christian," Gilly said. "Marcus put the French up to capturing you. I suspect Marcus let Girard know you were spoiling for a chance to kill him."

"Marcus is my heir," Christian spat. "You're both spouting nonsense."

"Not nonsense," Girard said. "Your cousin dealt not with me, but with Anduvoir. I commanded a garrison. I did not take captives. They were brought to me by my superiors, you among them. Your circumstances were not..." He scowled, as if the English words had evaporated with the low-lying mist. "They were not right. You were betrayed, and to allow you to leave captivity in wartime would have been to sign your death warrant. I agreed to meet you today, yes, but to warn you, not kill you."

The Frenchman was trying to mitigate his role in Christian's torment, though he was also, perhaps, telling the truth.

In her peripheral vision, Gilly saw Stoneleigh edge into the clearing. He led Chessie, who'd been pressed into service in the traces of a sleek, well-sprung curricle. A tense silence spread, broken only when Chessie shook his head, making his bit jingle.

Christian's gaze shifted to take in his horse.

"Think, Your Grace," Girard said patiently, wearily. "I was your enemy, and for that you may kill me, of course, but I am not your enemy now, and I did not kill you on the many occasions when the opportunity presented itself."

Gilly hated Girard, but Christian was listening to him—*even* to him—and the swords were safely back in the hands of the seconds.

"He had my horse," Christian said softly. "*Marcus had my personal mount.* The last thing I recall of the day I was taken captive is Chessie being led off, a French private on his back. I wished to God I'd at least freed my horse before I was captured. And then Marcus had my horse, my personal mount..."

A muscle in his jaw ticked twice.

"Bloody goddamned right I had your horse." Marcus pushed through the bushes on the far side of the clearing. "I nearly had your wife too, but she was too fond of her tiara. She didn't appreciate that I'd had you taken captive, and her unfortunate accident with the laudanum was easy to orchestrate after that. Providence took care of the boy—never let it be said I preyed on a child."

Gilly's whole being suffused with revulsion at the sight of Marcus, the embodiment of the same casual violence her husband had harbored, in a yet more malignant form.

"So you'll kill me in cold blood, before witnesses," Christian mused, "when I have no comparable weapon?" He took a fistful of Gilly's cape, pulling her behind him and into St. Just's arms, Stoneleigh's curricle beside her.

"*He* was supposed to kill you in France," Marcus said, jerking the barrel of an ugly horse pistol toward Girard. "Anduvoir promised me he'd arrange for that. Then I learned the generals always sent their best prizes off to Girard for special handling. I was a fool to trust a bloody Frog with something so important. Then you had to go and outlast the entire war and take up with her." The gun barrel waved toward Gilly, and Christian *and* *Girard* both shifted to step in front of her.

"So you tried to engineer Gilly's death," Christian said, "and you failed at that too."

"Of course I tried to kill her. If she dropped a brat within a year of Greendale's death, I would have been disinherited of the personal fortune. A male child would have seen me lose the title as well. The alternative was to live as a pauper at Greendale and hope you hadn't taken an intimate fancy to her."

"Marcus, you cannot prevail here," Christian said. "Too many witnesses can testify to your violent schemes."

"But with you gone, I will be tried in the Lords, and they never convict one of their own. Besides, who will take the word of a reviled Frenchman, a Scottish traitor, or a lawyer over that of a peer of the realm?"

Marcus raised his pistol, the muzzle aimed squarely at Christian.

Rage unlike anything Gilly had felt toward her deceased spouse suffused her. Marcus had known exactly the circumstances Greendale had forced on her. Marcus had destroyed Christian's family, preyed on Lucy, and he intended now to do *murder* in cold blood—

Gilly did not think. Her hand closed around Stoneleigh's buggy whip, an elegant length of black leather with a corded lash several feet long. She darted around the men shielding her, raised her arm, and brought the whip down with all her strength across Marcus's face.

"For Christian, damn you," she spat, raising her arm again. "For Helene, for Evan—"

Nothing had ever, ever felt as right as striking

Marcus with all her might, as seeing outrage and disbelief twist his handsome features while she raised three angry red welts on his cheeks and nose.

She, Gilly, the least powerful of his present adversaries, would hold him accountable for his crimes. The *bliss* of striking him, of hurting him when he'd planned harm to so many, gave her endless strength and a towering indifference to her own fate.

He shifted, of course, away from Christian, to defend himself against Gilly's whip, and his aim shifted as well.

Between landing the third blow and raising her arm again, Gilly perceived that she would in fact die. The ugly snout of the horse pistol took aim at her, the distance was a handful of feet, and she would in the next moment breathe her last.

So be it. Christian and Lucy would live, Marcus's crimes would be exposed, and Gilly would die protecting those she loved.

Fighting for them.

A shot rang out, obscenely loud in the cool morning air, and the scent of sulfur wafted on the breeze. Gilly stood clutching the whip, inventorying her body for pain, shock, anything.

Girard blew smoke from the end of a pistol, and surprise bloomed on Marcus's face amid the lacerations Gilly had given him.

While a bright red stain spread over the center of his chest.

He looked at the wound then at Girard, before crumpling on the ground in a heap.

Gilly dropped the whip and wrapped her arms

around Christian, while Stoneleigh turned to quiet the horses, and St. Just approached the body to lay his hand on Marcus's neck.

"Dead before he hit the ground," St. Just said, closing Marcus's eyes with curious gentleness.

Girard passed the gun to his second, much as he might have passed a spent fowling piece over in the middle of a pheasant shoot.

"This does not reconcile our accounts. I understand that, Duke." Girard ambled over to Marcus's prone form and extracted something from his watch pocket. "I am, however, rid of a portion of my guilt."

"Tell him to *be silent*," Gilly said, pressing her nose to Christian's chest. "I cannot bear to hear his stupid, French-accented voice. I am not myself, and I cannot answer for my actions. Christian, I struck Marcus, I gloried in striking Marcus. I would still be beating him if—" She couldn't talk and get her breath, and still she held on to Christian.

"Gilly, hush. Please hush. You're safe."

The violence reverberated in her, part horror, part surprise, and also—God help her, God help her—part relief.

"Hold me. Don't ever let me go."

"I have you." Christian's chin came to rest against her temple, and his fingers made slow circles on her nape. He pitched his next words to a whisper. "Unless you need to be sick. Most soldiers are, after their first battle. I certainly was, even though, like you, my first battle was a resounding victory."

She canvassed her physical state, and if anything,

felt as if she'd purged herself of a toxin. "I need you to hold me, and tell Mr. Stoneleigh to retrieve his whip."

Heat and cold shivered through her, weakness, and wonder.

She could fight back. If she had to, if she ever again found herself endangered, *she could fight back*.

A woman who could fight back could manage to stand unassisted, though Christian only turned loose of her enough to dab at her cheeks with his white handkerchief.

"Apologies for the intrusion," Girard said. "Mercia, I believe this is yours." He tossed what looked like a blue-and-gold signet ring to St. Just. "And, my lady, you do not know the lengths I traveled to keep your duke alive when my superiors clamored to have him quietly executed or worse.

"I sent the horse to that one"—Girard gestured toward Marcus—"thinking the English would solve the puzzle of how Mercia was taken, but the English did not make the attempt. I suspect the late colonel opined to his superiors that such diligence was unnecessary. I had a letter sent through the diplomatic channels, which I'm sure was dismissed at Easterbrook's urging. I instigated rumor, I—"

Gilly glowered at Girard, for his litany had a pleading quality, as if he longed for Christian to absolve him of his trespasses, when Gilly longed to take a buggy whip to him.

She remained bundled against her duke, as a nasty insight wiggled past her ire: at no time had Christian described Girard as a man who delighted in violence for its own sake, while she, under certain circumstances, apparently possessed that trait.

And was not ashamed of it—just yet.

"Why keep me alive?" Christian asked.

Girard arranged the two silver foils in their case and closed the lid.

"For two reasons. First, I know what it is to be in dire circumstances, far from home, with no good options. I was a boy when the Peace of Amiens stranded me among my mother's people in France. My choices were to join the English captives or, eventually, to join the French army—to kill my father's people or be held prisoner by my mother's. Delightful options, *non*? Your choices were no better—treason or torture—and yet you found a way to prevail with your honor intact. I respected your tenacity. I was inspired by it, in fact."

Girard spoke softly, much as Christian had weeks ago when Gilly had first barged into the ducal parlor, dreading the confrontation even as she handed a duke of the realm orders.

And while part of Gilly wanted to drag Christian away from the sunlit clearing, another part of her ached for a boy—not a cavalry officer, a boy—who'd fallen victim to the pervasive injustice of war.

Girard turned his face up to the sun slanting through the trees. Viewed objectively, he was a handsome man, and, Gilly also admitted—grudgingly—a man who bore the marks of a soul-deep exhaustion.

"You should also know Anduvoir caused significant awkwardness by capturing a duke who was quite obviously an officer in possession of a uniform," Girard went on. "And he further humiliated himself by failing to extract any intelligence from you whatsoever. As a consequence, Anduvoir was denied every possible promotion, which prevented him from much foolishness. There is more to it, but your silence saved not only English lives, but French lives; therefore, on the peculiar abacus that passes for my moral reckoning, you were condemned to live."

Girard's manner was patience edged with a detachment that bore a tincture of madness—or perhaps the confessional zeal of a misguided, heathen saint.

And while Gilly could on an abstract level feel compassion for the wreck war had made of Girard, she had no wish to linger in the man's presence.

"The other reason?" Christian asked.

Girard smiled faintly, a sad, tired caricature of what might have been a charming grin, and somewhere above, a songbird offered the day a silvery, sweet greeting. "You will have your confession of me, eh, Mercia?"

"I will have the truth."

"You are owed that." Girard regarded the body as he went on speaking, his accent becoming all but undetectable. "We are of an age, Your Grace. Had war not intervened, I would have started at Eton after spending time with my grandparents in France. You and I would have been in the same form, probably belonged to the same clubs, played on the same cricket team. We would have been nearly neighbors, for the St. Clair seat is less than a day's ride from your own home. One could say your battle was my own, and you fought well enough for both of us."

Girard looked away, but not before Gilly caught a hint of self-consciousness in his frown. Or perhaps he was bewildered to be making this confession without benefit of torture, bewildered that Christian would even listen to him.

As Gilly herself was bewildered to find a man—a flesh-and-blood man, with regrets and scars of his own—behind the beast who'd haunted Christian's dreams.

As the bird paused in its serenade to the new day, Stoneleigh spoke up: "This Frenchman has committed murder in peacetime on English soil. Greendale's gun was not trained on him, and Girard cannot claim he was defending his loved ones."

Girard examined his fingernails, as if the threat of hanging was of no moment to him, and perhaps it wasn't.

"Gilly?" Christian looped his arms around her, which was fortunate given that the state of her knees had become unreliable. "What shall be Girard's fate?"

The big Frenchman—Englishman?—shot her a look. His green eyes were flint hard, but in them, Gilly saw…a plea, and not for freedom. For understanding, perhaps?

All she knew was that the man she loved was no longer driven by a need to do murder—and *neither was she*—and indirectly, she had Girard to thank for her own survival.

Also Christian's. "His fate is up to you, Christian."

Christian must decide for himself when the war ended and life began anew. All that remained for Gilly was to love him, regardless of his decision.

He closed his eyes and leaned on Gilly, truly leaned on her, as he had when she'd first joined his household and he'd barely been able to sleep through the night, keep down a cup of tea, or sign his name.

"Then Girard goes about his business, and I go about mine."

"My thanks, Your Grace, for your mercy." Girard bowed low to Gilly, collected his second, and disappeared into the morning fog.

❧

"Lucy is more taken with the adventure of riding all the way up to Town with you than she is traumatized to know Marcus is dead." Christian might have been discussing the weather, not murder most foul, and murder narrowly averted.

While Gilly remained seated at St. Just's library desk, Christian moved pieces around on a chessboard near the window.

"We were so lucky," Gilly said, fiddling with a letter opener sporting what had to be the Moreland crest.

Unicorns seemed appropriate for St. Just. He hadn't come home yet, for he'd had an unfortunate accident to report involving the late Lord Greendale and firearms affected by morning damp.

"How were we lucky?" Christian returned the pieces, one by one, to their starting positions.

"On the way up from Surrey, the roads were dry, we met little traffic, and George and John were able to get us household funds and to pack our saddlebags with food and drink. The groom knew exactly where we were going, and Mr. Stoneleigh was all that was hospitable. Lucy thought we were merely out for a hack until we left the lanes. She rides very well."

"She's a Severn, of course she rides well."

"One hopes she'll sleep well."

Christian's mouth quirked, the first hint of a smile Gilly had seen from him all day. They'd been busy collecting Lucy from Stoneleigh's, staying in touch with St. Just as he dealt with the authorities, and putting together the story of Marcus's perfidy.

And of course, Lucy and her papa had had much, *much,* to say to each other.

"One hopes I'll sleep well." Christian examined the white queen, a smiling little study in carved marble. "What were you thinking, trying to stop a duel? What if Girard and I had already engaged? You could have got me killed, or worse, been hurt yourself."

Did he want to toss the little queen as much as Gilly wanted to upend the entire chessboard? She rose from the safety of the desk and went to the sofa.

"I had to see you, had to talk to you. Come sit with me." She held out a hand, and he hesitated.

That instant's hesitation devastated Gilly, though in some corner of her soul, she'd anticipated it.

What man could be attracted to a woman who had judged him bitterly for his instinct for justice, then had fallen prey herself to ungovernable violent impulses?

"If I touch you, Countess, I'll want to take you to bed."

She let her hand drop. "Why? I might have killed Marcus, had I been able. And now, my temper seems to plague me without ceasing. I fear for Girard if my path ever crosses his, Christian, though what he imparted in that clearing should at least earn the man my forbearance. Any who seek to harm you or Lucy will find a madwoman—"

His expression was unreadable, but he at least sat beside her and took her hand.

"The protectiveness you exhibited with that buggy whip, which arguably saved my life, is the antithesis of what drove Greendale, Gilly, and had nothing in common with Marcus's ruthless self-interest. They were men of hatred. You are a woman who loves."

He spoke slowly, quietly, as if she might bolt off the sofa and run into the street howling did he get a single word wrong. The composure Gilly had fought so hard to learn threatened to desert her—again.

"About that." But then the words wouldn't come, wouldn't push past the ache in her throat.

"Gillian?" Christian slid his free arm around her, and Gilly turned her face into his shoulder. He smelled good, of lemon and ginger, and understanding.

"I hate embroidery. Needlework makes my head hurt and my eyes sting, and I was never competent at it as a girl."

"You made your needle a weapon. But you no longer need to wield it."

"Yes. Exactly. You understand better than I did myself. I thought I was above doing battle. I thought I'd chosen the better path. I hadn't. I'd chosen only silent battles, though—until today. What does that make me?"

"Brave. Determined, shrewd, resilient. Formidable."

He kissed her hand with each word, as a knight might kiss a damsel's hand, and Gilly's heart nearly broke for the absolution he offered.

"You are a war hero," she said, lifting her face. "The victim of betrayal by your own heir, a man who preyed on your wife and children."

"Victim is not a word a proud man wants associated with him in any sense," Christian said. "Nor a proud lady."

"I was not a prisoner of war. I was a *wife*."

"Unless you accept that you were a prisoner of war too, Gilly, then you will always struggle with being my wife." His voice was gentle, and his thumb brushed back and forth over the small scar on her knuckle. "You were betrayed by family, as I was. You were tortured, as I was. You were toyed with and paraded about as a trophy of war, as I was. You fought back in the small ways available to you, as I did, and you prevailed in the end, whereas I merely endured."

"I did not prevail," she whispered. "I did not. My enemy simply died, and even in death, he nearly defeated me. Had Girard not shot Marcus, I would cheerfully have died, provided I could have hurt Marcus further as I breathed my last."

Her consternation at this realization was immeasurable, a complete departure from what she'd believed herself to be, and yet, she'd take up that whip against Marcus in the next instant if given the chance again.

"You took a few swats with a horsewhip at a man who deserved far worse. While I understand you are uncomfortable with having done violence to Marcus's person, don't you think his instructions to his solicitors were left in such a way as to cast the gravest suspicion on you when Greendale died? You prevailed, Gilly. Against Greendale, against his heir, and against all the demons haunting me, and even those haunting my daughter. You won." He scooped her into his lap and held her close. "My duchess must be proud of her victories, as I am proud of her."

"I almost do feel p-proud," she said. "Marcus would have killed you. He nearly did, and I was almost too late, and, and, oh, God, he killed Helene, and all for a stupid t-title. I love you. I love you so, and Marcus has been trying to have you killed for so l-long."

She sobbed into his neck, holding on to him as if she were drowning, wetting his shirt and telling him over and over she loved him. When he carried her to the bed, she tore his clothes from him and had him naked on his back in moments.

A lady who will fight for her love will fight for her pleasure, too.

Then his will prevailed, by degrees, until they were savoring each other and speaking in whispers and sighs between the times when their bodies spoke in silence.

She wanted a quiet wedding; he wanted St. George's with all the trimmings.

She wanted to wait until spring out of respect for Helene and Evan. He wanted their vows said the day after the banns had been cried for the third time.

She wanted to remove to Severn immediately; he wanted to flaunt her on his arm before every hostess and title in Town.

They did not argue, though. They talked, they listened, they even tussled a time or two, though into the dawn and for the rest of their lives, most of all, they *loved*.

Read on for a sneak peek at the next two
books in the groundbreaking
Captive Hearts series

The Traitor

The Laird

Coming soon from Grace Burrowes and
Sourcebooks Casablanca

The Traitor

THE BULLET WHISTLED PAST SEBASTIAN'S EAR, COMING within an inch of solving all of his problems, and half an inch of making a significant mess instead.

"Die, goddamn you!" Lieutenant Lord Hector Pierpont fired his second shot, but rage apparently made the man careless. A venerable oak lost a few bare twigs to the field of honor.

"I shall die, *bien sûr*," Sebastian said, a prayer as much as a promise. "But not today."

He took aim on Pierpont's lapel. An English officer to his very bones, Pierpont stood still, eyes closed, waiting for death to claim him. In the frosty air, his breath clouded before him in the same shallow pants that might have characterized postcoital exertion.

Such drama. Sebastian cocked his elbow and dealt another wound to the innocent oak branches. "And neither shall you die today. It was war, Pierpont. For the sake of your womenfolk, let it be over."

Sebastian fired the second bullet overhead to punctuate that sentiment, also to ensure no loaded weapons remained within Pierpont's ambit. When

Pierpont opened his eyes, Sebastian gazed into loathing so intense as to confirm his lordship would rather be dead than suffer any more of Sebastian's clemency or sermonizing.

Sebastian walked up to him and spoke quietly enough that the seconds could not hear.

"You gave away nothing. What little scraps you threw me had long since reached the ears of French intelligence. Go home, kiss your wife, and give her more babies, but leave me and mine in peace. Next time, I will not delope, *mon ami*."

He slapped Pierpont lightly on the cheek, a small, friendly reminder of other blows, and walked away.

"You are not fit to breathe the air of England, St. Clair."

This merited a dismissive parting wave of Sebastian's hand. Curses were mere bagatelles to a man who'd dealt in screams and nightmares for years. "*Au revoir*, Pierpont. My regards to your wife and daughters."

The former captain and his missus were up to two. Charming little demoiselles with Pierpont's dark eyes. Perhaps from their mother they might inherit some common sense and humor.

"Cold bastard."

That, from Captain Anderson, one of Pierpont's seconds. Anderson was a twitchy, well-fed blond fellow with a luxurious mustache. Threaten the mustache, and Monsieur Bold Condescension would chirp out the location of his mother's valuables like a horny nightingale in spring.

Michael Brodie snatched the pistol from Sebastian's grasp, took Sebastian by the arm, and led him toward their horses. "You've had your fun, now come along like a good baron."

"Insubordinate, you are. I thought the English were bad, but you Irish give the term realms of meaning Dr. Johnson never dreamed."

"You are *English*, lest we forget the reason yon righteous arse wants to perforate your heart at thirty paces. Get on the horse, Baron, and I'm only half-Irish."

A fact dear *Michel* had kept quiet until recently.

Sebastian pretended to test the tightness of Fable's girth, but used the moment to study Pierpont, who was in conversation with his seconds. Pierpont was in good enough weight, and he was angry—furious—but not insane with it. Nothing about his complexion or his eyes suggested habitual drunkenness, and he had two small, adorable daughters who needed their papa's love and adoration.

Maybe today's little exchange would allow them to have it.

"You fret, *Michel*, and one wants to strike you for it. The English are violent with their servants, *non*? Perhaps today I will be English after all."

"The French were violent with the entire Continent, best as I recall, and bits of Africa and the high seas into the bargain. You ought not to begrudge the English some violence with their help from time to time. Keeps us on our toes."

Michael climbed aboard his bay, and Sebastian swung up on Fable.

Burnished red eyebrows lowered into a predictable scowl. "You would have to ride a white horse," Michael groused. "Might as well paint a target on your back and send a boy ahead to warn all and sundry the Traitor Baron approaches."

Sebastian nudged his horse forward.

"Fable was black as the Pit when he was born. I cannot help what my horse decides to do with his hair. That is between him and his God. Stop looking over your shoulder, *Michel*. Pierpont was an officer. He will not shoot me in the back, and he will not blame you for sparing all others the burden of seconding me."

Michael took one more look over his shoulder— both the Irish half of him and the Scottish half were well endowed with contrariness.

"How many duels does that make, your lordship? Four? Five? One of these honorable former officers will put paid to your existence, and where will Lady Freddy be, then? Think on that the next time you're costing me and Fable our beauty sleep."

He took out a flask and imbibed a hefty swallow, suggesting his nerves were truly in bad repair.

"I am sorry." Such flaccid words Sebastian offered, but sincere. "You should not worry about my early outings. These men do not want to kill me any more than I wanted to kill them."

Michael knew better than to offer his flask. "You didn't kill them, that's the problem. What you did was worse, and even if they don't want to kill you—which questionable conclusion we can attribute to your woe-fully generous complement of Gallic arrogance—the rest of England, along with a few loyal Scots, some bored Welshmen, and six days a week, an occasional sober Irishman, would rather you died. I'm in the employ of a dead man."

"Melodrama does not become you." Sebastian cued Fable into a canter, lest Michael point out that melodrama, becoming or not, had long enjoyed respect as a socially acceptable means of exposing painful and inconvenient truths.

❦

In Millicent Danforth's experience, the elderly, like most stripes of human being, came in two varieties: fearful and brave. Her grandmother had been fearful, asking incessantly for tisanes or tea, for cosseting and humoring. Like a small child, Grandmother had wanted distracting from the inevitability of her own demise.

By contrast, Lady Frederica, Baroness St. Clair, viewed her eventual death as a diversion. She would threaten the help with it, lament it gently with her many friends, and use it as an excuse for very blunt speech indeed.

"You are to be a companion, not a nursemaid. You will not vex me with your presence when I attend my correspondence after breakfast. You will appear at my side when I take the landau out for a turn in the park. Shall you write this down?"

Milly returned her prospective employer's beady-eyed glower calmly.

"I will not bother you after breakfast unless you ask it of me. I will join you when you take the air in the park. I believe I can recall that much, my lady. What will my other duties involve?"

She asked because Mr. Loomis at the agency had been spotty on the details, except for the need to show up at an unseemly early hour for this interview.

"A companion—you keep Lady St. Clair company!" he'd barked. "Step, fetch, soothe, entertain. Now, be off with you!"

The way he'd smoothed his wisp of suspiciously dark hair over his pate suggested more would be involved, a great deal more. Perhaps her ladyship tippled, gambled, or neglected to pay the trades—all to be managed by a companion whom the baroness might also forget to regularly compensate.

"You will dine with me in the evening and assist me to endure the company of my rascal of a nephew if he deigns to join us. What, I ask you, is so enticing about a rare beefsteak and an undercooked potato with a side of gossip? I can provide that here, as well as a superior cellar, but no, the boy must away to his flower-lovers' club. Never mind, though. He's well-mannered enough that he won't terrorize you—or no more than I will. Are you sure you don't need to write any of this down?"

Yes, Milly was quite sure. "I gather you are a list maker, my lady?"

Blue eyes lit up as her ladyship reached for the teapot.

"Yes! I am never so happy as when I'm organizing. I should have been a general, the late baron used to say. Do you enjoy the opera? One hopes you do, because nothing is more unendurable than the opera if one hasn't a taste for it."

Her ladyship chattered on about London openings she'd attended, who had conducted them, and what she had thought of the score, the sets, the crowd in attendance, and the various solos, duets, and ensemble numbers. Her diatribe was like a conversational stiff wind, banging the windows open all at once, setting curtains flapping, papers flying, and lapdogs barking.

"You're not drinking your tea, Miss Danforth."

"I am attending your ladyship's recitation of my duties."

The baroness clinked her teacup down on its saucer. "You were estimating the value of this tea service. Jasperware is more practical, but it's so heavy. I prefer the Sèvres, and Sebastian likes it too."

Sebastian might well be a follower. Milly had stolen a moment while waiting for this audience to glance over the cards sitting in a crystal bowl on the sideboard in the front hall. Her ladyship's social life was quite lively, and by no means were her callers all female.

"The service is pretty," Milly observed, though it was more than pretty, and perfectly suited to the pastel and sunshine of her ladyship's breakfast parlor. They were using the older style of Sèvres, more easily broken, but also impressively hued. Her ladyship's service boasted brilliant pink roses, soft green foliage, and gold trim over a white glaze. "Meissen or Dresden aren't as decorative, though they are sturdier."

The baroness used silver tongs to put a flaky golden croissant on a plate. "So you are a lady fallen on hard times?"

She was a lady who'd blundered. Paid companions did not need to know that fifteen years ago, Sèvres was made without kaolin, fired at a lower temperature, and capable of taking a wider and more bold palette of hues as a result.

"My mother was a lady fallen on hard times. I am

a poor relation who would make her own way rather than burden my cousins any further."

"Kicked you out, did they?" Her ladyship's tone suggested she did not approve of such cousins. "Or perhaps they realized that underneath all that red hair, you're quite pretty, though brown eyes are not quite the rage. One hopes you aren't delicate?"

She passed Milly the pastry and shifted the butter a few inches closer to Milly's side of the table.

"I enjoy excellent health, thank you, your ladyship." Excellent physical health, anyway. "And I prefer to call my hair auburn."

The baroness snorted at that gambit, then poured herself more tea. "Will these cousins come around to plague you?"

They would have to bother to find her first. "I doubt it."

"You wouldn't be married to one of them, would you?"

Milly nearly choked on soft, buttery pastry. "I am not married." For which she might someday be grateful.

"Then I will regularly scandalize your innocent ears and enjoy doing it. Eat up. When Sebastian gets back from his morning ride, he'll go through that sideboard like a plague of locusts. If you prefer coffee, you'd best get your servings before he comes down in the morning. The man cannot abide tea in any form."

"The plague of locusts has arrived."

Milly's head snapped around at the mocking baritone. She beheld...her opposite. Whereas she was female, short—petite, when the occasion was polite—red-haired, and brown-eyed, the plague before her was male, tall, green-eyed, and sable-haired. The divergence didn't stop there.

This fellow sauntered into the parlor, displaying a casual elegance about his riding attire that suggested time on the Continent. His tailoring was exquisite, but his movement was also so relaxed as to approach languid. The lace at his throat came within a whisker of being excessive, and the emerald winking from its snowy depths stayed barely on the acceptable side of ostentatious, for men seldom wore jewels during daylight hours, and certainly not for so mundane an undertaking as a hack in the park.

This biblical plague had…sartorial éclat.

Again, the opposite of Milly, who generally bustled through life, wore the plainest gowns she could get away with, and had never set foot outside London and the Home Counties.

"Aunt, you will observe the courtesies, please?"

This was the rascal of a nephew then, though as Milly endured his scrutiny, the term rascal struck her as incongruously affectionate for the specimen before her.

"Miss Millicent Danforth, may I make known to you my scamp of a nephew, Sebastian, Baron St. Clair. St. Clair, Miss Danforth—my new companion. You are not to terrorize her before she and I have negotiated terms."

"Of course not. I terrorize your staff only *after* you've obligated them to a contract."

If this was teasing, Milly did not regard it as humorous. Her ladyship, however, graced her nephew with a smile.

"Rotten boy. You may take your plate to the library, and read your newspapers in peace."

His lordship, who was not a boy in any sense, bowed to Milly with a Continental flourish, bowed again over Lady St. Clair's hand, tucked some newspapers under his arm, and strolled from the room.

"He's been dueling again." The baroness might have reported that her nephew had been dicing in the mews, her tone truculent rather than aghast. "They leave the poor boy no peace, those gallant buffoons old Arthur is so proud of."

For all his smoothness, something about St. Clair had not sat exactly plumb, but then, what did it say about a man if he could face death at sunrise and appear completely unaffected by the time he downed his morning coffee?

"How can you tell he was dueling?" For ladies weren't supposed to know of such things, much less small elderly ladies who lived for their correspondence and tattle.

"He's sad. Dueling always makes him sad. Just when I think he's making some progress, another one of these imbeciles finds a bit of courage, and off to some sheep meadow they go. I swear, if women ruled the world, it would be a damned sight better place. Have I shocked you?"

"Several times, my lady."

"Excellent. Have another pastry."

Milly munched away on a confection filled with chocolate crème—one could learn to appreciate such fare all too easily—while Lady St. Clair waxed enthusiastic about the affairs of Wellington—for who else could "old Arthur" be?—and his officers.

And still, something about the Baron St. Clair lodged in Milly's awareness like a smudge on her spectacles. He was quite handsome—an embarrassment of handsome was his to command—but cold. His smile reached his eyes only when he beheld his elderly aunt.

Perhaps dueling had taxed his store of charm.

"…and the ladies *très jolie*, you know?" Lady St. Clair was saying. "Half the fellows in government claimed they needed to go to Paris to make peace, but the soiled doves of London went into a decline until the negotiations were complete. Making peace is lusty work, methinks."

"I'm shocked yet again, my lady." Though not by the baroness's bawdy talk.

St. Clair—a baron and peer of the English realm— had spoken with a slight aristocratic *French* accent.

"Excellent. We shall get on famously, Miss Danforth, provided you aren't one to quibble about terms."

"I have not the luxury of quibbling, my lady."

The baroness peered at her over a pretty teacup. "Truly odious cousins?"

"Very. And parsimonious in the extreme."

"My condolences. Have another pastry."

The Laird

"ELSPETH, I BELIEVE A VIKING HAS COME CALLING."

At Brenna's puzzled observation, her maid set aside the embroidery hoop serving as a pretext for enjoying the Scottish summer sun, rose off the stone bench, and joined Brenna at the parapets.

"If Vikings are to ruin your afternoon tea, better if they arrive one at a time," Elspeth said, peering down at the castle's main gate. "Though that's a big one, even for a Viking."

The gate hadn't been manned for at least two centuries, and yet, some instinct had Brenna wishing she'd given the command to lower the portcullis before the lone rider had crossed into the cobbled keep.

"Lovely horse," Elspeth remarked.

The beast was an enormous, elegant bay, though its coat was matted with sweat and dust. From her vantage point high on Castle Brodie's walls, all Brenna could tell about the rider was that he was big, broad-shouldered, and blond. "Our visitor is alone, likely far from home, hungry and tired. If we're to offer him hospitality, I'd best inform the kitchen."

Highland hospitality had grown tattered and threadbare in some locations, but not at Castle Brodie, and it would not, as long as Brenna had the running of the place.

"He looks familiar," Elspeth said as the rider swung off his beast.

"The horse?"

No, Elspeth hadn't meant the horse, because now that the rider was walking his mount toward the groom approaching from the stables, Brenna had the same sense of nagging familiarity. She knew that loose-limbed stride, knew that exact manner of stroking a horse's neck, knew—

Foreboding prickled up Brenna's arms, an instant before recognition landed in a cold heap in her belly.

"Michael has come home." Nine years of waiting and worrying while the Corsican had wreaked havoc on the Continent, of not knowing what to wish for.

Her damned husband hadn't even had the courtesy to warn her of his return.

Elspeth peered over the stone crenellations, her expression dubious. "If that's the laird, you'd best go welcome him, though I don't see much in the way of baggage. Perhaps, if you're lucky, he'll soon be off larking about on some new battlefield."

"For shame, Elspeth Fraser."

A woman ought not to talk that way about her laird, and a wife ought not to think that way about her husband. Brenna wound down through the castle and took herself out into the courtyard, both rage and gratitude speeding her along.

She'd had endless Highland winters to rehearse the speech Michael deserved, years to practice the dignified reserve she'd exhibit before him should he ever recall he had a home. Alas for her, the cobbles were wet from a recent scrubbing, so her dignified reserve more or less skidded to a halt before her husband.

Strong hands steadied her as she gazed up, and up some more, into green eyes both familiar and unknown.

"You've come home." Not at all what she'd meant to say.

"That I have. If you would be so good, madam, as to allow the lady of the—*Brenna*?"

His hands fell away, and Brenna stepped back, wrapping her tartan shawl around her more closely.

"Welcome to Brodie Castle, Michael." Because somebody ought to say the words, she added, "Welcome home."

"You used to be chubby." He leveled this accusation as if put out that somebody had made off with that chubby girl.

"You used to be skinny." Now he was all-over muscle. He'd gone away a tall, gangly fellow, and come back not simply a man, but a warrior. "Perhaps you're hungry?"

She did not know what to do with a husband, much less *this* husband, who bore so little resemblance to the young man she'd married, but Brenna knew well what to do with a hungry man.

"I am..." His gaze traveled the courtyard the way a skilled gunner might swivel his sights on a moving target, making a circuit of the granite walls rising some thirty feet on three sides of the bailey. His expression suggested he was making sure the castle, at least, had remained where he'd left it. "I am famished."

"Come along then." Brenna turned and started for the entrance to the main hall, but Michael remained in the middle of the courtyard, still peering about. Potted geraniums were in riot, pink roses climbed trellises under the first-floor windows, and window boxes held all manner of blooms.

"You've planted flowers."

Another near accusation, for nine years ago, the only flowers in the keep were stray shrubs of heather springing up in sheltered corners.

Brenna returned to her husband's side, trying to see the courtyard from his perspective. "One must occupy oneself somehow while waiting for her spouse to come home—or be killed."

He needed to know that for nine years, despite anger, bewilderment, and even the occasional period of striving for indifference toward him and his fate, Brenna had gone to bed every night praying that death did not end his travels.

"One must, indeed, occupy oneself." He offered her his arm, which underscored how long they'd been separated and how far he'd wandered.

The men of the castle and its tenancies knew to keep their hands to themselves where Brenna MacLogan Brodie was concerned. They did not hold her chair for her, did not assist her in and out of coaches, or on and off of her horse.

And yet, Michael stood there, a muscular arm winged at her, while the scent of slippery cobbles, blooming roses, and a whiff of vetiver filled the air.

"Brenna Maureen, every arrow slit and window of that castle is occupied by a servant or relation watching our reunion. I would like to walk into my home arm in arm with my wife. Will you permit me that courtesy?"

He'd been among the English, the *military* English, which might explain this fussing over appearances, but he hadn't lost his Scottish common sense.

Michael had *asked* her to accommodate him. Brenna wrapped one hand around his thick forearm and allowed him to escort her to the castle.

❧

He could bed his wife. The relief Michael Brodie felt at that sentiment eclipsed the relief of hearing again the languages of his childhood, Gaelic and Scots, both increasingly common as he'd traveled farther north.

To know he could feel desire for his wedded wife surpassed his relief at seeing the castle in good repair, and even eclipsed his relief that the woman didn't indulge in strong hysterics at the sight of him.

For the wife he'd left behind had been more child than woman, the antithesis of this red-haired Celtic goddess wrapped in the clan's hunting tartan and so much wounded dignity.

They reached the steps leading up to the great wooden door at the castle entrance. "I wrote to you."

Brenna did not turn her head. "Perhaps your letters went astray."

Such gracious indifference. He was capable of bedding his wife—any young man with red blood in his veins would desire the woman at Michael's side—but clearly, ability did not guarantee he'd have the opportunity.

"I meant, I wrote from Edinburgh to let you know I was coming home."

"Edinburgh is lovely in summer."

All of Scotland was lovely in summer, and to a man who'd scorched his back raw under the Andalusian sun, lovely in deepest winter too. "I was in France, Brenna. The King's post did not frequent Toulouse."

Outside the door, she paused and studied the scrolled iron plate around the ancient lock.

"We heard you'd deserted, then we heard you'd died. Some of the fellows from your regiment paid calls here, and intimated army gossip is not to be trusted. Then some officer came trotting up the lane a month after the victory, expecting to pay a call on you."

Standing outside that impenetrable, ancient door, Michael accepted that his decision to serve King and Country had left wounded at home as well as on the Continent.

And yet, apologizing now would only make things worse.

"Had you seen the retreat to Corunna, Brenna, had you seen even one battle—" Because the women saw it all, right along with their husbands and children. Trailing immediately behind the soldiers came a smaller, far more vulnerable army of dependents, suffering and dying in company with their menfolk.

"I *begged* you to take me with you." She wrenched the door open, but stepped back, that Michael might precede her into the castle.

She had pleaded and cried for half their wedding night, sounding not so much like a distressed bride as an inconsolable child, and because he'd been only five years her senior, he'd stolen away in the morning while she'd slept, tears still streaking her pale cheeks.

He searched for honest words that would not wound her further.

"I prayed for your well-being every night. The idea that you were here, safe and sound, comforted me."

She plucked a thorny pink rose from a trellis beside the door and passed the bloom to him.

"Who or what was supposed to comfort me, Michael Brodie? When I was told you'd gone over to the enemy? When I was told you were dead? When I imagined you captured by the French, or worse?"

They stood on the castle steps, their every word available to any in the great hall or lurking at nearby windows. Rather than fret over the possibility that his wife had been unfaithful to him—her questions were offered in rhetorical tones—Michael stepped closer.

"Your husband has come home, and it will be his pleasure to make your comfort his greatest concern."

He even tried a smile, letting her see that *man and wife* might have some patching up to do, but *man and woman* could deal together well and very soon.

She looked baffled—or peevish. He could not read his own wife accurately enough to distinguish between the two.

"Have you baggage, Husband?"

Yes, he did. He gestured for her to go ahead of him into the hall. "Last I heard, the coach was following, but I haven't much in the way of worldly goods."

"I'll have your things put in the blue bedroom."

When she would have gone swishing off into the

bowels of the castle, Michael grabbed her wrist and kept her at his side. She remained facing half-away from him, an ambiguous pose, not resisting, and not exactly drinking in the sight of her long-lost husband, either.

"What's different?" He studied the great hall he'd stopped seeing in any detail by his third birthday. "Something is different. This place used to be…dark. Like a great ice cave."

And full of mice and cobwebs.

She twisted her hand free of his.

"Nothing much is different. I had the men enlarge the windows, whitewash the walls, polish the floors. The room wanted light, we had a bit of coin at the time, and the fellows needed something to do."

"You put a balcony over the fireplace." She'd also had the place scrubbed from the black-and-white marble floor to the blackened crossbeams, freeing it of literally centuries of dirt.

"The ceilings are so high we lose all the warmth. When we keep the fires going, the reading balcony is warmer than the hall below it."

She'd taken a medieval hall and domesticated it without ruining its essential nature, made it… comfortable. Or comforting? Bouquets of pink roses graced four of the deep windowsills, and every chair and sofa sported a Brodie plaid folded over the back. Not the darker, more complicated hunting plaid Brenna wore, but the cheerful red, black, and yellow used every day.

"I like it very much, Brenna. The hall is welcoming." Even if the lady was not.

She studied the great beams twenty feet over-head—or perhaps entreated the heavens for aid—while Michael caught a hint of a smile at his compliment.

That he'd made his wife smile must be considered progress, however miniscule.

Then her smile died. "Angus, good day."

Michael followed her line of sight to a sturdy kilted fellow standing in the doorway of the shadowed corridor that led to the kitchens. Even in the obscure light, Michael recognized an uncle who had been part older brother and part father, the sight of whom now was every part dear.

"Never say the village gossip was for once true! Our Michael has come home at last." Angus hustled across the great hall, his kilt flapping against his knees. "Welcome, lad! Welcome at long last, and God be thanked you're hale and in one grand piece, aren't you now?"

A hug complete with resounding thumps on the back followed, and in his uncle's greeting, Michael found the enthusiasm he'd hoped for from his wife.

From anybody.

"Surely the occasion calls for a wee dram," Angus said. His hair was now completely white, though he was less than twenty years Michael's senior. He wasn't as tall as Michael, but his build was muscular, and he looked in great good health.

"The man needs to eat before you're getting him drunk," Brenna interjected. She stood a few feet off, directly under crossed claymores that gleamed with the same shine as the rest of the hall.

"We can take a tray in the library, woman," Angus replied. "When a man hasn't seen his nephew for nigh ten years, the moment calls for whiskey and none of your fussy little crumpets, aye?"

Brenna twitched the tail of her plaid over her shoulder, a gesture about as casual as a French dragoon swinging into the saddle.

"I will feed my husband a proper meal at a proper table, Angus Brodie, and your wee dram will wait its turn."

Angus widened his stance, fists going to his hips, suggesting not all battlefields were found on the Continent.

"Uncle, Brenna has the right of it. I haven't eaten since this morning. One glass of good spirits, and I'd be disgracing my heritage. Food first, and then we'll find some sipping whiskey."

Brenna moved off to stick her finger in a white crockery bowl of roses, while Angus treated Michael to a look of good-humored disgruntlement.

"She runs a fine kitchen, does our Brenna. Do it justice, and find me in the office when you've eaten your fill. I'm that glad you're back, lad."

He strode off, the tassels on his sporran bouncing against his thick thighs, while Brenna shook droplets of water off the end of her finger.

"Does my uncle often cross swords with you?"

She wiped her finger on her plaid. "He does not, not now. He leaves the castle to me. I'm sure your arrival is the only thing that tempted him past the door. What are you hungry for?"

He was hungry for her smiles. A soldier home from war had a right to be hungry for his wife's smiles.

"Anything will do, though I've a longing for a decent scone. The English can't get them right, you know, and they skimp with the butter and must dab everything with their infernal jams, when what's wanted is some heather honey."

Compared to the little curve of her lips he'd seen earlier, this smile was…riveting. Brenna had grown into a lovely woman, but when she aimed that smile at Michael, he had the first inkling she might be a *lovable* woman, too. Her smile held warmth and welcome, maybe even a touch of approval.

"A batch of scones has just come out of the oven, Michael Brodie. If we hurry, you can get your share before the cousins come raiding."

He followed her into the depths of the house, watching her skirts twitch, and entertaining naughty, husbandly thoughts.

Until he recalled that the blue bedroom where Brenna was sending his baggage was a guest chamber, across a cold, drafty hallway and several doors down from the laird's apartments.

About the Author

New York Times and USA Today bestselling author Grace Burrowes hit the bestseller lists with her debut, The Heir, followed by The Soldier, Lady Maggie's Secret Scandal, and Lady Eve's Indiscretion. The Heir was a Publishers Weekly Best Book of 2010, The Soldier was a Publishers Weekly Best Spring Romance of 2011, Lady Sophie's Christmas Wish won Best Historical Romance of the Year in 2011 from RT Reviewers' Choice Awards, Lady Louisa's Christmas Knight was a Library Journal Best Book of 2012, and The Bridegroom Wore Plaid, the first in her trilogy of Scotland-set Victorian romances, was a Publishers Weekly Best Book of 2012. All of her Regency and Victorian romances have received extensive praise, including starred reviews from Publishers Weekly and Booklist. Darius, the first in her groundbreaking Regency series The Lonely Lords, was named one of iBookstores Best Romances of 2013.

Grace is a practicing family law attorney and lives in rural Maryland. She loves to hear from her readers and can be reached through her website at graceburrowes .com.